THE SHEPHERD

A.J. Busa

PHYLUM
PUBLISHING

Phylum Publishing, LLC.

Book Cover by A.J. Busa

Illustrations by A.J. Busa

1st edition 2026

For my loving parents John and Pat.
Thank you for instilling my passion for telling stories and your un-
wavering support.
I couldn't have accomplished this without you.

PROLOGUE

The sound of ringing bells sliced through the thick, dusty silence that clung to the village of Gu Mei. In this sleepy town, nothing changed but the seasons. The discordant jingling alone startled farmers from the endless toil of scratching life from dirt.

Old Jian appeared from the blanket of dust like a spirit made flesh. His donkey Chong plodded beside him, laden with a cart that clinked and rattled with each step. The villagers saw a wizened figure whose face was etched with a roadmap of wrinkles from long days in the wind and sun. Thin wisps of a long grey beard framed his features, while his eyes were shrewd, holding the experience of a man who had seen much in his travels.

The duo strolled by dozens of homes made from weathered stone and thatched roofs, where old women and children peeked out of open windows at the unexpected sight of them. Villagers began to spill from their doorways, gathering excitedly behind the cart, drawn by the promise of novelty in a place where tomorrow looked exactly like yesterday.

"Wares! Wares for sale!" he croaked, his voice raspy as dry leaves. After pulling Chong to a stop in the village square, he chocked a wheel with a piece of wood and, with a dramatic flourish, undid a latch.

Trays holding wares popped into place along the sides of the wooden cart, while a canopy sprang outward, offering patrons much-needed shade from the scorching sun. Children squealed in delight at the spectacle.

"Beautiful silks for that special lady! Spices that'll make your tongue sing! Tools to ease that burden on your back! Potions guaranteed to enhance your fertility—" He lowered his voice and leaned towards some younger men nearby, and with a wink added, "—and virility."

Among the crowd, Yu lingered at the edges, a shy and invisible ghost in her own village. Once, she had been the pride of Gu Mei—a beauty that made young men stumble over their words. Now, three months after her husband's sudden death, she was a shell of her former self.

Hollow eyes, hollow spirit, hollow everything, except for the weight of the infant pressed against her chest. Her husband, a shepherd like many, had been taken by a swift sickness, leaving her to tend the local temple and raise their son, Bao, alone.

She clutched the baby close, his warmth radiating through her thin garb. Bao was a fussy child, prone to fits of crying that would echo out of their stone temple and down the hill overlooking the village. Yu had tried everything—herbs, prayers, the old women's remedies—but nothing could quiet the child's restless spirit. A familiar fussing began from her shoulder.

Yu stood patiently on the outside of the crowd, waiting for the other villagers to finish pushing and bartering as her baby wailed. When the crowd eventually settled down and most had dispersed, she crept forward, her steps hesitant as a deer approaching water.

"Anything to help him sleep?" Yu asked, her voice barely a whisper. She gestured towards Bao, who screwed up his face in a prelude to another wail.

Old Jian peered at her with a surprisingly gentle gaze. He saw the exhaustion in her eyes, the desperation in the set of her mouth. He knew the hardships of village life, the constant struggle to survive.

"Sleep, eh?" he rumbled, stroking his beard. "I have special teas, herbs... but those cost a heavy coin." He knew she likely had very little.

Yu's shoulders slumped. She could barely afford the staples, let alone luxuries like sleep remedies. She fingered the few copper coins in her pouch, enough for a handful of needed seeds for her garden, or perhaps a small amount of tea if she bargained well. She preferred not to part with what little she had, though. She rubbed the small bundle of cloth she'd brought—her own weaving, intricate and beautiful, but worthless in a world that counted only copper and silver.

"I... I have some weaving," she offered hopefully, slowly handing over a handful of colorful fabric. "It's not much, but..."

Jian examined the material Yu handed him, his fingers tracing the intricate pattern woven into the cloth. It was good work, skilled work, but it wouldn't fetch much in the market.

He peered over at her, a flicker of an old, deep pain in his eyes. He thought of his own wife, taken by fever decades ago, and the child they'd never had. His fingers began rubbing the smooth cloth while he was lost in thought before responding.

"You know, it's been a long ride for me and old Chong here," Jian said, lovingly patting the donkey's head. He pointedly looked down at Yu's waterskin at her belt. "Perhaps you could spare a few drops for two weary old travelers?"

Smiling in understanding, Yu unhooked the waterskin from her belt and handed it over enthusiastically. Jian took a ceremonial sip, smacked his lips with exaggerated satisfaction, then handed it back. Chong brayed in annoyance at being overlooked.

"There is one thing..." he muttered, more to himself than to Yu.

Jian turned back to his cart, rummaging through a pile of trinkets and baubles before carefully pulling out an intricately designed device of brass. Miniature sheep, crafted with remarkable detail, hung from a central column topped by tiny sails that would catch the heat from candles at the base and spin them around and around.

Yu let out a quiet gasp as he held it up with a flourish and smiled at seeing the look on her face.

"I found it abandoned by an old well in the far north," he explained. "They have different stories there, you know? They whisper this lamp keeps the bad dreams away. Been carrying it for many moons, waiting for the right person."

He didn't mention the other stories, the ones about shadows that moved when no one was looking.

You are doing the right thing. A voice inside his head whispered, a constant companion since he had found the lamp. *You are so kind.*

It was a beautiful thing, utterly out of place in this dusty, impoverished village. The shiny device pulsed with inner light, and something stirred in her chest—a longing so sudden and intense it was almost painful. The object was calling to her, promising the one thing she needed most.

It was perfect.

She looked down at Bao who started to squirm and whimper.

"How... how much?" she asked, her voice barely audible. She knew it was a foolish question. She could never afford such a thing.

Old Jian chuckled, a dry, rustling sound.

"For you, my dear? And for that little lamb who needs his rest?" He waved a dismissive hand. "The road is long, and a peddler grows weary. Sometimes, a kind face and a shared moment are worth more than coin."

He carefully wrapped the candle lamp in a piece of cloth she had handed him earlier, to protect its delicate metalwork.

"Consider it a gift. A blessing for your little one. May it bring him peaceful sleep, and you a moment's respite."

Yu's eyes widened, disbelief warring with a surge of overwhelming gratitude.

"I... I don't know what to say," she stammered, tears welling up. "Thank you, Jian. You are too kind."

"Kindness is a rare spice these days, my dear," Jian said with a wink. "Use it sparingly but savor it when you find it."

He handed her the wrapped candle holder.

"Just—" he paused and cocked his head to the side as though straining to hear something before continuing. "—be careful."

The words felt flimsy, a half-hearted warning against the guilt he'd carried like a stone for eight months. He'd tried to sell the device before, or to discard it, but the voice in his head—his constant companion since finding the lamp—always talked him out of it. This woman's raw need, however, had finally silenced that uncooperative whisper in his mind.

Yu accepted the gift with trembling hands, cradling it as if it were made of spun glass.

"I will. I promise." She bowed her head in appreciation, her heart singing with hope for the first time in months.

As she walked away, a renewed conviction in her step, the wind began to pick up. Old Jian watched her go, a flicker of regret crossing his weathered face. He reminded himself he was doing a good deed, easing the burden of a struggling mother. But another voice in the back of his mind whispered that he'd just made a mistake he didn't understand, something potentially dangerous. He shook his head, trying to dispel the voices. He was just an old peddler, not a seer.

He noticed the remaining villagers were staring past Yu. He followed their gaze up towards the crest of a mountain and to where a temple sat watching over the village like a silent sentinel. Dark clouds gathered on the horizon behind the temple, moving faster than any natural storm.

With a sudden, urgent haste, Jian began to pack away his cart, the bells ringing like rattled bones. One villager offered Jian his home as shelter for the night, but he waved him away with a half-hearted thanks.

Something was wrong—had been wrong since the moment he'd given away the lamp. The voice in his head was silent now, and somehow that was worse than its constant whisper.

"Come on, Chong," he muttered, kicking the donkey into motion. Lightning flashed in the distance. A tremor of something cold and dreadful ran through him. "Time to go."

Chong brayed in agreement, its ears twitching nervously, seemingly sensing the approaching storm as well. With one last look back at the village, Jian sighed, then plodded on as the two of them disappeared into the gathering darkness, the sounds of their bells fading away.

Yu reached the temple just as the sun set and the storm crashed overhead. The wind blew so hard she struggled to close the door while holding both Bao and the lamp. Pressing her back against the heavy wood she pushed as hard as she could with her legs until the door slowly slid into place.

Inside, the temple felt different—older somehow, as if the storm had awakened something in the ancient stones. Yu moved through the darkness with practiced ease. She placed Bao on his straw mat before unwrapping the lamp with reverent care, setting it on a rickety table beside the crying baby.

The brass gleamed with each lightning flash, the tiny sheep caught in perfect detail. Their metal eyes seemed to track her movements, and for a moment, she could have sworn she saw them blink.

Yu fumbled with her flint and steel, her hands shaking slightly. The storm raged outside, wind howling like a hungry wolf, rain lashing against the thick walls of the stone temple. Finally, a spark caught, and she lit the candles nestled within the brass lamp. A warm, flickering glow bathed the tiny animals.

Bao, however, continued to wail, his little face red and contorted. Yu sighed, exhaustion pulling at her. She settled in beside him on the dirt floor, and began to hum a lullaby, a traditional melody passed down from her mother, and her mother before her. The words spoke of gentle streams, plum trees, and the watchful moon. It was a song of peace, of protection, of the deep, unbroken sleep of the innocent.

She gently picked him up, exposed a breast from her gown and tried to feed him, but he didn't seem interested.

As she continued singing, the candle's heat began to turn the carousel. The miniature brass sheep began their circular journey, casting dancing shadows on the rough stone walls.

At first, the movement was excruciatingly slow, but gradually, it picked up speed. One by one they went around—their tiny metal hooves began ticking softly against the base of the lamp in a comforting rhythmic pattern.

Tick. Tick. Tick.

Outside, lightning flashed, the crash of thunder quickly followed.

Yu closed her eyes and laid her head back against the wall as she continued her soft lullaby. Lost in her song, she didn't notice one of the shadows lingering for just a moment, suspended on the wall, before it joined the other silhouettes in their dance.

She continued patiently humming and singing to Bao, gently bouncing him up and down, then side to side. His wailing eventually died down to an occasional whimper as he began to finally feed.

It was working.

Relief flooded over Yu. The promise of finally getting sleep made her singing more upbeat and hopeful.

On the wall, one of the dark shapes began to change. Imperceptible at first, but slowly it stretched and elongated, no longer mimicking the gentle curves of the sculpted sheep. They became angular, sharp, their movements jerky and unnatural. They detached themselves from the wall, writhing and twisting like living things. With every rotation they seemed to change, but always staring down at Yu and Bao with penetrating eyes.

Tick. Tick. Tick.

That shadow stopped spinning.

A sudden cold prickled on the back of her neck, as if she were being watched. Then a thick, cloying scent, like wet wool and blood hit her nose.

Tick. Tick. Tick.

Thunder crashed.

Bao's whimpers abruptly ceased.

Yu stopped singing as her heart leaped with a sudden fear—every instinct in her told her something was wrong. She opened her eyes and looked down at her son. His gaze was wide, but it was not focused on her, it was fixed on the spinning shadows.

His mouth hung open, no longer attached to her bosom feeding. He was unnaturally still. Not even the smallest tremor of breath disturbed the tiny rise and fall of his chest.

"Bao?" she whispered, her voice trembling. She reached out a hand to touch his cheek, her fingers brushing against skin that felt strangely cold.

Tick. Tick. Tick.

Then, all the ghostly figures stopped. Yu looked up in confusion at the lamp, which was still lit and spinning.

Tick. Tick. Tick.

One of the shadows began to shift. It didn't move like any shadow should—sliding across the stone—but something impossibly real. Something with weight and substance and terrible purpose. It began peeling itself from the wall with a sound like tearing silk, its arm stretching impossibly long, reaching across the room toward the silent infant.

Yu stared, frozen between horror and disbelief. Maybe she had fallen asleep, and this was a dream, a nightmare. The black formless arm stretched, snaking across the stone until it hovered directly above them.

Then, with that same tearing sound, a claw-like hand began to pull free from the wall, a physical thing born of shadow. It reached down, its phantom tendrils extending towards the still infant.

Yu recoiled, a silent scream trapped in her throat. She scrambled back, her eyes wide with horror, unable to tear her gaze away from the monstrous shade that loomed over her child.

The apparition suddenly paused above them, so close she could reach out and touch the now physical arm. The room fell silent except for the unrelenting rhythmic ticking.

Tick. Tick. Tick.

Bao shifted in her arms. She dared a quick look down at him and gasped. Bao stared back, his eyes unblinking and black as polished stone. His mouth opened slowly, and a low, guttural bleat croaked out.

The cry grew louder, distorting into something inhuman, something ancient and terrifying. The bleating became a sustained, piercing shriek, a sound that vibrated the very air in the temple, a sound that spoke of nightmares made real.

Yu screamed, a desperate, primal cry of terror and denial. But her scream was swallowed by the impossibly loud shriek from the infant. The candles blew out suddenly and violently, plunging the room into absolute, suffocating darkness.

All that remained was the echo of a mother and her son's screams being ripped away.

Outside, the storm let up and a silence fell over the village below.

Little Bo-Peep has lost her sheep
And doesn't know where to find them.
Leave them alone and they'll come
home,
Bringing their tails behind them.

Chapter 1

The world tilted, a familiar morning lurch that sent the floor swimming. Sarah gripped the edge of her nightstand, knuckles white, waiting for the wave of dizziness to pass. She took a deep, deliberate breath and held it for a moment, then slowly released it. This daily ritual fought the woozy phantom of her epilepsy medication.

It was only when the room settled that she saw the constellation of small white pills scattered across the hardwood floor, the consequence of her earlier, blind slap at the buzzing phone alarm. 6:00 AM. On any other day, she might have cursed. But today was different. Today marked the seventh anniversary of when her mother walked into the Chinese village of Gu Mei and vanished without a trace.

And today, Sarah was going back to find her.

Sarah let out a small squeal of pent-up excitement. She and her mismatched group of friends were actually doing this. Years of dreaming and planning, and the time was finally here.

She glanced at the framed photo on the dresser: Mei-Lin. Her mother. It was a faded image of a young woman mid-laugh, with dark sparkling eyes and a cascade of jet-black hair.

Sarah's memories of her resembled that photo—fragmented, sun-bleached, and brittle. The trace of jasmine perfume. A lullaby sung that she could barely remember. Mei-Lin had been erased from her life when Sarah was thirteen. Seven years carved off the calendar like skin from bone. A simple family trip that had shattered her world.

The official story amounted to nothing but shrugged shoulders and tight-lipped silence. One day she was there; the next, she was gone. Her father, Dr. David Láng, had flown back and forth for months, his scientific certainty crumbling against a wall of provincial superstitious whispers. The village had never even sent out a damn search party.

He finally settled on a narrative of his own, one he clung to like a crucifix in a horror movie: that Mei-Lin, overwhelmed with stress, had simply left them. Not suicide, she'd never do that, but a voluntary reset. A tidy, clinical explanation that insulated him from the messy horror of the alternative—murder.

Sarah, however, had gotten more than her mother's high cheekbones—she'd inherited her belief in things that slithered just at the edge of sight. The whispers her father dismissed, she held onto. It was a quiet, fungal growth of suspicion in her heart; the truth was something uglier, something that couldn't be easily dismissed.

Her mother would never leave them, not by choice. And murder? In that sleepy village?

It was a raw, festering wound of opposing beliefs, one Sarah intended to lance open the second she set foot on Gu Mei's soil. She wanted some goddamn answers.

Pills rattling back into their bottle, Sarah padded over to the open suitcase on the floor where a jumble of clothes, toiletries, and travel essentials spilled out the top. She picked up a small, intricately carved wooden jewelry box, a gift from her Auntie Lin during a brief, awkward visit to New York years ago. Sarah didn't actually wear jewelry; she hated the feel of it. Her mother hadn't either.

She knew it was foolish to carry expensive trinkets across the world, especially if she didn't plan on wearing them. But leaving them felt like betrayal—like abandoning her mother's spirit. After convincing herself to take them, she buried the box under a pile of dark, functional clothes.

In the cramped bathroom, the smudged mirror reflected a pale, petite Asian woman in her early twenties, with her mother's high cheekbones and her father's kind, catlike dark brown eyes. Her smooth jet-black hair, once long, was currently chopped into a no-nonsense, chin-length bob that complemented her roundish face. The severe style change made her features look more determined than beautiful—at least she hoped so.

She splashed cold water over her, the shock helping to clear the lingering fog of sleep and medication. Water droplets clung to her pale, almost translucent skin, amplifying the faint blue veins visible just beneath the surface. A small, barely noticeable scar traced a line above her left eyebrow, a souvenir from a childhood fall, that in hindsight, might have been from her first seizure.

While brushing her teeth, she studied her reflection with a critical eye. She looked tired, the circles under her eyes pronounced. Stress lines, too deep for her age, etched around her mouth. She sighed, knowing that no amount of concealer would completely erase the evidence of sleepless nights and anxieties.

Back in her bedroom, she dressed quickly and efficiently, prioritizing practicality over style. She pulled on a pair of loose-fitting, dark linen pants and a simple, grey, short-sleeved shirt. Comfort and breathability were key. She avoided anything tight or constricting, the ever-present need to feel unconfined.

The loose fit felt essential—tight spaces, even the feeling of restrictive clothing against her skin, could trigger a prickle of panic, making her breath catch in her throat. This vulnerability, a quiet dread of being trapped, represented another challenge she managed. It was a fear forged with her friends; on an anniversary they never spoke of.

She chose sturdy, well-worn walking shoes over the more fashionable sandals she'd considered. Function over form, she reminded herself, always. A thin, silver chain, almost invisible against her skin, was the only adornment she allowed herself. It held a tiny, silver St. Christopher medal, a gift from her father, a silent prayer for safe travels. She tucked it beneath her shirt, a private gesture of hope and protection.

Sarah surveyed herself one last time in the full-length mirror on the back of her door. She looked... unremarkable. And that was exactly the point. She didn't want to draw attention to herself. She wanted to blend in, to observe, to uncover the truth about her mother's disappearance without becoming the focus of anyone's curiosity. She wanted to be a shadow, a ghost, moving through the village unnoticed, gathering the pieces of a puzzle she'd been trying to solve for half her life.

A sudden knock on her door made her flinch.

"Sarah? You up?"

"Yep. You can come in."

Dr. Láng opened her door a crack and peeked through the opening to make sure she was decent before stepping inside. Her father, a tall and slender man with graying temples and kind, intelligent eyes was dressed in his usual attire—a crisp button-down shirt and slacks, even though it was a Saturday. He always looked like he was on his way to a lecture or a conference.

"I see you managed to wake up early," he said, his gaze sweeping the room—the suitcase, her medicine bottle and the general state of pre-travel chaos.

"Couldn't sleep," Sarah replied, forcing a smile. "Too excited, I guess."

"Excited or anxious?" he asked, his voice laced with gentle probing as he picked up her medicine bottle and began silently counting the pills. He knew her better than she knew herself.

Sarah shrugged. "Both, maybe." She avoided his eyes, pretending to fold a stray T-shirt.

Dr. Láng rubbed his eyes. He'd tried to dissuade her from going on this trip, insistent even, worried about the emotional toll it might take on her. He knew how deeply she yearned to connect with her mother's past, but he also feared what she might uncover. The village of Gu Mei held its own painful memories for him, secrets he'd buried deep.

"Sarah," he began, his voice taking on that serious, clinical tone he used when he was about to dissect something uncomfortable. "I know this trip is important. But you need to be careful. For your own sake. Don't... don't go digging. Some things are better left buried."

Sarah met his gaze, a flicker of defiance in her eyes. "She's not buried, Dad. She's *missing*. That's the problem."

He hesitated, then shook his head. "The *problem* is that damn village. Going back there, stirring up the past won't bring her back."

"But maybe it will. Maybe I'll find her and bring her back," she replied, holding his gaze defiantly.

Her dad managed a thin smile. "You remind me of her, you know," he said after a short pause. "Just promise me you'll be careful, Sarah. And that you'll listen to your instincts. If something feels wrong, *don't* ignore it."

"Like you ignored mom?"

Sarah immediately regretted her snarky response when she saw her dad wince. He didn't deserve that. She knew her father's concerns stemmed from a place of love and protection, but she also felt a responsibility to her mother whose beliefs were always ignored, if not openly mocked.

"Sorry." She flashed him an apologetic smile. "It's just that of all people, you, who needs proof of everything, just accepted their *theories* without question. I need to find my own answers."

A sudden buzz from her phone interrupted them before her dad could respond. It was a text from Maya.

> *I'm here.*

A jolt of adrenaline shot through her. It was time. "That's Maya," she said, lifting her suitcase then grabbing her backpack and the pill bottle, stuffing the meds inside the bag. "Gotta go!"

Before she could escape past him, he pulled her into a hug that felt more like a desperate attempt to hold her back.

"Be safe," he whispered into her hair, the words a prayer and a warning.

She flashed him a sincere smile, pulling away, then fled, taking the stairs two at a time, not looking back. From the window, he watched the whirlwind of her fragile bravado, hurtling headfirst toward the same quiet, suffocating mystery that had swallowed his wife whole seven years ago.

Outside, the air was already warm, even though the sun had barely risen. Summer had gripped New York hard this year and refused to let go. Probably all that global warming she kept hearing about on the news.

Her friend Maya was leaned against the driver-side door of their slightly beat-up SUV. The resident pragmatist of the group, their heavy-set build showed even beneath their dark green hoodie, cargo pants, and sturdy hiking boots. Despite the heat, they were still wearing their familiar oversized clothing—pretending to be comfortable in this hellish weather. Sarah wasn't complaining though, she thought they looked cute in the outfit.

"You ready for this?" Maya asked, reaching through the window and popping the back hatch.

"As I'll ever be," Sarah replied, wrestling her suitcase into the back.

Maya came around the car to help, flashing Sarah a warm grin while rearranging the luggage. Sarah's cheeks flushed at their simple kindness, and her attempt to return the smile felt very awkward.

"Did you remember your passport? And charging adapters?" they asked.

Sarah looked up at them. They stood a head taller than Sarah, their straight, dark brown hair was pulled back into a tight ponytail, revealing a face that was both intelligent and kind. Wiccan jewelry covered their tan body—their own quiet faith against the world's chaos.

"Yep," Sarah said. "I used the list you gave us. Checked it twice." The simple, practical questions were a comfort, a small anchor of normalcy in the swirling emotions of the morning.

"Alright," Maya said, closing the hatch with a loud *thunk*. "Let's go get the rest of the chaos crew."

Sarah laughed and slid into the passenger seat, moving Maya's large journal so she had room to sit. The familiar scent of sage and old books that permeated the car enveloped her in its comforting embrace. Maya hopped in the driver's seat, started the engine, and the SUV lurched forward, pulling away from the curb. Sarah waved goodbye at her dad who was still standing at her bedroom window watching.

A sense of finality washed over her as her father faded away behind them. She was leaving behind the familiar, the safe, the known. She was heading into the unknown, into the heart of her family's past, and into the shadow of a mystery that had haunted her for most of her life. She took a deep breath, trying to quell the rising tide of anxiety. It was too late to turn back now. China awaited.

As they drove, Sarah gazed out the window, watching the familiar cityscape of New York blur past. The towering skyscrapers, the bustling streets, the constant hum of activity—it was all so... ordinary. But with every mile they traveled, a sense of unease grew within her. She was leaving all of this behind, venturing into a world that was both foreign and deeply personal.

"You okay?" Maya asked, noticing her quiet contemplation in the rearview mirror. "You seem a little... off."

Sarah forced a smile. "Just thinking about my mom," she said. "It's weird, you know? Going back to the place where she grew up, where she..." The word died in her throat. *Died. Ran away. Vanished.* She silently berated herself for allowing her mood to sour already. It hadn't even been an hour. She was working on that with her psychologist.

Maya nodded understandingly. "It's going to be intense," they said. "But we're here for you, okay? We're all in this together."

"Thanks, El," Sarah replied, using Maya's occasional nickname taken from their favorite Broadway play Wicked. "Speaking of... the gravity of the situation..."

Sarah gently nudged Maya and gave them a sly wink. Maya, smirking back in understanding, reached over and started a song. She released a squeal of happiness as 'Defying Gravity' from the Wicked soundtrack started playing. The two of them began singing together in a duet, laughing the whole time.

The song was finishing for the third time when they pulled up to Chloe's apartment. Maya paused the music just as Chloe burst out the front door, a vibrant splash of pink hair against the brick, her phone already held aloft. "They're here!" she chirped to her followers, a rainbow fanny pack slung across the cropped tie-dye shirt exposing her midriff.

Chloe bounded over to them with her usual bright smile and bubbly personality, a stark contrast to Sarah's more subdued demeanor. Her fingers, each adorned with multiple rings, flashed as she gestured excitedly, her phone raised, capturing every moment. "And here she is, guys," Chloe narrated into her phone, before turning the camera on Sarah. "The lady of the hour. Are you ready for this adventure?" Chloe asked, her voice full of infectious enthusiasm.

Sarah stuck out her tongue and flipped off the camera.

Trailing behind her was Chris, looking effortlessly cool in a worn leather jacket and scuffed converse but struggling under the weight of Chloe's designer luggage. He swaggered over as best he could under the load. "You still have time to chicken out, Láng," he said, lowering his sunglasses.

"And miss you getting lost on another hike? Not a chance." Sarah replied, as Chris started wrestling Chloe's brightly colored, designer luggage into the back.

"That was *one* time!" he yelled from behind the SUV, before turning to Chloe. "Jesus Christ, babe. You have so much shit, there's no room for Ben's suitcase."

"He can hold it on his lap," She replied in a bubbly voice while climbing into the second row of seats. "He won't mind."

Which was true, Ben wouldn't mind. It was no secret how Ben felt about Chloe and there was no doubt he would bend over backwards to appease her—a fact that Chloe constantly took advantage of.

"Shotgun!" Chris suddenly barked, slamming the back hatch closed then bolting around the car and sliding to a halt in front of Sarah. With a sigh, Sarah crawled out of the front seat and into the back next to Chloe.

"That's not how it's supposed to work, Chris," she said in a flat voice as she sat down. "You can't call shotgun when someone is already in it."

He laughed. So, Sarah reached over the front seat and tousled his artfully crafted hair.

"Hey!" He cried out in fake indignation. "Hair is off limits Láng." She answered him with a mocking laugh.

"You deserved it." Chloe said to Chris, flashing Sarah a smirk in support. Chris turned around and gave them an exaggerated scowl.

As Maya put the car into gear and pulled away, Chris reached over to the radio controls and pressed play. The soundtrack to Wicked began blasting from the speakers.

"Ugh! What is this shit?" He groaned, while turning the volume down. Sarah and Maya both giggled. Chris frowned and started pressing buttons on the radio before Master of Puppets by Metallica began playing. "Now, *this* is some real music."

The group started head banging as they drove to pick up Ben in Sunnyside. It wasn't a far drive, but the crazy morning traffic made it take much longer than it should have. Still, they pulled up to his old, cramped apartment complex right on time. After sending him a dozen texts that they were there, Maya had to lay on the horn for a full ten seconds before the door finally opened.

Ben, or Glitch as his friends called him, already submerged himself in the blue glow of his phone as he emerged from the basement unit. Physically slight, almost fragile-looking, with a mop of unruly, sandy-blond hair that perpetually fell into his eyes. Like Maya, he was wearing an oversized hoodie in the stifling heat, along with baggy jeans, and worn-out generic sneakers. His pale skin made it obvious that he rarely saw sunlight, preferring the glow of a computer screen.

"Yeah, yeah. I'm here." He mumbled, pushing up the slim wire-framed glasses that started sliding down his short nose as he walked around the car looking for a place to put his suitcase. When he realized there was no room for his bag in the back, he leaned through the passenger window. "You guys forget I was coming?"

Chloe pouted her lips and fluttered her eyelashes. "Can you hold it on your lap, Glitch?"

After a short pause, Ben unsurprisingly agreed. "Fine. Scoot over, Sarah."

"Thank you, Ben!" Chloe said with way too much enthusiasm.

He grumbled under his breath as he squeezed in beside Sarah, laying the suitcase across his lap.

"You have your passport, Glitch?" Maya called out from the front.

"Relax, El," he said. "You reminded me six times yesterday. The pre-flight check is complete."

Maya rolled their eyes, but a small smile played on their lips. They were used to Ben's sharp tongue. Despite his introverted nature and geeky appearance, Ben possessed a sharp wit and a sense of humor that often-caught people off guard.

They were all so different, a collection of mismatched parts forced to fit together in the burning aftermath of... *that* day. The day they had aptly named themselves the 'Still Alive Five.' They were a trauma-bonded family, and that shared history—a link forged in fire—was the only reason they had all agreed to come.

Maya pulled the car away from the curb and the Still Alive Five were officially on the way.

"What game are you playing?" Sarah asked Ben next to her.

"Some new lit mobile RPG," Ben mumbled, his thumbs flying across the screen. "Gotta grind those levels before we lose service in the sticks."

Sarah chuckled. Ben's dedication to his virtual worlds was both endearing and slightly exasperating. She knew it was his armor, his own way of coping. She sometimes wondered if his constant joking was another form of escape as well.

The conversation in the car drifted to topics about the trip—their itinerary, the food they wanted to try, the sights they wanted to see. Chloe, of course, had a detailed plan for documenting every moment of their trip for her followers. Chris was eager to explore the countryside and try some "off-roading" escapades, much to Chloe's dismay. Ben just wanted to find a decent Wi-Fi connection.

But beneath the surface chatter, Sarah couldn't shake the feeling of apprehension that gnawed at her. *Don't go digging,* her father's voice echoed. But she planned to do exactly that. It was in her blood.

They made it to the airport earlier than they planned but still rushed in excitement for the trip ahead. During the security checkpoint shuffle, as they took their shoes off, Chris nudged Ben.

"You gonna be ok without the phone for a few minutes Glitch?"

Ben didn't miss a beat. "Maybe. Just make sure you took all those extra-small condoms out of your wallet before it goes through the scanner. Wouldn't want to embarrass yourself."

They shoved each other playfully, their laughter sharp in the tense noise of security yelling at everyone.

The line moved slowly, but they eventually made it through, the only incident being Ben making a terrible joke to a stone-faced TSA agent about a photon having no luggage because it was traveling light, which earned a pained groan from Maya.

As soon as their phones were back in hand, Chloe was filming again. At their gate, they sat down with some pizza they grabbed at the nearby eatery and chatted with an excited energy.

For a moment, watching them, a pang of genuine, uncomplicated happiness washed over Sarah. Maya, who was normally reserved, was even bantering back-and-forth with Ben while Chris was attacking Chloe's neck with kisses, making her squeal with laughter.

Sarah grinned to herself. It was all so perfect.

After a few bites of pizza Sarah caught Ben staring at Chloe with a visible frown, and a sad look of longing in his eyes, as she giggled and playfully tried to push Chris off her as he assaulted her with even more neck kisses. When he noticed Sarah was looking at him, he quickly looked away with a blush and mumbled a lame joke about needing more pepperoni fuel while stuffing the pizza in his mouth.

The crackle of the PA system interrupted her thoughts.

"We are now boarding group C for flight CA982 to Beijing."

"That's us!" Chloe sang, snapping her phone shut and jumping to her feet by pushing off Chris with an almost theatrical flourish. They each gathered their own gear, except for Chris, who was Chloe's pack-mule and made their way towards the gate. Grumbling the whole time, Chris followed, juggling bright pink designer luggage and bags, while somehow balancing his own suitcase.

Ben, ever the charmer, flashed a wide grin at the gate agent, who offered a polite, professional smile in return. Chloe rolled her eyes good-naturedly and pushed him along. Maya, calm and collected as always, handed over their documents with a quiet nod. Chris, predictably with his hands full, fumbled with his boarding pass, nearly dropping his phone, and muttered something about carrying all of Chloe's shit.

Once on the plane, they easily found their assigned seats and settled in. The arrangement suited Sarah, who usually preferred a window seat on short flights but took the aisle for more room on this long trip. Maya and Ben sat next to her while Chloe and Chris took two seats in front of them.

Ben was already hunched over in the window seat, fingers flying, trying to see if the plane's Wi-Fi was active, his brow furrowed in intense concentration.

"Wi-Fi won't turn on until we hit around ten thousand feet, Glitch." Sarah told him, while she shifted in her seat to buckle the seatbelt.

"You underestimate my power," he replied without looking up, his thumbs still dancing across his screen. "The Wi-Fi gods are fickle and demand tribute, probably in the form of overpriced satellite internet packages."

Chloe was already turning around in her seat, phone poised.

"Quick selfie before takeoff, guys. Airborne edition!"

Sarah forced a small smile for the camera. Chris leaned over the seat, making a peace sign and a goofy face. Maya gave a simple wave, their eyes crinkling at the corners while Ben gave the middle finger to the camera without looking up from his phone.

The plane lurched as the tow vehicle began pushing them away from the gate. Chris, tightening his grip on the seat, looked at each of them.

"Alright, nerds," he said, tapping his chest. "One."

Chloe lowered her phone, a small, genuine smile replacing her influencer grin. "Two," she said softly.

Ben, without looking up from his phone, mumbled, "Three."

Maya, settling into their seat, looked over at Sarah. "Four."

Sarah met their gaze and completed the ritual. "Five."

"Still alive," they whispered in near unison, the words a familiar, comfortable chant against the jitters of takeoff. It was their mantra, their check-in, a quiet acknowledgment of everything they had survived together. The Still Alive Five. For a brief moment, they knew they could survive anything.

As the plane taxied, Sarah gazed out the small, oval window, though the view was partially obscured by the wing. The airport buildings gave way to a patchwork of runways and the distant, hazy silhouette of New York City.

The engines began spooling up, whined, then roared, pressing everyone back into their seats. The plane lifted its nose, and the sensation of ascent pulled at their stomachs, the ground falling away with surprising speed.

There was no turning back now.

CHAPTER 2

The long flight dragged on, and after the initial excitement wore off, even Chloe with her endless energy agreed to try and get some sleep. Sarah tried to rest as well, but mostly just tossed and turned in her aisle seat to fight off her claustrophobia in the cramped space.

Occasionally she would doze off, her dreams filled with vague images of shadows, and a storm that chased her until its final, violent arrival woke her with a jolt.

She rubbed the sleep from her eyes and sat up. The inside of the cabin hung eerily still and dark, the only illumination from the faint floor lights and a couple of bulbs near the lavatories.

A small smile escaped her lips at the sight of Maya sleeping peacefully in the middle seat next to her, their head resting against the divider. With each breath, Maya let out a soft purring noise, just shy of an actual snore.

Surprisingly, even Chris, who normally snored like a lion, remained quiet from the row in front of her. From her vantage point, she could clearly see that he and Chloe were asleep, their heads leaning against each other's.

In the window seat next to Maya, Ben slept as well, his phone still clutched in hand. Sarah scanned around the cabin and noticed everyone, it seemed, was out cold. Surely a flight attendant or two would be walking around, she thought.

Confused, but needing to use the restroom, she unbuckled her seatbelt. She moved the items from her lap as quietly as she could, trying not to wake Maya, and stood. Her stiff muscles protested as she stretched them out.

The bathroom lights closest to her at the rear of the plane glowed red, signifying occupied. With a soft groan, she moved towards the middle of the plane instead. Stepping sideways, she navigated the aisle, trying not to bump into anyone while passing row after row of silent, sleeping passengers. No one made a sound. No coughing or sneezing, no one clearing their throat. Nothing.

Except one sound.

A faint rhythmic ticking she noticed over the hum of the engines, coming from somewhere near the front of the plane.

As she approached the mid-cabin lavatories, the green 'unoccupied' sign on both doors simultaneously flickered, spasmed, then turned red. Sarah froze in confusion.

No one had gone in the restrooms. She reached out and tried to open one of the doors, but it wouldn't budge. She turned around and tried the other one, but it was stuck as well.

"*What the hell?*"

In the periphery of her vision, towards first-class, a light along the floor abruptly went out. She turned to look just as another bulb turned off. Then another, but closer this time.

Row by row, one after another, they were extinguished. A slow, deliberate smothering, as if an unseen hand were moving down the aisle, snuffing out each light like a candle. The wave of darkness advanced slowly, swallowing the plane.

The ticking grew louder.

Tick. Tick. Tick.

She risked a glance back and gasped, a sharp intake of breath that caught in her throat. Every passenger in the rows behind her stared directly at her, their empty eyes wide and reflecting the dim cabin lights like a field of dark, wet stones. Heads swiveled on necks at unnatural angles, tracking her every move.

"What... what the hell is going on?" she choked out, her voice quivering in fear. "Ben, this isn't funny." She knew as soon as the words left her mouth that it wasn't another one of Ben's pranks.

The void continued its relentless advance. Row by row, the lights blinked out.

Closer. Closer.

And in perfect, horrifying unison, every mouth in the seats behind her opened. They opened wide, stretching much too far, but no sound came out. It was a silent, collective scream.

Their heads swiveled on their necks, tracking her movement as she scrambled backwards, away from the advancing dark, away from the silent screams. The gloom was approaching faster now; she couldn't outpace the rolling void. The aisle lengthened, the seats pressing in.

She couldn't find her row. Where was Maya?

Tick. Tick. Tick.

She turned and faced the oncoming blackness. Unable to outrun it, she stood her ground and waited. Silence fell over her, even the hum of the engines faded, the only sound was that of her heart about to burst from her chest. She stared hard into the void, straining to penetrate the pitch black.

Tick. Tick. Tick.

The ticking sounded right beside her ear now; the maddening noise worming its way inside her head. The darkness reached her. It wrapped around her like a thick blanket, but it was cold. So cold. She shivered uncontrollably as the total nothingness engulfed her.

She held her breath, her heart a frantic drum against her ribs.

And from behind her, out of the gloom, an icy-cold hand clamped down on her shoulder. Her mother's voice suddenly screamed in her ear.

"Sarah!"

She screamed.

"Sarah! It's going to be okay, Sarah."

Sarah's eyes flew open. Chris was leaning over her, his face a mask of frantic concern. He had her pinned to the floor of the plane. Above them, Ben and a flight attendant hovered, their expressions a mixture of alarm and confusion.

Maya stretched over from the seat to the side, their hand firmly holding hers. "It's okay, Sarah. You're okay. Just breathe."

Sarah's body trembled uncontrollably. The remnants of the nightmare clung to her—the suffocating darkness, the ticking sound, the silent, staring eyes. It had felt so *real*.

Shit. Shit. Shit.

The realization hit her, a wave of mortification even colder than the nightmare's touch. She wasn't trembling from a dream—she had just had a seizure.

She groaned as Chris and Maya helped her sit up, her entire body aching from the spasms. The thought of all those pitying eyes watching her sent a hot flush of shame across her cheeks.

Half crawling, she gingerly slipped past Maya and collapsed next to the window, hiding her face from the sea of curious, pitying eyes. The flight attendants, ever professional, verbally made sure she was ok and buckled in safely, before handing her a glass of water.

Chloe jumped to her feet, fiercely telling people to "mind their own damn business." Maya handled the flight attendants with their calm efficiency. And Ben, for the first time Sarah could remember, stayed utterly silent, his face pale, his usual armor of jokes gone.

Maya eventually slipped into the seat next to her, took her hand, and Sarah finally let the silent, hot tears come, her body shaking in her friend's steady hold.

When they finally landed in China, a strange mix of disorientation and familiarity made Sarah dizzy. The air smelled different, the sounds were different, the language was different. Yet, something in the atmosphere, something in the very soil beneath her feet, resonated with a part of her.

After a connecting flight to a smaller city, they boarded a rattling bus that took them deeper and deeper into the heartland. As the bus bumped along the winding mountain roads, the landscape grew increasingly green and rural. Rice paddies stretched out like emerald carpets, water buffalo grazed in lush meadows, and traditional houses with curved roofs dotted the hillsides.

Sarah gazed out the window of the bus, her heart pounding with a mixture of anticipation and dread. She was getting closer to the place where her life had changed forever, closer to the answers she craved.

A sudden hand on her shoulder made her flinch—the nightmare still fresh in her mind—and turned to see Maya looking at her with concern.

"You hanging in there?" Maya asked, their voice soft.

Sarah took a deep breath and nodded.

"Yeah," she said, trying to sound more confident than she felt. "I'm feeling better now. Just... mentally preparing myself."

Sarah hesitated, tempted to tell Maya about the nightmare, but decided against it—it was just a stupid dream, after all. Her answer seemed to satisfy Maya, who didn't probe any further.

As the bus rumbled on, carrying her deeper into the core of her family's past, Sarah couldn't shake the feeling that she was also heading straight into the heart of a nightmare. The landscape, however beautiful, held its breath, waiting.

The bus driver, a thin man with a face like a leather map, turned around and announced in a strange mix of local dialects that they were almost there.

She was almost home.

Chapter 3

The bus creaked and rattled, its aging engine protesting as it navigated the increasingly steep and winding mountain road. The landscape outside the grimy windows of the vehicle had transformed from the seemingly never-ending urban sprawl to a panorama of rural China straight out of a painting.

Terraced rice paddies cascaded up the hillsides like giant steps leading to the clouds. Water buffalo, beasts of burden and myth, wallowed in muddy pools, their movements slow and deliberate. Flocks of sheep grazed on green pastures, their white fleece standing out like scattered bones against the colorful hillside. Traditional homes clung to the slopes, their paper-covered windows like vacant eyes watching the road below.

Sarah pressed her forehead against the cool glass, captivated by the landscape rolling by. This place felt like a world away from the concrete canyons and relentless energy of New York City. A world both alien and beautiful, yet strangely familiar to her. Perhaps, she thought, her mother's spirit connected her to this magnificent land.

"Okay, this view is straight-up *gorgeous*," Chloe exclaimed as if reading Sarah's thoughts, while snapping a rapid series of photos with her phone. "My social feed is gonna *be lit*."

"Just don't drop your cell out the window," Maya cautioned.

"Yeah, I doubt there's a repair shop next to all the buffalo," Ben quipped.

"Chill, guys," Chloe said, rolling her eyes. "I've got a grip. Besides, I need to document every single second of this trip. This is *content*, people!"

Chris, who had been surprisingly quiet during the bus ride, leaned forward, his eyes scanning the passing scenery.

"Imagine tearing through these roads in a souped-up WRX," he muttered, a wistful note in his voice. "The drifts you could do..."

"Or imagine *not* driving like a maniac on these narrow mountain roads," Chloe retorted, giving him a pointed look.

"Live a little, babe," Chris said with a grin. "Where's your sense of adventure?"

"My sense of adventure doesn't involve me livestreaming our plunge to a fiery death, thanks," Chloe replied with a frown. "Though, I gotta admit, the stream would probably break the internet."

Ben, who was engrossed in a game on his phone, suddenly let out a cry of anguish.

"Guys, I'm losing signal," he announced, his voice tinged with a panic that Sarah couldn't be sure was real or not. "We're in the dark ages. The honest-to-god dark ages."

"Welcome to the real world, Glitch," Sarah said, a small smile playing on her lips. "Now you'll have to, you know, interact with us actual humans."

Ben shuddered dramatically. "Just kill me now. Throw me out the bus window."

Chris grabbed Ben by the shoulders and pretended to lift him out of the window. Ben laughed and grabbed Chris's arm as they started to wrestle, bumping into Chloe.

"Stop! I swear to God, Chris," Chloe said, playfully slapping Chris's arm. "It's like I am surrounded by children."

Ben gave Chris one last playful shove before settling back down into their seats. The two of them giggling.

The chatter inside faded, becoming a distant hum. Sarah traced a far-off peak with her finger, her own world shrinking to the tight knot in her chest. The closer they got, the less excited she felt. Tendrils of doubt began creeping in—was she truly ready for the answers she might find?

As the bus rounded a particularly sharp bend, its tires kicking up loose dirt, Sarah caught a glimpse of two figures standing on a rocky outcrop overlooking the road. An old man, his form stooped and weathered like a gnarled root, with wisps of a long thin beard blowing in the wind, stood beside a donkey. Hitched behind the dusty animal was a brightly colored cart, its sides painted with gaudy, peeling flowers.

They both seemed to be staring at her.

As the bus pulled away, the old man's arm rose, slow and deliberate. His finger, crooked and bony, pointed directly at Sarah.

Sarah blinked in disbelief, goosebumps rolling over her skin like a cold wave.

"Does anyone see that?" she asked, her voice shaky.

Her friends looked at her, puzzled. "See what?" Chloe asked.

"An old man standing on the ridge back there. With a donkey." Sarah pointed back towards the outcrop.

They all craned their necks, but the outcrop had already disappeared from view.

"Was it Shrek and his donkey?" Ben asked with a terrible Scottish accent. "Looking for his swamp?"

Chris and Chloe both shared a laugh, while Maya simply gave Ben an exasperated glance. Sarah sat quietly, too troubled over what she saw to find humor in the moment. Something about them sparked a flicker of recognition, but she couldn't put her finger on it. She glanced back in the direction of the strange pair, but they were long gone.

Just what she needed. Another mystery.

Finally, they crested a plateau, and the village of Gu Mei came into view. It was larger than Sarah had imagined, a cluster of a couple dozen shops huddled together around a central square, and homes stretched wide in either direction. Terraced fields and looming mountains surrounded the village itself. Smoke curled lazily from chimneys, carrying the scent of woodsmoke and cooking spices.

A thick cloud of dust hung over the valley, but Sarah welcomed the change over the polluted air of a big city.

"Jesus, look at the dust. Hope no one has allergies," Ben quipped.

As the bus hissed to a stop in the village square, a wave of emotion washed over her. This was it. The first and last place her mother had visited. Her origin story and her final chapter, all in one.

A small crowd had gathered, their faces a mix of curiosity and welcome. A woman stepped forward out of the throng, a slash of vibrant color in the dusty brown landscape. A silk scarf, stitched with impossibly bright plum blossoms, was slung around her neck. Sarah recognized her Auntie Lin immediately, her face a beautiful, weathered map, and in her eyes, the ghost of Mei-Lin. A surge of warmth filled her, a sense of connection to this place and these people.

The group hopped out, where Ben started sneezing immediately. Sarah ran to Auntie Lin with open arms, where they embraced in a tight hug. Her Aunt was smiling wide as she stood back and looked her over.

"Sarah! Look how much you have grown!" she said in Mandarin, gripping her shoulders warmly. "Welcome home."

"Thank you, Auntie."

The introduction of her friends was a blur of polite nods and their awkward attempts at Mandarin. The villagers helped with the luggage, their movements efficient, their eyes constantly flicking back to the newcomers, a mixture of curiosity and appraisal in their gazes. It wasn't every day distant relatives visited, not to mention foreigners.

Auntie Lin led them through the village to a traditional-style house that sat near the end. Rammed earth formed its walls, and intricately carved wooden eaves adorned its roof. The house, simple but charming, had a small courtyard filled with potted plants and a well-worn stone path leading to the front door. The villagers placed their luggage down by the old home and headed back to their own lives with a brief farewell.

"This was your mother's," Auntie Lin said, once the villagers were out of earshot, resting her hand on the weathered wooden door. "I use it mostly for storage now, but I cleaned it out for you."

She gingerly stepped inside.

The air felt heavy and thick with unspoken memories. Incense, dried herbs, woodsmoke—the scents overwhelmed her, both alien and achingly familiar. A lump formed in her throat.

Dim light filtered through small, paper-covered windows, leaving the interior shadowed. Old, worn furniture stood carefully arranged throughout the room. Family photos adorned the walls, offering glimpses into a past Sarah had never known—a gallery of ghosts. She saw pictures of her mother as a child, as a teenager, as a young woman, her smile radiant and full of life. A pang of grief, sharp and unexpected, pierced Sarah's heart.

"I'm so happy you all could make it," Auntie Lin said warmly.

"It's great to be here!" Chloe responded, trying her best at Mandarin.

"Yeah, thank you!" Chris said, attempting the local dialect as well.

Auntie Lin chuckled at the honest attempts.

"Make yourself at home, and we will eat soon!" Auntie Lin said as she gestured towards a large wooden table.

The friends began to unpack and collectively decided on sleeping arrangements without much fuss. Once their bags were opened, Maya immediately began taking notes in their large journal.

"This is surreal," Maya stated out loud to Sarah. "So much history here. What do you know about this village? Are there any local lore?"

Sarah shook her head.

"Not much, my dad never really talked about it."

"Well, you're about to get a major dose of culture shock, I hope you're ready," Chloe said laughing as she walked around holding her phone up high, trying to get a signal on her phone.

"I thought you would be happy to get away from the tech for a while?" Sarah asked.

"If I can't update my socials, that will literally be the worst thing that can happen to me right now!" Chloe exclaimed as Maya rolled their eyes.

Sarah noticed Chris was already outside doing stretches, probably preparing for later hikes and to take photos, she thought.

As the group started to settle in, the weight of the last seven years pressed down on Sarah. The excited chatter of her friends faded, replaced by a low hum of anxiety in her own head. This was the house where her mother had last slept, the air she had last breathed. Excusing herself, she found a back door near the kitchen and escaped into the unknown.

CHAPTER 4

Sarah stepped through the door into a small, enclosed courtyard, a haven of relative quiet compared to the bustle of unpacking and the excited chatter of her friends. Her eyes instantly settled on a stone well, resting in the center of the modest square, its mouth sealed shut by a moss-covered wooden lid. A wave of goosebumps washed over her as she neared it. She couldn't explain why; maybe it was the thought of the tight space triggering her claustrophobia.

An old peach tree leaned next to the well, its branches twisted like arthritic limbs and covered with sparse leaves which offered a meager shade. Sarah sat down on a low bench beneath the tree, feeling the cool, smooth stone beneath her fingertips.

And then it hit her: the smell of jasmine.

It wasn't a memory this time, it was here, and it was real. The scent triggered a dizzying cascade of images—her mother's hand, a lullaby, the weight of a hug. Tears pricked Sarah's eyes. She blinked, fighting them back. She was here for truth, not for crying. She needed to be strong, to focus on her purpose. But being here, in her mother's home, surrounded by the echoes of her past, made that resolve feel incredibly fragile.

She closed her eyes, taking a deep breath, trying to center herself. The sounds of the village faded into the background—the distant chatter of villagers, the clucking of chickens, the rhythmic creak of the wooden door to the house. She focused on the gentle rustling of the leaves in the peach tree, the chirping of unseen birds, the soft jingle of bells on the wind and the warmth of the late afternoon sun on her skin.

"Lost in thought?"

Sarah's eyes snapped open. Auntie Lin stood in the doorway, a gentle smile on her face. She held two steaming cups in her hands.

"Just... taking it all in," Sarah replied, managing a weak smile in return.

Auntie Lin walked over and sat beside her on the bench. "Chamomile tea," she said, offering her one of the steaming cups. "It will help you relax."

Sarah accepted the mug gratefully, the warmth seeping into her hands. The fragrant, soothing tea calmed her frayed nerves. "Thank you, Auntie," Sarah said, accepting the warm cup. "This is... it's all so much to take in. Standing where she last stood."

Auntie Lin nodded, her gaze drifting towards the well. "This place holds many memories," she said softly. "Some good, others... not so much."

There was the opening. Sarah seized it.

"Auntie Lin," she began, her voice trembling slightly, "I have to know. What *really* happened? My father thinks she just up and left. I don't believe that. You must know something."

Auntie Lin's expression softened, then faded into sadness and a hint of... was it fear? She looked down at her teacup, her fingers tracing the rim. "It was a long time ago, Sarah," she said evasively. "Your mother was a good woman. A fierce spirit. But she was... delving into things. Things better left undisturbed."

"What things?" Sarah pressed, her heart pounding.

Auntie Lin exhaled between pursed lips, a deep, weary sound. "Your mother... she was always drawn to the old ways, the old stories. She had a...connection to this land, to the spirits of our ancestors." She paused, choosing her words carefully. "There are... *things* in these mountains older than the mountains themselves. Towards the day she disappeared, she was fixated on a whisper, consumed by it even. She was determined to finish the story, but..." She trailed off, her gaze fixed on the well.

"But what?"

Auntie Lin finally met her eyes, and Sarah saw a flicker of something dark and unsettling in their depths. "She told me not to follow her that night. She said... she was going to end it."

Sarah leaned forward, her grip tightening on the teacup. "End what? Her life?"

Auntie Lin shook her head slowly, her eyes clouding with a mixture of sadness and a haunted look that Sarah couldn't decipher. "No, not her life." She stood up abruptly, her movements stiff and awkward. "Come, let's go inside. I need to finish cooking, and your friends will be wondering where you are."

Sarah wanted to protest, to demand more answers, but she sensed that her aunt was genuinely distressed. Pushing her now wouldn't help. She needed to be patient, to gain her aunt's trust. "Okay, Auntie," she said softly, rising from the bench.

As they walked back to the house, Sarah couldn't tear her eyes from the well. The heavy wooden lid seemed to press down on the darkness beneath, containing something ancient and unseen. She shivered, despite the warm evening air.

Inside, the comforting aroma of cooking food filled the house. Chloe, Chris, Ben, and Maya were gathered around the large wooden table, chatting animatedly about the upcoming adventures. A shared sense of excitement and anticipation replaced any previous exhaustion.

"There you are!" Chloe exclaimed, seeing Sarah enter. "We were starting to think you'd started an adventure without us!" She laughed, while patting the empty spot next to her for Sarah to sit.

"Just catching some fresh air," Sarah replied, forcing a smile and plopping down into the seat next to Chloe.

"This place is amazing, Sarah," Maya said, journal in hand, their eyes shining with enthusiasm. "I was just writing down what your auntie was telling us about the history of the village. It's incredibly fascinating!"

"Yeah," Ben chimed in, "Apparently, this place is, like, totally off the grid. No Wi-Fi, no cell service... it's like stepping into one of my RPG's." He didn't seem entirely displeased by this fact, surprisingly.

"Check out these cool things," Chris said, while examining a collection of old farming tools hanging on one of the walls. "They look like they were made centuries ago."

Auntie Lin, who had busied herself in the kitchen area, smiled. "Some of them are," she said. "We still use many of the old ways here. Those tools have been handed down for generations."

Sarah looked over at a wall adorned with family photographs. She studied the faces of her ancestors, searching for some resemblance to herself, some connection to this place that felt both alien and deeply familiar. She paused at a photo of her mother, Mei-Lin, as a young woman, her smile radiant, her eyes full of life. Sarah's heart swelled with longing.

In the periphery of the glass, something moved.

It wasn't one of her friends. She squinted her eyes trying to see it better. The distorted glass revealed a figure standing directly behind her.

It was the old man from the outcrop.

His mouth was a black gash, a silent scream, and his crooked bony finger was pointing right at her.

Sarah stumbled back with a gasp, colliding with Maya.

"She was beau—" Maya started to say when Sarah collided with them. Sarah twisted around and scanned the room with darting eyes.

There was no sign of the old man.

"Did... did you see that?" Sarah looked back at the picture; the reflection of the old man was gone. Only Maya could be seen, shaking their head and squinting over her shoulder at the image with a worried look on their face.

She was losing it, she thought. *Going crazy. Did her mom go crazy too*? *No*! She wasn't going down that road, so she took that thought and ripped it to shreds.

"See what?"

Sarah rubbed her eyes and took a deep breath before answering. "Nothing. Never mind."

"Well, as I was saying, she was beautiful and your auntie says she was quite the storyteller," Maya continued, pointing at the photo of Mei-Lin, while keeping a close eye on Sarah for any more erratic behavior. "She knew all the old legends and myths of this region."

Sarah looked at Maya, surprised. "She did?"

Maya nodded. "Apparently, she was quite famous for it in the village. People would come from miles around just to hear her tell stories."

"Yes, Mei-Lin had a gift," Auntie Lin replied, unprompted, from the small kitchen, somehow overhearing their discussion over the clamoring of her cooking. "The ancestors spoke through her. The whole village would gather to hear her tales... but—" her smile faltered for a fraction of a second, "—She couldn't cook as well as me."

They all shared a laugh.

"Okay, who is hungry?" Auntie Lin asked, as she carried a full tray of traditional dishes over to the table. Some of the recipes looked familiar to Sarah, they were similar to her father's watered-down versions back in New York. There was fragrant rice, savory stir-fried vegetables, succulent roasted meats, bao buns and a variety of very spicy sauces. The group quickly sat down and started eating.

Across the table, Chris's face had turned the color of a ripe tomato. A single bead of sweat tracked through Ben's dust-caked stubble as he reached blindly for his water, his eyes glassing over with tears. They were trying to be polite, but the Sichuan peppercorns were clearly winning. Sarah laughed but was impressed that her friends put on such brave faces without complaint in front of Auntie Lin. She found herself thoroughly enjoying the food and the company.

As the evening wore on, however, Sarah couldn't stop the thoughts of her past creeping in. The well in the courtyard, her aunt's evasiveness, the fragmented memories triggered by the scent of jasmine—it all pointed to something hidden, something lurking beneath the surface of this idyllic village. And she was determined to uncover it, no matter the cost.

As Auntie Lin was pointing out the location of the outhouse, something else caught Sarah's eye. In the distance, an old crumbling building stood outlined against the growing dusk at the crest of a mountain.

She shivered.

"What's that?" She asked, pointing her finger.

Her aunt turned around following her gaze. "Oh, that is just the old temple ruins. No one goes there anymore."

"Old temple ruins?" Chris piped up, his ears perking up at the mention of something potentially explorable. "What kind of temple?"

Auntie Lin hesitated, a flicker of unease crossing her face. "It's... just very old," she said vaguely. "From a time, long before our ancestors settled this valley. Best not to disturb such places."

"Disturb?" Ben asked, his adventurous spirit clearly ignited. "Ghosts?" He chuckled, but Sarah noticed a slight tremor in his voice.

"Just old dangerous stones," Auntie Lin said firmly, dismissing the topic with a wave of her hand. "Now, finish your dinner. You must be tired after your long journey."

The conversation shifted back to more mundane topics, but Sarah couldn't shake the image of the ruined temple from her mind. It loomed in the distance, a silent relic of the past watching over the village. She wondered what secrets it held, what stories it could tell.

After dinner, the friends helped clear the table and wash the dishes, a task that became surprisingly comical due to their lack of familiarity with the traditional methods. Ben, attempting to use a hand-operated water pump, ended up soaking himself and Maya, much to everyone's amusement. Even Sarah found herself laughing, the tension momentarily forgotten.

As the evening drew to a close, Auntie Lin decided it was time to call it a night and opened the front door to leave, letting in an air that blew cool and fresh. She slung the vibrant scarf she always carried with her around her neck to stave off the chill.

"Sleep well," Auntie Lin said, her voice warm and genuine. "Tomorrow, I will show you more of our village." She left, gently closing the door behind her.

Once the group of friends were alone, they gathered in Sarah and Maya's room, the largest of the sleeping areas. Chloe, despite her earlier exhaustion, buzzed with energy, scrolling through her phone, editing photos and videos for her social media.

"This place is *amazing*," she gushed. "The light, the scenery, the *authenticity*... my followers are going to go *crazy*."

"Just try not to step into any animal shit while you're livestreaming," Ben quipped, earning a playful shove from Chloe.

"Seriously, though," Maya said, looking at Sarah, "are you okay? You were pretty quiet at dinner."

Sarah hesitated, unsure how much to reveal. She didn't want to alarm her friends unnecessarily, but she also couldn't shake the feeling that something was wrong. "I'm just... processing everything," she said finally. "It's a lot to take in."

"She's probably embarrassed that I handled the spice better than her," Ben said with a chuckle.

Sarah laughed, trying to appear more relaxed than she felt. "Yeah, maybe," she conceded to Ben, "let's see how well you handle it tonight though."

Ben squinted his eyes in confusion. "What does that mean?"

Everyone else had a laugh in understanding. "You'll see," Sarah replied cryptically.

"So," Chloe said, changing the subject and plopping down on the large, shared mattress, "what's the plan for tomorrow? Auntie Lin said she'd show us around. I'm dying to see the market – I need some authentic souvenirs!"

"I want to see those old farming tools up close," Ben said, stretching his arms above his head. "Maybe even try my hand at using some of them. Learn how things were done 'back in the day'."

Chris, who had been surprisingly quiet since dinner, spoke up. "I'm still kind of curious about that old temple," he admitted, avoiding eye contact with Sarah. "Even if it's just... old rocks. It sounds... interesting."

"We should probably stick with Auntie Lin's plan, at least for the morning. Get a feel for the village, maybe learn their customs," Maya remarked. "We don't want to offend anyone by wandering off where we're not supposed to."

Sarah appreciated Maya's caution. It was a sensible approach, but a small, rebellious voice inside her whispered that she might need to push boundaries to get the answers she sought. This wasn't a carefree vacation to her like it was for her friends. She needed to find the truth—her truth. Spending time with Auntie Lin and her friends seemed appealing, but she wanted to explore her mother's home free of outside distractions. And to simply *feel* the village in solitude.

"Sorry, Maya," Sarah said, trying to keep her voice steady. "You guys can see what Auntie Lin has planned, but I need to explore on my own."

Maya started to say something but stopped themselves and simply nodded.

"Okay. Sounds like a plan," Chloe replied distractedly, already composing a caption for her next Instagram post. "Authentic Village Life, Day One! #AdventureTime, #CultureVulture, #OffTheGrid." Her voice trailed off as she continued in her own internal world.

"Well, whatever we do there better be good food," Chris stated. "I'm starving again."

A chuckle rippled through the room.

"I think Auntie Lin has you covered, Chris," Sarah said, a genuine smile finally reaching her lips. Despite her somber mood, she found a measure of comfort in the familiar banter of her friends. They were here for her, supportive and understanding, even if they didn't fully grasp the depth of her personal quest.

They talked for a while longer, sharing their impressions of the village, their hopes for the trip, and their amusement at Ben's near-constant mishaps. Gradually, the conversation died down, replaced by the sounds of yawns and rustling blankets. One by one they excused themselves to their beds until only Sarah and Maya were left.

Before laying down for bed Sarah rummaged in her backpack, pulling out the familiar pill organizer and shaking out a single pill, swallowing it quickly with the last sip of water from her bottle. Maya gave her a small, satisfied nod, already pulling out pajamas from their bag.

They changed quietly, the only sounds the rustle of fabric and the distant chirping of crickets outside. Finding their respective spots on the large mattress, they pulled the thin blankets up, the relative silence of the village night settling around them like a heavy shroud.

Sarah laid in bed, staring up at the wooden beams of the ceiling as she allowed herself to be immersed in the harmony of sounds surrounding her. She could already hear the soft snores of Maya next to her, the rhythmic creak of bedsprings from Chris and Chloe's room, the rustling of leaves outside the window, the distant barking of a dog, and a faint, rhythmic jingling of bells.

The moonlight streamed through the gaps in the shutters, casting long, dancing shadows on the walls. The scent of jasmine, still lingering faintly in the air, brought with it a fresh wave of memories—fragmented images of her mother, whispers of stories, the chilling echo of Auntie Lin's words about a story.

She closed her eyes, focusing on the rhythmic bells to help her fall asleep and to distract from the creaking bed in the room next to her. And as she finally slipped into a troubled sleep, the sound of distant bells playing a hypnotic lullaby was the last thing she heard as they weaved into her dreams.

CHAPTER 5

Sarah sat at the edge of her bed, basking in the sounds of Gu Mei stirring to life—the sharp crowing of a rooster, the bleating of a nearby sheep, and a wet, heavy *thump-thump-thump* from a nearby courtyard—a pestle, she guessed, crushing something soft in a stone mortar. This was much different than the urban symphony of sirens and garbage trucks she was used to from New York.

She stretched, her muscles stiff from the unfamiliar bed and the lingering tension from the previous night. The faint jingling that had followed her to sleep the night before was gone, replaced by the cheerful chirping of birds.

Maya sat cross-legged on the floor, scribbling furiously in their journal.

"Hey, El," Sarah mumbled, stifling a yawn. "You been feeling okay lately?"

"Feeling okay?" Maya repeated, looking up with a smile. "Okay? Like I was dragged on an adventure, literally, halfway around the world with Ben?"

Sarah managed a weak laugh that came out like a croak. "Something like that." She rubbed the sleep out of her eyes and grabbed for her pill bottle. "I had some bad dreams."

Maya nodded understandingly. "It's this place... the energy here," Maya tapped their chin with their pen. "It talks. We need to learn how to listen."

Sarah knew exactly what they meant. There was something about the village, something about the ancient watchful mountains and the way the wind whispered that made her feel connected and yet deeply unsettled.

Sarah swallowed her pill and got ready for the day. They soon joined the others for a simple breakfast of congee and pickled vegetables that Auntie Lin prepared for them.

Chloe was already in her element, phone perched on a selfie stick, narrating her 'authentic rustic breakfast experience' for a legion of Lululemon-clad followers. Chris, itching for adventure, gulped down his meal and started lacing up his hiking boots. Ben, surprisingly, took his time eating, he seemed in no rush to just wander around the village and observe. Maya, of course, had already started scribbling in their journal.

Sarah, however, had a different agenda. She wasn't here as a tourist; she was here as a detective to a museum of her own past, searching for the ghost of her mother, Mei-Lin. She decided to start by exploring the village itself, hoping to find some trace of Mei-Lin's presence, some clue that might lead her to the truth. She needed to walk where her mother had walked.

After helping clear the bowls, Sarah offered a quiet word of thanks to Auntie Lin and slipped out into the morning bustle of the village.

The name, Gu Mei, meant 'Looking after plum blossoms,' but there was nothing sweet about it. Narrow, winding lanes turned the village into a labyrinth. The houses of rammed earth and stone huddled together like old women sharing a secret, their tiled roofs sagging with age.

Woodsmoke, cooking spices, and the ever-present dust filled the air, covering everything like a blanket. Chickens scratched in the dirt, children played in the courtyards, and elderly villagers sat in the sun, gossiping and watching the world go by. As far as she could see, there wasn't a plum blossom in sight.

A disorienting sense of déjà vu swept over her, as if she were walking through a landscape she'd visited in her dreams. The curve of a stone wall, the particular shade of peeling red paint on a door, the ghost of a melody hummed by a woman washing clothes in a plastic tub—each triggered a phantom limb of a memory, an itch she couldn't scratch.

Her wandering led her to the temple that stood sentinel over the hillside cemetery, the one where her aunt worked. A stoic, weary-looking building greeted her. Two stone lions whose fangs had been worn to nubs by centuries of rain and wind, stood guard. Inside, the gloom was pricked by the faint, trembling light of butter lamps.

The faint scent of incense caught her nose. A part of her, the part that craved tranquility, wanted to step inside, to breathe in the relaxing air. But she hesitated. Now was not the time. She would wait for her aunt, who was still probably trying to get a slothful Ben out the door.

Further on, she came to a small sun-drenched square that served as a market, where villagers were selling their wares—fresh vegetables, dried herbs, handcrafted tools, and colorful fabrics. The scene pulsed with vibrant, bustling life, a testament to the self-sufficiency and resilience of the community.

She stopped at a stall where an elderly woman with a face like a dried apricot sat before a stack of flat, woven trays. The woman's wrinkled hands were stained purple from years of handling dyes, her eyes bright and intelligent. Using the Mandarin her mother had insisted she learn, a language that now felt alien in her mouth, Sarah complimented the woman's weaving then jumped right into the reason she was there.

"Excuse me, Popo," she said, using what she hoped was the respectful term for her elder. "Did you know my mother? Mei-Lin? She went missing here about seven years ago."

The woman's eyes widened slightly, and a shadow of recognition crossed her face. "Mei-Lin?" she repeated, her voice raspy with age. The woman's hands stilled in her lap. "A long time ago. A pretty girl. A sad story."

Sarah's heart quickened. "Do you remember what happened to her?"

The woman's smile was gone. Her face was a mask of polite, unassailable sorrow. Fear, too. Sarah saw it flicker in her eyes, a tiny, trapped thing. "A story," she said, her hand waving dismissively, a gesture that was meant to end the conversation. "A superstition. Nothing more."

A superstition? What the hell does that mean?

When Sarah pressed for more details, the woman's face became a mask of genuine fright. She leaned forward and hissed, her voice a wet rattle. "No more. To speak of this is to invite it. We do not tell that story here." She paused, looking around. "It listens."

She then immediately turned away, her shoulders hunched as if protecting herself from an unseen wind. Sarah tried to ask more, but the woman had turned her attention to rearranging her trays. The wall of silence was absolute. The discussion was over.

It was the same everywhere she went. A mention of Mei-Lin's name was met with sad smiles, nods, and a sudden, shared deafness when she asked about her disappearance. Sarah stood in the middle of the dusty square, surrounded by the chatter, the bartering, the laughter—and felt utterly alone, as if she were separated from it all by a sheet of invisible glass. It was a wall, and she was on the outside. It was no wonder her father never got anywhere with the villagers.

With no immediate answers, Sarah decided to give up on her mission, at least temporarily, and focus instead on the beauty of the village. She wandered for hours, shopping and chatting, until her feet eventually led her back around to the temple.

Auntie Lin was there now, sweeping the stone steps between the two lions with a broom of bound twigs. She looked up and gave Sarah a tired but genuine smile. Sarah, returning her smile, lifted a small bag of dried fruit she'd bought for the group, and waved it.

"Save some for me," Auntie Lin called out. "I will be over for supper soon."

"No promises!" Sarah called back with a grin.

Auntie Lin chuckled and went back to work.

Sarah arrived at her mother's house just as the sun began its descent in the hazy sky. The home was empty; a hollow space filled only with the ghosts of the past. Her friends were still out, chasing their own versions of adventure. She wandered through the rooms, analyzing familial objects, studying faded photographs hanging on the walls, just searching for any clue to her mother's past.

She walked along the edge of the room gently trailing her fingers along its cold rough surface. *If only walls could speak*, she thought, *what secrets would they share?* With a sigh, she let her hand drop from the surface. Maybe Maya had some Wiccan magic to let them see through the wall's eyes, Sarah mused, a smile playing at her lips.

The air around her suddenly grew heavy, pressing in, thick and cloying as mud. The walls of her mother's home began to shrink.

Oh god. Not now.

Her eyes shot to the back door, to the rectangular opening that promised escape. She needed fresh air before the weight of the house, the history, the grief, crushed her. She half stumbled—half charged through the door.

She gasped for the clean air of the courtyard, her hands finding the heavy wooden lid of the old stone well for support. The suffocating pressure in her chest began to ease, but the memory of the crushing darkness in her nightmare, the feeling of being trapped—threatened to renew the assault. With a few forced deep steady breaths, she regained control, and the pressure released.

God, she hated her fucking spells of claustrophobia, not to mention her epilepsy. A litany of afflictions. Why couldn't she just be normal?

Her fingers began unconsciously tracing the grain of the lid, a map of deep grooves and moss-covered edges. She felt a sudden, inexplicable urge to lift the lid, to peer into the darkness below. She somehow knew, with chilling certainty, that this well held a key to the mystery of her mother. She heard her father's words in the back of her mind *Don't go digging,* but she ignored it.

Unable to resist the compulsion, she went to work on the covering. The bolt, thick with rust, resisted, groaning in protest. She put her shoulder into it before it finally slid free with a grating screech. She paused, then heaved the heavy lid aside.

A blast of cold, damp air rushed up to meet her, carrying an unpleasant smell of mildew and decay that made her wrinkle her nose. It was followed by a sound—a low, resonant hum, like a single, drawn-out moan that vibrated in her teeth. For the briefest of moments, she thought she could hear whispers behind the humming before the sounds drifted away, carried by the warm dry breeze. A heavy silence followed, settling over the courtyard like the calm before a storm.

Sarah peered over the stone lip, down into absolute blackness. It wasn't an absence of light; it was a presence of dark. She stood there for a few moments, panting, then turned on her phone's flashlight. Her hand trembling, she aimed the light into the gaping maw. The well's stone lining shone, slick with moss and dark slime. The light failed to reach the bottom. It was just... swallowed by the hole.

The void below called to her, coaxed her, beckoned her. It seemed a thing alive, reaching for her.

The space wasn't just absorbing all the light; it pulled the sound from the very world around her. The cheerful village noises dimmed. Stretched. Vanished into that inky silence.

She wasn't sure if she was leaning in closer or being pulled, but the rough rim was pressing into her stomach, the darkness rising to meet her.

Just a little closer, a thought slithered into her mind, a thought that was not her own. *All your answers are down here...*

"Whoa! Easy there, Láng!"

A hand clamped down on her arm, yanking her back so hard she stumbled. The sounds of the village crashed back in, loud and jarring. It was Chris. He looked from her wide, staring eyes to the open, black mouth of the well.

"You trying to climb in?"

"No," she said, startled. "I was just looking."

"At what? The bottom of the world?" He casually stepped past her, leaned over the edge and spat. A long, white glob of saliva vanished instantly into the void.

"Oh my god," Sarah said, smacking his arm. "You are so disgusting."

He laughed, the sound loud and sharp.

"Yeah, yeah. Well, I just got back from some actual recon. You're not gonna believe what I found," he said grinning, a flash of mischief in his eyes. "Come on. I'll tell everyone after dinner." He tugged her gently away from the well, toward the house.

Dinner?

She glanced upward and stumbled. The light was wrong. The sun, high in the sky only moments before, now touched the mountain peaks, bleeding orange and violet across the horizon.

An entire afternoon had vanished.

The smell of roasted duck and ginger welcomed them as they entered. The others were already gathered on cushions around the low table—their faces flushed from their day's adventures.

"There she is," Ben said, gesturing with a greasy drumstick. "We were about to send out a search party."

Search party? She was only gone a few minutes...

"Just exploring," Sarah said, forcing a smile. She slid into a vacant spot on the floor cushions next to Maya.

"Find anything good?" Maya asked, pushing a bowl of rice toward her.

Sarah opened her mouth to respond, but Chris interrupted, unable to contain himself as he launched into a boisterous account of his afternoon hike. Maya rolled their eyes and mimicked hanging themself. The two of them shared a quiet giggle as Chris went on.

"...and then, I swear, I saw this *massive* snake," Chris was saying, holding his hands wide apart to demonstrate its size. "Must have been at least ten feet long and *almost* as thick as my bicep! The thing was so big it crushed trees as it slithered away into the woods. I think the damn thing was poisonous too."

"Venomous, not pois—" Maya stopped themself from correcting him. "Never mind."

Chloe, ever the influencer, was already lamenting the missed photo opportunity. "A snake that big though? That would have been *epic* content!"

"You sure it was a snake," Ben interrupted, "and not a sandworm with all this fucking dust." He joked, earning a playful shove from Chris. Then promptly sneezed.

"Just be glad I wasn't there," Maya added. "I would've freaked out. I *hate* snakes."

Auntie Lin entered the room, carrying a large platter piled high with steaming food. She placed it in the center of the table, and everyone eagerly began to serve themselves. All talk of snakes forgotten as they sampled new and unique foods.

"So, Sarah," Auntie Lin said, turning to her niece with a warm smile. "What do you think of our village so far?"

Sarah hesitated, unsure how to answer. "It's... beautiful," she said, choosing her words carefully. "And... very different from New York."

Auntie Lin nodded. "Life is slower here," she said. "More connected to the land, to the old ways. Smells better too."

Sarah chuckled at her joke while plopping some steaming dumplings onto her plate. "Maya was telling me about the history of the village," Sarah said, glancing at her friend. "You mentioned my mom was a storyteller last night. That she had a gift."

Auntie Lin's smile softened, a glint of sadness in her eyes. "A gift?" She looked over at Sarah. "Yes. Some called it that."

"Did she... ever talk about any... evil?" Sarah asked, trying to sound casual, as if it were just an idle question.

Auntie Lin's expression tightened, and she glanced nervously around the room, as if checking to see if anyone was listening. "That is not dinner conversation Xiao Láng," she said dismissively. "Let us talk of more positive things."

"But the well—" Sarah began, then stopped herself. She didn't want to reveal her experience, not yet, not until she knew she wasn't going crazy.

"The well is just an old well," Auntie Lin said firmly. "It's been covered for years. There's nothing down there but water and—" She stopped herself then deliberately changed the topic. "Now eat, you are too thin."

Sarah picked at her food, her appetite gone. Auntie Lin's evasiveness only confirmed her suspicions: there was something she wasn't telling her, something about the well, about her mother. The village, with all its seemingly picturesque beauty, held secrets from those who came from the outside.

As dinner progressed, Sarah found herself increasingly withdrawn, lost in her own thoughts. She observed her friends, their laughter and easy banter with a pang of envy. They were enjoying a simple adventure, a cultural experience.

She, on the other hand, was caught in a web of mystery and dread, a nightmare that bled into her waking life. She needed answers, and she knew, with a growing certainty, that she wouldn't find them by playing the role of a curious tourist. She would have to dig deeper, to confront the darkness that lurked beneath the surface of this seemingly peaceful village, even if it meant facing her own deepest fears.

After dinner, Auntie Lin stood to leave, gathering her things.

"Good job on the dishes tonight, Ben. We'll make a housewife of you yet." Everyone but Ben had a good laugh at that. Auntie Lin paused at the door, looking up into the sky before visibly shivering. "Feels like a storm is coming, best be on my way quickly."

With a final wave she disappeared out into the village.

"Okay," Chris said, his voice dropping to a conspiratorial whisper. "Now that she's gone. You guys are not going to believe this."

He pulled his chair around and leaned forward, his eyes alight with mischief.

"I went up to those ruins."

"Chris!" Chloe and Maya said in unison.

"Guys, C'mon," Sarah interrupted, her interest piqued at what he found. Maybe he had found something that could help her. "Let's hear him out."

They both looked incredulous. "Seriously, Sarah? You're taking *his* side?" Chloe demanded. "We all know what happens when he goes 'exploring'."

"I just want to hear what he found," Sarah said calmly. "It might be interesting."

Chris, emboldened by Sarah's support, grinned. "Thank you! See, Chloe? Láng gets it. I'm telling you guys—this place was *epic*." He leaned forward to build suspense. "So, I was hiking up towards those ruins your aunt told us to avoid—"

"Naturally," Chloe muttered, rolling her eyes.

"—and I found this crevice," Chris continued, ignoring Chloe's interruption. "It was hidden behind some rocks, almost like it was deliberately concealed. And inside..." He paused for dramatic effect. "...was a shrine filled with old shit. Like *really* old shit."

"And you took stuff, didn't you?" Sarah asked, even though she most likely knew the answer already.

Chris's grin was sheepish. "Souvenirs." He dug into his pack and laid his haul on the table. A shard of pottery with a faded glaze. A rusted, hand-forged nail. And a lump of dark stone, slick and cool to the touch, carved with symbols that seemed to writhe in the lantern light.

Chloe gasped. "Chris! You can't just take things from historical sites! That's, like... I dunno. Super illegal or something."

"Relax," Chris said dismissively. "No one's going to miss this stuff. It's been sitting there for centuries. Besides," he added with a wink, "it's *way* cooler than anything we'd find in a gift shop."

Maya, however, was examining the objects with a frown. "These symbols... they're not just decorative," Maya said, their finger hovering over the stone. "I've seen versions of them before. In texts about binding rituals."

"Binding what? Ghosts?" Ben scoffed.

"Not just ghosts," Maya replied quietly, their eyes distant. "Spirits. Curses. They're meant to trap an influence... to bind it to an object. Or sometimes, even to a story, to keep it from spreading."

"See?" Chris exclaimed triumphantly. "I told you it was cool!"

"Or maybe it's a warning," Maya said quietly, their voice filled with a sudden concern.

A heavy silence fell over the table, broken only by the first patter of rain against the window. The stone on the table seemed to pulse with a coldness that had nothing to do with the night air.

"We should go back there," Sarah said, her voice firm. "Tomorrow."

Chloe stared at her, aghast. "Are you *crazy*? Your aunt specifically told us to stay away from those ruins! And besides," she added, gesturing towards the objects Chris had taken, "We already have our souvenirs. Mission accomplished."

"This isn't about souvenirs, Chloe," Sarah said, her gaze fixed on the object. "It's not that I *want* to go. It's that I think I'm being *pulled* there. What if *that's* where my mother went?"

"Oh, come on, Sarah," Chloe said, rolling her eyes. "Seriously? Don't tell me you're buying into all that spooky village folklore. It's just stories."

"No. Out at the well—"

"Look," Ben said quickly, interrupting Sarah. "I'm with Sarah. I think we should check it out. It could be, at worst, a cool adventure.

And at best," he added with a wink at Sarah in support, "awesome hidden loot."

Maya still looked hesitant, but they nodded slowly. "I guess it wouldn't hurt to take a look. But we need to be careful. If there are any... protective wards or anything."

"Wards?" Chris scoffed. "You're serious? I was already in there!"

"Maybe you're already cursed then," Maya said half-jokingly. "Seriously though, we need to be respectful and cautious."

"I don't know, guys," Chloe said, still unconvinced. "This all seems a little... extreme. Can't we just, like, relax here and enjoy our vacation?"

"Chloe," Sarah said, her voice pleading, "Please. This is important to me."

Chloe looked at Sarah's face, at the desperation in her eyes, and finally relented. "Fine," she sighed. "But if we get cursed or possessed by some ancient mountain spirit, I'm blaming you all."

Chris clapped his hands loudly and stood up.

"Then it's settled. Operation spooky ruins is a go. Ben, help me get the supplies ready. We'll need food, water, flashlights, rope..."

Sarah stopped listening as her thoughts turned inward. Could there really be answers out there she wondered. Or was her sense of adventure and desperation for answers tricking her into a false sense of hope. She was sure of one thing though—she wouldn't find peace until she found the truth.

CHAPTER 6

The next morning dawned bright and sunny, the small storm from the previous night having passed, leaving the air washed clean and the mountains gleaming in the sunlight. Despite the seemingly peaceful atmosphere, a current of nervous energy ran through the group as they gathered for breakfast.

Auntie Lin had brought over a basket of local fruits, bread and some eggs this time. Sarah had a suspicion that she was trying to make them a more traditional American breakfast, but she kept that to herself.

As the group finished their breakfast, Auntie Lin rose to depart for work. "I hope everyone enjoys their day," she announced, moving toward the exit. "Last night's rain is a good omen."

"We will, Auntie," Sarah assured her, offering a comforting hug. She intentionally omitted any mention of their plans to investigate ancient, dangerous ruins.

"I'll see you all at dinner. I've prepared something special for this evening." She held Sarah's gaze for a moment before continuing. "And Sarah, you should come visit me at the Temple today."

Sarah could only nod, afraid her words would betray her lie if she were to agree. She had every intention of visiting her aunt's Temple, eventually, just not today. Satisfied, Auntie Lin swung her vibrant plum blossom scarf around her neck and left.

Chris, as expected, sprang into action almost before the door clicked shut. He hopped on the balls of his feet, nearly quivering with anticipation. "Okay, team," he declared, clapping his hands. "Time to go! Adventure calls!"

Chloe, although complaining about the unreliable Wi-Fi and the possibility of ruining her manicure, attempted to stay upbeat for her followers. She pulled out her phone, recording a brief update.

"Hello, Wanderlusters! It's day three in the Chinese countryside, and we're about to start an incredible trek to visit some old ruins. Keep watching for breathtaking scenery and perhaps a couple of eerie encounters!" She gave the camera a wink, before facing Chris. "Please promise me that we won't get lost like our last hike."

Chris scoffed. "I didn't get us lost," he protested. "I was... exploring alternative routes."

"Uh-huh," Maya said dryly, adjusting the straps of their large, canvas bag. "And I suppose that giant snake you saw was just an 'alternative' earthworm?"

"Hey, that snake was *real*," Chris insisted. "And it was *huge*."

Ben, who had spent most of the morning trying to coax a signal out of his phone, finally gave up with a sigh. "I'm going in blind, people," he announced. "No maps, no GPS, no connection to the outside world. This is either going to be the best day ever or a complete disaster."

"Let's just try to be careful, okay?" Sarah said, looking up from her still full plate. She hadn't eaten much, just mindlessly pushed scraps around with a finger. "And stick together." The memory of the well, of that hungry darkness, made the thought of being alone out there terrifying.

Chris took the lead, consulting a crudely drawn map he'd sketched the previous day. "Alright, follow me, intrepid explorers!" he declared, striking a heroic pose. "The lost ruins await!"

Chloe rolled her eyes, but she followed him, already filming their departure. Ben trudged along behind, giving silent thanks to the rain for settling the dust.

Maya, ever practical, checked the list in their journal one last time. "Did everyone bring water?" they asked. "And extra batteries? Who knows how deep those caves go."

"Yes, *Mom*," Ben said, feigning exasperation.

"Just making sure," Maya replied calmly. "Someone has to be responsible."

"Hey, El," Chloe said, stopping Maya. "Speaking of responsible. Can I put the water and stuff in your bag? My Chanel is not made for hiking."

Maya frowned but opened it for Chloe, who dropped her items inside. "Fine, but if anything gets crushed, it's on you."

"Thanks for bringing it," Sarah said, as she fell into step beside Maya, where a faint whiff of sage hit her nose. "I didn't even think about half of the supplies we'd need."

Maya shrugged. "It's my 'witch bag'," they said with a wink. "You never know what you might need when you're venturing into the unknown." Their tone was teasing, but Sarah had a feeling they were only half joking.

The trek began easily enough, following a well-worn path that wound its way through the terraced rice paddies and seemed to lead straight up to the ruins standing watch above the village. The scenery took all their breaths away. Lush green fields, sparkling streams, and the majestic mountains looming in the distance. Fresh, clean air, scented with wildflowers and damp earth filled their lungs.

The group bantered back and forth, jokes and light conversation filling the time. Sarah stayed mostly quiet while fiddling with the strap of her backpack, a nervous habit she'd never quite been able to kick.

She focused on the vibrant colors of the wildflowers dotting the path, the musical chirping of unseen birds, and the playful small talk of her friends, but a shroud of nervousness clung to her. Despite the cheerful mood of the group, she found herself subtly scanning the surrounding forest in apprehension, her senses on high alert for any sign of... something. She wasn't sure what, but Auntie Lin's cryptic words and the lingering feeling from the well left her deeply unsettled.

"So, Maya," Chris said, breaking Sarah out of her thoughts, "you've been awfully quiet. What mystical secrets are you pondering?" He playfully nudged them with his elbow. "Are you communing with the ancient spirits of this place?"

"Maybe Maya's getting psychic vibes!" Chloe chimed in. Ever attuned to an audience, she held her phone up to capture the moment. "Tell us, oh wise one, what do the spirits say? Will we find buried treasure? Or maybe just a really good Wi-Fi hotspot?"

Maya chuckled, and even Ben cracked a smile, momentarily forgetting his digital deprivation. Sarah forced a smile, trying to shake off her apprehension. She watched as Maya rolled their eyes playfully at Chris and Chloe's teasing.

"Oh, I'm definitely communing," they said, voice dripping with mock seriousness. "The spirits are telling me..." They paused for dramatic effect, extending a hand towards Ben, who looked up from his phone, a flash of curiosity in his eyes. "...that someone here is surrounded by a very... *dark* aura."

Ben blinked, then a slow grin spread across his face. "Dark aura? Me? I'm the most optimistic one here, aside from maybe Chris. What does that even mean?"

Maya continued the charade, circling Ben slowly, their eyes narrowed as if scrutinizing him. "It means... it means you're blocking the positive energy flow! All that longing for a five-bar signal is creating a vortex of technological despair!" They dramatically waved their hand over his phone. "I sense... frustration! Disappointment! The crushing weight of missed guild meetings!"

Chloe giggled, turning her phone to capture Ben's reaction. "Maybe Maya needs to perform an exorcism of his phone! Banish the digital demons!"

Sarah chuckled along with the others, the tension easing slightly from her shoulders. Maya's playful performance was a welcome distraction. Even Ben was laughing now, shaking his head at Maya's antics. But for a brief moment, she caught Maya's playful smile drop, like they actually saw... something, but El quickly forced the smile back.

"Alright, alright," Ben conceded, holding up his hands in mock surrender. "I'll try to embrace the digital detox. But if the old temple has a charging station, I'm claiming it."

"See?" Maya said triumphantly, turning back to Chris. "The spirits *are* wise. They know all about Ben's technology addiction."

"Okay, you've made your point," Chris said, laughing. "But seriously, Maya, do you actually... you know... *believe* in all that Wiccan stuff?"

Maya shrugged, a mischievous glint in their eyes. "Let's just say I believe in keeping an open mind," they said. "There's more to this world than we can see, measure, or explain with science. And sometimes," they added, giving Sarah a quick, knowing glance, "a little bit of 'witchcraft' can come in handy."

A slight shiver ran down Sarah's spine, despite the warm sunlight. She couldn't tell if Maya was still joking or if there was a hint of truth behind their words. It made her think of the well, and her encounter with... whatever it was. She pushed the thought away, reminding herself that it was probably just her imagination running wild. Still, she couldn't quite shake the feeling that Maya knew more than they were letting on.

The conversation continued, the air alive with her friends' optimistic jokes, but a small knot of worry began to form in the pit of her stomach the further they walked. As they climbed higher, the path became steeper and rockier. The vegetation grew thicker, the trees taller, casting long shadows that danced across the trail. Chris, despite his claims of knowing the way, seemed increasingly uncertain. He consulted his map frequently, frowning and muttering to himself.

"Are you sure this is the right way, Chris?" Chloe asked, her voice tinged with annoyance.

"Yeah," Chris said, his voice lacking its usual confidence. "I... think so. It's just... further than I remember."

"You *think*?" Maya said sharply. "You were just here yesterday, and you *think* you know where we're going?"

"Relax, Elphaba," Ben said, trying to defuse the tension. "We'll find it. It's probably just around the next bend."

But the next bend revealed only more trees, more rocks, and more winding trails. They continued to hike for another hour, their initial enthusiasm waning with each passing minute. The playful banter died down, replaced by frustrated sighs and muttered complaints.

"My feet are killing me," Chloe whined. "And my phone's about to die. This is *not* the epic adventure I signed up for."

"Maybe we should turn back," Maya suggested, their voice laced with concern. "We're clearly lost, and my feet are aching too."

"No way," Chris argued stubbornly. "I know it's close. We just have to keep going." He squinted intensely at his drawn map, then mumbled under his breath. "It doesn't make any sense—it should be right here."

The sky, which had been clear and blue earlier, began to darken. Ominous clouds gathered above the mountain peaks, their shadows creeping down the slopes like advancing armies. A distant rumble of thunder echoed through the valley.

"Great," Ben muttered, pointing up at the approaching storm. "Just what we needed."

The tension within the group reached a breaking point. Chloe and Chris started bickering, their voices sharp and accusatory. Maya tried to mediate, but their pleas for calm were drowned out by the rising wind and the increasingly frequent thunderclaps.

The hairs on the back of Sarah's neck suddenly stood up. She stopped, listening intently. Beneath the commotion of her arguing friends, a faint, rhythmic ticking reached Sarah's ears, like the sound of an old grandfather clock. She recognized it instantly.

It was the same noise from her nightmare on the plane.

"Do you guys hear that?" Sarah asked, but everyone else was too busy arguing to hear her.

Without another word, Sarah turned and walked away from the group, following the noise. The ticking, barely audible, appeared to be guiding her off the path, drawing her deeper into the forest. She pushed through thick undergrowth, ignoring the scratches on her arms and the growing weight in her heart. As she made her way over the rough terrain the sound grew louder, clearer. The air grew heavy with the scent of damp earth and something... old.

The sudden ringing of tiny bells carried on the wind, rose from the opposite direction. Her feet slid on the damp soil as she slid to a stop, straining to listen. Her eyes widened in recognition; it was the same jingling that lulled her to sleep from the night before, but clearer, more insistent.

She now felt compelled in two directions, as if the sounds were fighting for her attention, calling her, urging her towards them. The bells were soft, promising comfort, safety, and peace. The mysterious ticking was sharp, urgent, a question demanding an answer.

Her father's voice warned her not to dig, but the memory of her mother urged her forward. She needed answers, and she wouldn't find them if she didn't take risks. She took a determined step in the direction of the ticking, of answers, and pushed aside a low hanging branch of thick leaves and stepped through. She emerged from the trees into a small clearing.

The bells went silent.

And there, before her, stood the ruins.

CHAPTER 7

The ruins presented no grand or imposing spectacle. Instead, Sarah found the remnants of something far humbler: a large stone building, its walls crumbling, the roof long collapsed, swallowed by the encroaching embrace of the forest. Moss and vines clung to the weathered stones, softening their edges, blurring the lines between nature and structure. She had discovered a place of quiet decay, of ancient neglect and memories long forgotten.

Sarah stood at the edge of the small clearing; her breath caught in her throat at the sight. A thick sense of... presence, hung in the air. It wasn't a feeling of being watched, exactly, but more like being *known*, being acknowledged by something ancient and unseen.

She took a tentative step forward, her eyes scanning the rubble. A section of wall, partially intact, revealed the outline of a doorway. A broken stone basin, perhaps once a well or a fountain, lay half-buried in the undergrowth. A scattering of broken pottery shards, their patterns faded and indistinct, hinted at the lives that had once unfolded here.

Brushing a strand of stray hair from her eyes, Sarah swept her gaze over the fragmented remains of a life she could only imagine. A large, flat stone, almost like a table, lay overturned near what might have been the center of the cluster of buildings. She wondered if it had been a place for communal meals, for sharing stories under the stars.

Had her mother been here? Was she searching for... something in these ruins? The thought sent goosebumps over her body, a prickle of connection to her mother and the long-gone inhabitants.

She moved closer, her steps crunching softly on fallen leaves and twigs. A profound silence pressed in, broken only by the whistling of the wind through the trees. The weight of it spoke volumes.

Turning slowly, Sarah followed the gentle slope of the land downwards with her eyes. The trees thinned, giving way to a breathtaking vista. There, nestled in the valley below, was the village they had left that morning.

But something was off. It looked... close. Far closer than it should have been after their arduous, hours-long hike up the winding mountain path. The houses were still distinct, their colored-tiled roofs gleaming in the afternoon sun, not tiny specks she expected from this height.

A frown creased Sarah's forehead. It had to be some optical illusion, she thought, trying to convince herself. The unsettling proximity defied the reality of the climb she remembered so vividly. Just great. Everywhere she went seemed to add another mystery.

Turning her attention back to the ruins, a sudden movement caught her eye. A dark shape, like a fleeting shadow, disappeared behind a crumbling wall, quickly swallowed up into a tangle of gnarled roots and overgrown vegetation. Sarah squinted, trying to make out what it was, but the dense foliage had already claimed it.

She froze, her heart leaping into her throat. It had been too fast to identify, but it was definitely *something*. A person? A dog? Chris's snake? Or something else entirely?

"Hello?" she called out in a weak, trembling voice which echoed unnaturally in the stillness of the ruins. There was no reply. Only the rustling of leaves in the wind and the threatening rumble of thunder.

She inched closer towards the crumbling wall and peeked around it. Behind the wall were large roots covered in thick vegetation. The rustling sounded again. *Something* was definitely in there.

"Ben," she said between gritted teeth. "This isn't funny!" She knew deep down it wasn't Ben, or any of her friends. It couldn't be. Every instinct screamed at her to flee, but a deeper, more desperate need for answers urged her on.

She pushed aside the brush. The sight that greeted her froze the scream in her throat.

A perversion of a sheep huddled in the roots. Its wool hung in a sickly mat of filth and pus. Its legs bent at angles bone should not allow. And its mouth, tearing at a mess of unidentifiable gore, was filled with vicious, needle-like teeth. Blood dripped thick and dark from its chin, staining the earth below.

Then, slowly, it lifted its black-colored head, and two points of malevolent, burning red lights fixed upon her.

Recoiling in horror she let go of the tangle of branches she had pushed aside and fell backwards. The scream she held in finally came out, a raw, piercing sound, shattering the quietness.

"SARAH!"

The sound of her friends' voices, distant but growing closer, cut through her panic. They had heard her scream.

Footsteps crashed through the undergrowth, and moments later, Ben, Maya, Chris, and Chloe burst into the clearing, their faces etched with concern.

"Sarah! What happened? Are you okay?" Maya rushed to her side, their eyes scanning for injuries. Sarah couldn't speak. She could only point, her hand trembling, towards the thick brush.

The others followed her gaze, their expressions shifting from confusion to amusement as a normal looking sheep stepped out from the bushes and bleated.

"A... goat?" Ben asked chuckling, his voice a mixture of relief and bewilderment. "What's so scary about a goat?"

Sarah felt her face flush with embarrassment. It was just a sheep. Matted wool, placid yellow eyes, a muddy hoof. There was no blood on its chin. No impossible teeth. It bleated, a soft, questioning sound—as if... confused.

"I... I thought..." Sarah stammered, trying to explain. "It was eating... and the blood..." She trailed off, feeling foolish. The adrenaline that had surged through her a moment ago was now replaced by a wave of embarrassment.

Maya leaned over to Ben. "It's a sheep," they whispered, "not a goat."

Ben groaned. "Jesus, Maya. Same thing."

Chloe started to laugh, a high-pitched sound that echoed through the stillness of the clearing. "Oh my god, Sarah! You nearly gave us all heart attacks! I swear, my heart skipped like, *ten* beats! My fans are gonna love this, though! This is, like, *peak* content!"

She immediately whipped out her phone and started filming the inquisitive animal, who walked away to graze at a patch of grass nearby, all the while narrating the scene with an exaggerated, breathless excitement for her online audience.

"Okay, well, false alarm," Chris said. He turned his back to the ruins and held his arms out. "But seriously, Láng, you found it! Check this place out! It looks even older than your aunt described."

Maya, ever observant, had noticed something else. "Sarah," they said, voice low and serious, "look at your hand."

Sarah looked down. Her hand, the one she'd used to push aside the brush, was covered in dirt and a dark, reddish-brown stain that looked disturbingly like dried blood.

She gasped, recoiling from her own hand. "What... what is that?"

Maya knelt down, examining the ground near the wall. "There's more here," they said, pointing to a patch of disturbed earth. "And... are those...?"

Sarah's gaze followed where Maya pointed. Partially hidden beneath a snarl of roots and dead leaves, almost entirely concealed by the rampant growth, lay remains.

They were small—the delicate, brittle bones of a baby.

Beside them, nestled amongst the tiny body, was another set: the larger bones and skull of an adult, its arm curved as if embracing the infant. Tattered strips of what appeared to be a once-vibrant dress, now faded with time, still clung to the adult's corpse.

The most horrifying thing of all though, was their skulls, both crushed in on top as if some monstrous predator chomped down on them. Nausea rolled over Sarah, and she staggered back, a strangled cry escaping her lips. This wasn't just some ancient ruin; this was a grave. A mother and child, lost to time and tragedy. The bones looked ancient, but the dark blood on her hands looked much fresher.

"Holy shit," Ben exclaimed, looking over Sarah's shoulder.

Before anyone could react to him, the storm that had been threatening all day finally broke. The sky opened up, unleashing a torrential downpour. The wind howled through the trees, whipping the rain into a frenzy.

"We have to find shelter!" Maya shouted, their words almost drowned out by the storm's roar.

Chris pointed towards the mountainous rock face, relief on his face. "Guys, over there!" Hidden amongst the rocks, partially obscured by overgrown vines and the driving rain, was a dark opening, a crevice in the mountainside. "It's the cave!" Chris yelled. "Come on!"

Without hesitation, Sarah and the others ran towards the shelter, the storm pressing at their backs. Sarah was relieved to leave the ruins of the ancient temple, and with it, the sheep and the corpse of a long-dead mother and child behind them.

With a desperation to get away from that animal more than the storm, she scrambled after Maya and Ben through the narrow opening, practically shoving them ahead of her, then followed closely by Chloe and Chris.

Unbothered out in the storm, the sheep watched.

CHAPTER 8

Inside the tight crevice, the air turned immediately cold and still. The wind, which had roared outside, was reduced to a low, mournful whistle as it snaked through the narrow passage, a sound that set everyone's teeth on edge. It was like the mountain itself was moaning.

"Well, this is cozy," Ben said, his voice echoing unnaturally in the cramped opening. He fumbled for his phone, then remembered, with a groan, that he had no signal. "Guess I'll have to entertain myself the old-fashioned way." He kicked at a loose pebble.

"Everyone, stay close," Maya said, their voice calm but firm. They had already pulled a small, powerful flashlight from their "Witch Bag," its beam cutting through the gloom. "And Chris, no wandering off. We stick together."

Chris, subdued by the unsettling atmosphere and perhaps still feeling the sting of Sarah's earlier scream, simply nodded. He pulled out his own, much larger flashlight, and shone it down the passage. The path narrowed ahead, barely wide enough for them to walk single file. Rough, uneven rock formed the slick, moist walls. Water trickled down the stone, forming small puddles on the uneven floor.

Sarah didn't like the suffocating atmosphere one bit. The air began to feel heavy, pressing down on her, making it difficult to breathe. The walls of the passage closed in on her the further they went. With a silent curse at herself for being claustrophobic, she focused on the small circle of light ahead, fighting the urge to turn back, to escape the crushing weight of the stone around her. Luckily relief came quickly as the cave began to widen after only a short distance.

"This is where I found those things yesterday," Chris said, his voice hushed, as if afraid to disturb the silence. He pointed to a small alcove in the wall, littered with broken pottery shards, rusted metal fragments, and what looked like pieces of bone. "I didn't go any further than this."

Chloe wrinkled her nose. "Gross. It smells like a tomb in here."

"Maybe it *is* a tomb," Ben quipped, then immediately regretted his words as Sarah stiffened, a sharp, almost imperceptible movement.

As if to reinforce Chloe's building fears, a large, glistening cave cricket with unnervingly long antennae scuttled over a rock near her designer sneaker. She let out a piercing shriek, scrambling backward and nearly tripping over her own feet.

"Oh my god, what *was* that? Did you see the legs on that thing? I can't. Chris, I literally cannot."

Chris shone his light on the now-empty rock. "Relax, babe, it's just a bug."

"Don't tell me to relax!" Chloe shot back, brushing imaginary bugs off her arms. "This whole place is probably crawling with... with creepy crawlies."

Sarah knelt down, ignoring the exchange behind her as she examined the objects in the alcove. They were clearly very old, remnants of ancestors that had long since vanished. She picked up a shard of pottery, its surface decorated with a faded, intricate pattern. It felt cold and strangely heavy in her hand. She ran her finger over the rim, it was smooth and worn, no doubt handled by many. She quietly wondered if her mother had ever stood in this very spot, had ever touched this very object, seven years ago.

"These are incredible," Maya breathed, shining their light on the carvings. "They could be centuries old, maybe even older." They carefully placed a few of the shards into a plastic bag they'd brought for collecting samples.

"Let's not disturb too much," they added, giving Chris a pointed look. "We don't want to upset the spirits."

Chris shrugged, but he didn't argue.

"This is some Lara Croft shit here," Ben said, then took a deep breath and blew off some dust from what looked to be some kind of statue half buried in the ground. "It's like being in a real-life video game."

Sarah grinned at his comment as she carefully placed the pottery shard she was holding back in the alcove, a strange sense of connection, almost like a residue of memory, clinging to her fingertips. She stood up, brushing dust from her jeans, her gaze sweeping the chamber. It felt more expansive now that they were fully inside, the initial claustrophobia giving way to a kind of hushed awe.

"I wonder what else is down here," Chris said, his voice bouncing off the walls. He pointed his oversized beam of light down the passage, which curved gently to the left, disappearing into darkness. "I mean, if this is where they left offerings, or whatever... imagine what's further in."

Chloe shifted uneasily. "I don't know, guys. That storm outside is pretty bad. Maybe we should just hunker down here for a bit, wait it out."

Maya nodded in agreement. "Chloe's right. We've already found some amazing artifacts. We can come back another day..."

Ben shook his head. "We've already come this far," he replied while looking at Sarah for support. "Isn't this why we are here?"

Sarah was pulled in both directions. Part of her, the cautious, logical part, echoed Chloe and Maya's concerns. But another part, a deeper, more instinctive part, thrummed with anticipation. This *was* why she was here. Every strange carving, every dusty relic, could be a clue. The answers to her mother's disappearance might be just around the corner.

"I think we should go a little further," Sarah said, the words surprising her as much as they did the others. It was as if another voice, one fueled by a desperate need for answers, had spoken for her. All eyes turned to her as the words slipped right off her tongue.

Ben, predictably, grinned ear-to-ear. "See? Sarah's with me. Come on, scaredy-cats, a little adventure never hurt anyone." He playfully punched Chris's arm. "Right?"

"Right," Chris answered with a weak smile.

Sarah stepped forward and added, "We don't have to go far. Just a peek around the corner. If it looks dangerous, we turn back. Deal?"

Maya hesitated, their gaze flickering between Sarah and the dark passage. Sarah knew Maya sensed it too, that pull, that undeniable magnetism of the unknown. Finally, Maya sighed, a reluctant smile curving their lips. "Okay, fine. But we stick *very* close together. And at the first sign of trouble, we're out of here. Agreed?"

A chorus of agreements followed, and with a renewed sense of excitement, albeit tinged with apprehension, the group began to move forward, their flashlights casting dancing shadows on the ancient walls. Sarah fell into step behind Chris, her own small beam adding to the pool of light, her heart pounding a rhythm of both fear and exhilaration. She felt they were on the verge of discovering something truly remarkable.

As they continued deeper into the winding and twisting tunnel, the air grew colder, the silence more profound, broken only by the drip, drip, drip of water and the occasional muffled sounds of their own footsteps. Luckily the tunnel didn't have any side passageways to get lost in, so the group continued on without fear of getting turned around.

Sarah could suddenly feel a growing sense of panic, the familiar feeling of being pressed from all sides. She forced herself to think of her mother which strengthened her resolve in order to push onward. *Besides*, she reasoned with herself, *this was her idea. She couldn't ask them to turn back now.*

She caught herself listening intently as they pushed further and further into the cave, straining to pick out any stray sound over the constant dripping.

"Wait!" Sarah hissed suddenly. Everyone stopped and stared at her. Chloe's eyes wide open in questioning fear. "Do you hear that?"

They looked around in confusion, not hearing anything. Ben raised one questioning eyebrow at her.

"Sarah," Chloe whimpered. "You'd better not be screwing with us right now."

"I'm not. Listen."

"I don't—" Ben was cut off by Sarah holding up a finger to shush him.

Then they all heard what Sarah was hearing. A soft rustle, like leaves blowing around on a fall day, building louder and louder. The air itself began to stir, no longer stagnant, but coming alive.

Chris held his flashlight higher. "What the hell?"

What started as a whisper was now a torrent of noise. Individual sounds of squeaks and clicks became clear. The cave's acoustics amplified the noise to a terrifying level, an auditory wave that rolled over them.

As soon as Sarah realized what it was, the noise was upon them.

Bats.

The sound became a physical force. The roar of countless wings was a buffeting, turbulent wind whipping past their faces and carrying with it the rustle and slap of leathery membranes. The high-pitched screeches beside their ears, sharp and piercing, a chaotic, disorienting shriek that threatened to overwhelm their senses.

Bats flying too close were caught in Sarah's hair, pulling wildly to get away. She waved her arms frantically, trying to keep them off. She recoiled in horror as her hand connected with one bat, the leathery wings fluttering against her palm.

The beam from each of their flashlights spun in a dizzying pattern on the cave wall as they all flung their arms around in a panic. The passing swarm of bats casting flickering shadows at sickening speed.

Sarah screamed, the sound lost in the cacophony of wings.

Then just as suddenly as it arrived, the storm of bats was gone. The roar of flapping wings gradually faded away, but Sarah and Chloe continued to scream long after the animals had left. Once their shrieks finally died and nerves calmed, Maya called out to the group.

"Anyone hurt? Anyone bit or scratched?"

"I'm good!" Chris shouted, his voice echoing in the tunnel.

A shaky "No vampire here," came from Ben.

Chloe just managed a wet, squeaking sound, swatting at her hair as if a bat were still tangled in it.

Maya swept their light over each of them in a frantic, head-to-toe check for bites or blood. Then let out a short, sharp bark of a laugh when they found none. It was such an absurd sound that Ben snorted in response. Then Chloe let out a high-pitched, hysterical giggle.

Suddenly, it was a contagion. The laughter erupted, raw and ragged, echoing off the damp cave walls. The sound of built-up adrenaline releasing in a torrent. And as Sarah doubled over, clutching her stomach, tears streaming down her face, she realized it was the first real breath she'd taken in minutes.

Sarah wiped the tears from her face as her laughter finally faded and started grabbing the supplies they dropped in their panic. Chris, still letting out random giggles, helped her gather their things and started back down the passageway.

It didn't take long before they came to a section where the shaft dipped sharply downwards, a steep, treacherous slope of loose rock and gravel.

"Careful here," Chris warned, testing the ground with their foot. "It looks slippery."

They descended slowly, clinging to the walls for support, their flashlights casting long, dancing shadows that began to take on monstrous shapes in their building paranoia. Sarah slipped once, her heart leaping into her throat, but Chris caught her arm, steadying her.

"Thanks," she mumbled, her voice echoing strangely in the confined space.

"No problem," Chris replied, his voice unusually subdued. He looked at her apologetically. He knew that they all, in some way, blamed him for their predicament. He didn't know she was blaming herself as well.

At the bottom of the slope, they all had to duck under the low ceiling, then climbed as the shaft rose upwards again in a gentle incline. At the crest, the view stopped them in their tracks.

The tight tunnel opened into a larger chamber, where a body of water lay in the center, its reflective surface clear as glass. Far above the pool, a small, circular opening in the rock allowed a shaft of pale, filtered sunlight to penetrate the gloom, illuminating the water with an ethereal glow. Rain, from the storm outside, spilled down the opening in a thin waterfall into the pool below.

Sarah gasped. "Guys, I think that is the well outside the house." She pointed her light up at the opening above the pool of water.

The others stared in stunned silence, their flashlights casting dancing arcs across the water's surface. A sense of ancient knowledge, of secrets long buried, permeated the air in the cavern.

"How can you tell?" Ben asked, looking over at Sarah.

"Just a... feeling," Sarah replied with a shudder. Her thoughts went to the other day when she peered into the blackness of the well, the pull she felt. And now she was in it, the darkness. She didn't know how to explain that to Ben.

"What... what *is* this place?" Chloe whispered, her voice trembling slightly.

"I don't know," Maya said, their eyes wide with a mixture of awe and apprehension. "But if this is the well, why is the water so low? We should be swimming right now, right?" Maya shone their light around the room to illustrate their point.

Sarah didn't really hear them. Her eyes were scanning the chamber, frantically searching the shadows, the water's edge.

"Mom?" she whispered to herself; the sound lost in the vastness of the cave. "Where are you?"

With tentative steps, the group of friends slowly approached the pools edge. Sarah immediately noticed something reflected in the still surface, something metallic, gleaming faintly in the dim light. And holding it was...

"Look!" She pointed towards the reflection, her heart pounding.

The others followed her gaze, their flashlights converging on the spot she indicated. As the beams joined, the reflection sharpened, resolving into a distinct shape. An old brass candle lamp rested on a rocky base, barely sticking out of the seemingly shallow, clear water.

It was ornate, clearly crafted with care, despite the tarnish of time and neglect. A carousel of tiny metal sheep, frozen mid-leap, encircled the base of the candle holder, hanging from thin, delicate brass sails, designed to catch a candle's heat and spin. A shiver ran down

Sarah's spine followed by a wave of goosebumps that had nothing to do with the cool air of the cavern.

The old device looked like it was waiting for them.

And it wasn't alone.

A decayed and mummified body lay draped over the stone, one skeletal hand still gripping the lamp.

Sarah's heart skipped a beat. Could it be her? She focused her beam on the strange, ancient relic and the corpse that held it. How had they ended up *here*, at the bottom of this pool, inside a cave? What had happened? The questions swirled in her mind, a dizzying mix of confusion and a growing, undeniable fear. This was more than just a cave; it was a connection to something just outside of her understanding. A connection to answers that were so close she could almost feel them.

The lamp was a key, unlocking a flood of sense-memories: her mother's voice humming a lullaby, the scent of jasmine tea, the soft glow of candles chasing sheep shadows from the corners of a room. It was all there, a ghost limb of a memory, and here, before her, was the source. The joy of recognition warred with the horror of the scene, creating a nauseating vertigo in her mind.

"Who is that? *What* is that? How did they get down here?" Chloe asked out loud, saying what they were all thinking.

"The object looks... almost pristine," Maya observed, leaning as close as they dared to the water's edge, their archaeologist's instincts kicking in. "Brass tarnishes somewhat easily, even in freshwater. But the shape itself... it's like it's been perfectly preserved."

Ben, recovering from his initial awe, piped up. "Who cares about the creepy relic, what about the stiff? Do you think they fell down the well?"

"No, I don't think so," Sarah answered. "If this is the well in my mother's courtyard, it was covered. Remember?"

Ben looked up at the opening and pointedly aimed his flashlight at it. "Looks open to me."

"I... opened it yesterday," Sarah replied meekly.

Chris, who had been uncharacteristically quiet, cleared his throat. "Yeah, I saved your ass from falling in." Everyone sat quietly for a moment, staring at the unfortunate custodian of the lamp.

Chloe broke the silence first. "It's beautiful though. My subscribers are gonna love this." Chloe turned on her phone and started recording. "So... can someone... get it?" Chloe pointedly looked over at Chris with widened doe eyes and gave a flutter of her lashes.

Maya was next to Chloe in a flash and whispered harshly in her ear. "What's wrong with you? What if that's Sarah's mom?"

Chloe blinked a few times like a deer in headlights before nodding her head and turning off the phone.

"I'll do it," Sarah said, ignoring the exchange. This was *her* family mystery after all. She felt a fierce determination, a need to know if that was her mother. And if it was, she wanted to be there first. "I'm the best swimmer here anyway," she added.

"You wish," Chris replied with a half-hearted chuckle but he didn't move to jump in.

"Are you sure?" Maya asked, concern etched on their face. "If that's—" Their eyes darted to the corpse as they cleared their throat. "Maybe someone else should go."

Sarah shook her head. "No, I'm doing this." She handed her flashlight to Chris, who took it with a slightly shaky hand. "Keep the light on the lamp."

She took a deep breath, the cold, damp air filling her lungs. The scent of wet musty stone was almost overwhelming now. She slipped off her shoes and socks, the cold stone chilling her feet. Then, slowly, she lowered herself into the water.

The shock of the cold was immediate, stealing her breath. It was far colder than she'd expected, a bone-chilling cold that seeped into her very marrow. "It's freezing!" She exclaimed, between chattering teeth. She took a deep breath, fighting back a shiver, and started to wade deeper. The bottom was surprisingly smooth, covered in a layer of fine silt that shifted under her feet.

The water quickly rose, past her knees, then past her waist. The pool was much deeper than it appeared from above, as if it were an optical illusion—or a trap. As she waded further, the lamp and its guardian seemed to move along with her, staying just out of reach. Its brass surface gleaming teasingly in Chris's beam.

"Almost there Sarah!" Maya said encouraging her on. The group joined in. "Just a few more steps!"

She froze as her foot touched something solid. It wasn't the smooth silt she'd been expecting. It was hard, ridged, and strangely brittle. Curiosity got the better of her, so she began probing with her toe, which nudged the long object. It shifted with a dull clack against something else. Another one. She bent down, keeping her head just above the surface, and reached into the dark water... her fingers wrapping around something long and hard. She pulled it out.

A shriek escaped her lips, a sharp sound that echoed around the cave. She snatched her hand back as if burned.

Chris, seeing her distress, lowered his light from the brass device and into the water around her feet. The light penetrated the still, clear water, illuminating not just one skeleton, but dozens. They littered the bottom of the well like discarded dolls. Skulls with empty sockets stared up at her from the silt, limbs tangled together in a silent, submerged graveyard.

Sarah stiffened, afraid to move and touch any more of the remains. "Oh god. Oh god. Oh god." She started to regret not letting Chris jump in the water.

Maya and Chloe began calling for Sarah to forget the damn thing and come back, while Chris encouraged her to ignore the bones and press on. But Sarah wasn't listening to them. She was scanning the submerged boneyard, her eyes frantically darting from one tangled skeleton to another, searching for a specific sign—a silver locket, the faded remnants of a silk dress, anything familiar. Searching for her mother. Her mind was a roaring torrent of denial.

She's not here. She can't be here.

Her earlier exhilaration drained away, replaced by an overwhelming panic. Every fiber of her being screamed at her to scramble out, to run back the way they came, to escape this nightmare.

Yet, amidst the rising tide of panic, a strange, stubborn refusal began to surface. Even if the worst was true, that lamp, lying there so close, was the reason. It was the clue. The answer. It *had* to be. She couldn't just leave it there. It was too perfect, too poignant, to be a coincidence.

A profound sadness, mixed with a chilling determination, began to push back against the fear. These skeletons weren't just random people to her. They were poor souls who were caught up in the same story as her mother, a story that was becoming hers as well. And that one corpse, resting calmly amidst the horror, felt like the next, crucial piece.

Taking a shuddering breath, Sarah forced herself to focus on the small, gleaming object that lay just beyond the sea of bones. It pulsed with a quiet significance, a silent promise of revelations.

With a deliberate, agonizing effort, she lifted her left foot, placing it down with painstaking slowness, trying to avoid any direct contact with the macabre floor. Her eyes were fixed solely on the brass lamp and the corpse, willing them closer, willing herself to overcome the overwhelming disgust and revulsion. Despite the water that still felt like liquid ice, she began to sweat.

Time slowed down as she got closer and closer. Sounds faded away. Each step felt like it wasn't her own, as if she were watching a stranger in her body. The cadaver looming larger and larger.

Then she was there.

The mummified body was hunched over, facing away from her; resting on the stone slab that held the brass device. The corpse was clearly preserved, but Sarah had no way of knowing just how long it had been resting there.

She studied it with her eyes, afraid to touch it, searching for any signs that this was her mother. The hair had fallen off long ago, the skin was shriveled and dry, and the clothes were old and faded. She couldn't be sure, but the way the remaining tattered cloth hung from the skin made her think it may have been a dress. Her mother wore loose dresses.

She carefully shuffled a few inches forward to try and get a good look at the face when her foot brushed against something solid again, causing her to instinctively flinch. But it wasn't the ridged feel of bone she'd been expecting. It was something smaller, smoother. With another shudder, she bent down, reaching into the water, her fingers brushing against something metallic, and smooth.

As her fingers wrapped around the small object, a jolt, like a static shock, ran up her arm. It wasn't painful, but it was startling, unexpected. She almost lost her grip but held on tight. And then, she heard it.

A whisper.

It wasn't a sound that came through her ears. It was... inside her head. A faint, fleeting voice, speaking an ancient language she didn't understand, yet somehow, *felt*. It was a sensation of yearning, of longing, and horror.

Sarah pulled the object from the water, holding it out so she could see it in the light. Water streamed off it, leaving it gleaming, impossibly bright in the dim light of the cave. She turned towards her friends without a word, holding the metal object high to show them.

It was her mother's locket.

That's when the ground began to shake.

CHAPTER 9

The walls of the chamber trembled, dust and loose rocks raining down from above. The water in the pool sloshed wildly, waves crashing against the edges. The rumbling grew louder, deeper, evolving into a deafening roar.

"Earthquake!" Chloe screamed, grabbing Chris's arm and pulling him towards the tunnel. "We need to get out of here! Now!"

Ben, his face white with terror, didn't need to be told twice. He scrambled after them, his usual jokes forgotten. Maya, though, hesitated, turning towards Sarah, still in the basin.

"Swim, Sarah!"

At the sound of Maya's frantic voice, Chris, Chloe and Ben spun around at the tunnel opening, fear in their eyes. The sight of Maya standing bravely at the edge of the pool, calling to their friend struggling in the water stopped them cold.

Sarah, disoriented and terrified, struggled to get her limbs moving, but her legs wouldn't stop shaking. Water suddenly started to gush down the well opening above. The once thin trickle grew into a powerful cascade, crashing down on her, threatening to suffocate her. She cursed her short height; the water level was quickly growing deeper, and she already struggled to walk along the bottom.

From just outside the cacophony of the rumbling cave, she could make out the sound of her friends encouraging her on. She flung the locket and its chain over her head then pushed as hard as she could with her legs.

She reached out and grabbed the brass lamp. It was snagged, caught in the unyielding grip of her mother's corpse. Sarah hesitated for only a heartbeat, the sacrilege of what she was about to do warring with the desperate need to survive. She closed her eyes and pulled. The lamp came free with a sharp, splintering crack.

She forced her eyes open, saw the limp, broken hand of the woman who gave her life, and a sob of pure self-loathing tore from her throat. Her mother's carcass rolled over from the force of her tug and floated away in the rising tide. For a horrifying second, her gaze locked onto the grisly remains of her mother's face, the lipless mouth seeming to hang open in silent disappointment.

I'm so, so sorry, Mom. She turned and swam, fleeing less from the crumbling rocks around her, and more the horror of what she had just done.

The floor of bones became a sea of horror, as the rushing flood churned up the corpses. Sarah flailed wildly in terror as skulls floated up out of the water and brushed against her; their empty eyes staring.

Her toes could no longer touch the bottom of the rising well. She desperately clawed for purchase near the pool's edge, trying to keep her head above the churning waterline. The roaring in her ears built to a crescendo—the earthquake, the waterfall, the desperate shouts of her friends.

But Maya's voice cut through it all, a beacon in the chaos. "Don't stop!"

Finally, the tips of her fingers felt the rough edge of the basin. Maya's surprisingly strong hands gripped hers and hauled her up out of the torrent. Sarah leaned over on all fours and began coughing up water, her lungs burning while struggling for precious air. Her foot slipped on loose gravel as she stood, the ground still vibrating beneath her.

Sarah raised her eyebrows in surprise when she realized she still held onto the brass lamp.

"Go, go!" Maya commanded, taking the lamp from her and shoving her towards the passage where Chris, Chloe, and Ben waited, their faces a mixture of relief and terror. Sarah didn't hesitate. She ran, her legs heavy and clumsy, Maya right behind her.

The corridor was narrow, forcing them into a single file. Chris led the way, his flashlight beam dancing erratically on the uneven walls. The rumbling started to subside, replaced by an abrupt, unnerving silence, punctuated only by their ragged breaths and the echoing flow of water.

They reached the dip in the passage from their earlier descent, but it was no longer just a steep slope. Water rushed in, rapidly filling the depression, which was already knee-deep, and the flow showed no signs of slowing.

Great, another fucking pool.

"We have to cross now!" Chris yelled, his voice tight with urgency. "It'll be flooded soon! Follow me!" Chris plunged into the freezing torrent, his flashlight beam disappearing beneath the surface, emitting a ghostly, green luminescence.

"Oh god, oh god..." Chloe chanted hysterically, stepping in after him. Ben followed close behind, jumping in without a word. Each of them gasped at the icy shock.

Sarah hesitated, her heart pounding. The water looked dark and menacing, and the memory of being trapped beneath the waterfall under the well remained fresh and terrifying.

"Sarah, it will be okay, I'll be right behind you." Maya's gentle reassurance gave her the final push.

She looked at Maya, and with a shared breath, they both stepped into the icy water. Even though Sarah had just been in it a few moments ago, the cold still shocked her, forcing her to gasp. She could hear Maya exhale sharply behind her as they entered the frigid water as well.

Ahead, Chris submerged underneath the low ceiling, the rising deluge nearly closing the gap completely. Chloe extended an arm and was yanked through by Chris, the rushing water fighting against his pull. Ben swiftly ducked under and powered through, leaving Sarah and Maya in the now-flooded tunnel.

Sarah's breath quickened, panic setting in again. The level rose to chest height, leaving mere inches of air below the ceiling. The ghostly green glow of Chris's submerged flashlight vanished, swallowed by the inky blackness of the water ahead. Chloe and Ben were through, but the raging current kept rising.

Panic clawed at her throat. The image of the waterfall, the crushing weight of the surge on top of her, the desperate struggle for air—it all flooded back, threatening to paralyze her. She could feel her legs start to shake again, the cold seeping into her bones, amplifying her fear.

"Sarah!" Maya's voice, though calm, held an edge of urgency. "You can do this. It's just a few strokes. Hold your breath and use the wall. I'm right behind you, I promise."

Sarah focused on Maya's words, clinging to them like a lifeline. *A few strokes. Use the wall. Maya's right behind me.* She repeated the mantra in her head, trying to push back the rising tide of terror. She had to do this. For herself, for her mother, for Maya, for all of them.

She took a deep, shuddering breath, filling her lungs to bursting. She could feel the cold water rising against her face. Sarah nodded, a tiny, almost imperceptible movement, more for herself than for Maya. Then, she ducked her head beneath the surface.

The world dissolved into a muffled roar and darkness. The cold came as a brutal shock that almost stole her breath. She squeezed her eyes shut, fighting the instinctive urge to gasp. Her hands, her only guide in the disorienting blackness, scrabbled against the rough, slimy rock of the passage wall. She kicked, pushing forward through the torrent with all her strength. Her head felt light, dizzy.

Just a little further.

Her lungs burned, a fiery ache spreading through her chest.

Her coordinated kicks and strokes started becoming more erratic. Her clothes felt like weights, dragging her down. The flooding water pushed against her. Was she even swimming forward at all? She reached out, trying to find anything to grab ahold of.

A sharp pain erupted from her arm, but she ignored it in her building panic.

She could feel her claustrophobia closing in around her, threatening to overwhelm her with panic. The water and the darkness pressed in on her.

She knew then, she wasn't going to make it.

She stopped kicking. A strange calmness settled over her, and a thought bubbled to the surface. How easy it would be to just... let go, to breathe in the liquid, to stop fighting and end all this pain. To end everything and join her mother. She wrapped a hand around her mother's locket hanging from her neck and held it tight.

Suddenly, her free arm was gripped by strong fingers that wrapped around her wrist, pulling her forward with a surge of power. She broke the surface, gasping, choking, gulping in the blessed air.

Chris's face, etched with relief, was inches from hers. He hauled her the last few feet, pulling her onto the slightly higher ground on the other side of the flooded dip. She collapsed onto the cold, damp stone, coughing and shivering uncontrollably.

"Maya!" Chris shouted, turning back to the submerged passage-way.

Sarah looked back at the rising water, but Maya was nowhere to be seen. There was no motion, no beam from her flashlight. Ben squeezed past Sarah to join Chris, both men plunging their hands into the pool, searching for any indication of Maya.

No, not Maya. If anything happens to them—

There was nothing. No sign of her friend. The two guys thrashed in the water for what felt like hours. Time slowed to a stand-still as Sarah watched Chris and Ben's frenzied searching stop. The cavern fell utterly silent, everyone holding their breath in anticipation. Waiting. Chris and Ben shared a look of profound worry.

An uncontrollable whimper left Sarah's lips as she gripped her mother's locket in one hand. Ben looked over at her and seeing her pained expression, turned back to the tunnel with renewed vigor. He reached in as far as he could and felt around with his arms.

"Easy, Glitch." Chris reached around Ben's waist, holding him back from jumping all the way in. "We don't want to lose both of you."

Suddenly, Ben yelled, shattering the quiet, "I have her!"

Maya's head burst through the surface; their dark hair stuck to their pallid face. Ben pulled them from the pool, helping them onto the solid floor. Maya fought for air, violently coughing out water from their lungs. But even through their spasms, a small, unsteady smile touched their lips as they locked eyes with Sarah.

Sarah stood, relief flooding her, and stumbled over to Maya, giving them a long tight hug. They held each other's gaze for a brief moment as they separated from their embrace.

"Sorry, guys, I dropped my flashlight down there," Maya said quietly, breaking the tension.

Sarah suddenly stepped back from Maya, looking her over in a panic.

"Wait, you still have the lamp?" Sarah asked, then immediately winced, regretting the words as soon as they left her mouth. Her friend had nearly died, and her concern was an old trinket.

"Yeah, I have it." Maya held up their bag. "In here. I'm ok too, thanks for asking."

Sarah was too embarrassed to reply so she simply hugged them again.

A profound silence followed, broken only by their ragged breathing and the relentless sound of rushing flood. The earthquake seemed to have truly passed, but the danger wasn't over. They were still deep underground, in a water-filled cave, with no idea what lay ahead. But for now, they were together, and they had survived. That, Sarah realized, was all that mattered.

They each took an unspoken, much-needed moment to regather their composure. Sarah used that time to look around at her friends, their faces illuminated by the dim, wavering light of Chris's flashlight. She saw Chloe's haunted look. Ben's vacant gaze. Chris's clenched jaw. And Maya... Maya was simply Maya, calm and steady, a quiet source of strength. With her voice raw and hoarse from coughing up water, she spoke first.

"One," she said, pointing at herself.

Chris answered, firm and immediate. "Two."

Chloe, trembling, added, "Three."

Ben managed a grin. "Four."

Maya finished. "Five."

"Still Alive," they murmured together, finishing the last part of the group mantra.

For only the second time in the group's shared history, they had survived a life and death situation. Together. The Still Alive Five had somehow, again, made it through impossible odds. A swell of pride filled Sarah at the camaraderie, giving her a small boost in energy.

"Sarah!" Maya suddenly said in surprise, reaching out and grabbing Sarah's arm and lifting it. "You're bleeding."

She looked down at her limb and was startled to see it was covered in blood. She hadn't even realized she'd been hurt. Chris walked over to study her wound along with Maya, who was already reaching into their "Witch Bag" searching for something. Maya pulled out a short, colorful piece of cloth and gently wiped at the blood on Sarah's arm, revealing a small gash. Chloe looked away with an exaggerated gagging sound.

"It's not too bad," Chris stated, seeming relieved. "We can dress it now easily enough until we get back to the village for better supplies."

"As long as it doesn't get infected and you turn into a zombie or some shit," Ben quipped, his humor back. Maya, who was already wrapping Sarah's injury, shot him an all-too-common annoyed look.

Once her arm was dressed, Sarah gave it a quick flex test and was satisfied the wrap would hold. She was thankful that it didn't hurt—yet. She knew it was only a matter of time until the adrenaline wore off.

Standing there, Sarah realized that they were all waiting on Chris, the de facto leader, for direction. He noticed everyone's eyes on him and took a deep breath of the damp cave air, his shoulders rising and falling.

"Alright," Chris said, his voice low but firm. "We can't stay here. The water is still rising. We need to keep moving." He didn't need to articulate the unspoken question: *What if another earthquake hits?* The thought hung in the air, a chilling reminder of their vulnerability.

He pointed the flashlight down the tunnel, the beam swallowed by the oppressive void. The sound of rushing water echoed around them. He set off down the treacherous passage without a word, and the group followed closely behind, vanishing into the darkness.

CHAPTER 10

The silent, treacherous trek back through the cave became an ordeal. The water, a mere trickle on their way in, now flowed as a steady stream, fueled by the storm outside and the mysterious earthquake. It tugged at their feet, threatening to sweep them away at any moment.

The narrow passages, which had seemed merely claustrophobic before, now felt like the jaws of a monstrous beast, eager to swallow them whole.

Maya's loss of her flashlight was a major blow. The darkness now became almost absolute, broken only by Chris's increasingly dimming beam. They stumbled blindly, their hands scraping against the cold, wet rock, their ears filled with the roar of rushing water and the pounding of their own hearts.

"How much further?" Chloe gasped, her voice hoarse with fear and exhaustion.

"I... I don't know," Chris replied, his usual bravado gone. "Can't be far now, just... keep moving."

"Does anyone have any battery left on their phones?" Ben's voice cut through the panic, surprisingly calm. "We could use the flashlight."

Hearing his voice made Sarah feel a little better. He had been uncharacteristically quiet since saving Maya back at the flooded tunnel.

"Good idea," Sarah said, checking her phone. "I've only got six percent on mine."

"I've got twenty-three, Glitch," Maya said, with a bit of optimism. "Chloe?"

But Chloe was shaking her head, her eyes still wide from the terror earlier. "Umm... I think it's dead."

"You *think?*" Chris blurted out with more anger than he intended. Everyone stopped and looked at him in surprise. He took a steadying breath before continuing. "I'm sorry, babe. Can you check please, my flashlight is almost dead."

As if on cue, Chris's flashlight beam flickered violently, then died, plunging them into a suffocating darkness.

"Shit!" Chris exclaimed, slapping the flashlight against his palm. "The batteries *are* dead. Chloe?"

"It's completely drained," Chloe answered meekly.

As Sarah's eyes adjusted to the darkness, she could just make out a faint glow ahead. "Look!" She gestured, pointing past Chris, who continued to smack the flashlight, but in the darkness, no one could follow her motion.

Ben, however, must have glanced in the same direction, because he suddenly gasped.

The faint, ethereal glow emanating from the distant crevice entrance was a beacon of hope in the overwhelming darkness.

"El, turn on your phone light since you have the most juice left," Chris instructed, taking charge. Maya turned on her phone, and even the faint light from the screen seemed so bright compared to the darkness earlier. She pressed a button, and the cave lit up.

Chris took the phone from Maya and headed off towards the distant light. They stumbled forward, their hands outstretched, guiding themselves along the cold, wet wall, their progress agonizingly slow.

Finally, after what seemed like an eternity, they reached the opening. They scrambled out, gasping for breath, their clothes soaked and clinging to their bodies, their limbs trembling with exhaustion and cold.

But their relief didn't last long. The storm outside, though abating slightly, continued raging. The wind whipped around them so hard, the rain stung as it pelted their faces. And the damn storm had transformed the landscape into a muddy, treacherous mess.

"We can't go back to the village in this," Maya said, her voice barely audible above the wind. "We'll never make it. We need to wait out the storm in the cave."

"I am *not* going back in there!" Chloe said, her voice sharp with panic. "I can't."

They huddled together, shivering, their teeth chattering, each unsure what to do next.

"Listen. There's a small overhang just inside the crevice," Chris finally said. "It's not far inside, and it'll provide some protection from the wind and rain. We can wait out the storm there."

Chloe nodded meekly. With no other options, they all agreed. They squeezed back into the narrow opening, finding a small, relatively dry patch of ground beneath the rock overhang. The cramped, uncomfortable space still offered a better shelter than the tempest outside.

Maya sat down next to Ben. "Thank you for saving my ass back there, Glitch," they said, wrapping Ben in a strong hug.

Ben blushed. "It was nothing," he stammered, trying to squirm free of Maya's hold. "But man, some weed would be nice right now." Everyone had a small chuckle, happy for the brief distraction from their misery.

"Well, I don't have weed, but I do have—" They began to rummage through their Witch Bag and pulled out a small bag of dried ground herbs. "—This." They tossed it to Ben, who caught it and flashed Maya a confused look.

"What is it?"

"That," they said, glancing at the herbs. "Is my proprietary magical mix to help calm us down. It's a blend of lavender, basil, and other herbs to help reduce anxiety and stress." They pulled out a lighter and handed it to Ben. He gingerly took it and stared at both items in his hands before nodding.

"As long as it doesn't turn me into a frog or something."

Chris, watching the two of them, suddenly got an idea.

"Wait, Glitch. Hand me that lighter." Ben tossed it over to him without lifting his head. Chris caught it and without a word, stood up and disappeared back into the cave; still using Maya's phone as a light. The group just looked at each other and shrugged.

He returned with an armful of artifacts and some sticks that had washed in with the rain. Without a word, he arranged the ancient pottery shards into a crude fire pit, then taking the herbs from Ben, piled all the tinder in the center. After several failed tries and numerous curses, he finally coaxed the tinder into flame. The small fire offered a welcome respite, providing both light and heat, its dancing glow painting shifting shadows upon the cave walls.

Ben clapped for Chris who gave a slight bow to the group.

"Good job, babe," Chloe said in encouragement, flashing Chris a warm smile.

They huddled around the small fire as the sweet scent of herbs filled the air; a much welcomed and pleasant smell compared to the damp and musty cave. They pressed close together for warmth, their faces illuminated by the firelight. The only sounds were the crackling of the flames, the howling of the wind, and the occasional rumble of thunder outside.

"I'm starting to not like this place," Chloe murmured, finally breaking the silence with a trembling voice.

"The cave, or..." Ben said sarcastically, gesturing all around.

Sarah took a deep breath, calming herself. She couldn't blame them—she knew it was her fault they were here.

Sarah looked around at her friends, their faces wavering in the firelight.

"I'm sorry I dragged you all into this. I really am. I just... I needed answers. I... miss my mom, ya know?" she said with a solemn tone.

Her friends sat in silence for a moment, their faces reflecting a mix of sympathy and tiredness. The weight of their shared predicament pressed down on them, heavy and suffocating.

Chloe noticed Sarah was holding the locket that she had found in the water and was gently rubbing it between two fingers. Sarah stared at it, lost in its reflection.

"Sarah, what is that?" Chloe asked.

Sarah didn't need to look up to know what Chloe meant. A wave of guilt for leaving her mom's body behind suddenly washed over her. She looked at Maya, who offered a weak but reassuring smile, the lines around her eyes crinkling with concern.

With a click, Sarah released the clasp on the locket and held it out for the group to see. Inside was a worn photo of Mei-Lin and Sarah.

"It's my mother's—" Her words caught in her throat.

The sudden realization hit the others all at once.

"Oh, shit, Sarah," Chloe responded with eyes wide in shock. "That means that body was... was your..." She couldn't say it out loud.

Maya was first to hug Sarah, wrapping her in a tight embrace, followed by Chloe, then Chris and Ben. Everyone hugging in the tight space wasn't a very comfortable position, but the gravity of the moment made them suffer in silence. Sitting amongst her friends in a large group embrace allowed her to finally face the reality of what had occurred.

The search for her mother was over. She supposed a small part of her had hoped that, just maybe, her mother *had* run away; at least she'd still be alive. But in truth, she had died all those years ago.

Alone, at the bottom of a well.

The adrenaline suddenly came crashing down all at once and was replaced with a grief so strong it physically hurt her chest. Tears burst from her eyes as she sobbed. She sobbed harder than she had ever sobbed before. Her friends didn't leave her side; they held her even tighter as she disappeared into her pain and sorrow.

She cried for so long, Chris had to let go to rekindle the flames in their makeshift firepit. Eventually her sobs dwindled away to silence causing the group to release their embrace and settle back down around the fire.

"Well, look at the bright side," Ben said, breaking the tension. "At least we weren't attacked by Chris's snake today."

Chris shot Ben a sly grin. "Don't worry, there's always the trek back."

"Well, if we *do* bump into it, just remember, I don't have to run faster than the snake," Ben leaned over and gave Chris a playful shove. "I just need to run faster than you."

Sarah let out a harsh laugh at their banter. She had always appreciated how they had a way of making her feel better. She watched them with a smile, as the firelight danced across their dirty faces. The warmth from the small fire Chris had managed to build felt like a godsend, chasing away some of the bone-deep chill. And the smell of Maya's herbs was so comforting.

But as the echoes of their laughter faded, replaced once more by the howl of the wind and the crackle of flames, the weight of their situation, and the reason they were stuck here, settled back onto Sarah's shoulders.

Chris shifted, leaning forward slightly, his expression softening as he looked directly at her. The playful glint in his eyes was gone, replaced by genuine concern.

"Sarah," he began, his voice lower now, careful, "What umm... what do we do now?"

Sarah swallowed, the dryness in her throat making it difficult to speak. She wasn't even really sure herself.

"I... I don't know," she admitted, her voice barely a whisper. "Now that I found my mother, I guess I need to figure out what happened. Someone up there," She gestured emphatically at the cave entrance. "Knows something. My mom always talked about this village, like it held some secret, some connection to her past. Everyone has been so vague about what happened, I thought I could piece together the mystery myself. Here, in this cave, I thought we would find something that would explain what happened. But... I just found more mysteries."

A wave of despair washed over her. The weight of her mother's absence, which had always been a heavy burden, now felt crushing. She had risked everything, dragged her friends into this mess, for... what?

Chris, seeing her distress, placed a hand on her shoulder.

"Look, whatever happened to her, whether it was... an illness or something else, you can't carry that weight alone."

His touch was surprisingly comforting, a small anchor in the storm of her emotions. The jesting between him and Ben had offered a brief reprieve, but the silence that followed felt heavy again, thick with the weight of Sarah's own uncertain quest.

She pulled her knees tighter to her chest, the rough fabric of her jeans scratching against her skin. Maybe Chris was right, too. Maybe there was no grand mystery, just illness and loss, and she was chasing shadows in a damp, dark hole. Just as the despair threatened to engulf her again, Chloe, who had been staring intently into the fire, suddenly looked up, her eyes wide but less panicked than before.

"Wait," Chloe said, her voice still shaky but gaining a thread of conviction. "We *did* find something," She glanced towards Maya's backpack, propped against the cave wall nearby. "The candle thingy."

Maya reached over with a groan, unzipped the side pocket of their pack, and carefully pulled out the object.

"It's heavier than it looks," Maya said, spinning it in their hands to better see it in the faint light of the fire. "And cold too."

Sarah had never seen anything like it before. It reminded her of those German Christmas pyramids; the holiday candle carousels made of wood, but this one was made of brass and definitely not festive. The lamp itself was intricately carved with swirling patterns that writhed in the flickering glow. The thinly designed sheep and sails on the carousel were, miraculously, in perfect shape.

"Weird, isn't it?" Maya murmured, while turning it over slowly then tracing one of the carved lines on the base with their finger.

"What is it supposed to be? Some kind of ancient paperweight?" Chris asked, leaning in and squinting.

"No, I don't think so," Maya answered without looking up from the object. "I think it's some kind of lamp. Maybe for kids. The candlelight will cast shadows from these sheep, and maybe the sails spin them too."

"Don't you think it's a little... cliché?" Ben asked, wrinkling his nose at the brass object. "The dirty old lamp in the hidden room? It's practically begging for a genie."

Chloe snorted. "God, I hope not, Ben. I don't even want to think about what you'd wish for." She reached over and ran a finger along the cool metal, a dreamy look in her eyes. "It is so beautiful though. And mysterious. It could be useful for—" She stopped herself, looking over at Sarah with a nervous glance.

Maya shivered slightly, pulling their jacket tighter around themself. "Its energy feels... creepy."

Sarah stared at it, her heart pounding a little faster. It was *something* at least. Looking at it now, cold and silent in Maya's hands, it offered no immediate answers, no sudden revelations. It was just another enigma, another piece of a puzzle she didn't know how to solve.

Sarah watched as Chloe leaned forward, her gaze locked onto the brass lamp that Maya held near the fire. An intense, almost unnerving fascination had taken over her. Chloe's eyes, usually wide with apprehension, were now narrowed slightly, fixed on the intricate sheep as if deciphering a hidden message.

"Can I see it?" Chloe asked, her voice barely above a whisper, yet carrying a strange weight. Maya hesitated, maybe sensing the same prickle of unease Sarah felt, but then carefully passed the object to Chloe. Chloe took it almost reverently, her fingers gently tracing the swirling patterns and the delicate, impossibly intact sheep, her expression one of deep concentration, almost bordering on entrancement.

Observing her friend, who had been in a small panic mere minutes ago, now handle this strange relic with such quiet intensity sent a shiver down Sarah's spine.

"Maya," Sarah said, her voice tight, hoping she sounded more casual than she felt, "maybe just... put it back in your bag for now?"

Maya nodded in understanding and reached out a hand to Chloe. Much to Sarah's relief, Chloe passed it over without any argument.

Ben looked over at Sarah with an annoyed frown on his face.

"Seriously though, do you think that *lamp* is somehow related to what happened to your mother?" He asked, gesturing at the brass object that Maya was putting back into their bag. "All that talk earlier about not bothering the spirits and shit. If anything is cursed here, it's *that* fucking thing.

Sarah couldn't argue with that logic. Maya sat up straighter and started to say something in defense of Sarah, but Sarah placed a gentle hand on their shoulder to stop them.

"You are right," she replied while looking around at her friends. "I can't honestly tell you why I needed that thing. I just thought maybe, maybe this is something important. That this holds the answer to what happened to my mom. Instead, I almost got us all killed over a useless... lamp. Or whatever it is." She dropped her head, unable to look her friends in the eyes. "I'm sorry."

Ben simply scoffed in reply, causing Maya to shoot him a dirty look.

Chloe chimed in to break the tension. "Well, regardless, we have the lamp thingy now and everyone is alive." Sarah peeked up at her and noticed she was staring at Maya's bag—no, staring *through* the bag and at what laid inside.

They fell into silence then, listening to the storm recede. The fire crackled in the center of their huddled circle, painting their exhausted faces with wavering, distorted shadows. Sarah watched as Maya scribbled furiously in their journal as Chris continued to idly stoke the fire with a small stick. The hours crawled by, and the storm gradually calmed, the relentless downpour easing to a steady drizzle. They pressed even closer together, sharing body heat, drifting into a fitful, uneasy sleep as exhaustion finally claimed them.

Sarah, however, found sleep elusive. Her mind raced, replaying the day's events, searching for a missed detail, a forgotten clue. She stared into the flames, the dancing light reflecting in her eyes. Her fingers mindlessly rubbing the locket at her chest. Images of her mother's decrepit face were relentlessly played back in her mind.

The gash in her arm began to throb, a dull pain pulsing as sticky blood began to soak through the thin cloth wrapped around her arm. So much for the St. Christopher medallion keeping her protected—then again, she *was* still alive. She let go of her mother's locket and reached for her father's medallion, but her fingers only found the thin fabric of her shirt.

She frantically felt under her collar, her breath catching in her throat. The chain was gone. She hadn't felt it break. She hadn't heard it fall. It was simply... lost. Her mind swirled with thoughts on where it could be. Back in the cave? In her mother's old home? Maybe at the airport? Hell, she couldn't remember the last time she had even seen it.

Wherever it was didn't even matter. The one flimsy shield from her father's world had vanished. A silent sob escaped her lips.

Dad. I'm sorry.

As the first faint rays of the sun peeking through the clouds crept into the cave, painting the entrance with a pale, watery light, Sarah knew she couldn't give up. Not yet. The answers were still out there, somewhere. Perhaps, in the Temple of the village where she felt her mother would want to be laid to rest—once they figured out how to get her body out.

She wasn't giving up on finding answers, for her mother, for her friends, and for herself.

The search wasn't over. It was just beginning.

CHAPTER 11

H olding her wounded arm, Sarah watched as the group slowly stood and stretched. The storm had ended, and they were finally free to head back to the comfort of the village. A cautious peek outside revealed a landscape transformed. The angry tempest had left behind a world washed clean and glistening in the late afternoon light. The route they had struggled up just hours before now presented a more treacherous mess of mud, rocks, and uprooted trees.

Sarah noted there was no sign of the sheep.

"We're going to have to be careful," Chris said, his brow furrowing as he surveyed the damage around them.

"At least we know the way," Maya chimed in, trying to sound optimistic, though a tremor still lingered in their voice.

They began their descent, carefully picking a safe course through the debris-strewn trail. The going was slow and arduous, each step requiring concentration and balance. They helped each other, paying special attention to Sarah and her injury, lending a hand over slippery rocks and fallen branches. A somber mood settled over them, the shared experience binding them together in a silent camaraderie.

The pace of the descent was unnervingly swift. At one point, Sarah stopped short, her boots skidding on the loose gravel.

"Wait," she said, her voice breathy. She turned, craning her neck to look back the way they had come. The same path that had felt like a brutal, never-ending climb just hours ago now seemed surprisingly brief. "Is it just me," she asked the group, "or is this... way too fast?" She squinted, as if trying to force the mountain to reveal its secret.

"It's always easier going down," Maya said, stating the obvious.

"No, I mean, it *feels* shorter," Sarah clarified. "Like, significantly quicker. This morning, climbing up felt like the ruins were so far away. This... it feels so much closer to the village."

Chris nodded in agreement. "Yeah... it does. This place is just fucking weird like that."

"Or maybe," Ben added, a hint of his usual mischievousness returning, "it's going quicker because we're not following Chris's map."

"Ha. Ha," Chris returned sarcastically. "You better hope we don't find my snake, because I'm going to feed you to it."

"Hopefully, Chloe has an easier time finding your *snake* than you do," Ben quipped, dodging a half-hearted jab from Chris as they both laughed.

Even through her exhaustion, Sarah managed a genuine smile at her friends jesting. Whatever the real reason for the strange perceptions in distance, they all welcomed the quicker pace.

As they neared the village, the first signs of habitation began to appear. The familiar scent of woodsmoke, animals, and a hint of floral filled the air, a comforting contrast to the wild, untamed scent of the mountain. The usual layer of dust around the village was gone, settled by the heavy rain.

But as they rounded the final bend, a scene of unexpected commotion unfolded before them. The quiet village buzzed with activity. People ran about, shouting and gesturing wildly. There was a palpable sense of urgency, of something terribly wrong.

Sarah felt a knot of worry tighten in her stomach. She quickened her pace, her heart pounding with a sense of foreboding. The others followed close behind, their faces reflecting a mixture of confusion and concern.

They approached a group of villagers clustered near the village square. The elderly woman Sarah had met at the market the other day was giving directions; her face etched with worry. She was speaking rapidly in their native dialect, her hands waving in the air. Several men were nodding their heads grimly, their expressions somber.

"What's going on?" Sarah asked, her voice slightly breathless.

The old lady turned to look at her and eyes softened when she saw Sarah.

"Oh, my dear. There was a mudslide in the storm. The Temple... The Temple is..." She couldn't finish.

Sarah's blood ran cold. A mudslide? The Temple? It was almost too much to comprehend after what they had just survived. They had all thought it was an earthquake not a mudslide. Sarah tried to imagine how large this mudslide would have to be to shake the very earth.

"My Auntie?" Sarah let the question hang. The old lady simply shrugged and shook her head.

Sarah's heart sank to her feet. The old lady gestured towards a group of men preparing to leave, carrying shovels and ropes.

"They're going to try to dig them out, but..." Her voice trailed off, the unspoken fear hanging heavy in the air.

She couldn't just stand there. She had to do *something*.

"Can we help?" Sarah asked, her voice surprisingly steady despite the turmoil raging inside her. "We're strong. We can dig."

The old woman looked pointedly at Sarah's bloody wrapped arm, then at Ben, Chris, Chloe and Maya, assessing their weary but determined faces.

"Yes," she answered with a slow nod. "Any help is welcome. But be careful. The ground is still unstable."

The five friends joined the rescue effort, following the men towards the site of the disaster. A scene of utter devastation greeted them. She now understood how the mudslide had shaken the cave—half the mountain they were under was simply... gone. The inconceivable scale of the destruction made her mind reel.

The ancient Temple, a beautiful structure of carved stone and weathered wood that had stood for centuries, now lay buried under a massive pile of mud, rocks, and shattered timber.

Sarah felt a surge of despair, but she pushed it down, forcing herself to focus on the task at hand. She grabbed a shovel and joined the line of villagers digging frantically into the mud. The work was grueling, the mud heavy and clinging, the rocks sharp and unforgiving. But the urgency of the situation, the knowledge that lives were at stake, fueled their efforts.

They worked in silence, the only sounds the scrape of shovels, the grunts of exertion, and the occasional sob from a grieving villager. Sarah's arm throbbed, her back ached in protest, and her hands were blistered and bleeding, but she didn't stop. She thought of Auntie Lin, of her gentle smile and her unwavering faith, and she dug with a surge of determination.

Hours passed. The sun began to set, casting long, ominous shadows over the scene. The rescuers had managed to clear a small section of the debris, but there was still so much more to do. Hope began to dwindle, replaced by a growing sense of futility.

Suddenly, a shout went up from one of the men.

"I hear something!" he cried, his voice hoarse with excitement. "I hear someone calling!"

Even though Sarah's friends couldn't understand the words being shouted, she didn't have to translate, they all knew instinctively. A hush fell over the crowd, and everyone strained to listen. Faintly, through the mud and rubble, Sarah could hear a muffled cry. It was weak, but it was definitely there.

A fresh wave of energy surged through the rescuers. They dug with a frantic intensity, their movements desperate but coordinated. Sarah felt a glimmer of hope flicker within her. Maybe, just maybe, they could save someone. Maybe, Auntie was still down there, and they'd be able to pull her to safety.

They focused on the area where the sound seemed to be coming from, clearing away the debris with painstaking care. Finally, they uncovered a small opening, a gap in the rubble just large enough for a person to squeeze through. A young boy, his face covered in mud and tears, was pulled from the wreckage. He was alive, but clearly terrified and exhausted. A cheer went up from the crowd, a mixture of relief and elation.

A choked sob of relief escaped Sarah at the sight of the boy, alive. The shovel suddenly felt lighter in her hands, her exhaustion momentarily burned away by a renewed fire inside her. She pushed the shovel back into the mud, the muscles in her arms screaming in protest.

Auntie Lin *had* to be alive. She just had to be.

The excavating continued, the rhythmic scrape of metal against earth and stone a somber counterpoint to the anxious whispers of the villagers. Another hour crawled by, marked only by the deepening gloom and the growing despair that gnawed at the edges of Sarah's resolve.

They found a couple more survivors, each rescue met with a wave of tearful relief and cheers, but each time, Sarah's heart sank a little further as Auntie Lin's familiar face remained absent.

Then, a choked cry of anguish rang out. Sarah's blood turned to ice. She knew, even before she saw the cluster of villagers gathering around a newly excavated area, what they had found. She pushed her way through the crowd, her legs moving on autopilot, her mind refusing to accept what her eyes were already seeing.

There, amidst the mud and broken timbers, was Auntie Lin. Her eyes closed shut, and her face ashen and swollen. Her mouth, filled with wet mud, hung open in a soundless scream. Her body lay twisted at a horrifying angle. The once vibrant silk scarf she always wore, the one with the intricate pattern of plum blossoms, was stained dark with mud and blood.

Sarah collapsed beside her, her hand trembling as she reached out to touch Auntie Lin's cold cheek. No breath. No pulse. Just the chilling stillness of death.

A wave of nausea washed over Sarah. The world tilted, the sounds of the rescue effort fading into a dull roar. She felt a hand on her shoulder, probably Chris, but she couldn't bring herself to look up. The reality crashed down on her, a crushing weight that stole the air from her lungs.

She wasn't sure how long she knelt there, lost in a haze of grief and disbelief. Vaguely, she was aware of people moving around her, of hushed voices and sympathetic glances. She heard Ben's voice, low and concerned, but his words didn't register. Maya's hand was squeezing hers, a small gesture of comfort that barely penetrated the numbness.

Someone, perhaps the elderly woman from the market, helped her to her feet. Her legs felt like lead, her body heavy and unresponsive. She stumbled away from the wreckage, away from the scene of devastation, her mind blank with shock.

She found herself walking, almost unconsciously, towards the small, weathered house where her mother had grown up. The structure that miraculously survived the devastation.

The front door stood unlocked, just as Auntie Lin always left it. Pushing it open, she stumbled into the now well-familiar scent of jasmine and sandalwood. The dimly lit home teased all of the commonplace objects—the hand-carved furniture, the faded photographs, the delicate porcelain teacups.

She heard the voices of her friends behind her, muted and indistinct, like sounds from a distant world. They were asking if she was okay, offering words of comfort, but she couldn't respond. She couldn't even look at them.

She moved through the home like a ghost, her footsteps silent on the worn wooden floor. She reached the small bedroom at the back of the house, the room that still held the faint scent of her mother.

Without bothering to change out of her mud-caked clothes, she collapsed onto the narrow bed, curling up into a fetal position. The exhaustion, both physical and emotional, finally overwhelmed her. She closed her eyes, seeking oblivion, a temporary escape from the unbearable reality. First her mother, and now poor Auntie Lin.

Sleep came quickly, a dark, dreamless void.

But it didn't last.

Little Bo-peep fell fast asleep,
And dreamt she heard them bleating;
But when she awoke, she found it a
joke,
For they were still all fleeting.

Chapter 12

Sarah stood in a vast, green pasture, bathed in the ethereal glow of a full moon. A sickly, swirling green sky cast the world in an ominous hue. The rolling hills, deceptively gentle, stretched endlessly in every direction—a suffocating, claustrophobic expanse.

Fences, made of twisted, gnarled branches, crisscrossed the landscape, creating a maze-like pattern with no discernible entrance or exit. The cool, crisp air carried the scent of wildflowers and damp earth. It was a scene of idyllic tranquility, yet a sense of wrongness prickled at Sarah's skin.

And the sheep. They were everywhere.

She scanned the flock, her eyes searching for the source of her apprehension. The sheep all appeared identical, their faces placid and unseeing, their movements slow and deliberate as they mindlessly grazed. They seemed unbothered by the wrongness of the place, uncaring, heedless.

A sudden motion caught her eye. Something dark slithered in between the sheep. The way it moved almost looked like a shark swimming in a sea of white.

Sarah froze, her eyes trying to follow the dark form as it weaved in and out of the apathetic animals. The sheep didn't react to whatever was crawling around, which was uncharacteristic of normally skittish animals. It was unsettling to watch hunted prey lacking any survival instinct.

The dark creature suddenly stopped at the edge of the flock and slowly stood up, stretching on its hind legs to tower over the grazing sheep. It was sheep like in appearance, but only in passing. It was covered in splotches of dark wool, its monstrous head an inky black. An overly large mouth, lined with razor-sharp teeth, rhythmically opened and closed, making a terrifying clicking sound. And its eyes, those familiar red pinpricks of glowing embers she would never forget—this was the thing she encountered at the ruins.

While the sheep idly grazed, the monstrous creature glided its hoof-like hands over the oblivious animals and casually walked among them. It inspected them, stopping every so often to pet one.

At first it seemed as if the monster was simply admiring its flock, like a proud parent watching their children play. But the way this creature moved, the way it clicked its mouth open and closed, felt more like a predator selecting its next meal.

A primal fear gripped her; a sense of dread so profound that it paralyzed her. She wanted to run, to scream, but she was rooted to the spot, her legs refusing to move. She was trapped in an open field with nowhere to go.

The creature paused, its arm held over one sheep's head. Something had caught its eye on the ground. From her vantage point she couldn't make out what it was. The monster bent over and lifted something up off the dirt.

"No!" Sarah cried out in anguish. In the creature's grasp hung a single vibrant scarf fluttering in the gentle wind.

It was Auntie Lin's scarf.

The beast lifted its head in surprise at her cry. Its gaze found her and its lips slowly pulled back into a hideous mockery of a smile—recognition flashing in its eyes. A low, guttural sound that mimicked a sheep's bleating erupted from its throat, sending a vibration deep within Sarah's bones.

The guttural rumble grew louder, morphing into a sickening, wet scream that clawed at Sarah's sanity. The monster, still holding her gaze with those terrifying, burning eyes, began to *change*.

It started subtly, a tremor that ran through its body, making its dark wool ripple like water disturbed by a stone. Then, the skin began to bulge and stretch, the muscles underneath contorting in ways that defied nature.

Sarah watched, frozen in a state of petrified horror, her mind struggling to process the vile spectacle unfolding before her.

A long, jagged tear appeared on the creature's flank, splitting the wool and skin like rotten fabric. A viscous, black fluid oozed from the wound, steaming slightly in the cool night air. The tear widened, growing with horrifying speed, accompanied by the sickening sound of ripping flesh and snapping bone.

From within the widening gash, something *pushed*.

It was an arm, but not a sheep's limb. This was something alien, something monstrous. The exoskeleton was a sickly green, covered by sharp, bony protrusions. It was impossibly thin, almost skeletal, yet possessed a disturbing, sinewy strength. The new arm ended in a clawed, four-fingered hand with talons that curved like obsidian daggers.

Another tear appeared on the opposite side of the creature's body, and a second arm emerged, mirroring the first. Then, more tears, more ripping, more of the black, viscous fluid. The thing's body was being torn apart from the inside, its wool falling away in ragged clumps to reveal the monstrous form beneath.

The monster's legs began to elongate, the bones cracking and reshaping themselves with audible snaps. The hooves split and splayed, forming clawed feet that dug into the soft earth. It rose slowly, unsteadily at first, onto its hind legs, towering over the other sheep that carried on grazing as if nothing out of the ordinary was occurring.

The abomination that stood before her was a nightmare made flesh. It was tall and gaunt, its body a grotesque mockery of the sheep-like animal it had once been. Its insectile arms, ending in those wickedly sharp claws, hung loosely at its sides.

The sheep's head remained, but it was distorted, elongated, the muzzle stretched into a foul, tooth-filled grin. The eyes, still burning with that malevolent light, were now set deep within sunken sockets, giving the monster a skull-like appearance.

It took an unsettling, jerky step towards Sarah, its clawed feet leaving deep imprints in the soft earth. It twitched and spasmed with each movement as if controlled by unseen strings. It tilted its head, the movement causing a sickening crackling pop from its neck then it let out another of those guttural cries. The sound was even louder this time, resonating in Sarah's chest.

Then, with a suddenness that stole Sarah's breath, it charged.

The creature moved with an impossible, blinding speed, a blur of dark wool and chitinous limbs. The ground trembled beneath its feet as it closed the distance between them in a heartbeat.

Sarah could see the saliva dripping from its fangs, the glint of moonlight on its razor-sharp claws, the evil fire in its eyes.

She wanted to scream, to run, to do *anything*, but she was paralyzed, her body locked in the grip of pure, unadulterated terror. The creature was upon her, its fetid breath washing over her face, its claws reaching, reaching...

Sarah bolted upright in bed, her heart hammering against her ribs like a trapped bird. A strangled gasp escaped her lips, her body drenched in a cold sweat. The remnants of the nightmare clung to her; the image of the monstrous sheep seared into her mind. The smell of the creature's breath fading from her nostrils.

She was back in her mom's house, in the small, familiar bedroom. The moonlight streamed through the window, casting long, dancing shadows on the walls. The room was silent, save for the rhythmic throbbing of rushing blood in her ears and her ragged breathing.

It had only been a dream, but her mind reeled trying to stitch all the horrifying pieces together. The sheep, so vacant and unseeing. The creature, a disguised predator tending to its flock. And Auntie Lin's scarf. No, this was more than a dream—she could feel it.

Sarah sat there for a long time, trembling uncontrollably in the darkness. She knew she wouldn't be able to sleep again even if she wanted to. The image of the nightmare would haunt her waking hours, a constant reminder of the day's horrors.

She finally dragged herself out of bed, every muscle in her body ached. She groaned with the effort of simply rolling over, like she was an old woman. Maya's spot beside her was notably empty, the blankets neatly folded. They must have risen early, or perhaps found another place to sleep, leaving Sarah to her ghosts.

She rested her hand on Maya's side of the bed for a brief moment; her thoughts on how thoughtful her friend was. Her eyes widened in surprise to see her wound freshly bandaged. Lifting her arm to inspect it, a slight hint of an herbal poultice tickled her nose. She gave her arm a quick flex and was reassured that it still worked properly.

Giving a silent thanks to whomever patched her up so nicely she stood up on shaky legs and stretched. Dear God, was she sore. The previous day's adventure and workload had taken its toll on her petite frame.

After a long deep stretch, she swallowed her daily pill then limped over to her door on stiff legs and opened it slowly. The home sat dark and silent. She found her way to the small kitchen, her bare feet gliding across the wooden floor. A stillness filled the house, a quiet melancholy for a place where life had once flourished, but now felt empty, hollow.

She lit the small oil lamp on the counter, the flickering flame casting dancing shadows on the walls, illuminating the familiar objects with a soft, golden glow. Grabbing the lamp, she looked around the room, and saw she was right about Maya.

They were asleep on the couch where Ben usually was, and he was sleeping on the floor next to them instead. He must've sacrificed his comfort for Maya. A wave of sadness washed over Sarah thinking of all the sacrifices her friends had made for her.

Not wanting to wake anyone else, Sarah snuffed out the lamp and made her way to the back courtyard. She shivered as the cold air washed over her. Making her way over to the stone bench and sitting down, she noticed the faint sounds of rescuers continuing their tireless work back at the mudslide.

A wave of guilt hit her for leaving the rescue attempts last night, but she refused to be too hard on herself after all she'd been through. She decided she would go back and search again, just as soon as she gathered her strength.

Her thoughts drifted all over the place as she sat in silence. Thoughts mostly of her family, friends, and the poor villagers. Thinking back on the mudslide made her realize she may never get the chance to recover her mother's body in the cave. The villagers would be too busy focusing on the more immediate issues at hand.

Frustration, or was it anger, began to set in; she slammed her hand against her thigh, the sting of pain a welcome distraction.

With the feeling of simmering anger building up, she made the conscious decision to do something about it before exploding. She stood and looked over at the open well, a well that no longer called to her. Feeling foolish for having put the closest people in her life in danger over the idea of getting answers, she decisively ignored the once mysterious hole.

Back in the kitchen, she quickly grabbed some dried fruit—anything to get some much-needed energy after that whole ordeal—Then laced up her shoes. Sighing in annoyance, she realized she was still wearing the same muddy clothes from the day before.

"Can't wait to hear what Ben says about this," she muttered to herself. Then as quietly as she could, Sarah slipped out the front door, careful not to wake anyone, and headed off towards the mudslide.

Sarah braced herself against the chill morning air as she walked. The mudslide, even from this distance, looked like a gaping wound on the landscape, a raw, brown scar against the otherwise vibrant green of the surrounding hills.

The sounds of the ongoing rescue effort, a low hum of activity punctuated by the occasional shout grew louder as she approached. The storm's moisture still held down the persistent dust. But with each muddy step she cursed under her breath. She never thought she'd prefer the damned dust over this wet dirt, but here she was. She would've breathed in dust for the rest of her life if it meant her Auntie could still be alive.

A sense of responsibility, mixed with a lingering dread, propelled Sarah forward. She'd rested, she'd eaten, and now she needed to *do* something. The inactivity, the quiet contemplation in the courtyard, had only amplified the frustration simmering inside her. This trip couldn't end without knowing *why*. She wouldn't let it.

As she neared the perimeter of the disaster zone, she saw familiar faces among the rescuers, faces that were masks of exhaustion, etched with a grief that went beyond mere sympathy. Bone-deep weariness, the kind known by those who had confronted death, weighed on everyone's shoulders. The sight felt all too familiar to Sarah, and the weight was one she thought she'd never have to carry again.

A uniformed police officer, his face caked in mud, came up to her.

"Miss Láng, isn't it? You should be resting."

"I was," Sarah replied, her voice firmer than she expected. "But I need to help."

The officer hesitated, his eyes scanning her dirty clothes, bandaged arm and the determined set of her jaw. He seemed to weigh the potential liability of an emotionally and physically drained volunteer against the undeniable value of another helping hand.

Finally, he nodded. "Alright," he said, his voice rough with fatigue. "But be careful and stay with the designated search teams. The mountain has taken enough from us already."

Sarah swallowed, the knot of anxiety in her stomach tightening. "I understand," she said, her voice barely a whisper.

He directed her towards a group of volunteers sifting through a section of debris near what had once been the village's main road. She joined the line, picking up a shovel and falling into the rhythm of the work. Dig, lift, sift, repeat. The physical exertion was a welcome distraction, a way to channel the roiling emotions inside her. She focused on the task at hand, her eyes scanning the mud and debris for any sign, any clue, any hint of life, or even... closure.

Hours passed in a blur of mud and sweat. Sarah worked alongside the other volunteers, their shared purpose creating a silent brotherhood. They exchanged few words, their faces grim, their movements driven by a desperate hope that began to dwindle with each passing hour.

Villagers, too weak to dig, showed up to help in their own way. Carrying buckets of water and carts of food from their pantries to help keep the volunteer's energy levels up. Eventually all of her friends, save for Ben, joined her as well, silently slipping into the same rhythm of work.

Beside her, Chris grunted, heaving a waterlogged timber aside. Following closely behind him was Chloe. She was a sharp contrast to the brown mud in her brightly colored clothing. Sarah was proud to see her clawing at the dirt, unafraid of breaking a nail in the seriousness of the disaster.

Sarah took a deep breath, trying to slow her racing heartbeat from the relentless exertion. The smell around the village was becoming overwhelming—wet earth, snapped pine, and the sickly sweet of rot. Maya, their face covered with a bandana, seemed unbothered by the smell. They shoveled methodically at the thick sludge, making a trench alongside what remained of shops and homes.

For a long time, no one spoke. There was only the rhythmic scrape of shovels and the shared, desperate language of effort. The sun climbed higher, beating down on the searchers. Sarah felt the sweat stinging her eyes, mixing with the grime already caked on her face. Her muscles ached, a dull throb that echoed the deeper ache in her heart.

The four of them, Chris, Chloe, Maya, and herself worked as a unit, their movements synchronized by a shared grief and a desperate, unspoken hope. They scanned every upturned root, every twisted piece of metal, every sodden scrap of fabric, searching for... something. Anything.

Around midday, the elderly woman from the previous night paid them a visit, her face etched with a sorrow that aged her another decade. She moved slowly, her steps deliberate, like someone carrying a weight far heavier than her frail frame could bear. She approached Sarah and her friends, her gaze sweeping over them with a mixture of pity and a strange, quiet understanding.

"We're holding a service," she said, her raspy voice barely above a whisper. "A mass funeral for those we've lost. It's... it's the best we can do right now." The words hung in the air, heavy and final. The unspoken truth that the search for survivors was now, realistically, a search for bodies. Sarah exchanged glances with her friends. There was no need for words. They put down their shovels, the metallic clang echoing in the sudden stillness.

They held the funeral in a small clearing a short distance from the mudslide. A makeshift altar had been erected, adorned with personal items, wildflowers and flickering candles. There, she found Ben, shuffling about, helping grieving family members with their sentimental items. A swell of pride filled her heart at the sight of him; she had half-expected to find him sleeping in.

The villagers slowly gathered, their faces a mixture of grief, exhaustion, and a stoic resilience that Sarah found both heartbreaking and inspiring. Sarah solemnly trudged up to the altar and placed her Auntie Lin's brightly colored scarf and a photo of her aunt and mother next to some lavender flowers. In a way, this felt like the true ceremony her mother deserved.

She closed her eyes, bowed her head in silence and said a few parting words for their spirits to hear.

Mom... I'm sorry. I'm sorry I wasn't here. I should have been asking what was wrong, not just... missing you. I don't know exactly what answers you were searching for out here, but I'll find them. I won't give up on you. I'll make this all mean something. God, I miss you. I hope I make you proud. I love you.

And you, Auntie Lin... my sweet, brave aunt. Thank you. That's all I can say. Thank you for every kind word, for every warm meal, for looking after us. For trying to hold back the darkness with just your love. I love you.

Goodbye for now. I'll see you when this is over.

The service itself remained simple, a mixture of prayers, chanting, and shared silences. Sarah didn't understand all the words, but the emotion, grief, was universal. Tears flowed freely, mingling with the ever-present mud. The names of the deceased were read aloud, each one a fresh wound, a reminder of the lives ripped away by the unforgiving earth.

As the service ended, the old woman approached Sarah as she was collecting the scarf and photo from the altar. "Your Auntie Lin," she said, her voice cracking with emotion. She pointed at the scarf. "Wore that to keep warm. May it always warm your heart. Come. I'll take you to her home."

The walk to Auntie Lin's house was short, but it felt like an eternity. Each step was heavy, laden with the weight of loss and the crushing disappointment of unanswered questions. The house, remarkably spared by the disaster, stood in stark contrast to the devastation surrounding it. It was a small, traditional dwelling, its walls painted a faded blue, its roof adorned with simple carvings.

The old woman ushered them inside the dim interior where the air was filled with the scent of incense and old wood. Family photos lined the walls, a silent testament to a life lived, a family loved. It was a space filled with memories, a space that felt both comforting and profoundly empty.

Sarah gently put down the colorful scarf on a table near the front door.

"Please," the old woman said, gesturing around the room. "Take what you need. Anything that will help you remember her."

Sarah, moved through the house slowly, her fingers tracing the edges of furniture, picking up small trinkets, each object imbued with the essence of Auntie Lin. Chris and Chloe waited by the front door, while Maya followed closely behind her in support. Ben must've waited outside, which was probably for the best considering how small the home was.

She found a worn photo album filled with pictures of a younger Auntie Lin, her mother, and other family members—all their smiles frozen in time. She clutched it to her chest, a tangible link to a past she could never fully reclaim. A past that she still believed held an answer, and with a bit of research, she might still get.

She and Maya continued their search into the one and only bedroom. The room was small and tidy, with very little in the way of sentimental items. She scanned around, but nothing immediately caught her eye. Maya bent down with a pained grunt and checked under the bed but came back up shaking their head. While Maya struggled to stand, using the bed for support, Sarah opened the closet door.

Her gaze instantly fell upon a small, wooden bin, tucked away on a high shelf. It was a container she hadn't seen in years, a box that belonged to her mother. She reached for it, pulling it down carefully.

Dark, polished wood formed the box which had intricately carved images of plum blossoms and swirling clouds. A built-in lock secured it shut, but Sarah knew exactly where her mom kept the key: in a small, ceramic dish shaped like a lotus flower on the shelf above the stove, all the way back home in New York. Why was the box here, she wondered; and locked at that.

This was it though, *this* was what she was searching for. She felt a weight lift off her shoulders. She turned to Maya with a huge grin on her face, holding up the chest for her to see.

Sarah's grin faded as she met Maya's eyes. Her friend's expression didn't mirror her excitement but rather held a mixture of relief and... concern. It was a look Sarah was getting used to seeing, especially these past few weeks.

"Are you alright, Sarah?" Maya asked, their voice soft while plac-ing a supportive hand gently on top of Sarah's. "You look... intense."

Sarah blinked, a little surprised. She looked down at her hand, which was white from gripping the bin so hard. She hadn't realized how tightly she was clutching the box, or how fiercely the hope had flared within her. She loosened her hold slightly.

"I... I think this is it, Maya," she said, her voice thick with emotion. "This is what holds the answers."

Maya nodded slowly, their gaze searching Sarah's.

"And if it doesn't?" they asked gently. "What if it's... empty?"

The question hung in the air, a small, sharp dart of reality piercing Sarah's bubble of anticipation. She hadn't allowed herself to consider that possibility, so focused had she been on the *idea* of answers, on the *need* for closure.

"It has to be it!" Sarah snapped, more to herself than to Maya. She couldn't bear the thought of another dead end, another layer of unanswered questions. She began to claw at the lid, digging her nails into the seam, trying to force it. It didn't budge. She shook it, the unknown contents shuffling around but the container held its secrets tight. The frustration was a fresh wave of grief.

"Sorry," Maya rested their hand on top of Sarah's, calming her rising aggravation. "Let's get back to the others," they said. "We can open it together, okay?"

Sarah nodded, dropping the issue, though irritated they weren't as optimistic as she was. The two of them returned to the main room, box in hand, only to find it empty. Chris and Chloe were gone.

Through the small, dusty window, she could see them stand-ing near a cluster of trees, away from the house. They weren't just waiting; they were arguing. Even from this distance, Sarah could see the tension in their shoulders. Chloe's hands were moving in sharp, pleading gestures. Chris was shaking his head, his arms crossed stubbornly over his chest.

Before heading outside to discover what was going on, she paused at a small collection of family photos displayed on a side table. She carefully picked up a few, the glossy paper cool against her fingertips. Images of happier times, of smiles and laughter before the shadows had crept in. Maybe, she thought, her father would want some of these, a tangible piece of the past to hold onto, something to remember the good old days.

She sighed. How could she ever tell her father she'd found his wife's body, only to leave it at the bottom of a collapsed well? The thought was gut-wrenching.

Satisfied there was nothing else worth searching for, Sarah scooped up her aunt's scarf, quickly wrapped it around her neck, and left the home without looking back.

Just as Sarah and Maya stepped out the front door, Chloe glanced over, her eyes widening slightly. The conversation between her and Chris snapped off as if severed by a knife. A placid, too-bright smile immediately plastered itself on Chloe's face. Chris just looked away, refusing to meet Sarah's gaze. Ben, who was casually leaning against a tree nearby, straightened up, his eyes questioning.

Sarah held up the chest. "I found it," she said, her voice a little shaky. "My mother's box. I think... I hope it might explain why she was here."

Ben's expression softened. He knew how much this meant to her. They all did. He walked over and held out his hands. She handed it to him reluctantly. "It's locked." He noted, while turning it over to admire the intricate patterns. "With my tools back home... and about 6 hours of YouTube, I could probably crack it."

"No need," Sarah replied. "I know exactly where the key is. It's back home in New York." Sarah gently took back the box and flashed Ben a thankful smile. Sliding past him with renewed hope; she made her way back to her mother's old home with a determined step. Her friends turned and followed without a word.

Each of them was lost in their own thoughts as they shuffled along the muddy road. The weight of the day, the exhaustion, the grief, and now this new, fragile hope, rested on their weary shoulders.

Once back inside, they gathered in the main room. The atmosphere was charged with a nervous energy, a blend of anticipation and trepidation. Sarah placed the bin on the low table in the center of the room.

The group stood around Sarah and her box in silent support. The intricate carvings shimmered in the soft light filtering through the windows. Sarah looked at her friends, then back at the chest. The answers were right there, sealed in dark, polished wood.

An entire ocean and a continent away, a tiny, forgotten key had just become the most important object in the world.

Chapter 13

The preparation for the journey back home was a dreary affair. The vibrant energy they had on their arrival in Gu Mei was completely gone, replaced by a heavy, oppressive lethargy. The vacation, once filled with the promise of adventure and excitement, had ended in tragedy and a gnawing sense of dread that clung to them like the damp, sticky mud of the landslide. Even after cleaning off the dirt and grime that clung to their skin and clothes, their mood had not improved.

They packed their belongings in a daze, the bright, colorful clothes they had brought seeming garish and out of place against the backdrop of their grief and exhaustion. The souvenirs they had purchased and collected as reminders of their shared journey, now felt like a sad weight tainted with tragedy. Even Ben's usually irrepressible humor had evaporated.

Chris and Chloe finished packing their suitcases first, and without a word, they both left to go load the van waiting for them outside.

Sarah paused in her packing, sitting in the far corner silently staring at the candle lamp in her suitcase. Maya noticed her and walked over to see what held her attention.

"Are you sure we should keep that, Sarah?" Maya asked, raising an eyebrow, their gaze also fixed on the lamp.

"Yeah," she replied, as she reached out and rubbed a finger along one of the intricate sheep. "It's... a reminder."

"Yeah, a reminder of us almost becoming bat food," Ben replied from the other side of the room, his joke landing flat.

"Ben, bats don't eat—" Maya bit their tongue. "Never mind."

Sarah ignored them; she simply wrapped the lamp in layers of cloth and placed it back carefully in her bag. Maya and Ben left her to join Chris and Chloe outside, their footsteps echoing faintly on the wooden floorboards.

She understood their concern; the candle lamp was a tangible link to the horror they had all experienced. But they didn't understand. It wasn't just a reminder of the *bad*. It was a reminder of—everything. Of the initial joy, the lush tapestry of the village, the fleeting connection she had felt with her heritage, with a past she barely knew. And yes, it was a reminder of the darkness, of the chilling reality that had lurked beneath the surface. But it was also a reminder of their resilience, their fight to survive.

She took one last, lingering look around the main room of the small house. The simple furniture, the faded photographs on the wall, the lingering scent of incense and her mother's old herbs and spices... it was a world away from her life in the city. A part of her, a newly awakened part, ached to stay. But another part, the part that had been shaken to its core, desperately needed to leave.

"Goodbye, māmā," she whispered, her voice catching in her throat. She touched the cool, rough surface of her ancestral home one last time, a silent farewell to a past she had only just begun to understand.

Outside, the midday sun beat down on the dusty village. The rain from days before had evaporated, leaving the air thick with dust again. The picturesque green of the surrounding hills seemed almost mockingly cheerful, a stark contrast to the melancholy mood that hung over them. Ben and Maya were loading their bags into the back of the rented van, while Chris and Chloe were already seated—impatient to leave.

Sarah joined them, her own suitcase feeling heavier than it should. The village, which had once been so welcoming, now felt strangely alien, its beauty tinged with a sense of disquiet. Even the familiar chatter of the villagers seemed muted, distant.

They crammed into the vehicle, the close quarters amplifying the unspoken tension. The driver, a local who they hired for the day, started the van and looked back at Sarah, waiting for confirmation. With one last somber look at her mother's home, Sarah let the driver know they were all set with a nod.

As they pulled away, Sarah looked back at the receding village; a single tear traced a path down her cheek, leaving a clean streak in the fine dust that had settled on her skin.

The bumpy dirt road started jostling them in their seats. No one spoke, only the sound of an occasional sniffle or sigh broke the silence. Sarah sat by the window, staring out at the passing landscape, subconsciously rubbing her bandaged arm, her mind a swirling vortex of images and emotions. The mudslide, Auntie Lin's lifeless face, the monstrous sheep from her nightmare, and the brass lamp, all blended together in a horrifying collage.

Sarah caught a flicker of movement in the rearview mirror. Chloe leaned towards Chris, whispering something Sarah couldn't hear. Chris met Chloe's gaze, a brief, almost imperceptible exchange passing between them before he gave a small, discouraging shake of his head. Chloe shifted in her seat, turning her attention forward, clearly disregarding his opinion.

"Hey, Sarah?" Chloe's voice, though quiet, sounded unnaturally loud in the oppressive silence.

"*Babe, don't,*" Chris mouthed quietly.

Sarah looked over her shoulder, meeting Chloe's gaze. Chloe offered a small, hesitant smile that didn't quite reach her eyes. "So, um... I was thinking," Chloe began, twisting a strand of her hair around her finger. Chris crossed his arms and turned away from Chloe. "That lamp thingy... the one you packed? Could I maybe borrow it when we get back? Just for a little while?"

Sarah's grip tightened instinctively on the edge of her seat. Borrow it? The lamp?

"Why?" Sarah asked, her voice flat, betraying none of the sudden possessiveness that flared within her.

Chloe glanced back at Chris for reassurance, but he ignored her. "Well, I had this idea... for a livestream. You know, talking about what happened... processing it all. And the relic... is perfect for what I want to do."

The idea felt jarring, almost disrespectful.

"Chloe, I don't think—"

"*Please?*" The word hissed in the air. "I *need* this, Sarah."

Sarah hesitated, looking from Chloe's pleading eyes to Chris's silent protest. Part of her wanted to refuse outright, to hold this one tangible piece of her experience close. She had risked everything for it. But as she looked at Chloe's pale, pleading face, a voice bloomed in her mind.

Look at her. So frightened. Because of you. She needs this. It's just a candle lamp, and you'll get it back. You owe her. What harm could it do?

The tension in Sarah's shoulders eased as she listened to the voice. With a heavy sigh, she found herself nodding.

"Okay, Chloe. Just... be careful with it."

Chloe's face broke into a relieved, almost manic smile. "Yes! Thank you, Sarah! I promise, I'll bring it back."

Sarah turned back to the window, a cold, hollow feeling settling in her stomach. She felt like she'd just lost a fight she hadn't even realized she was in. Outside the scenery was changing from the idyllic village to the narrow mountainous road. As they approached the same rocky outcropping where she had first seen the strange peddler in what now seemed to be a lifetime ago, Sarah took a sharp breath.

"Stop the car!" she cried out, her voice cracking with urgency. "Please, stop the car!"

The driver looked at her in the rearview mirror, his expression a mixture of confusion and alarm. He slammed on the brakes, the car swerving slightly on the gravel road before coming to a jarring halt.

"Miss? What is wrong?" he asked, his English heavily accented.

"The man... the peddler... he's there!" Sarah pointed towards the outcropping, her hand trembling.

"Sarah, what are you talking about?" Chris said, following her gaze.

This time, however, he saw him. They all did.

The peddler stood on the same rocky ledge, his silhouette stark against the pale morning sky. He and the donkey stood even further away this time though. He no longer merely gestured; he *yelled*, but no sound came out, his mouth in a wide, black O of silent desperation, his arms flailing wildly, his whole body contorted in an agony of unspoken communication.

"Holy shit," Ben breathed, his eyes wide with disbelief. "It *is* him. The creepy Shrek guy you told us about."

"He looks... sad," Maya said in a hushed voice.

Sarah frowned. She didn't quite get that same vibe, the old man looked angry to her, but Maya had always been more perceptive.

Chloe, however, was staring at the figure with a growing horror that mirrored Sarah's own. "Do you think he's trying to tell us something?" she whispered, her voice strained.

The peddler continued his silent pantomime, his movements frantic, almost convulsive. It was like watching a horror movie with the sound turned off, the silence amplifying the terror, making it all the more unsettling.

"I think he is. We have to go back," Sarah said, her voice pleading. "We have to talk to him. If he knows something, I need to talk to him."

Chris, however, was shaking his head. "Sarah, we can't. We'll miss our flight. And besides," he added, trying to inject a note of reason into the increasingly surreal situation, "he's probably just some local eccentric. He's probably crazy."

"Crazy?" Sarah turned to him, her eyes blazing with a mixture of disbelief and fear. "I don't think so. He's screaming *something*, Chris! Can't you see? He's trying to warn us!"

"Sarah, calm do—" Chris cut himself off with a groan, aggressively running his hands through his hair. "Sorry, that's not what I meant. We're all stressed, we're all tired. We're just not thinking clearly."

"I am thinking clearly!" Sarah insisted. "More clearly than I have in days. We need to go back."

The argument was cut short by the blare of a horn behind them. Another car had pulled up, its driver impatient to pass. Everyone turned to look at the car behind them, and when they swiveled back, the peddler and donkey were gone.

"What the fuck..." Ben said quietly, mirroring all their thoughts.

"Miss, we must go," the driver interrupted in an agitated voice. "The airport is very far. You will miss the plane."

As he put the car in drive and started to pull away, Sarah thought she heard him whisper something about them being "crazy" in Cantonese. The group all shared a look of concern and fear. The driver was right; they didn't have time to investigate with their flight so soon. With nothing to do about it, they all reluctantly sat back in their seats. Sarah and her friends simply sat in a chilled silence again for the remainder of the drive.

What was one more unsolved mystery, she thought.

CHAPTER 14

The flight to New York was, for the most part, long and un-eventful. The perpetual drone of the engines was a poor substitute for the easy banter that had once filled the air at the start of their vacation. Maybe it was just stress catching up with them, but Sarah couldn't help but notice the subtle changes in her friends.

It started while boarding. Chloe, who always presented a meticulously maintained public image, looked a mess. Her disheveled hair, wrinkled clothing, and amateurish makeup shattered her usual facade. She grunted as she struggled to lift her suitcase into the overhead bin.

"Chris, a little help?" she snapped.

Chris, who would normally leap at the chance to play the hero, didn't even turn his head. He just continued to stare blankly out the window. "Just do it yourself, for once," he mumbled, his voice flat and distant.

A flight attendant, seeing the struggle, gave a stunned Chloe a hand. "Rough trip?" the attendant asked with a polite smile.

Chloe just glared, her usual bubbly personality gone. "You have no idea." Then with a growl of anger, Chloe plopped down into her seat next to him. She began fidgeting with her purse; clearly frustrated.

Sarah watched the exchange, a knot of unease tightening in her stomach. She turned to say something to Maya, but paused. They scratched at their journal, their hand moving mechanically across the page, not with the focused curiosity of before, but with a mindless, automatic rhythm.

"Maya," Sarah said gently, trying to get her attention. They didn't respond. "Maya!"

They stopped writing, looking up at her slowly as if coming out of a deep trance. "Huh?"

Sarah scrunched her eyes, then gestured to the seatbelt.

"Oh," Maya mumbled. They struggled with the buckle, their usual calm efficiency replaced by a clumsy frustration. They went back to scrawling in their book without an apology.

Even Ben seemed off. He had predictably retreated into the blue glow of his phone, but he constantly rubbed his temples as if fighting off a migraine. When the flight attendant made a corny joke during the safety briefing, he didn't laugh. He didn't even crack a smile. He just stared at his screen, his face pale and drawn. It was the low-hanging fruit he would normally snatch out of the air, but it hung there, unnoticed.

None of them, Sarah included, were able to get any real rest, despite the long flight and the deep desire for sleep. The pressurized cabin provided a strange sense of detachment from the horrors they had left behind. Yet, despite the physical distance, the emotional weight of their experience remained, constantly pressing down on them.

With sleep elusive, Sarah's thoughts kept returning to the secrets locked in her mother's box. She kept it tucked away in her carry-on bag, a tangible link to the past she wanted to hold close to her, a reminder of the mystery she was determined to unravel.

After what felt like an eternity in the air, the plane finally landed at JFK. The familiar sights and sounds of the airport—the crowds of people, the announcements over the loudspeaker, the smell of unwashed passengers and fast food—all of it should have been comforting in its familiarity, but they only served to amplify Sarah's sense of displacement, her feeling of being an outsider in her own world.

They collected their luggage, their movements slow and lethargic. Just a short walk from the baggage claim area they all squeezed into Maya's SUV, then began the drive back to Sarah's home in Queens. Above them, the city skyline loomed like a concrete and steel jungle that felt just as alien and threatening as the mountains of China. The usual cacophony of the city—the honking horns, the sirens, the shouts of street vendors—grated on Sarah's nerves, amplifying her sense of anxiety.

"You gonna be okay?" Chris asked, twisting around from the front passenger seat to study her.

"Yeah," Sarah lied. "I just need some sleep."

He didn't press her, sensing that she needed space, that she needed time to process the events of the past handful of days.

"Text me if you need anything, okay?" Maya said, a bit of their caring personality returning.

"I will," Sarah said, managing a weak smile.

They pulled up to her home and Sarah felt a sudden wave of homesickness wash over her. She got out of the car, her legs feeling heavy and unsteady. After grabbing her luggage out of the back of the SUV, she placed her carry-on bag down, unzipped the top and reached in and pulled out the candle lamp. She paused for only a moment before handing it over to Chloe.

"Thank you, Sarah," Chloe said, taking the relic carefully. "I promise to take care of it."

Sarah couldn't trust herself to answer so she simply smiled. Her friends said their goodbyes one last time before driving away. She watched as the taillights of Maya's car disappeared around the corner, leaving her alone on the sidewalk, facing the daunting prospect of confronting her father, of confronting the truth.

Her father stood in the living room, bent over in the process of grabbing his work bag, as she walked in. He looked up and his face lit up at the sight of her. He dropped the bag and ran to her, his arms outstretched. "Sarah," he said, his voice thick with emotion. "Thank goodness you're home."

"Dad," she sobbed. "I found her."

Her father looked at her, his expression confused, wary. "What are you talking about?"

"She's dead, Dad," Sarah whispered. "She's dead. I was in the cave. I... I found her body."

Her father's face drained of all color. "No," he breathed. "No, that's not possible. You're mistaken. It was... it must've been someone else."

"It was her," Sarah insisted, her voice breaking. "I found this." Sarah pulled the locket out from under her shirt. His eyes widened in disbelief and shock at the sight.

"No..."

"Dad, she was at the bottom of the well, holding this... this lamp."

"The well? No. That's impossible," he stammered, pacing now. "There must be an explanation. You were traumatized; you were in a dark cave. The mind can play tricks, Sarah. It's grief, it's—"

"Dad," she whimpered, the pain in her voice giving him pause. Her teary eyes met his. He enveloped her in a tight hug as she collapsed in his arms, his embrace a haven of warmth and security in the storm of her emotions. Sarah clung to him, tears streaming down her face, the dam of her grief finally breaking.

He held her, stroking her hair, murmuring words of comfort. He didn't ask for details, not yet. He simply let her cry, letting her release the pent-up fear and sorrow that had been building inside her.

After a long while, her tears subsided, leaving her feeling depleted and empty. She pulled away from him, wiping her eyes with the back of her hand.

"I need to tell you everything," she said, her voice hoarse.

The story poured out of her in a jumbled rush. She told him about the cave, finding her mother's corpse with the brass lamp, the mudslide, Auntie Lin's death, the terrifying nightmares, the strange peddler, the box of her mother's things.

Her father listened patiently, his eyes misting over when she mentioned how she found Mei-Lin then his expression grew increasingly grim as she continued recounting her story. He didn't interrupt, didn't question, didn't dismiss her fears as the product of an overactive imagination. He simply sat there, his presence a solid, grounding force in the swirling chaos of her emotions.

When she was finished, he was silent for a long moment, his gaze fixed on her bandaged arm, his brow furrowed in thought.

"Poor Mei-Lin. Alone, all this time," he finally responded in a soft voice. "I knew this trip was a mistake. I should have listened to my gut. I should have stopped you."

"Stopped me?" Sarah exclaimed in disbelief, stepping away from him. "I had to go. I needed to find... Mom. I *found* Mom."

He sighed, running a hand through his thinning hair, a gesture of weariness that mirrored her own exhaustion. "No... I never told—" He cut himself off, his face scrunched as if he fought an internal battle.

"What, Dad?" Sarah pushed. "Never told me *what*?"

"Nothing," he replied, brushing a stray hair from her face. "Go unpack your things, I'll cook us dinner—Your favorite. Pizza delivery."

Sarah's first instinct was to demand answers right then and there, but she held her tongue. She was just so tired, emotionally and physically drained from her ordeal that she couldn't push the issue. Her father looked relieved when she didn't argue.

"I'm sorry I can't stay here and spend more time with you; I was just on my way to the clinic. You'll have to save me a slice," he picked up his work bag off the floor and headed for the front door before pausing, turning to look at her over his shoulder. "Thank you, Sarah. For finding her."

With that, he walked out, leaving her alone with the weight of her own thoughts.

Later that evening, after licking the last of the savory pizza sauce from her fingers, she finally built up the nerve to open the box. She stood on her toes and reached for the bowl above the stove where her mother kept her keys, still untouched since her disappearance.

Inside the bowl she quickly located the one key she had hoped to find. Prize in hand, she sat down at the small kitchen table, the single overhead light casting harsh shadows on the walls, making the familiar objects of her home seem alien and unfamiliar.

Holding her breath, she inserted the key into the lock and sighed in relief as it slid in perfectly, confirming her expectations. A twist of her wrist unlatched the lock with a soft click, and the lid opened slightly. With trembling hands, she lifted the lid. A faint scent of sandalwood and dried flowers wafted out, a scent that instantly transported her back to her childhood, to a time when her mother was still alive, when the world felt safe and secure.

The first thing she noticed was a vibrant scarf, a perfect match to the one Auntie Lin had worn. She smiled, thankful at having taken the scarf home from China; it felt right, having a piece of her mom and her aunt together again. She picked up the soft silk cloth, and held it to her face, inhaling the faint scent of jasmine, a scent that instantly transported her back to aunt's house, to the warmth and comfort that had been shattered by the mudslide.

Putting the scarf aside for the moment she continued searching the box. On top, was a small, plain looking journal with an elastic band wrapped around it. Dozens of photos and handwritten notes lay scattered underneath the bound book. Sarah felt a surprising pang of disappointment at how empty the chest was.

She pushed the bound book aside and picked up some of the photographs and began flipping through them one by one. Each picture was faded and worn, capturing moments from her mother's life in Gu Mei before she had moved to America.

Sarah saw her mother as a young girl, her face full of youthful innocence, playing in the rice paddies with other children, their laughter echoing across the years. She saw Mei-Lin and Auntie Lin together, their arms wrapped around each other, their smiles reflecting a deep bond of sisterhood that even death could not erase. She saw her mother standing in front of the temple, the intricate carvings of the ancient structure a backdrop to her radiant face, a beauty that now seemed tinged with a subtle sadness, a hint of the darkness that would eventually consume her.

Sarah gently tossed the photos back into the box and removed the letters. They were written in her mother's elegant, flowing script, and addressed to friends and family in America. They spoke of her daily life in the village, of the changing seasons, of the local festivals, of her hopes and dreams for the future. They painted a picture of a vibrant, close-knit community, a world far removed from the bustling streets of New York City. But even in these seemingly mundane accounts,

Sarah detected a subtle undercurrent of disquiet, a sense of something lurking beneath the surface of everyday life.

Sarah lifted the journal out last and undid the band holding it shut. Before she could open it, scraps of paper, torn from notebooks, napkins, even the backs of envelopes, filled with her mother's frantic, almost illegible handwriting fell out from between the pages. They were disjointed, fragmented, like pieces of a shattered mirror reflecting a terrifying truth. They were the raw, unfiltered expressions of a mind grappling with an unspeakable horror.

"The dreams are getting worse. So vivid. So real. The sheep... its eyes... they're watching me. Always watching."

"I can hear the demon whispering my name, calling to me from the darkness. It's getting closer. I can feel it, a cold, suffocating presence."

"It is a shapeshifter that goes by many names: the Grave Goat, the Shepherd, the Wool Eater."

"It's not only in the lamp anymore. It learned. It wants new eyes. It wants out."

"They think it is a story. But the story is the cage. When the story is told, the cage door opens."

"The symptoms. They're starting again. The fatigue, the headaches, the feeling of being disconnected, of not being myself. It's happening again. Just like before."

The symptoms. The fatigue, the headaches, the feeling of disconnection. She had seen those same signs, almost exactly, from her friends just hours before. She remembered Chloe, her usually vibrant face pale and drawn, complaining and disheveled looking. She remembered Ben, his usual boundless energy depleted, his sense of humor absent. She thought of Chris, his strong, athletic frame weakened, his usual confidence replaced by a hesitant uncertainty and aloofness. She pictured Maya, their stoic facade crumbling, and their unusual inattentiveness.

Then there was the sheep.

It *couldn't* be a coincidence.

Her gaze fell on one last photograph, tucked away at the bottom of the box, almost hidden beneath the other mementos. It was a small, square Polaroid, its colors faded and distorted.

She picked it up, her fingers trembling, her heart pounding in her chest. She held a picture of herself as a child, no more than four or five years old being cradled in her mother's arms. They were standing in front of a worn and ancient well that she recognized immediately—the one at her mother's home, in Gu Mei.

Dawning realization chilled her to the bone. She had been to Gu Mei as a child. Her head began to spin, the floor beneath her lurching.

That was it, that was the connection.

Suddenly, the weird feeling of familiarity, the unsettling déjà vu she'd experienced the entire time she was in China, made a terrifying kind of sense. It wasn't just a feeling; it was a *memory*.

With a sudden thought, she snatched up the remaining photographs and began sifting through them frantically. Her fingers fumbled with the glossy paper, each image a blur of faces and places until her suspicion was confirmed.

She found it.

Her breath caught in her throat, a strangled gasp, and her blood ran cold, like ice water in her veins. In one particular photograph, positioned innocuously behind her smiling mother and Auntie Lin, an object sat on the table between them.

It was the *lamp*.

CHAPTER 15

Every pothole in the road sent a bouncing jolt through Chloe's skull, amplifying the dull, persistent throb behind her eyes. God, she was *tired*. Not just normal, end-of-a-long-trip tired, but a deep, bone-weary exhaustion that seeped into her very soul.

China had been... intense. Way more intense than she'd bargained for. The cave, the earthquake, Auntie Lin... Chloe shivered, pushing the memories away. No point dwelling on it. Not now.

In the seat next to her, Chris suddenly shouted—at least it sounded like a shout with her headache. "You good up there, El?" he asked, checking Maya for any signs of driver fatigue. Even he looked rough, his usual energetic spark dimmed. If she and Chris felt this bad... well, she was just glad she wasn't the one driving right now.

"Yeah, fine," Maya said, their smile clearly forced. "Just beat. Can't wait to crash."

"Ha, ha," Ben mocked from the back, where he was struggling to keep his eyes open as well. "And you thought MY jokes were bad."

Maya just nodded absent-mindedly, unaware of their accidental pun, their gaze fixed on the lines in the road passing by.

Chloe, fighting her own drooping eyelids, watched Maya as well. Unsurprisingly, Maya's head, previously fixed forward, began a slow, almost imperceptible nod. Once. Twice. Then, their chin dipped sharply towards their chest.

The SUV drifted into oncoming traffic.

"Maya!" Chloe shrieked, leaning forward and grabbing their shoulder. Maya jolted awake, yanking the wheel hard as an oncoming car blared its horn, its headlights flooding the cabin. The near miss left a ringing silence in the car.

"Shit," Maya whispered, stabbing at the window button. A rush of cold, damp air flooded the cabin. They shook their head vigorously, trying to dispel the fog of sleep.

"What the hell, El?" Ben shouted from the back. "You said you were okay."

"Yeah, pull over, El," Chris said, his voice low and tight. "Let me drive."

"No, I'm good now," Maya insisted, though their voice trembled. They glanced back at Chris and with all the confidence they could muster, said, "I'm good."

"Just watch the road!" Chris cried, while pulling his hair.

"Sorry," Maya replied sheepishly.

"Jesus Christ, Maya," Ben mumbled from the back. The accusation in his quiet voice was worse than a yell.

The rest of the short drive to Chloe's apartment was quiet as the passengers tried to regain their composure. Until they arrived safely, Chloe kept a much closer eye on Maya for any signs of them passing out again. When they finally pulled up outside Chloe's apartment building, the relief was palpable.

"Okay, nerds, my bed awaits," Chloe announced, trying to inject some of her usual cheerfulness into her voice. "Thanks for not killing me, El."

Chris got out of the SUV and surprisingly helped her with the luggage, his touch lingering on her arm. "You want me to stay here tonight?" he asked, his brow furrowed with concern.

"Not tonight," she replied, maybe a little too sharply. "Let's just get some sleep. Lots and lots of sleep." She wasn't really in the mood for his drama right now. Their on-again, off-again thing felt decidedly *off* after the stress of the trip.

"Alright," he said, backing off slightly. "I'll text you when I get home."

"Okay, sure," she replied, while waving him away. She grabbed her bags and waved goodbye to her friends with a struggling free hand. As she made her way inside, she heard Chris's voice from the SUV behind her, ordering Maya out of the driver's seat.

Inside, her apartment felt strangely alien after the rustic simplicity of Gu Mei. The familiar chic decor, the carefully curated collection of art prints, the neatly arranged shelves of makeup and skincare products—it all seemed... surreal.

She dropped her bags by the door, kicking off her shoes with a sigh of relief. She stood there for a moment, looking around her apartment that felt a tad unfamiliar after her long trip. She took a deep breath through her nose and was surprised at how different her apartment smelled too.

Did it always smell this... potent?

With an exaggerated groan Chloe picked up her bags by the straps and dragged them into the kitchen. She slapped the light switch, and the sudden flare of fluorescent light sent an ice pick of pain jabbing behind her eyes. The pain was getting worse, a relentless pounding that made the room swim. And the weariness... it was becoming a deep, crushing, fatigue, an anchor pulling her down into the dark. She desperately needed sleep. But the thought of closing her eyes, of the fragmented nightmares that clawed at the edges of sleep since the cave... that was its own kind of terror.

"Fucking Sarah," she muttered under her breath as she plopped down her designer luggage in the middle of the room. The energy drink she pulled from the fridge hissed open, the cold liquid caffeine sliding down her throat a welcome shock. She loved the girl, but Christ, trouble clung to Sarah like a second skin. If she believed half the occult crap Maya always spewed, she'd think Sarah was literally cursed.

She'd known going to China was a bad idea, but she'd gone anyway. Let them think she'd tagged along for the content. Let Chris think he'd convinced her. It was easier than admitting the truth, easier on his fragile ego. The truth was, Sarah had saved her life on *that* day. Amidst the horror, something had screamed at her to follow Sarah, not Chris. A choice that had kept her alive. She replayed that split-second decision over and over, a fucking viral reel stuck on a loop in her head.

Cursed and blessed. For every insane, world-ending event Sarah stumbled into, she somehow clawed her way out alive. So Chloe had made a choice: stick to Sarah. Stick to the group—the Still Alive Five. How the hell could one person be both a lightning rod for disaster and the goddamn shelter from the storm?

She shambled into her bedroom, the room bathed in the soft, diffused light filtering through the blinds. The bright and cheerful colors decorating the room did little to lift her mood. As she stripped off her clothing her thoughts kept bouncing around from one to another. From the craziness of what happened in China to her clearly depressed friend Sarah, and to her next live stream.

A voice whispered inside her exhausted brain, an unfamiliar urging cutting through the fog.

The sheep lamp thingy. The challenge.

Yes—It was perfect.

She hadn't been able to post much real content from China with the lack of signal and all. Her followers were getting restless.

Yes, they need something new, something exciting, something... authentic.

Right? And what was more authentic than sharing her struggles, her real-life insomnia, her desperate search for rest?

You should do the livestream. Tonight.

People loved mysterious stories. And this lamp... it was ancient, mysterious, maybe even a little bit cursed—perfect for generating buzz. She could frame it as a desperate attempt, a last resort to sleep. Maybe it would actually work? And even if it didn't, the spectacle alone would be worth thousands of views.

A surge of energy, fueled by the familiar rush of creative inspiration, momentarily pushed back the tiredness. She went and grabbed the luggage in the kitchen and brought them to her room. She pulled out the lamp with its gleaming sheep from the suitcase and carefully unwrapped it. It felt heavier than she remembered.

She gently rubbed her fingers over the surface, tracing the intricate shapes, its brass surface cool against her skin. She then ran her fingers down over the miniature sheep, their tiny forms frozen in mid-leap.

Cute, but also... kind of creepy.

Perfect.

As she ran her fingers down below the sheep and underneath the base, she felt something sticking out. Turning the lamp over to see what it was, she lifted her eyebrows in surprise at what she found. Tucked there, almost hidden, was a small, aged rectangle of parchment stuffed into a small crevice. She pulled it out and unfolded it. Curiously, it had English writing on it, but in a peculiar, stylized script.

"Little Bo-Peep has lost her sheep,
And doesn't know where to find them;
Leave them alone, and they'll come home,
Bringing their tails behind them..."

It continued on for more verses, but she stopped reading. She sat there staring at the parchment with the nursery rhyme. Why was a nursery rhyme written down in English hiding in an ancient Chinese lamp, she wondered. And how did they all miss it before? She shrugged, deciding that however it ended up there was to her viewers benefit.

Okay. Time to set the stage.

She spent the next half hour meticulously preparing her bedroom for the livestream. Setting up her ring light, adjusting the camera angle on her phone, arranging pillows and blankets on her bed to create a cozy, inviting atmosphere. She changed into her favorite silk pajamas, applied a fresh layer of makeup and positioned the brass lamp prominently on her nightstand.

As she worked, the headache intensified, a sharp, stabbing agony behind her right eye. Lethargy washed over her in waves, making her limbs feel heavy, her movements sluggish. She felt... off. Disconnected. Like she was watching herself move through the motions from a distance.

Weird. Probably just jet lag, Chloe told herself, pushing the thought away.

She checked her phone and was relieved to see her friends had all texted her in group chat letting her know they were safely home. She texted a quick reply back bidding them all a goodnight then made sure the livestreaming app was setup.

Finally, everything was ready. She took a deep breath, trying to quell the nervous flutter in her stomach. This was it. Time to go live. She tapped the screen, her face instantly illuminated by the phone's glow.

"Hey, Wanderlusters!" she began, forcing her signature bright smile, though it felt strained, unnatural. "It's your girl, Chloe, back from the wilds of China and dealing with some *serious* insomnia."

She launched into her tale, weaving a narrative of travel fatigue, stress, and the desperate search for sleep. She described her adventure in China in detail, with barely any exaggeration, then with the suspense built up properly she introduced the lamp.

She held it up to the camera, the light reflecting off its polished surface which highlighted its intricate design, and the "creepy-cute" sheep. She also held up the aged piece of paper and showed the chat the nursery rhyme.

The chat scrolled wildly, a mix of sympathetic comments, skeptical questions, and demands for her to start the challenge. The view count climbed steadily. First hundreds. Then thousands.

Perfect.

"Okay, guys," she said, trying to inject excitement into her voice. "What should we call this challenge?"

Her chat scrolled by with all sorts of suggestions until one caught her eye.

"Yes!" she squealed, using a fake, overly excited voice. "Viewer WoolEater69, the '40 Winks Challenge' is perfect. Okay, moment of truth. I'm lighting the candle."

The light gleaming off the lamp made the sheep's eyes seem alive, as if they were watching her. Goosebumps ran down her back. Chloe rubbed her own eyes with the back of her hand, trying to scrub away the exhaustion but just wound up inadvertently smearing her makeup.

That voice in the back of her mind whispered again.

Your viewers are watching... judging. Don't leave them waiting.

The voice was right, she couldn't let her fans down now, by losing her mind.

"The exhaustion is killing me, guys. Let's do this! Here we go!"

Her hands trembled slightly as she struck a match, the small flame flaring to life. She carefully lit the candle she had placed within the center of the carousel. The flame flickered, casting a warm, inviting glow. As the wick started to heat up, she turned off her ring light and settled down on her bed, being careful to position herself in the frame of the video at the perfect angle to catch both her and the lamp together.

The tiny sails at the top began to turn, slowly at first, then picking up speed as the heat rose. The sheep shadows began their circular dance on the wall behind her bed. As the carousel began to spin, the tiny metallic hooves of each sheep began to tick on the base with each pass.

Tick. Tick. Tick.

"It's beautiful guys," Chloe whispered, as she watched the shadows in fascination. "Imagine how many generations of families have used this. Picture how many children have fallen asleep watching these same shadows."

Chloe yawned. "Okay, everyone, now *we* get to experience this, together." She held the paper closer as she laid down on her bed, her eyes scanning the words, and began to chant, her voice soft and rhythmic, almost hypnotic.

"Little Bo-Peep has lost her sheep,

And doesn't know where to find them;"

It *was* kind of hypnotic. Her eyelids felt heavy, the lassitude pressing down on her like a physical weight. Maybe this crazy rhyme thing was actually working?

"Leave them alone, and they'll come home,

Bringing their tails behind them.

Little Bo-Peep fell fast asleep,

And dreamt she heard them bleating;"

The shadows on the walls began to spin faster. Their forms elongating. Changing. Becoming less and less sheep-like. The ticking grew faster.

Tick. Tick. Tick.

"But when she awoke, she found it a joke,

For they were still a-fleeting."

Her voice faltered. A sudden wave of dizziness washed over her. The room tilted slightly, the shadows swirling with a nauseating intensity. The air grew thick, heavy, pressing in on her. And that smell... she wrinkled her nose. What *was* that? Like wet wool left out in the rain too long, mixed with something metallic, almost coppery. Like... blood?

A jolt of animalistic panic shot through her. *Stop this. NOW.* The thought was sharp, instinctual. But another, calmer thought immediately washed over it, smoothing the edges of her fear.

It's just the old brass. Tarnish and rust. Relax. The viewers are watching.

She took a shaky breath, forcing the panic down. She needed to remain professional.

"Then up she took her little crook,

Determined for to find them,

She found them indeed, but it made her heart bleed,

For they'd left their tails behind them."

The candle flame sputtered as if blown by a gentle breeze, causing the shadows to dance as they journeyed around her room. All the shadows stretched and twisted in different ways. Some shadows cried out in silent pain, others reached outwards as if trying to escape. All but one shadow. One silhouette went around and around the room without any shifting. Staring at Chloe with each pass. She was so tired and focused on the parchment in front of her that she didn't notice.

"It happened one day, as Bo-Peep did stray

Into a meadow hard by,"

The rhythmic sound of the tiny metal sheep hitting the base of the lamp, once soothing, now sounded like... like tiny hooves tapping on stone. Or maybe like fingernails tapping on glass. It was getting louder, more insistent, grating on her nerves.

Tick. Tick. Tick.

"There she espied their tails side by side,

All hung on a tree to dry."

The sheep spun faster and faster. Their twisted shadows no longer resembling sheep but horrifying angular shapes writhing in torture. The lone shadow that mysteriously didn't change shape like the others, inexplicably stopped spinning, hovering on the wall above Chloe, the other shadows continued spinning around it. Its eyes now glowing an evil red, stared at her with hunger.

Slowly the shadow detached itself from the wall, pulling itself free from the flat surface. This sheep shadow no longer had short stubby legs, instead they stretched and popped into long insect-like arms ending in sharp claws.

Tick. Tick. Tick.

She risked a glance at the chat as she continued chanting. Some viewers were definitely picking up on the creepy vibes now.

"*OMG Chloe those shadows r freaking me out,*" one comment read.

"*Is that part of the challenge??*" asked another.

A third comment appeared: "*Dude, she looks scared af.*"

Fear, cold and sharp, lanced through her. She *was* scared. Something was wrong. Terribly wrong. This wasn't just a weird sheep carousel or a creepy nursery rhyme. This felt... alive. Malignant.

Then she saw it.

In the reflection on her screen, just to the side of the chat window, she saw the shadow pull away from the wall behind her. She wanted to stop, to blow out the candle, end the stream, scream, run out of the room. But she couldn't. She was frozen, her body locked in place, her voice continuing the chant automatically, as if compelled by some outside force.

"And tried what she could, as a shepherdess should,

To tack each again to its lambkin."

The large shadow unfolded, rising, expanding, filling the space behind her bed. It wasn't just a shadow anymore; it had depth, substance, a three-dimensional presence that defied logic. Chloe watched its reflection in the dark screen of her laptop nearby, her eyes wide with terror.

It was tall and impossibly thin, a grotesque silhouette against the wavering light of the lamp. Its limbs were like snapped twigs, ending in impossibly sharp claws. Its head... its head was vaguely sheep-like, but elongated, distorted, the muzzle stretched into a hideous rictus grin filled with too many teeth. And the eyes... two points of burning, malevolent red light fixed on her reflection.

She tried to move, to turn, to look directly at the horror behind her, but her muscles wouldn't obey. She was trapped, pinned beneath the weight of its terrifying gaze.

A small pathetic whimper escaped her lips.

The chat scroll was a blur of frantic messages now. People were freaking out, asking what was happening, demanding to know if this was real. But Chloe couldn't answer. She couldn't speak. She could only watch, helplessly, as the monstrosity raised one of its long, insectile arms.

It reached out, its shadowy tendril extending towards her reflection in the laptop screen. The movement was slow, deliberate, almost teasing. Chloe squeezed her eyes shut, bracing for... she didn't know what. Pain? Oblivion?

She felt a touch, feather-light, but impossibly cold, on the top of her head. Then, nothing. The world dissolved into blackness, the frantic scroll of the chat, the dancing candlelight, the monstrous shadow; all disappeared. She didn't even feel the sickening crack of her head on the nightstand as her body collapsed.

The livestream continued broadcasting the image of her still, silent form with open, unseeing eyes, staring into the camera. Then, as the candle abruptly blew out, the livestream ended.

The last thing the viewers heard was the rhythmic ticking of the brass sheep as they spun on their carousel.

Tick. Tick. Tick.

CHAPTER 16

The insistent buzzing of her phone on the nightstand woke Sarah sharply from a dreamless sleep. The loud vibrations shot through the old wood and into her bones.

With a silent curse, she reached for the offending device. The screen lit up, blindingly bright in the dim bedroom. Dozens of notifications flooded in—texts, missed calls, social media alerts, and news headlines pinging with alarming frequency.

Maya

SARAH CALL ME NOW!!!

Chris

Dude wtf is going on with Chloe???

Ben

Check the stream link NOW Sarah holy shit

#ChloeUpdate, #WanderlustersWorry: Influencer Chloe unre-sponsive after bizarre livestream, NYPD conducting wellness check after streamer...

Sarah's blood ran cold.

Chloe. The livestream. The lamp.

Her fingers, clumsy with sleep and a sudden, nauseating wave of fear, fumbled to unlock the phone. She bypassed the texts, her thumb stabbing at the social media icon, bringing up the platform Chloe used. A notification banner flashed across the top: *Chloe's "40 Winks Challenge" Livestream - ENDED ABRUPTLY.* Below it, the chat replay showed a chaotic mess, a digital riot of panicked emojis, terrified questions, and wild speculation.

"What happened?" she whispered, scrolling rapidly through the timestamped comments. The early messages were full of sleepy emojis and jokes, viewers settling in for Chloe's promised sleep hack. Then, a shift. Comments about the weird shadows, Chloe looking scared, the stream cutting out...

Maya's contact popped up on her screen as the phone buzzed again. Sarah answered their call with shaking hands.

"Sarah? Oh my god, did you see?" Maya's voice sounded tight with panic, breathless.

"I... I just woke up," Sarah stammered. "What happened? Is she okay?"

"She's definitely *not* okay! Paramedics are here—they're taking her to the hospital! Chris called me, he got there first. She's... she's completely unresponsive. Like... like she's in a coma or something."

A coma. The word hung in the air, heavy and chillingly familiar.

"The lamp," Sarah breathed, the connection hitting her hard. "It was the lamp. I shouldn't have let her take it."

"Really?" Maya sounded confused, scared. "How?"

"I opened my mom's box last night, and you won't believe what I found, El."

"Okay," Maya interjected quickly. "Let's go over this later. Can you be ready in ten minutes?"

"Yeah," Sarah said, already throwing off the covers, ignoring the dizziness that threatened to overwhelm her. "Where are they taking her?"

The sound from Maya's end became muffled as they lowered the phone. Sarah could just make out someone talking in the background, but couldn't hear it clearly enough to understand. She took the brief pause in her conversation to swallow one of her epilepsy pills. Maya's voice abruptly returned.

"Chris just told me he heard Brooklyn Methodist," Maya said. "He's on his way there now. Ben and I will pick you up. Be outside in ten." The line clicked dead.

Sarah moved on autopilot; her mind numb with shock and a sickening sense of guilt. This was her fault. She knew the thing was dangerous, she'd felt its pull, seen the warnings in her mother's notes. And she had let Chloe take it. For *content*.

She threw on the first clothes she could find—jeans, a faded floral-patterned t-shirt, and some fresh socks. She splashed cold water on her face, barely glancing at her reflection, too ashamed to look herself in the eye.

She grabbed her pills, keys, her wallet, and her phone, stuffing them into her pockets. She turned to leave when the wooden box sitting on her kitchen table— the tangible link to her mother, and to the curse—made her stop.

Answers. She needed answers. And she knew this box was intertwined with Chloe's fate. With a surge of desperate resolve, she snatched it up too, shoving it into her backpack.

She practically flew down the stairs of her home, past her father's closed bedroom door where he was still sleeping and burst out onto the street just as Maya's familiar SUV screeched to a halt at the curb.

Sarah wrenched open the passenger door and threw herself inside. Ben, who was sitting in the backseat, didn't say a word.

Maya's pale face had lost its usual calm, replaced by a raw anxiety.

"Any update?" Sarah asked, her voice tight.

Maya shook their head, pulling away from the curb with a squeal of tires. "Chris just texted. They're admitting her now. Doctors have no idea what's wrong. All vitals are normal, but she's just..." They glanced at Sarah, their eyes dark with worry.

Ben let out a low, steady whistling sound, like a flatline. Sarah turned to snap at Ben, but when she saw how pale and worried he looked, she bit her tongue.

They drove in silence, the city flashing past in a blur of noise and color, a stark contrast to the suffocating quiet inside the car. Maya, usually the practical and safe one, was pushing the limits of the law. Sarah clutched at her backpack and checked that her seatbelt was fastened.

They arrived at the hospital in record time and found Chris pacing like a caged animal in the waiting room, his face grim. He looked like he hadn't slept at all; he even wore the same clothes as the day before. The usual swagger he carried was completely gone.

"Any news?" Maya asked, as they rushed towards him.

Chris shook his head, running a hand through his already messy hair. "Nothing. They're running tests, scans... but they're baffled. Her eyes are open, but no one is home. They keep asking if she took something, drugs, pills... but she didn't! I *know* she didn't. I should've been there though—I shouldn't have fucking left her." His voice cracked with a mixture of frustration and fear.

"It wasn't drugs," Sarah insisted quietly, her voice heavy with certainty.

The others turned to look at her, their expressions questioning.

"It was the lamp," Sarah continued, her voice gaining strength. "The one from the cave. The one I let Chloe borrow."

"Sarah, come on," Chris started, a hint of exasperation creeping back into his tone. "We talked about this. It's just an old trinket."

"No, it isn't," Sarah insisted, pulling the wooden box from her backpack and placing it on one of the waiting room chairs. "That lamp belonged to my mother. And I think... I think it's cursed."

Chris stared at Sarah, his face a mask of disbelief and raw grief. "Cursed?" he repeated, his voice dangerously low. "Are you fucking kidding me right now, Sarah? Chloe is in there," he jerked his head towards the emergency room doors, "Fighting for her life, maybe brain-dead for all we know, and you're talking about cursed objects and... and what?" He ran a shaking hand through his hair again, his knuckles white.

"I have proof, Chris. My mother's notes—"

"Get a grip, Láng! This isn't some spooky story you heard in that village. This is *real*."

"It *is* real, Chris!" Sarah implored, stung by his dismissal, her own fear and guilt bubbling into anger. She fumbled with the latch on the wooden box, wanting to show them, to make them *see*. "My mother knew! She wrote about it! The fatigue we all have, the nightmares, the *thing* that she saw... it's all connected! The lam—"

"Enough!" Chris exploded, slamming his fist against the waiting room wall. The sound echoed flatly in the sterile space, making a nearby nurse flinch. "I don't want to hear about your mother's fucking diary or some ancient curse! Chloe needs help! Real help! Not... not ghost stories!"

He turned away, his shoulders slumped, burying his face in his hands. The anger drained out of him, leaving only a hollow despair. A male nurse stood up near the front desk, watching Chris with a critical eye.

"Chris, man, take it easy," Ben said, placing a hesitant hand on Chris's shoulder. He looked pale and shaky himself, the usual sarcastic armor completely gone. "We're all worried for her." He glanced nervously between Chris and Sarah, clearly uncomfortable with the escalating tension.

Maya stepped between Sarah and Chris, their expression calm but firm.

"Okay, both of you, listen. Yelling isn't helping anyone right now." They looked at Sarah, their eyes searching. "Sarah, I... I believe you felt something, saw something. In China, in the cave... I admit it was weird." They sighed, rubbing their temples where a persistent ache lingered. "It's a lot to process. We're all exhausted, scared..."

"But the symptoms, Maya!" Sarah insisted, desperate to make them understand. "You all felt it on the plane! Hell, you all still feel it! I can see it. The fatigue, the headaches, the feeling of disconnection! My mother described the *exact same things* in her notes right before she died!" She fumbled with the box again. "Look, I can show you—"

"Wait," Ben interrupted, holding up a hand. He looked at Sarah, his brow furrowed. "Have you seen Chloe's livestream? Have you actually *watched* the recording yet?"

Sarah blinked. In the panic and rush to get to the hospital, she hadn't had a chance. She'd only seen the frantic chat replay.

"No, I... I scrolled through the comments, but I didn't watch the video itself."

"Then maybe we should," Ben said, pulling out his own phone, his fingers already tapping rapidly on the screen. "Maybe we can see what actually happened. See if it matches up with whatever you have in there." He nodded at the box in Sarah's hand.

Chris looked up, his expression skeptical but weary.

"I don't know if I can do that. Watch her... you know... before..." He stopped, unable to say it out loud.

"We'll watch, okay?" Maya said, pulling a few chairs together so they could huddle around Ben's phone. "We understand if you can't, Chris."

Sarah hesitated, a knot of dread tightening in her stomach. Like Chris, she wasn't sure she *wanted* to see it, to relive Chloe's terror, to witness the moment the curse claimed her. But Ben was already tapping play.

Chloe's face filled the small screen, bright and bubbly, though the strain around her eyes was more obvious now, knowing what came next. They watched in silence as she launched into her "40 Winks Challenge," setting up the candle holder, her voice taking on that soft, rhythmic quality as she began to chant the "Little Bo-Peep" rhyme. Hearing his girlfriend's voice, Chris couldn't help himself and slid next to Sarah to watch.

"Little Bo-Peep has lost her sheep, and doesn't know where to find them..."

As the sheep on the carousel started to spin faster, the shadows began their macabre dance around the room. Each pass of a sheep around the candle caused a subtle flickering of light against the wall—a flickering that increased in speed and intensity and began to give Sarah a headache. But each flicker was also followed by a faint familiar ticking sound—a sound she immediately recognized from Gu Mei. She held her breath, waiting, her eyes scanning the shadows on the walls behind Chloe.

There. The shadows began to shift, twisting, elongating.

"She found them indeed, but it made her heart bleed..."

"Yeah, that's... creepy," Ben muttered, leaning closer. "The lighting's weird."

"It's just the shadows from the sheep spinning," Chris said dismissively, though his knuckles were white where he gripped the armrest. "That's what they are supposed to look like."

"There she espied their tails side by side..."

"No," Sarah whispered, her voice trembling. "Look. *Look.*"

Behind Chloe, the shadows weren't just flickering anymore. They were *coalescing*. Darker shapes swirled within the indistinct gloom, forming... something. Sarah could see it clearly now—the tall, gaunt figure, the impossibly thin limbs, the vaguely sheep-like head, the two points of burning red light where its eyes should be. It was the monster from her nightmares. The demon pushed and squirmed its way out of the wall behind Chloe.

"She heaved a sigh and wiped her eye..."

Chloe's chanting faltered on screen. Her eyes widened in terror. Sarah felt a choked sob escape her own throat.

"Do you see that?" Sarah gasped, pointing frantically at the phone screen. "Right there! Behind her! It's... it's the demon!"

"Where?" Ben asked, squinting at the screen. "I can kind of see a shape in the compression artifacts. It looks like a person, maybe? But it's just digital noise. It has to be."

"I don't see shit," Chris said, shaking his head. "It just looks like... weird shadows. Maybe a trick of the light?"

"No!" Sarah insisted, frustration and a terrifying sense of isolation bubbling up inside her. "It's *right there*! How the hell can you not see it?"

Maya rewound the video slightly, pausing it at the exact moment Sarah had pointed out. They peered intently at the screen.

"Okay," they said slowly, "I see... *something*. Maybe. I think there's a pareidolia effect happening here. But... gods, it *is* a creepy one."

Sarah stared at them, her heart sinking. They couldn't see it. Not really. They saw creepy shadows, weird lighting, but not the distinct, terrifying form that was so horrifyingly clear to *her*. Was she going crazy? Was Maya right? Was the stress, the grief making her see things that weren't there? The nightmare on the plane... had that just been a hallucination too? Doubt, cold and insidious, began to creep in, undermining the certainty she had felt just moments before.

Chris looked over at Ben and mouthed. "What the fuck is a pareidolia?" Ben shrugged as Maya pressed play, continuing the video. Bile began to rise in Sarah's throat as the lights on the wall behind Chloe flickered even faster—her head pounding in pain with each flash. She knew her epilepsy might be activating, but she couldn't look away. Not yet.

Flicker. Tick. Flicker. Tick. Flicker. Tick.

Her headache was becoming unbearable, the nausea overwhelming. Sarah couldn't help it—she tore her eyes away from the video just as the shadowy form reached out towards Chloe. With her eyes closed Sarah heard her friends all gasp in unison. The room was spinning under her feet.

With a lurch, the nausea she was fighting bubbled up. She shoved past a shaken Chris, and over to a trashcan just in time. Her throat erupted in a fiery burn as her stomach emptied.

Maya quickly closed the video.

"Okay," Ben muttered, his voice shaky. "That was... disturbing. Cursed object or not, something seriously messed up happened to her."

Maya handed Sarah a soft cloth from their bag. She took it with a trembling hand and cleaned the spittle off her lips as the group sat in silence. The video had offered only terrifying ambiguity, at least for everyone but Sarah. To her it offered terrifying clarity.

"We need that object," Sarah said finally, the words quiet but firm.

"What good is that going to do, Láng?" Chris asked.

"I don't know," she admitted honestly. "But it's the only thing I *know* is connected to this. I discovered I've been to Gu Mei before, when I was younger. I just don't remember, maybe because of the trauma or maybe because I was too young, I'm not sure."

Her words were pouring out in a rush. "And the lamp, I found a photo of me, my mom and Auntie Lin standing next to that damn thing. My mother knew it was dangerous. Chloe used it, and now... now she's like this. And you guys," she looked pointedly at Maya, Ben, and Chris, "are all feeling the same warning signs my mom described before she died."

Ben, who had been staring blankly at his phone screen since closing the app, finally looked up. His usual smirk was gone, replaced by a worried frown.

"Okay, Sarah," he said, his voice quieter than usual. "You keep mentioning your mom's notes. What exactly did she write? How... how does it connect to *that*?" He gestured vaguely towards the phone, clearly still shaken by the video.

Sarah took a deep, shuddering breath, grateful that someone was finally willing to listen. She plopped down into a chair against the wall behind her.

"She wrote about the candle lamp," Sarah began explaining, her voice thick with emotion as she clutched the wooden box on her lap. "She described how it worked, the rhyme, the spinning sheep... but she also wrote about the shadows. How they weren't just shadows. She saw something *in* them, something forming, something malevolent."

Sarah's gaze drifted towards the waiting room doors, picturing Chloe lying unresponsive inside, just like her mother must have been.

"She described a figure, tall and thin, with a head like a sheep's skull and burning eyes. Just like what I saw behind Chloe in the video—what I saw in my dreams—even if you guys couldn't see it clearly. And the feeling, Ben... the dread, the headache, the feeling of being watched, drained... it's all in there. She wrote about it happening to her right before..."

Sarah couldn't finish the sentence, the implication hanging heavy in the air. The video wasn't just a recording of Chloe's stream; it was a terrifying echo of her mother's final warnings—warnings Sarah now carried in this box.

She paused, taking another shaky breath, trying to regain control.

"It's the only lead we have," she repeated, looking pleadingly at her friends. "Maybe Mr. Chen can figure something out. Maybe he can tell us what it is, how to stop it."

Maya nodded slowly.

"She's right. We can't just sit here. Doing nothing feels... wrong. We need to understand what we're dealing with." They looked at Sarah. "I'll take you to Chloe's apartment. You guys," they indicated towards Chris and Ben, "stay here. Keep us updated if there's any news."

Ben nodded wordlessly, looking relieved not to have to go any-where near the object again or maybe not having to leave Chloe—either way Ben didn't argue. Chris hesitated, clearly torn between staying for Chloe and wanting to do *something*, anything.

"Fine," he said weakly. "But call me the second you know any-thing. Anything at all."

"We will," Sarah promised. She stood up and reached out, laying her hand on Chris's shoulder to reassure him before turning to Maya. "Let's go get that lamp."

Chapter 17

A palpable heaviness hung in the silent car. So much had changed since the morning they left for Gu Mei, when they were happy. Sarah wanted so badly to reach over and play the Wicked soundtrack with her friend, to sing as loud as they used to. But instead of Broadway musicals, she listened to the sound of the wind whistle by outside the car.

Maya navigated the traffic with their usual focused efficiency, though Sarah noticed their gaze still seemed distant, slightly unfocused.

"You hanging in there, El?" Sarah asked gently, breaking the silence.

Maya blinked, as if startled out of a deep thought. "Hmm? Oh, yeah. Fine." They offered a small, unconvincing smile. "Just... tired. And this headache..." They rubbed their temples again. "It's killer."

The symptoms were spreading. The fatigue, the headaches, the disconnection. It was affecting the others. But why not her? She felt the psychological toll, the nightmares, but the deep, bone-weary sickness her friends described... it hadn't taken root in her. Was she somehow immune?

"This lamp..." Maya began, their voice low, hesitant, their knuckles white on the steering wheel. "To be holding it when she... when she died, must mean something, right? What do you think she was *doing* with it? Was she trying to use it? Or maybe trying to destroy it?"

Sarah's mouth grew tight. She didn't have an answer to Maya's question. Not yet. She hugged the backpack containing her mother's box tighter.

"I have an idea," Maya continued. "Something I read in one of my Wiccan books. We could perform a scrying ritual to see what we're dealing with, then perhaps a binding spell. I never thought I'd actually use it, so I'll have to find that book to remember the details."

Sarah felt a spark of hope. Maya's knowledge, their connection to practices outside the realm of conventional understanding, might be exactly what they needed.

"Mr. Chen will know something, or at least he'll be able to find answers." Sarah said with confidence.

They pulled up outside Chloe's apartment building, a trendy, upscale, and modern structure that seemed jarringly incongruous with the ancient horror they were confronting. They got out of the car, and the familiar sounds of sirens, traffic, and distant music swirled around them.

Chloe's apartment was up on the third floor and Sarah whispered a prayer that the elevator would be working. With how sore her body was, she didn't think she could climb the stairs if she had to. She let out an audible sigh of relief when the elevator doors opened.

As they rode the elevator up, Sarah felt a sudden wave of dizziness wash over her, accompanied by a faint, almost imperceptible sound.

Tick. Tick. Tick.

She shook her head, trying to clear it. Just exhaustion, she told herself. Stress. Lack of sleep. It wasn't real.

Once they reached the apartment, Maya unlocked the door with the spare key Chloe had given all of them—and they stepped inside. To Sarah's slight surprise, the apartment remained exactly as Chloe had left it for her livestream: meticulously clean and stylishly decorated. She had half-expected to find traces of the evil, or maybe signs of a struggle, even though she knew there hadn't been one.

The ring light still stood beside the bed, though knocked slightly askew. Pillows were scattered on the floor—most likely from first responders and not the demon. Chloe's phone sat upright on its stand next to her bed, its screen now spiderwebbed with cracks.

On the nightstand sat the still and silent candle lamp.

It looked smaller than Sarah remembered, almost innocuous in the bright afternoon light streaming through the large windows. But Sarah could feel it. A chill radiating from the metal, a subtle vibration in the air around it, a sense of ancient malice barely contained.

She heard it again.

Tick. Tick. Tick.

Faint, rhythmic, insistent. Like tiny hooves on stone.

"Do you hear that?" Sarah whispered, her eyes fixed on the ancient device.

Maya frowned, tilting their head. "Hear what? I don't hear anything." They walked further into the room with slow cautious steps. Their hand went instinctively to the protective amulets they wore around their neck. They appeared even more detached now, their gaze slightly unfocused, as if looking through a haze.

Sarah felt a surge of panic. Maya couldn't hear it. Just like they couldn't *see* the Shepherd clearly in the video. Was she the only one attuned to this thing? Was she losing her mind?

She forced herself to focus, pushing back the rising tide of fear.

"I'll grab the lamp," Sarah said, her voice steadier than she felt.

Maya nodded slowly, their eyes still scanning the room, lingering on the shadows in the corners.

"Okay. But be careful, Sarah. Don't touch the metal directly if you can help it."

Sarah looked around, her eyes landing on the cloth draped over the back of Chloe's desk chair—the cloth Sarah had taken from Auntie Lin's house, a memento now stained with grief. She picked it up, the soft warm silk making a soothing rustling sound as it slid off the chair.

Carefully, using the cloth to shield her hands, Sarah picked up the brass lamp. It felt heavier than it looked, unnaturally dense, and cold; a deep, penetrating cold that leached the warmth from her hands even through the layers of silk. The faint ticking sound intensified in her ears, a maddening, rhythmic pulse that seemed to emanate from the object itself.

She held her breath, half-expecting the damn thing to shock her, or for the shadows in the room to coalesce, for the Shepherd to manifest before her eyes. But nothing happened. The ancient object remained inert, its brass surface gleaming dully, its tiny sheep frozen in their eternal leap.

"Okay, got it," Sarah said, her voice tight.

Maya opened the large canvas bag they wryly called their "Witch Bag," and held it open towards Sarah.

"Put it in here," they instructed. "This bag has protections woven into it. Sigils. Herbs. It should help contain... whatever energy it's putting out."

Sarah gingerly lowered the brass lamp, still wrapped in Auntie Lin's cloth, into the depths of Maya's bag. Maya drew the drawstring tight with a precise, almost ritualistic motion. The ticking sound in Sarah's ears faded immediately, leaving only the dull throb of her new headache and the frantic pounding of her own heart. The heavy, oppressive atmosphere in the room lifted slightly, though the underlying sense of dread remained.

"Holy shit, Maya," Sarah said with a laugh of disbelief. "It actually worked. The ticking noise is gone."

Maya looked almost as surprised as Sarah did.

With the lamp in hand, they surveyed the room one last time. Sarah saw Chloe's vibrant personality stamped everywhere—the colorful artwork, the overflowing makeup vanity, the diligently curated collection of jewelry and succulents. It felt wrong to be here without her, like they were snooping.

Sarah spotted the small, aged piece of paper with the "Little Bo-Peep" rhyme lying on the floor near the bed, likely knocked off the nightstand when Chloe collapsed. She bent down and picked it up, then shoved it into her pocket. Another piece of the puzzle. Another remnant of her mother's doomed fight.

"Let's go," Maya said, their voice hollow as they avoided Sarah's gaze. "Let's get this thing to Mr. Chen."

Sarah nodded, taking one last look at Chloe's empty bed, a silent promise echoing in her heart.

We'll figure this out, Chloe. We'll bring you back.

They stepped out of the apartment, closing the door gently behind them, leaving the scene of Chloe's silent horror. As they walked towards the elevator to take them downstairs, Sarah kept glancing at the bag in Maya's hand. Even though the lamp was tucked safely away inside, Sarah couldn't shake the feeling it was watching her.

Chapter 18

The drive from Chloe's over to Chinatown stretched to an almost unbearable length for Sarah. The constant waiting began fraying her patience. She felt like a horse led by a dangling carrot, and the frustration pissed her off. Every time she finally thought she had the answers in her grasp, they were ripped from her hands, and a new prize was teased.

Just mystery on top of mystery. And each minute that ticked by was another minute Chloe lay unresponsive, another minute the curse potentially tightened its grip on Ben, Chris, and Maya.

Yet, Sarah also felt a desperate need for more time—time to think, time to process the fragmented horrors revealed in her mother's box, time to prepare herself for whatever answers, or further questions, awaited them at Mr. Chen's shop.

Maya's silence became the new normal. The easy camaraderie, the playful banter that usually defined their friendship, had evaporated. The group had never been so strained before. Not like this. Hell, even after that fateful day that brought the Still Alive Five together felt better than this. This time was different, and Sarah began to realize she didn't recognize her friends anymore.

Sarah glanced over at Maya, whom she considered her best friend out of the group. Their eyes were fixed on the road, but their gaze was distant, that same unsettling disconnection Sarah had noticed earlier. Studying them, she figured the headache they'd mentioned still pounded behind their temples—a pain brought on by the curse, or demon, or whatever it was.

She felt a similar throb behind her eyes, but hers had a different cause.

The rhythmic sweep of sunlight peeking through each building as they drove by flashed across the window like insistent, stabbing attacks against her, each pulse reverberating in her head. The air in the small car began pressing in on Sarah until her lungs felt constricted. It wasn't just the physical confines; the whole situation felt suffocating, a tightening knot of fear with no room to breathe, no clear escape route from the nightmare she found herself in.

She quickly popped one of her pills, swallowing it dry and squeezed her eyes shut for a second, trying to anchor herself to the worn fabric of the seat beneath her fingertips. With deep, steady breaths and a mental effort born of years of practice, she found a center of calm. Once her heart rate settled down and she felt confident she was back in control of her body she opened her eyes to see they had arrived in Chinatown.

They quickly found a parking spot—a minor miracle—on a crowded side street just off the main road. Stepping out of the SUV, they were immediately enveloped by the unique sensory assault of Chinatown: the rapid-fire cadence of Cantonese and Mandarin chatter, the pungent aromas of roasting duck, fermented bean curd, and exotic spices mingling with the less romantic scents of exhaust fumes and overflowing dumpsters.

It was a world away from Gu Mei yet immediately gave her a sense of familiarity that was comforting.

Maya slung their heavy canvas Witch Bag—now containing the suspicious lamp wrapped in silk—over their shoulder, the weight seeming both literal and metaphorical. They navigated the crowded sidewalks, dodging tourists snapping photos and elderly women pushing grocery carts laden with bok choy and ginger root.

They arrived at a narrow storefront squeezed between a bustling dim sum restaurant and a shop selling traditional herbal remedies. The sign above the door, painted in faded gold calligraphy, read "Thorne's Curios," a name that seemed both whimsical and slightly ominous.

Below it, in smaller English letters, read: *Antiques — Oddities — Consultations.*

Sarah and her mother used to visit here years ago—when she was still alive—the two of them drawn to the shop by the strange objects and Mr. Chen's quiet wisdom. She felt so comfortable at the shop that she started working part-time there after her mother's death—never imagining she'd be returning under such terrifying circumstances.

Sarah pushed open the heavy wooden door and flinched as the small brass bell above it announced their arrival with a discordant jingle—a sound chillingly reminiscent of the bells she'd heard in her nightmares and on the mountain path.

The interior of the shop was a world unto itself, a dimly lit labyrinth crammed floor-to-ceiling with an eclectic, almost overwhelming, collection of artifacts from every corner of the globe and every conceivable era. Dusty tapestries hung alongside African masks with vacant eyes; porcelain dolls with cracked faces shared shelf space with Tibetan singing bowls and tarnished silver lockets; stacks of brittle, leather-bound books leaned precariously against glass cabinets filled with strange medical instruments and taxidermized animals frozen in unnatural poses.

The smoke of incense mixed with a hint of old paper, dust, dried herbs, and the faint, lingering aroma of the jasmine tea Mr. Chen perpetually brewed filled the air. Sarah found the familiar scent comforting and nostalgic. Soft, melodic wind chimes tinkled somewhere in the back, adding another layer to the shop's unique soundscape, punctuated by the muffled rumble of the city outside.

"Mr. Chen?" Sarah called out, her voice echoing slightly in the cluttered space. "It's Sarah."

A rustling sound came from behind a towering bookcase overflowing with scrolls and maps. A moment later, a small, slender man, older than Sarah's father and with kind eyes, emerged while wiping his hands on a dusty apron. Mr. Chen broke into a warm smile when he saw Sarah. He moved with a quiet, deliberate grace, like a scholar navigating his library. Despite his age, there was an alertness about him, a sharp intelligence that belied his gentle demeanor.

"Ah, Xiao Yáng!" he greeted her, using the affectionate nickname "Little Lamb" he'd given her when she first started visiting him as a child. A name that now struck her as deeply ironic. "Back from your journey already? I trust the trip was... enlightening?" His smile faltered slightly as he took in their expressions, the exhaustion etched on Sarah's face, the pale anxiety clinging to Maya. "Is everything alright?"

Sarah swallowed, the lump in her throat making it difficult to speak. "Not exactly, Mr. Chen," she managed, her voice trembling slightly. "Something terrible happened. To our friend, Chloe."

"Come, sit. I'll get you tea and you can tell me," he said, gesturing towards two worn velvet armchairs tucked in a corner beside a low table.

Sarah and Maya sank into the chairs, the plush velvet a small comfort. She accepted the warm tea, and then, as briefly and coherently as she could, she recounted the recent events: the trip to Gu Mei, the earthquake, Auntie Lin's death, Chloe's disastrous livestream and her subsequent catatonic state. She described finding the ruins and the cave Chris had discovered.

Mr. Chen listened patiently the entire time, his expression growing increasingly grave. He asked few questions, but when Sarah mentioned the cave opening into a chamber at the bottom of a well, his eyes narrowed almost imperceptibly.

"A well," he repeated softly. "You found a chamber at the bottom of a well?"

Sarah took a shuddering breath, the memory raw and visceral. "It wasn't just a chamber, Mr. Chen. It was... it was more like a tomb. There were bones everywhere. And in the center, on a stone slab... I found her."

Mr. Chen leaned forward, his face paling. "Found who, Xiao Yáng?"

She subconsciously rubbed the locket under shirt before pulling out her mother's wooden box and laying it gently on the table. "My mother," Sarah whispered, the words tasting like ash. "I found my mother's body. She was... she was holding something."

The air in the shop grew heavy, thick with unspoken grief. Maya shifted uncomfortably in their chair; their gaze fixed on the floor.

Mr. Chen was silent for a long moment, absorbing the weight of her words. His eyes, staring at Mei-Lin's box, began to moisten. Finally, he spoke, his voice gentle but laced with a new, grim urgency.

"The object she was holding, was it this box?"

Sarah shook her head.

"What then? Do you have it with you?"

Maya hesitated, then carefully lifted their heavy bag onto their lap. They loosened the drawstring and, using the edges of the silk cloth wrapped around the relic, gingerly lifted it, placing it carefully on the table between them.

Even here, in the cluttered confines of the antique shop, the candle lamp possessed a strange aura. The brass gleamed dully, the miniature sheep seemed poised to leap, and Sarah could just about hear that faint, rhythmic clicking sound emanating from its base.

Mr. Chen leaned forward, his eyes magnified by his thin wire-framed glasses, examining the object intently. He didn't touch it, but hovered his hand over it, his brow furrowed in concentration. Sarah felt a strange energy shift in the small space, a subtle hum, like static electricity before a storm.

"Ancient," Mr. Chen murmured, his voice barely a whisper. "Very ancient. And... powerful." He looked up, his gaze meeting Sarah's, and she saw not just concern, but a deep, unsettling knowledge in his eyes. "Your poor mother... Mei-Lin... she asked me about objects like this, many years ago."

Sarah's heart leaped. "She did? What did she say? Did she tell you about the curse? About the demon?"

He let out a large breath between tight lips, leaning back in his chair. Maya took out their journal and began writing.

"Hmm, yes. She spoke of curses. Of a darkness that clung to her family and her village. She felt... haunted. Pursued by something she referred to as 'The Shepherd'." He gestured vaguely at the towering shelves surrounding them. "She came here often, looking through my older texts, researching folklore, protection rituals, wards..."

Sarah looked around at the mass of unorganized curiosities. The thought of her mother digging through hundreds, if not thousands of items made her head swim. Where would someone even start looking?

Mr. Chen ran a hand through his thin gray hair, then started rummaging through a stack of scattered parchments on the table.

"Hmm. She was searching for answers, just as you are now. But she was very private, very guarded. She never confided the full extent of her fears, or the specific nature of the entity she believed was after her."

He paused, his gaze returning to the brass lamp before continuing.

"She did, however, describe something very similar to this once. An artifact... a vessel... capable of bridging worlds." His voice trailed off into a whisper as he stared at it.

"Bridging worlds?" Sarah repeated, the phrase sending a fresh wave of ice through her veins. "What does that mean? What kind of vessel?"

He shook his head slowly, his eyes still fixed on the relic, though he maintained a careful distance. "Hmm. Not a vessel like a container, Xiao Yáng. More like a key. A focal point. Some objects, through craftsmanship, intent, or accidental tragedy, become imbued with energy. They absorb echoes of events, of emotions. Sometimes," his voice dropped lower, "They become resonant points for forces... entities... that exist outside our normal perception.

"Sometimes it is a crafted object, like this candle lamp. Sometimes it is a place, like the well you mentioned. And sometimes," his gaze drifted towards a shelf of ancient, leather-bound books, "the most powerful vessels are the stories themselves. A tale that is told and retold can build its own energy, create its own doorway."

Maya looked up from their journal, the earlier skepticism seemingly evaporating in the face of Mr. Chen's quiet certainty and the object's palpable aura. "Like a psychopomp object? Something that guides or attracts spirits?"

Mr. Chen looked at Maya, a flicker of surprise and respect in his eyes. "Something like that, yes. Though not always guiding benevolent spirits."

He lifted his glasses for a moment to rub his eyes then looked back at Sarah.

"Your mother understood this. She felt the pull of such things. She spoke of feeling drained. Plagued by nightmares she couldn't shake."

"The... Shepherd," Sarah whispered, testing the new name on her tongue. "Do you know if you have any books that mention that?"

Mr. Chen frowned, tapping a long, thin finger against his chin. "The Shepherd? Hmm, no, I do not recall that specific name in my books. Maybe your mother found one though. She suspected the origin was connected to her village, Gu Mei, but she never said how. One thing she *did* confide in me, was her fear. A terrible, consuming fear. Especially for you, Xiao Yáng. She was desperate to protect you."

Sarah opened her mother's box and pulled out the notes, the frantic script, the disturbing sketches of the brass lamp and the demonic sheep and handed it to him. Mr. Chen examined them closely, his brow furrowing deeper, his breathing shallowing almost imperceptibly. He gently touched the edge of the paper depicting the Shepherd, recoiling slightly as if burned.

"Hmm, the energy is strong, even in this drawing," he murmured. "Dangerous." He looked from the notes to the object, then back to Sarah, his expression grim. "You say this... livestream? Your friend Chloe chanted a rhyme while using the lamp?"

"Yes. She chanted Little Bo Peep of all things," Sarah answered in a tight voice.

"And now she is unresponsive?"

"In a coma, though her eyes are open," Maya confirmed, their voice strained. "The doctors have no explanation."

Mr. Chen stood up, his movements suddenly brisk, agitated. He began pacing the small space between the armchairs and a cabinet filled with grinning porcelain masks.

"The rhyme... the relic... the symptoms... the connection to Gu Mei..." He stopped, turning to face them, his eyes bright with a disturbing mix of intellectual curiosity and genuine alarm. "This is not good. Not good at all."

"What is it, Mr. Chen?" Sarah asked, her heart pounding. "What do you think it is?"

"Hmm, I have a theory," he said slowly. "Based on Mei-Lin's research long ago, on the symbols I vaguely recall... this 'Shepherd'... yes, I believe it fits. An earth-bound entity, drawn to places of death, capable of influencing dreams..." His voice trailed off as he seemed to get lost in his own thoughts.

"But how?" Maya interjected, shaking Mr. Chen out of his internal daydreaming. "How does a candle lamp connect to an ancient Chinese Earth demon?"

"That," Mr. Chen said, gesturing towards the device, "is the vessel. The conduit. Perhaps originally crafted to contain it, or perhaps simply an object that became attuned to its energy through proximity to its resting place—you mentioned a well..."

He paused in thought while rubbing his eyes.

"Hmm, I seem to recall something about a well." He shook his head. "Regardless, the lamp became a key. And your friend Chloe, by performing the ritual—the rhyme, the focused intent, amplified by the livestream's digital reach—she didn't just unlock the door, she rang a dinner bell."

"So, what do we do?" Sarah asked, her voice tight with urgency. "Can we destroy it?"

Mr. Chen looked at the Relic, his expression a mixture of grief and scholarly focus. "Destroy it? Hmm. Mei-Lin was holding it, you said. As if in her final moments, she chose to cling to it... or was unable to let it go." He shook his head grimly. "That suggests its power over its wielder is immense. To destroy it might unleash the entity entirely. No, no it's too dangerous a gamble."

He began muttering to himself, scanning the chaotic shelves.

"There was a book... seventeenth century, I believe... a treatise on *Yaoguai* and subterranean spirits... compiled by a rather eccentric Daoist monk... Where did I put it?"

A cloud of dust erupted as he started rummaging through a teetering pile of items near the back. Books tumbled, scrolls unrolled, small carved figures clattered to the floor. It was a scene of utter, almost comical, disarray, yet Sarah sensed an underlying order known only to Mr. Chen.

"It discussed bindings, wardings... specifically entities tied to the earth, to burial sites..." he continued muttering, oblivious to the mess he was creating. "Ah! Perhaps behind the Qing dynasty scrolls?" He disappeared behind a bookcase. Muffled curses followed.

"He really does have everything in here, doesn't he?" Maya whispered to Sarah as they watched him rummage around, a glint of amusement crossing their face despite the gravity of the situation.

Sarah nodded, a small, sad smile touching her lips. "He and Mom used to spend hours back here, digging through books and scrolls, talking about history, folklore... Dad never understood it. He always said it 'filled her head with superstitious nonsense.' "

Mr. Chen suddenly reappeared, looking flustered, dust smudging his glasses. "Not there. Hmm. Perhaps I lent it to Professor Albright? No, he never returned my notes on Confucius's Guoyu." He sighed, rubbing his eyes again beneath his glasses. "It will take time, I'm afraid. My filing system is slightly disorderly." He looked at Sarah and Maya apologetically. "Give me some time. I will search. I know it is here somewhere. I have a hypothesis and need to verify."

Sarah nodded, unable to hide the disappointment from her face but Mr. Chen was too preoccupied to notice.

He glanced at the relic, then quickly away, as if its presence disturbed him. "That thing may have once been used to lull a child to sleep, but no longer. Do not mistake it for an ordinary lamp. Safe to simply call it the Relic for now, so as not to confuse anyone into complacency. Also, leave the cursed thing here," he said as he took off his glasses to rub his eyes. "It is safer contained within these walls. I have ways of dampening its influence somewhat."

He didn't elaborate.

"Okay," Sarah said, feeling a mixture of disappointment and relief. They had a lead, an expert, but no immediate solution. "Thank you, Mr. Chen. Please, call us as soon as you find anything."

"I will, Xiao Yáng. I promise." He paused, his gaze softening as he looked at Sarah. "Your mother... she fought very hard against her darkness. Your father... he tried to understand, in his scientific way, but he could never truly accept what she felt, what she believed she was facing. Stubborn man, David." He chuckled sadly. "Always needed empirical proof, even when the proof was screaming in his face."

A sudden, cold clarity cut through Sarah's grief.

Your father... he tried to understand.

Mr. Chen's sympathetic words twisted in her mind, becoming an indictment. No, he hadn't *tried* to understand; he had actively chosen *not* to. The promise to talk "tomorrow" was a stalling tactic. All those years, he had kept the truth locked away, just as surely as her mother had locked her secrets in that wooden box.

He hadn't been protecting her from a painful story; he had been hiding behind his own failure to believe in the woman he loved.

"Maya," Sarah said abruptly, standing up, the wooden box clutched tightly in her hand. "We need to go."

Maya looked surprised but nodded, sensing the sudden shift in Sarah's demeanor.

"Where?"

"Home," Sarah said, her voice tight with a new resolve. "I need to talk to my dad." Without another word, she turned, a blur of motion, squeezing herself between the messy aisles of the shop. Maya quickly followed, their eyes wide but unquestioning. As Sarah shoved the front door open, those familiar welcoming bells rang again, but this time it sounded less like an announcement and more of a desperate warning.

Then up she took her little crook,
  Determined for to find them;
She found them indeed, but it made
    her heart bleed,
For they'd left their tails behind
    them.

CHAPTER 19

The bell above Mr. Chen's door followed Sarah out onto the bustling sidewalk. The air outside, although thick with the scents of Chinatown, felt strangely thin compared to the weighted atmosphere of the antique shop. Dark clouds had rolled in while they were inside, but Sarah still blinked against the sudden brightness.

Mr. Chen's words swirled in her head.

A vessel—bridging worlds—epilepsy.

Sarah, her mind distracted, stumbled on a crack in the sidewalk. Maya, walking beside her, caught her by the arm. Sarah mumbled "thanks" and noticed Maya's brow was furrowed tight as if listening to something far away or perhaps struggling against that headache. Whatever symptom it was, it seemed to be getting worse. Probably for Chris and Ben too.

Everyone except her.

They walked past a busy street vendor selling some skewers, the fragrant smell making her stomach rumble. She pushed her hunger aside and focused on the knowledge that Mr. Chen had shared with them. "He knows more than he's saying," Sarah said, clutching the backpack containing her mother's box tighter. The weight of it felt immense, a burden of secrets and unspoken horrors.

"Definitely," Maya replied. "He was... intense. And the way he looked at the lamp..." They shivered slightly, despite the mild afternoon air. "He recognized it, or at least its type. He's scared, Sarah."

"So am I." Sarah admitted, the words strangely therapeutic to say aloud. "But my dad... Mr. Chen said he never accepted what my mom was feeling. Called it superstition."

Hot anger began to bubble beneath the surface of her fear and grief. Her father had *promised* her answers. He had known, all these years, that her mother believed she was being haunted, pursued by something evil, and he had dismissed it, hidden it.

"We need to talk to him, Maya," Sarah said, her voice hardening with resolve. "No more waiting until 'tomorrow.' Right now." Maya didn't argue. They simply nodded again, unlocked the SUV, and slid into the driver's seat.

The drive back to Queens was a blur, the miles consumed by Sarah's simmering anger and Maya's quiet, desperate urgency. The usual city traffic parted before them, as if even the universe sensed the need for this confrontation.

A slight drizzle began to fall just as they pulled up to Sarah's familiar brownstone home. Without waiting for Maya, Sarah threw open the door and was out of the car before it had fully stopped, sprinting up the front steps, her keys already in hand. She burst through the front door, her backpack banging against the frame.

Her father was in the living room, sitting in his usual armchair, a medical journal open on his lap, though Sarah could tell he hadn't actually been reading. Worry lines that hadn't been there yesterday etched his face while a sleeplessness that mirrored her own shadowed his eyes. He looked up, startled as she stormed in.

"Sarah! Where did you go? Is everyth—?"

"You lied to me," Sarah cut him off, her voice trembling with a mixture of rage and hurt. "All these years you let me believe she just *left* us! You let me believe she was selfish and overwhelmed, when you knew she was terrified! You knew something was hunting her!" She threw her backpack onto the floor, the wooden box inside thudding heavily.

Dr. Láng froze in the middle of standing up. His expression gradually shifted from surprise to a familiar, weary sadness. He licked his lips and slowly finished standing up before responding. "Sarah, please, let me explain. Let's make some warm tea—"

"No!" Sarah screeched, pacing back and forth, unable to stand still. The confining walls of the apartment suddenly felt suffocating, echoing the oppressive tightness she'd felt in the cave. "No more 'tomorrow'! I talked to Mr. Chen. He told me Mom came to him all those years ago, researching curses, demons! She was terrified, Dad! Terrified of something from Gu Mei! Something she called the Shepherd!"

She stopped pacing, planting herself directly in front of her father, forcing him to meet her gaze. Forcing him to listen. "She went back there to protect me, didn't she? That's why she died there. It wasn't because she was overwhelmed or stressed. It was the fucking demon. It got her."

Her dad flinched as if struck. He sank back into his armchair, rubbing his temples, the picture of a man cornered by truths he refused to accept. "Sarah," he began, his voice low, pleading. "Your mother was always prone to flights of fancy. She convinced herself that some old village superstition, some folktale, was real."

Sarah's laugh was short and sharp. She began sputtering in disbelief. "Flights of fancy?" she finally managed, echoing his words. "Dad, I have her notes! Her journal!"

She knelt, yanking the wooden box from her backpack, fumbling with the key she'd retrieved earlier. She unlocked it, pulling out the diary and the handful of frantic, ink-stained notes.

"Look!" She shoved them towards him. "Read them! Does this sound like 'flights of fancy'?"

He recoiled slightly from the papers, as if they were contaminated. "I don't need to read them, Sarah. I lived through it. I saw how consumed she became, how irrational. She believed these things, yes. Intensely. But belief doesn't make them real."

"Then explain Chloe. And explain how I found my mother's body holding that piece of shit candle thing. Are those 'flights of fancy' too?" Sarah demanded, her voice rising again. "Explain how Chloe used the exact Relic from Mom's photo," she jabbed a finger toward the sketch of the monstrous sheep, "chanted that stupid rhyme, and now lies in a coma doctors can't explain!"

Maya, who had quietly entered the apartment after Sarah, now stood awkwardly by the door, shifting uncomfortably.

Dr. Láng looked cornered, his scientific certainty warring with the undeniable evidence Sarah was throwing at him. "There could be explanations," he insisted, though his voice lacked conviction. "A toxin in the lamp's metal, perhaps released by the candle heat. Mass hysteria amplified by Chloe's livestream. Simple psychological suggestion..."

"Suggestion?" Sarah laughed, a harsh, broken sound. "Oh my god, Dad! Did psychological suggestion cause the mudslide? Did it make me see that... that *thing* behind Chloe in the video?"

"You saw something?" Dr. Láng seized on that. "Now you sound like her. Sarah, your epilepsy... you know stress and lack of sleep can trigger visual disturbances, even hallucinations. The nightmare on the plane, what you think you saw in the video... it could all be linked to your condition, amplified by everything you've been through."

The familiar explanation, the one she'd half-believed herself just hours ago, now felt like a deliberate deflection, a denial of the terrifying reality. "So that's it?" she cried, tears streaming down her face. "Mom and I are just crazy? I'm hallucinating?"

"I didn't say that," her father said gently, his voice laced with pain. "I'm saying there are logical, scientific explanations we haven't explored yet. Grief, trauma, neurological conditions... they can manifest in complex ways. Your mother... she *did* go back to Gu Mei because she was afraid. Afraid of these legends. She believed, rightly or wrongly, that something there threatened you, and she went back to confront it, to perform some kind of ritual she'd read about. And yes," his voice broke, "she died there..."

He looked away, unable to meet Sarah's gaze.

Maya cleared their throat softly from the doorway. "Dr. Láng... Sarah... maybe I should give you two some space."

Sarah barely registered Maya leaving, closing the apartment door quietly behind them. She stood facing her father, the raw pain of years of unanswered questions, of buried grief and unspoken secrets, laid bare between them. He believed her mother was delusional. He thought Sarah was hallucinating. He refused to see the goddamn truth that was screaming from her mother's notes, from Chloe's hospital bed, from the very air around them.

"You didn't fight for her?" Sarah asked, incredulously. "Dad, she died alone in a cave, forgotten, and you just lied to yourself—to me—that she ran away?"

Her dad sank further into his armchair, avoiding her gaze. His shoulders slumped, the posture of a man defeated by the sheer weight of memory. "What could I do, Sarah?" His voice was barely a whisper, thick with a grief Sarah had rarely witnessed. "It was... plausible."

"Plausible?" Sarah scoffed, the sound harsh in the quiet room. "Or convenient? Easier than accepting what Mom *knew* was happening? Easier than admitting you couldn't protect her from it?"

He looked up then, his eyes flashing with pain and a flicker of anger. "Protect her from *what*, Sarah? From stories? From shadows? From her own mind turning against her? I tried! I begged her not to go back to Gu Mei. I told her these fears, these nightmares, were symptoms of stress, of unresolved trauma from her childhood perhaps. I offered medication, therapy..."

"Because you thought she was crazy!" Sarah accused, tears stinging her eyes again. "Just like you think *I'm* crazy now!"

"I don't think—" he stopped himself and groaned, digging his fingers hard into his temples. "Look, I think you're grieving. I think you've experienced significant trauma—the earthquake, the cave, Auntie Lin's horrific death, Chloe..."

He gestured around helplessly. "It's understandable that your mind is trying to make sense of it, latching onto these patterns, these connections. Especially given your mother's history and your own predisposition..." He trailed off, clearly referring to her epilepsy.

"My predisposition?" Sarah seized on the word. "You mean the epilepsy? Mr. Chen mentioned it too. He said the demon... this Shepherd, as Mom called it, is known to cause it in children."

She took a step closer, lowering her voice, her words intense. "Dad, *when* did my epilepsy start? Was it after we were in Gu Mei? The time I don't remember?"

Her father blinked, his face paling slightly. He opened his mouth, then closed it again, conflict warring in his eyes. "Sarah..."

"Tell me!"

He sighed. "Yes," he admitted reluctantly. "Now that you mention it... your first seizure... the one that led to the diagnosis, happened a few days after you and your mother returned from that trip. The doctors could never find a specific cause. They called it idiopathic."

Sarah gasped, then stumbled backwards as if pushed, her thigh bumping into the coffee table. Idiopathic or unknown cause. But

Sarah knew now. Her childhood trip, her mother's growing terror, the Relic, the onset of her epilepsy, it was all connected. She began to see the big picture forming as the pieces of this damn puzzle came together.

"You knew," she breathed, barely hearing her own voice. "You knew and you kept it from me—"

"Is the timing a little suspicious?" he interrupted. "Sure. But correlation does not equal causation, Sarah."

"Then what about this photo?" she pressed, grabbing a Polaroid out of the box and thrusting it under his nose. "The one of me and Mom, at the well? With the *Relic* right there? Was that just 'a little suspicious' too?"

He flinched as his gaze fixed on the image of his broken family. "I remember this day," he breathed, voice wavering. "I'm the one who took that photograph, Sarah, and your mother—" He swallowed. "She was never the same after this day."

"But you knew about the lamp," Sarah persisted, refusing to let him evade. "You knew Mom was afraid of it."

He ran a hand over his face, his composure finally breaking. "Yes," he admitted, his voice barely audible. "Yes, she became obsessed with it after that trip. Said it whispered to her, called to her. She wanted to destroy it, but she was also... afraid of it. Afraid of releasing whatever she believed was inside. She was under the impression she knew how to 'end it' as she put it."

Sarah felt a surge of disbelief.

"You knew it was dangerous, possibly cursed, and you just ignored it? You didn't try to find out what it was? You didn't warn anyone?"

"Warn them about what?" he countered, his voice rising slightly, defensiveness creeping back in. "A folktale? A delusion? I deal in science, in observable phenomena! Not demons and curses!"

"Observable phenomena?" Sarah spat, snatching up her phone from her backpack, her fingers flying across the screen. "Then observe *this*!" She thrust the phone towards him, replaying the end of Chloe's horrifying livestream.

He closed his eyes tight, turning his head away. "I saw the news reports, Sarah. The video... it's disturbing, yes. But the shadows... it's pareidolia, the mind seeing patterns where none exist. Stress, exhaustion, the power of suggestion from the rhyme..."

"You didn't even look!" Sarah cried, frustration boiling over. "You won't even *look*! Just like you wouldn't look at Mom's fear. You hide behind your science because you're afraid! Afraid to admit that there are things you can't explain, things you can't control!"

"That's enough!" he shouted, standing up abruptly, his eyes shooting open. The sudden movement, the raw anger in his voice, startled Sarah into silence. He rarely raised his voice. "I loved your mother more than anything. I watched her become consumed by these fears. I thought if I could just get her away from that place, she'd be safe. I thought she *had* left... that she was alive somewhere."

His fists clenched for a moment before he quickly let them go. He looked up at Sarah, his eyes narrowed and focused.

"Maybe," he continued. "I was wrong not to listen more closely to Mei-Lin's tales. Maybe I was blinded by my own grief, my own denial. But I will *not* stand here and let you endanger yourself and your friends by chasing after shadows, by embracing the same superstitions that may have contributed to your mother's..."

He couldn't finish the sentence. The raw pain in his voice, the conflicting emotions warring on his face—grief, fear, anger, love—finally pierced through Sarah's own anger. She saw not just a stubborn scientist, but a grieving husband, a terrified father, desperately trying to protect his daughter from a pain he couldn't comprehend.

His eyes softened. "Don't forget, I was there with you two," he forced out with a sob while pointing at the photo of Sarah and her mom at the well. "If there was a curse, why did it take Mei-Lin and not me? Why?"

Sarah's throat tightened. She hadn't actually thought of that, and the pain in his voice almost broke her heart. She never stopped to consider that, maybe, he blamed himself.

The fight drained out of both of them simultaneously. Her shoulders, which had been tight with rage, slumped. She sank onto the couch, the adrenaline leaving a roaring sound in her ears. Her father remained standing as he stared at a photograph of Mei-Lin on the mantelpiece, his eyes blinking rapidly. The tension remained, a thick, palpable presence in the room, but the anger subsided, leaving behind a shared, weary sadness.

The silence stretched, heavy and uncomfortable. What now? Where do they go from here? He still didn't truly believe, not in the way she needed him to. He wouldn't help her fight this thing, not if he thought it was all in her head. She felt utterly alone. The demon was hunting her, but it was her own father's denial that truly isolated her.

Just as the silence became unbearable, Sarah's phone, lying forgotten on the coffee table amidst her mother's scattered notes, buzzed loudly, rattling across the wood. Both she and her father jumped at the sudden sound.

Sarah glanced at the caller ID. It was Ben.

Her heart lurched. Had something happened? Was there news about Chloe?

She snatched up the phone and answered. "Ben? What is it? Is Chloe okay?" She quickly put the call on speaker so her dad could hear.

"Okay? Well, yes, but no. She's the same." Ben's voice was feverish, laced with a near-hysterical panic she'd never heard from him before.

In the background, Sarah could faintly hear a cacophony of urgent sounds: rapid, clipped voices calling out medical terms she didn't understand—punctuated by the rhythmic beeping of machines and the distressed cries of grieving families. The sense of chaos and rising alarm was palpable even through the phone. "But you need to see this. Turn on the news! Check online! Anywhere!"

"Ben, what are you talking about? Slow down!" Chills ran down her spine, the background noise beginning to paint a terrifying picture.

"It's Chloe's stream, Sarah! It's everywhere! It's gone viral! #40WinksChallenge is trending worldwide! People in comas are being brought in by the dozens!"

CHAPTER 20

S arah woke with a gasp, bolting upright in bed, her chest heaving with panicked breaths. The phantom sensation of claws scratching at her skin lingered from the depths of the nightmare. The now familiar sickly green sky of the Shepherd's pasture dissolved, replaced by the familiar grey gloom of her bedroom walls.

She flinched as a crack of thunder rumbled outside. Rain lashed against the windowpane, driven by a wind that moaned against the glass. The storm had arrived overnight.

A frantic scratching sound next to her caught her attention.

She glanced over at Maya on the makeshift bed on her floor. They were curled up under a spare duvet, but they weren't asleep. They were scribbling furiously in their journal with wide, hyper-focused eyes. Their pale face drawn tight with concentration in the dim morning light. Sarah couldn't make out what they were writing, but the intensity Maya was using left deep grooves in the soft paper.

"Maya?" Sarah whispered, her voice hoarse.

Maya stopped their frenzied pen-strokes then slowly blinked, turning their head towards Sarah. "Huh?" they murmured, their voice flat, distant. That unsettling disconnection Sarah had noticed yesterday seemed more pronounced, a veil drawn between Maya and the world.

"What are you writing?"

"Huh? Writing?" Maya looked down in confusion. "Oh, just my thoughts I guess." Maya quickly snapped the book closed and tucked it under the duvet.

Sarah swung her legs out of bed, the cold floorboards beneath her bare feet instantly evoking the memory of the cold water from the caves. She grabbed a pill from the bottle on the nightstand and quickly swallowed it dry. As she stood up and stretched, she studied Maya out of the corner of her eye. While Maya appeared incredibly unwell, their normally dark skin pale and sickly, Sarah felt... strangely fine. Tired, sure, but the profound physical exhaustion, the headaches, the mental fog that plagued the others hadn't touched her.

She couldn't help but wonder—Was the demon toying with her, saving her for last? Had her mother found a way to protect her? These thoughts swirled, mixing with all the others over the past few days into a bitter vortex in her head.

She padded into the kitchen, the scent of stale pizza and old secrets still hanging in the air from last night's confrontation with her father. He had already left for the university, leaving only a hastily scribbled note on the counter: *"Sarah, need to gather my thoughts. We WILL talk more tonight. Be safe. Love you. Dad."*

With her emotions still raw from the day before, she crumpled the note up and tossed it in the trash. Sarah flicked on the small kitchen TV for an update on Chloe's viral video, keeping the volume low, as to not bother Maya. The local news channel popped up, the screen filled with images of wind-whipped trees and flooded streets. But then the headline shifted.

"'40 Winks Challenge' Spreads Alarm as More Teens Fall Victim to Unexplained Comas."

She turned up the volume, her hand trembling. Standing outside Brooklyn Methodist, the reporter spoke gravely about the viral phenomenon that had exploded overnight. Videos of Chloe's disastrous livestream, edited and re-uploaded countless times, were interspersed with clips of teenagers across the country attempting the challenge, chanting the rhyme, while replaying Chloe's video.

Then came more chilling reports: a high school student in Ohio found unresponsive by his parents after trying the viral stunt; two college roommates in California discovered in a catatonic state; a cluster of cases emerging in Florida. All young, all healthy, all linked by the same viral trend, the same baffling symptoms. Doctors were expressing confusion, warning parents, citing potential dangers of hypoxia from strange breathing patterns encouraged by some versions of the challenge, or even mass hysteria.

But Sarah knew better. It wasn't hysteria.

Her phone buzzed. It was a group text from Chris.

Hospital. It's getting worse here. Could use some company.

"Maya, we need to go," Sarah called out loudly to the other room, her voice tight with urgency.

Maya shuffled out from Sarah's room, their movements stiff. "More... comas?" they asked, their eyes wide with dawning horror as they caught sight of the TV screen.

Sarah didn't answer. She didn't need to.

The two of them didn't waste any time getting ready. Sarah was dressed, grabbed a slice of cold pizza, and was out the door before the news report was even over.

Once they arrived, walking into the hospital felt like walking into a war zone. Chaos swirled around them. Dozens of families huddled together; their faces etched with fear and confusion. Paramedics wheeled in another gurney carrying a pale, still teenager, their clothing soaked from the rain. Medical staff rushed around shouting terms and codes that Sarah didn't understand.

They found Chris through the crowd, slumped in a chair, his head in his hands. He looked up as they approached, his eyes bloodshot, his usual energy completely absent.

"How's Chloe?" Maya asked, as they squeezed around another family sitting next to him.

"No real change, other than her looking even worse than she did yesterday," Chris said in a somber tone. "The doctors aren't even helping her anymore. Not with all of these new patients coming in," he waved his hand in the general direction of the waiting crowd. "They just keep coming."

To the side, Ben was sitting on the floor, hunched in a corner, furiously tapping away on his phone. His face was pale and gaunt. He looked thinner than he had just a day ago, the skin stretched tight over his cheekbones. He barely acknowledged their arrival, his irritation a palpable wave rolling off him.

"How are you guys feeling?" Sarah asked, her voice low, studying her friends with growing alarm.

Chris just gave a noncommittal grunt.

"Peachy. Just love the smell of hospitals," Ben answered without looking up. His sarcasm came out lacking its usual bite.

Maya sank onto the floor beside Ben, pulling out their journal, shivering despite the stuffy heat of the waiting room. "I'm just... tired," they murmured, their gaze focused on the pages in their book. "And... anxious. Like something bad is about to happen."

Just as Sarah sat down on the floor next to Chris's chair, she heard something faint, almost imperceptible beneath the background of hospital noise.

Tick. Tick. Tick.

She looked sharply at Maya. "Do you hear that?"

Maya frowned, tilting their head. "Hear what? Just the rain, the..." They trailed off, their eyes widening slightly. "Wait. That... ticking sound?"

Ben looked up from his phone, his expression suddenly alert, fearful. "You hear it too?"

Chris lifted his head slowly, his eyes unfocused. "Ticking? Yeah, been hearing it on and off all morning. Thought it was just in my head."

They stared at each other, a shared horror dawning in their eyes.

All of them heard it now. The rhythmic ticking, the sound that had permeated Sarah's nightmares. The curse wasn't just causing fatigue and headaches; it was manifesting, auditorily, weaving itself into their perception of reality. The Shepherd was reaching for them.

"Okay," Sarah said, her voice low and urgent, pulling them into a tight huddle. "We need to talk. Seriously talk. Forget what my dad said, forget trying to find logical explanations. This is *not* normal. This is the Relic's doing. It's the Shepherd—or whatever *it* is."

Sarah sat up onto her knees, and leaned forward. She held each of their gazes to make sure they were listening.

"We don't know exactly how, yet," Sarah admitted, frustration clawing at her. "But my mother knew. She was terrified of it. And now it's happening to us. To Chloe. And worst of all we..." She gestured at the group of friends huddled around her. "Watched Chloe's video which means you are all affected."

"So, what do we do?" Ben asked, lowering his phone, his voice tight with fear. "Do we... do we smash the damn thing? Like, 'Lord of the Rings' style, chuck it into Mount Doom?" Despite the situation, Sarah was happy to see a flicker of his old self surfacing.

"Mr. Chen said that might be dangerous," Sarah replied. "That it could release whatever's inside."

"So, we use it?" Chris suggested, his voice rough. "Try to... I don't know... talk to it? Figure out what it wants?" He shuddered. "Maybe... maybe it wants the lamp thingy back in the cave?"

"Are you insane?" Maya snapped, their anxiety making them sharp. "Talk to it? Use it? I'm pretty sure it doesn't want to 'talk'. We could end up like Chloe. Or worse! Remember those bones, Chris?"

"So, we do nothing?" Chris shot back, his lethargy snapping into a desperate anger. "We just sit here and wait for our brains to turn to mush while this thing picks us off one by one?"

"Maybe it *is* just hysteria," Ben offered weakly. "Maybe we're just freaking out because of what happened in China... with Chloe..."

"Do you really believe that, Ben?" Sarah asked quietly, meeting his gaze.

He looked away, unable to hold her stare. She didn't blame him for grasping at denial—it was easier to accept than the truth. They were trapped, caught between the seemingly impossible and the undeniably horrific reality unfolding around them.

Destroy the Relic, use the Relic, hide the Relic, none of the options felt right, none felt safe. Their desperation mounted with each passing moment—with each new victim wheeled through the emergency room doors.

Sarah pressed on. "Look, I know this is all crazy, but we need to stop making excuses and face this for what it is. Mr. Chen already has an idea of what we are dealing with and once we hear back from him, we should know what to do."

"What *are* we dealing with?" Ben asked.

With some help from Maya on the vernacular, Sarah explained to Ben and Chris what Mr. Chen had told her the day before. Once she was finished, Chris opened his mouth to question her but was interrupted by Sarah's phone ringing with an incoming call.

The sudden sound made them all jump. With trembling hands, her heart pounding, she answered, then immediately exhaled in relief—It was Mr. Chen.

"Xiao Yáng! You must listen! Are your friends there?"

She placed the call on speaker so her friends could hear. His usually calm, measured voice sounded thin and reedy, stretched taut with an emotion Sarah had never heard from him before: pure, undiluted panic.

"Yes, Mr. Chen, we're all here," Sarah replied, glancing at the pale faces huddled around the phone. "At the hospital. What did you find?"

"The Relic... the descriptions your mother gave... it is worse than I feared." He took a ragged breath. "The book... so old... brittle... speaks of an entity... ancient and powerful..."

"What entity, Mr. Chen?" Maya urged, leaning closer to the phone. "What is it called?"

There was a pause, filled only by the distant rumble of thunder outside and the frantic pounding of Sarah's heart. Then, Mr. Chen spoke the name, his voice barely a whisper, heavy with dread.

"Fén Yáng."

The Mandarin words hung in the air.

"Fén Yáng?" Ben repeated, frowning. "What the hell is that?"

"*That*... is the 'Grave Goat'," Mr. Chen translated. Sarah raised her eyebrows in recognition. "A demon of the Earth. A subterranean horror. Some texts say it is born from stagnant water in deep wells—"

Sarah gasped, exchanging a horrified look with Maya. The well. The pool in the cave.

"—others that it coalesces in places of decay, of death. Tombs. Ruins." Mr. Chen continued, his voice gaining a frantic edge. "It haunts desolate places. It feeds on corpses, yes, but more than that...

it feeds on life force. On despair. It drains its victims, leaving them...
empty." He paused, and Sarah could hear the rustle of fragile pages
over the line.

"What else?" Sarah asked, dread coiling in her stomach, already
suspecting the answer.

"Much, more," Mr. Chen whispered cryptically.

A heavy, suffocating silence fell over the small group, broken
only by the relentless *tick-tick-tick* that they could all hear now. Her
mother's frantic notes about protection. Her forgotten trip to Gu
Mei as a toddler. The photo of her by the well. The brass lamp in the
background. It all fit together, a horrifying mosaic of interconnected
dread.

Chris stared blankly ahead, his lethargy seeming to deepen, as if
the confirmation of a specific demon was too much for his exhausted
mind to process.

Ben, however, reacted with anger. "So what? That's it? Some lame
ass goat-demon-thing from an old book is responsible for... for all
this?" He gestured wildly around the chaotic waiting room. "For
Chloe? For those other kids?"

"It is certainly not lame, Ben," Sarah insisted, her voice shaking
but firm. "It's ancient, powerful, and it's real. My mother knew it.
She fought it."

"And lost," Chris muttered darkly from his chair.

"Mr. Chen," Sarah spoke urgently into the phone, ignoring
Chris's comment. "The book... does it say how to stop it? How to
fight it?"

"I... I do not know yet," Mr. Chen stammered. "The text is archaic, fragmented. Difficult to decipher. There are mentions of rituals,
wardings... iron, salt, jade... the usual defenses against earth spirits,
but Fén Yá—" He cleared his throat, afraid to say the demon's name
out loud. "—The Shepherd, it is old and cunning. It requires... specific countermeasures. I need more time, Xiao Yáng. More research."

"Time?" Chris laughed harshly. "We don't *have* time!"

Ben let out a shaky, humorless laugh. He looked up from the phone to the chaotic waiting room, a grim realization dawning on his face. "Guess the genie really is out of its bottle now," he muttered.

"You must come here," Mr. Chen demanded suddenly, his voice regaining a sliver of its usual command. "All of you. It is not safe where you are. The hospital... places of sickness, of death... they draw such entities. Come to the shop. Now. I have protections here. We will be safer while I search."

"Okay," Sarah agreed immediately. "Okay, Mr. Chen, we're on our way." She disconnected the call, her mind racing. Fén Yáng. Grave Goat. Epilepsy. It was too much, yet it explained almost everything.

"Let's go," she said, turning to her friends, grabbing her backpack.

"Whoa, hang on," Ben said, holding up a hand. He hadn't stood up. "You guys go. I'm staying here. With Chloe."

"Ben, no," Sarah protested. "Mr. Chen said it's not safe here. We should stick together."

"Exactly," Ben shot back, a rare flash of defiance in his eyes. "What if she wakes up? What if something happens? Someone needs to be here for her." He looked towards the emergency room doors, his expression a mixture of fear and a stubborn loyalty that touched Sarah despite the circumstances. "I'm not leaving her."

Sarah looked over at Chris. He returned her gaze and shrugged. "If Mr. Chen finds a way for me to fight this thing, then I'm going. I need to do something other than sit around whining." She gave him a small smile and looked over at Maya who didn't offer any objection.

"Okay, Glitch," Sarah said reluctantly. "Okay. But be careful. Keep your phone on. Call us the *second* anything changes. And don't wander off."

"Wouldn't dream of it," Ben mumbled, turning his attention back to his phone, though Sarah noticed his thumbs weren't moving. He was just staring at the screen.

With a worried glance at Ben, Sarah turned to leave, but his voice stopped her.

"One," he called out from behind.

She turned back and saw him standing there, more vulnerable than she had ever seen him. He was pointing at himself with a shaky thumb.

Chris's face hardened, his grief and fear lashing out as anger. "No," he snarled, taking a step back towards Ben. "Don't you dare. She's not dead. The count is five. We're not doing this without her."

Sarah tilted her head in sympathy for Ben. He was looking for comfort, for any sort of confirmation that they were okay. But Chris was right. To count now would mean accepting Chloe was gone.

Maya gently pulled on Chris's arm. "Come on," they whispered.

Sarah looked at Ben one last time, the broken, unfinished chant hanging in the air between them like a ghost. She gave him a small, apologetic smile, then turned and walked out into the storm.

Chapter 21

Ben stood in a sea of grieving families as he watched his friends disappear out the sliding glass doors. Although he was surrounded by hundreds of other people—all of them there for the same reason he was—he had never felt so alone.

Chloe couldn't be left by herself. Not now. *He* needed to stay. Chris, roid-raging around the hospital like a caged bull, wasn't helping. It was best if Chris left to go punch something far away while he stayed and watched over her.

He leaned his back against the cool wall outside her room and shoved his earbuds in, a desperate attempt to build a shield against the outside world. He started scrolling aimlessly through social media but all the posts and comments about Chloe grated on his nerves, so he switched to one of his favorite games instead.

His thumbs flew across the glass, muscle memory guiding them through familiar combos, slaying digital monsters while the real demons gathered just outside his perception. Although he relished the distraction from the real world, playing games was more about control than zoning out. In the digital world, the rules were clear, the threats predictable, the victories achievable. Out in the real world?

Out there was chaos, helplessness, that same sickening lurch in his stomach he hadn't felt since... *that* day.

The day that had forged the group's strange, trauma-bonded friendship. He hated feeling powerless, of being useless. So, he retreated inwards. Into the code, into the pixels, into the predictable world where he could be brave, and where he could be the *hero*. He just wished, for once, it worked the same in the real world.

Just the fleeting thought of that fateful day—the day that proved he was a coward—was enough to make his hands sweat, causing him to mistime a combo. His short movements became frantic as he began to lose control. Ben's digital character exploded into a shower of pixels.

He lost, again, like he always did.

"Fuck!" He threw the hand holding the phone back in frustration, poised to smash the device on the ground, but stopped himself just short. He ignored the concerned glances from medical staff walking nearby. Taking a few deep breaths to calm himself, he checked his phone for any good news instead.

He frowned when he saw the reports. The #40WinksChallenge still trended but was now accompanied by darker hashtags: #CityOfSleep, #BrooklynBlackout. The stories did not improve his mood.

He felt exhausted, his eyelids heavy, his head pounding, but sleep had been eluding him. No matter how hard he tried he just couldn't stay asleep. And that damn ticking sound was starting to really irritate him. It had started subtly this morning, a faint *tick-tick-tick* like an old watch, almost lost beneath the hospital sounds. But now it was louder, more insistent, a rhythmic counterpoint to the frantic beating of his own heart. He pressed his fingers into his ears, trying to block it out, but it seemed to be coming from *inside* his head.

"I need some damn caffeine," he mumbled to himself, as he pushed himself up and peeked in on Chloe. His heart seized—she was staring right at him... but her eyes were vacant. He realized with a shudder that she was still "sleeping," trapped in that bizarre, eyes-open coma.

With another shiver at how freaky it all was, he left her room and shuffled towards the elevators, navigating the crowded corridors filled with harried nurses, anxious families, and the constant beeping of medical equipment. The lights overhead flickered intermittently, casting jarring shadows, a result of the ongoing storm straining the hospital's power grid. It added another layer of unsettling tension to the already chaotic atmosphere.

Downstairs, he was in the middle of pouring a coffee when his pocket started to vibrate. He put down the half-filled cup and pulled out his phone, expecting a text from Maya or Chris. But the name on the screen stopped his heart: the text was from Chloe.

Ben? Where r u??

Chloe?? OMG! Ur awake?? I'm here. At the hospital!

Thank God! The nurse said something about surgery? Idk. Kinda groggy. I'm scared Ben. I need you.

OMW!!! Stay put! Don't be scared I'm coming!

He turned, abandoning his coffee, and navigated the labyrinthine hospital corridors back towards the elevator to take him up to the fifth floor. The lights around him continued to strobe along the corridor, casting long, dancing shadows that played tricks on his eyes. The ticking in his head intensified with each step.

He reached the elevator and jumped inside, frantically pushing the number 5. "C'mon. C'mon! You piece of shit," he growled in impatience. The doors finally closed, and the elevator started its journey up. A sudden rumble of thunder shook the building, followed by a brief, stomach-dropping lurch of the elevator car. When the doors opened, he practically sprinted out into a seemingly empty hallway.

Tick. Tick. Tick.

He half-ran through the empty halls, his shoes squeaking on the floor with each step. As he barreled around a corner, he barely noticed the lights were out at the very far end of this particular hallway before he dashed into her room.

Chloe lay in bed, staring blankly with unseeing eyes, still very much comatose. The rhythmic beep of the heart monitor was still at the same steady rate. Ben took two large strides to stand by her bedside.

"Chloe?"

She didn't respond. Her eyes and mouth were wide open, fixed in the same vacant expression since the coma, but she was staring off into nothing. Clearly still under the demon's curse. Ben pulled out his phone to check his messages and gasped when he saw that they were gone. Vanished.

"What in the Christ," he said aloud, slumping hard into the visitor's chair. The cheap vinyl groaned. "I'm losing it, Chloe."

Outside, large drops of rain pelted the fifth-floor window, the sky a storm that mirrored his feelings. He stared longingly at Chloe; a nasal cannula rested below her nostrils, barely covering her pale face—a face he had always considered as perfect. She looked so fragile lying there tucked under the blanket with cords and tubes wrapped around her. So fragile.

He'd made a promise to himself, a long time ago—even before that fateful day brought them together—that he would always protect her. He wished he could tell her how he felt, *truly* felt, but he couldn't, not with Chris always there, a loud, annoying presence. Chris wasn't a bad guy, necessarily; he just wasn't a good match for Chloe. It was only a matter of time until the two of them broke up permanently; he just had to wait. He needed her to wake up—figuratively and literally.

To stop himself from screaming, or crying, he did what he always did. He stared at his phone and started doomscrolling. #CityOfSleep was going viral, already at over a million views. Posts included grainy videos of slumped-over figures on subways and trending theories about contaminated water and government conspiracies. It was a familiar tapestry of societal panic, and Ben consumed it numbly, the blue light of the screen painting his face in its ghoulish glow.

A vibration against his palm from an incoming message shook him from the mind-numbing social feed. He swiped down the notification bar, expecting another useless news alert but goosebumps crawled down his spine at what he saw.

The name on the screen again was Chloe.

Ice ran down his spine. His head snapped up to look at her. She hadn't moved. Her chest rose and fell in the same shallow, machine-assisted rhythm. Her own phone was dark on the bedside table, right next to a plastic cup of water. He shook his head—this was absurd. His thumb trembled as he tapped the notification.

u need to see this! <u>LINK</u>

Her text included a link.

It had to be a dream. He fell asleep and this was all in his head. Or maybe, a hallucination brought on by stress and too little caffeine. But his curiosity got the better of him, and he pressed the link before his brain could protest.

A webpage loaded, buffering for a heart-stopping second before a video player stuttered to life. The connection was shaky—the image filmed through a window streaked with rain. The only sounds coming through the video were the howl of the wind mixed with a shallow breathing from *something* behind the camera. The breathing was wet and rattled like someone's last gasp of air. The video itself was looking down at the hospital from across the street.

He could see the grid of windows, could count the floors up. He held his phone up, trying to align the view. There. The fifth floor. He could just make out the corner of the window to the room he was in. The video zoomed closer, the image pixelating before steadying. The camera focused, and he saw himself standing there in the stream. He waved and watched his digital duplicate mirror his movement.

He looked at Chloe's bed behind him in the livestream. Even though the video was slightly pixelated, the bed was clearly empty. The sheets were pulled tight, the pillow fluffed. A perfectly sterile, unoccupied hospital bed.

"What the fuck?" He lowered the phone, his eyes darting to Chloe, lying in the bed, the monitor beeping its steady, lying rhythm. He looked back at the screen. Empty. He was watching a ghost room. A feed from a minute ago? An hour ago? Before she was admitted? No, he had just seen himself in the video, the feed was definitely live.

Ben turned and scanned the apartment across the street, searching for any sign of the live streamer. He found nothing but black windows staring back at him. Even the roof was empty, which wasn't surprising in this storm. He scratched his head in confusion.

Ben glanced back down at the stream on his phone and turned up the volume. The video feed panned, jerky and unstable, across the building's face. It settled on the far end of his hall, where a single window suddenly blinked out, becoming an abrupt black square in the grid.

A flash of lightning split the sky, and for a brief moment, that darkened window was backlit, illuminating a form standing at the glass. At first glance it appeared human, but it was too tall and angular. The figure quickly disappeared deeper into the shadows of the room and lurched out of sight.

He felt the air in his lungs turn to ice.

He kept watching the livestream, the phone a heavy weight in his hand. The rattled breathing continued as another window closer towards him went black. Then another. The lightning flashed, a percussive, strobing light, and with each flash he saw *it* getting closer. A jagged silhouette, contorting in a way that wasn't human, its form briefly, horribly visible before it vanished into the new darkness it had created. It wasn't moving down the hallway. It was moving *through the goddamn walls.*

One by one, the lights were going out, a wave of blackness creeping steadily across the hospital's face on his phone screen. Each time a room went dark, the lightning would flash, and he would see *it* through the window. He could see a creature slowly and methodically shambling along through each room.

Ben's heart hammered against his ribs, a frantic counter-rhythm to the steady beep of Chloe's monitor. He was frozen with indecision in his chair. His instinct was to flee, but a part of him couldn't abandon Chloe. But what could he do if he stayed? He looked around the room for anything to use as a weapon. Nothing but cotton balls, tongue depressors, and Chloe's designer bag were nearby.

"Shit. Shit. Shit."

He glanced at the livestream. The room directly next to his went dark. The lightning flashed, and the thing was right there, pressed against the glass, a pale, featureless face turning slowly, impossibly, to stare directly at the camera across the street. To stare at Ben through the live feed. The breathing stopped.

With a surge of adrenaline, Ben jumped up from his chair and stood between Chloe and the wall to the next room. He held his breath in anticipation. The power in the room suddenly flickered, then went off. The abrupt plunge into darkness left him momentarily blind as his eyes tried adjusting. The only light remaining was from a small emergency sign above the door that bathed the room in a faint, hellish red.

He waited. Straining his ears. His heart pounded so hard in his chest he could hear each pulse in the silence. He felt a pang of guilt for being thankful that the beeping from Chloe's monitor had stopped. He just hoped she'd be fine without it for a minute. He needed to *listen*.

He let out the air he was holding and took a deep breath. Maybe the thing wasn't coming for their room or maybe he was imagining it like Chloe's texts? Just as he started to check the livestream, the power turned back on. The room was empty.

Chloe's monitor beeped back to life causing him to jump. With a sharp laugh, more a release of terror than humor, Ben walked over to the window and checked the stream.

In the video, Chloe was standing right behind him.

He spun around just as the power went out again, plunging the room into a dark void. The beeping monitor went silent as well. He waved his shaking arms out in front of him, feeling for any sign of Chloe but only felt the chill hospital air.

"Chloe?" He squeaked. "Is... that you?"

Tick. Tick. Tick.

There was no answer, only silence.

The power surged back on with a single, brilliant flash that seared in his eyes then died again, plunging the room back into darkness. He couldn't be sure, but he thought he saw an afterimage of someone standing in front of him. Each cycle of the lights made his senses reel, disorienting him as it reset his night vision and his ability to see. With his heart practically pounding out of his chest he waited, frozen in terror.

"Chloe?"

The only sound was from the rain that continued to drum against the glass behind him. No beeping from her monitor, no breathing, just the muffled roar of a barely contained storm outside. He wanted to check her bed and make sure she was okay, but his legs wouldn't move.

The bleating of a sheep suddenly erupted from his phone. Ben jumped at the loud noise, falling backwards against the window. The hair on the back of his neck stood on end at the sound. He instinctively lifted his shoulders in pain, trying to block out the unnatural howling that tore at his eardrums in its relentless, sustained shriek. He fumbled with his phone, trying to close the livestream with his trembling fingers. With years of muscle memory and some luck, he managed to silence the damn noise.

With his ears still ringing, he lifted his phone out in front of him slowly and turned on the flashlight. Standing right in front of him, unmoving, was Chloe. Shriveled, dry skin hung on her frail bones like a loose sheet. Her jaw hung agape, the lower lip having receded to expose a row of yellowed teeth and blackened gums in a permanent, silent moan. One eye was gone, the socket a dark, weeping pit from which pus oozed. The other eye remained, a clouded, milky marble staring at him, yet seeing nothing.

With a cry, he recoiled, but he had nowhere to go with his back already pressed against the window. His gaze flickered to Chloe's bed, where she still slept soundly, the gentle rise and fall of her chest a steady, impossible paradox. He shifted his eyes back to the decaying form of his friend. The corpse of Chloe was inexplicably there, unmoving, its single milky eye staring back at him.

What was real? He again peeked over towards Chloe's hospital bed, then in confusion, looked back at the corpse. His eyes had barely focused on Chloe's rotting form when it suddenly lunged at him, accompanied by a shriek of digital static that assaulted his ears.

It happened so quickly, he didn't even have time to flinch before he felt a concussive force crash against his chest, knocking the wind out of him and throwing him backward through the fifth-story window.

The glass shattered, the shards tearing at his skin as he fell out into the storm. The cold rain whipped at him, the wind a roar in his ears. The last thing he saw as he tumbled through the air, the window shrinking away from him at a terrifying speed, was a face in that broken window.

The face of Chloe, smiling down at him.

The power in the hospital flickered back on, just as the world went dark for Ben forever.

CHAPTER 22

Sarah flinched when the brass bell above the door to Thorne's Curios rang out in a dissonant toll, like a funeral knell cutting through the storm's howl. A gust of wind shoved them over the threshold, herding her, Maya, and Chris inside before the heavy door slammed shut, sealing them in with the shop's dusty, incense-laden air. The clutter of artifacts instantly pressed in on her, the shadows in the corners deeper and more watchful than before. She resisted the urge to bolt back outside, to escape.

Mr. Chen waited for them near the front counter. His usual serene composure had been replaced by a frantic, almost bird-like energy. His wire-rimmed glasses sat slightly askew, his wispy white hair stood on end as if he'd been running his hands through it repeatedly, and his eyes, magnified behind the thick lenses, looked tired and worn. He wrung his hands together, his knuckles pale.

"You came," he breathed, relief washing over his features, quickly followed by renewed urgency. "Quickly, quickly. Back here." He didn't wait for a reply, turning and hurrying towards the small, cluttered alcove where they had sat just the day before—a day that felt like a lifetime ago.

Sarah exchanged a worried glance with Maya and Chris. Mr. Chen's visible panic was far more terrifying than any cryptic warning. Chris was the first to follow, as he nervously ran a hand through his thick hair. Despite his lethargy, the adrenaline from Mr. Chen's call seemed to have sharpened his focus.

Maya clutched their Witch Bag close to their side; one free hand hovered near the protective amulets around their neck. The ticking sound, which had plagued them at the hospital, seemed momentarily ignored in the face of Mr. Chen's distress, but Sarah felt a residual tension, a listening quality in her friends that hadn't been there before.

Sarah trailed Chris to the back where Mr. Chen waited, weaving through the maze of stacked books and neglected treasures. Ancient, brittle-looking texts now covered the low table in the alcove. Scrolls bound with faded ribbon lay partially unrolled, revealing intricate calligraphy and unsettling illustrations. Open books, their pages yellowed and fragile, displayed diagrams of constellations, talismans, and grotesque, half-human creatures.

As always, the air here felt different, thick with the comforting weight of ancient knowledge. But Sarah immediately noticed the air was missing one thing.

"Mr. Chen," Sarah asked, her voice quiet, "do you have any tea?" He always had tea and she desperately needed a moment of familiar comfort.

"Tea? Ah, yes. Of course," Mr. Chen murmured, as he shuffled over to a cold, empty teapot. "I have some tea right—" He lifted the empty pot and squinted at it in confusion. "Hmm, I seem to have forgotten to make some." He placed it back with a shake of his head before shuffling back over to the table.

Sarah shared a worried look with Maya.

"It's okay," she assured him, turning back to the table, her own urgency overriding the need for comfort.

"Besides, there is no time for tea, Xiao Yáng. No, none at all. I found it," Mr. Chen said, his voice trembling slightly as he gestured towards a particularly large, leather-bound volume lying open in the center of the table. The pages were covered in dense, archaic Chinese characters, interspersed with disturbing, finely detailed ink drawings.

"What is it?" Chris asked, peering over Mr. Chen's shoulder.

"The treatise on *Yaoguai*. It took hours... my filing system..." He trailed off, shaking his head dismissively. "No matter. Listen. I was right in my suspicions."

He pointed a shaking finger towards an illustration on the open page. Sarah leaned closer to get a better look at the image. It depicted a creature rising from cracked earth beside a crumbling stone well.

It was horrifyingly familiar. Tall, gaunt, with unnaturally long, insect-like limbs ending in vicious claws. Its body was covered in patches of dark, matted wool, clinging to sickly green, chitinous skin. Its head was a nightmare fusion—the elongated skull of a sheep, twisted into a grotesque grin revealing rows of needle-sharp teeth—with deep-set sockets from which burned two points of malevolent red light. It bore an undeniable, terrifying resemblance to the figure Sarah had seen in Chloe's livestream and the monster from her own nightmares.

"Fén Yáng," Mr. Chen breathed, the name sounding like a curse on his lips. He tapped the characters written beside the illustration. "The Grave Goat."

Chris let out a low whistle, his skepticism seemingly evaporating in the face of the grotesque image and Mr. Chen's obvious terror. Maya stared at the drawing, their face pale, their hand unconsciously tightening its grip on their bag.

"It speaks of it as a subterranean demon," Mr. Chen continued, his voice regaining some strength, fueled now by the urgency of sharing his findings. "A creature born of the earth itself, specifically from places associated with death and decay. Tombs, burial grounds, ancient ruins... and wells." Mr. Chen paused at the last word, raising an eyebrow, looking pointedly at Sarah. "Particularly old, deep wells where the water has gone stagnant, where the earth's energy pools and festers."

Sarah felt the connection like two magnets snapping together. The ruins where they found the bones. The cave. The pool under the well where they found her mother. It all converged, a nexus of darkness pinpointed in the ancient text before them.

Finally. Finally, she was getting answers.

"The book calls it a *necrophage*," Mr. Chen said, his voice dropping again. "A feeder on the dead." He pointed to another disturbing illustration depicting skeletal figures clawing their way out of graves towards a shadowy, sheep-like form. "Some scholars believed its existence was invoked simply to explain decomposition, a process they could not understand. But this text... it insists it is more than that. It doesn't just consume the body—it consumes the *spirit*, trapping souls, feeding on life force..."

Mr. Chen flipped a fragile page, revealing more text and another series of illustrations—stylized depictions of people suffering, wasting away, their eyes vacant. Sarah glanced over at Chris, who was staring at the drawing. It was an illustration that looked a hell of a lot like Chloe in her coma. Chris didn't return her look, but she saw him take a hard swallow.

"How appropriate that your mother called it the Shepherd," Mr. Chen said grimly, "it tends to its flock of souls with a cruel, cosmic irony—a wolf in sheep's skin, you might say."

He let out a small chuckle at the idea, before clearing his throat and continuing. "It also speaks of hauntings, of the demon attaching itself to families, to bloodlines, often through cursed objects or desecrated ground. It describes the symptoms..."

He looked directly at Maya and Chris, then hesitantly at Sarah.

"A profound lethargy, headaches, a growing sense of disconnection from reality, irritability, anxiety..."

Maya groaned softly, their hand flying to their head. Chris leaned heavily against a bookcase, his face ashen. Even Ben, miles away in the hospital, fit in Mr. Chen's description.

"And," Mr. Chen continued, lowering his voice even more, his gaze fixed on Sarah with pity and fear, "it has an affinity for children. The text mentions afflictions. Unexplained illnesses." He took a deep breath. "It speaks specifically of inducing miscarriages and..." He paused, letting the word hang in the air, "...causing the 'falling sickness'—epilepsy."

Epilepsy. The word made the floor begin to spin under her. The trip she couldn't remember, the sudden onset of seizures weeks after returning... it wasn't idiopathic. It was *him*. She looked at Mr. Chen, her voice barely a whisper, laced with a chilling new fear.

"But, if Fén Yá—"

"Shhh!" Mr. Chen held up a finger, interrupting her. "Best not call its attention too much by using its true name."

Sarah gulped.

"The... Shepherd," she continued carefully, using the name her mother preferred. "Affects children like that... if it caused *this*," she gestured implicitly at herself, "why am I still alive? Why didn't it *take* me back then, when I was a child, near the well, near the device?"

The image of the ancient bones flashed in her mind—the crushed skulls of the mother and infant. Why had she been spared that fate, only to be marked?

Mr. Chen met her terrified gaze, his own eyes clouded with thought.

"Hmm, a difficult question, Xiao Yáng," he said softly, rubbing his tired eyes again. "Surely your mother performed some ritual, incomplete or flawed, yet enough to shield you from the worst of it. Or perhaps—" he tapped a finger against his chin, studying the lamp and its carousel of sheep with deep unease, "Perhaps the demon prefers to torture. To watch. To wait." He shook his head. "The texts are unclear on the specifics of its choices. But it marked you, child. That much is certain."

Sarah gripped the edge of the table for support, her knuckles white. She felt Maya's hand on her arm, a grounding presence in the swirling vortex of horror and revelation.

"How?" Sarah choked out the word. "How do we stop it? How do we fight it, Mr. Chen?"

Mr. Chen looked down at an ancient scroll, tracing his fingers across the faded characters. He removed his glasses and started rubbing his eyes again with a constant, almost unconscious gesture.

"Are you okay?"

"Hmm? Oh, yes, yes, child," he dismissed quickly, waving a hand. He placed his glasses back over his short nose, his eyes blinking rapidly. "Just dust. So much dust in these old books." He squinted at the text again, before continuing. "Fighting this demon is not simple. The ritual your mother attempted, perhaps it is mentioned here. Hmm, a severing ritual, but the details... they are obscure. The dialect is ancient, and parts of the text are even damaged..."

He shook his head in frustration then suddenly stiffened, his finger hovering over a torn piece of parchment. He cocked his head to the side as if listening to a distant sound.

He held up a single, trembling finger for silence.

"Listen," he hissed, his eyes wide behind his glasses. "Do you hear that?"

Chris and Maya exchanged a worried look. "The ticking?" Chris asked, his voice a low rasp. "Yeah. It's getting louder."

Mr. Chen shook his head, his gaze darting into the darkest, most unused corner of the shop. "No, not ticking. Something else." His voice was barely audible. "A rustling. Like dry leaves skittering across pavement. Or... maybe like the pages of a book, fluttering in a soft breeze."

Sarah held her breath, straining her ears, but she could hear nothing beyond the storm, the city's hum, and the heavy pounding of her own heart. Maya and Chris looked equally bewildered. Sarah scrunched her brow, wondering if he too was affected by the demon's curse.

"Must be a draft," Mr. Chen murmured, rubbing his eyes. "You said you hear ticking?" Sarah nodded. "This is not good. Not good at all." He took a deep, steadying breath and forced his attention back to the book on the table, though his glance kept flicking back to the corner.

"There are mentions of weaknesses," he continued. "Peachwood, blessed iron, maybe even mirrors—but these seem more like deterrents, temporary wards, not a true solution. Destroying the object is too risky. And appeasing the demon... the sacrifices mentioned are... unthinkable."

He raised his head, his face etched with worry and helplessness.

"I need more time, children. I must cross-reference with other texts, consult sources that are not readily available. There may be a way, a specific ritual perhaps... but I must find it." His eyes pleaded for their understanding, for their patience, even as the urgency of the situation screamed for immediate action.

More time again. The words hung heavy in the dusty air of the shop, a stark contrast to the frantic urgency pounding in Sarah's chest. More time felt like a luxury they couldn't afford. Chloe was already lost, trapped in that silent void. Chris, Ben, and Maya were fading, the Shepherd's tendrils tightening around them with every tick of an unseen clock.

Even Mr. Chen, their supposed expert, looked unnerved, rubbing his eyes with a frequency that sent prickles of alarm down Sarah's spine. Was he just tired? Or was the entity's influence reaching even here, within these walls supposedly protected by ancient wards?

"More time?" Chris questioned, echoing Sarah's thoughts, his voice rough with exhaustion. He pushed himself away from the bookcase he'd been leaning against, his movements slow, lethargic. "Mr. Chen, with all due respect, look at us! Look at what happened to Chloe! We don't *have* more time!"

"Patience, young man," Mr. Chen said, though his own voice lacked its usual calm authority. "Rushing into battle with an enemy you do not understand is suicide. This... Shepherd," he glanced at Sarah before continuing, "is ancient and powerful. Its patterns, its weaknesses... they are buried deep in obscure lore. A misstep, a wrongly performed ritual, could strengthen it, bind it to you more deeply. We must be certain."

"There are other ways, Mr. Chen," Maya said, while staring intently at the grotesque illustrations in front of them. They tore their gaze from the drawings and opened their canvas bag, revealing rows of neatly organized pouches filled with dried herbs, candles, crystals tied with twine, and small, hand-carved wooden figures. "My practice, Wicca, deals with earth spirits, with entities that cause illness and drain energy as well. There are cleansing rituals, banishing spells, protective circles..."

"Hmm," Mr. Chen studied Maya's collection, his expression softening slightly with respect for their belief, but he shook his head firmly. "Your path has power, young one, I do not doubt it. But it is a different power, rooted in different soil."

He gestured at the ancient Chinese scrolls scattered across the table before continuing. "The Shepherd is born of *this* land, *this* history, *this* specific confluence of energies. Its nature, its vulnerabilities, are tied to *our* traditions, *our* understanding of the balance between worlds. Western magic... it may be ineffective. At worst," his eyes darkened, "it could be perceived as a challenge, an intrusion. It could provoke the entity, make it... angry."

Maya appeared unconvinced, their fingers tightening around a smooth piece of crystal they'd pulled from their bag. "So, we just wait?" they asked.

"Not entirely," Mr. Chen said, pushing his glasses further up his nose. He turned back to the cluttered shelves, scanning them with a renewed focus. "While I search for the specific ritual needed to confront the Shepherd directly—whether it be binding, banishing, or... destruction—there are precautions you can take. Traditional defenses."

He rummaged behind a large porcelain vase, emerging with a small bundle of dark, reddish branches tied with twine. "Peachwood," he explained, handing a branch to each of them. "From a tree grown near flowing water, ideally. The Shepherd, being an earth demon, dislikes the vibrant, life-affirming energy of peach blossoms and the wood itself. It is said to ward off lesser spirits and ghosts, and it may offer some small measure of protection against the demon's direct influence. Keep it near you. Place it above doorways, near your beds."

Sarah took the smooth branch with a sharpened tip, its wood cool against her palm. It felt fragile, insignificant against the overwhelming power they were facing. A twig against a tidal wave. But it was something.

"Thank you, Mr. Chen," she said sincerely.

"It is a small measure," he cautioned again, rubbing his eyes tiredly. "Do not rely on it entirely. The true danger lies in the brass candle holder, the conduit. And in your own minds. The Shepherd feeds on fear, on exhaustion and will twist your reality. Stay together. Support each other. Do not give in to despondence." He looked pointedly at Chris and Maya, whose fatigue and anxiety were plainly visible.

The advice, though sound, felt almost impossible to follow. How could they not despair? Sarah looked over at her friends. Chris was leaning heavily against a bookcase, his eyes glassy and unfocused, as if he had trouble processing any words. Maya, turned, then sluggishly walked away towards the dark corner that Mr. Chen had stared at earlier.

"And Sarah, one more thing," Mr. Chen added, his voice trembling as he pulled out another ancient scroll. "The name of your mother's village... Gu Mei. We all assumed it was this"—he pointed at some writing—"which means 'To look after the plum blossoms.' A peaceful, poetic name to be sure, however, these older texts... they use a different character, a different tone," he flipped a page and pointed at another set of characters. "Guǐ Mèi. It is pronounced almost the same, but it does not mean 'plum blossom'. It means—"

"Demon," Sarah said, translating it herself.

"Exactly," Mr. Chen said standing up straight. "The villagers, either intentionally changed the name centuries ago, or it was slowly misinterpreted over the years. Regardless of how, the fact is, it's not named to honor a flower, but to hide a fiend."

Sarah's head reeled at the implications. It made complete sense now that she thought about it, and it explained why she never actually saw any plums in Gu Mei.

Silence settled over the group as they digested all this information. Mr. Chen stood back, watching them while wringing his hands together. Sarah laid a hand over his shoulder and gave him a small squeeze of appreciation. He smiled at her.

"We should go," Chris said, breaking the quiet. "We need to rest. And figure out our next move."

"Yes," Maya agreed from the dark corner of the shop, their back turned towards them. "Rest... that sounds like a good idea."

"My place," Sarah offered immediately. "My father isn't home right now. And it feels... safer than being alone." The thought of staying in her own home, with the memory of her father's denial still raw, was unbearable. But being together, facing this thing as a unit... it felt like their only option.

"Okay," Chris agreed.

Maya stood unmoving in the shadows.

"We need to tell Ben," Sarah said, pulling out her phone, her fingers hovering over the screen. A wave of guilt washed over her as she thought of him alone at the hospital, keeping vigil over Chloe while they consulted with Mr. Chen. He needed to know what they had learned. He needed to be with them.

She quickly typed out a message:

Sarah:

Hey Glitch. Heading back to my place. Things are... complicated. Mr. Chen confirmed it's bad. He thinks it's this demon Fén Yáng. We need to stick together. Also, don't say its name out loud! Meet us at my place. Text me back.

She hit send, her thumb trembling slightly. They waited in tense silence, the only sounds the crackling of Mr. Chen's small desk lamp and the distant rumble of the ongoing storm. After a minute that stretched like an eternity, her phone chimed. A reply from Ben.

Ben:

Demon? Seriously? U guys r crazy lol. But yeah, fine. Need 2 grab stuff from my place first. B there later.

Sarah frowned at the screen. The message sounded like Ben—the skepticism, the casual dismissal couched in humor. But something felt off.

"He says he'll meet us there later," Sarah told the others, trying to push down the flicker of suspicion. "He needs to grab stuff from his apartment first."

"Okay," Maya said, her back still turned.

Sarah narrowed her eyes; she wasn't positive, since it was so dark back there, but it looked like Maya took something out of their bag and placed it on a shelf. She reached out a hand to get their attention and question them, but then Maya looked back over their shoulder. For a brief second, their eyes became unfocused, glassy, as if looking through Sarah rather than at her, before they pulled away from her reach and stomped past without another word.

"Okay, then," Sarah said, staring at Maya with an annoyed look, before turning back to Mr. Chen. "Thank you for your help. Please... call us the moment you find anything else."

"Hmm, I will," Mr. Chen said, his gaze lingering on the lamp next to him. "Be vigilant. And do not underestimate the power of the Shepherd."

Sarah gave him a brief, tight hug, before turning to follow Maya and Chris. She hesitated at the door, looking back one last time. Her gaze lingered not just on her old friend, but on the dark shelf as well. With a shiver, she stepped out into the rain-soaked streets of Chinatown. As the door clicked shut behind her, she thought she heard Mr. Chen whispering to someone.

It happened one day, as Bo-Peep did stray
Into a meadow hard by,
There she espied their tails side by side,
All hung on a tree to dry.

CHAPTER 23

When they finally reached Sarah's house, the brownstone seemed less like a sanctuary and more like a fragile barricade against the encroaching darkness. It reminded Sarah of a nursery rhyme her mother used to read to her, one about—ironically—a wolf, that blew down some pigs' homes. She prayed they weren't the pigs in their own story, running into a house of straw.

They hurried inside, relieved to be out of the building storm. The sound of the front door closing behind them echoed unnervingly in the sudden quiet.

Sarah shivered in the surprisingly cold air, despite the warm summer storm boiling outside. Being soaking wet made it worse. She grabbed Auntie Lin's scarf off the coat rack next to the front door and wrapped it around her neck to help keep warm. The faint scent of sandalwood and jasmine, a ghost of her family's presence, hit her nose.

Her father still wasn't home from the university. In a way, she was glad he wasn't back yet, though the thought made her feel terrible. She just wasn't sure she could face another confrontation, another round of his well-meaning but ultimately dismissive scientific explanations. Not now. Not after what Mr. Chen had told them.

"Okay," Maya said, kicking off their wet shoes. "Let's get these wards in place." They dropped their Witch Bag onto the coffee table with a thud that reverberated through the small living room.

"You really think these... twigs... are going to stop *it*?" Chris scoffed, as Maya pulled out some of the peachwood from their bag and handed them over. The *tick-tick-tick* in his head seemed to punctuate his question.

"It's what Mr. Chen recommended as a deterrent," Sarah replied, holding the peachwood up to the light, studying it. "It's worth a try."

Chris, held up his own branch with a frown, clearly unconvinced that it had the ability to protect them. Sarah wasn't sure it did either, but she kept that to herself.

They then moved through the home, placing the peachwood branches above the front and back doorway, her bedroom door, then wedging smaller pieces into the window frames. The simple act felt almost childishly inadequate, like hiding under bed sheets to protect you from the monsters hiding in your closet. Yet, there was a primal, ritualistic comfort in the action, a small assertion of control in a situation that felt terrifyingly out of their hands.

Maya, despite Mr. Chen's uncertainty about the efficacy of Western magic against an Eastern demon, began to pull items from their bag: small pouches of dried herbs, salt, lavender, rosemary, and sage for cleansing—a black tourmaline crystal for grounding, and a small vial of what looked like salt water, likely moon water they'd consecrated themselves.

"Can't hurt," they muttered to no one in particular. "Something Mr. Chen said made me think. Salt is an earth purifier. If this thing is born from the earth..." they trailed off, letting the implication hang in the air. "It's a long shot, but it's *our* magic." They then sprinkled a fine line of salt across the threshold of the front door and dabbed a bit of the water on each windowpane, their lips moving silently, reciting words Sarah couldn't quite catch.

Sarah couldn't argue with that logic. Right now she was just thankful they had *any ideas.* She gave Maya a reassuring clap on the back.

"I really hope that stuff works, El." Chris muttered, watching them with his arms crossed, a deep line of doubt etched between his brows. Sarah could practically feel his skepticism radiating across the room.

Maya shrugged, not meeting his gaze. "Energy is energy, Chris. Intent is intent. At the very least, it makes *us* feel a little less helpless."

Sarah understood. The small acts of protection, whether peach-wood or salted thresholds, were as much for their own sanity as for any real defense against the Grave Goat. They needed to *do* something, anything, to fight back against the suffocating tide of fear and hopelessness.

Once the home was as "warded" as they could make it, an uneasy silence settled over them again. They huddled in the living room, the sound of the storm outside a relentless counterpoint to the frantic beating of their own hearts.

"So," Chris began finally, his voice hoarse, "what now? We just... wait? Wait for Mr. Chen to find some magic spell in one of his dusty books? Wait for Fén—" He cut himself off. "—the Shepherd to pick us off one by one by one, like Chloe? Like maybe even... Ben?"

The flippant, out-of-character text message echoed in Sarah's mind. It had been hours with no further word. No response to their increasingly frantic calls and texts.

"No. Ben will be here any minute," Sarah answered defiantly, though it didn't sound very convincing, even to herself.

"Or maybe that *thing* got to him," Chris muttered darkly, voicing the fear they all shared. The *tick-tick-tick* in his head grew louder, more insistent.

"Don't say that!" Maya snapped, their built-up anxiety making them sharp. "We don't know that. We can't assume the worst." But their eyes darted nervously towards the windows, as if expecting to see something monstrous peering in from the storm-lashed darkness.

"We need a plan," Sarah insisted, trying to take control, trying to push back the rising tide of despair. "Mr. Chen said the Shepherd preys on weakness, on exhaustion. We need to stay strong. We need to stay together."

"Easier said than done when you feel like your brain is being squeezed in a vise and there's a damn metronome in your ear," Chris grumbled, rubbing his temples.

Suddenly, a loud, sharp *knock* on the apartment door made them all jump, a collective gasp escaping their lips. They stared at each other, their faces pale, their eyes wide with a mixture of hope and terror.

"Ben?" Chris whispered, his voice hoarse.

Another knock, harder this time, more insistent. *KNOCK. KNOCK. KNOCK.* The sound echoed through the quiet home—each rap a hammer blow against their frayed nerves.

Sarah's heart pounded against her ribs. It *had* to be Ben. Who else could it be? Her dad wouldn't knock. She moved towards the door, her legs feeling strangely heavy, her hand trembling as she reached for the doorknob.

"Sarah, wait!" Maya hissed, grabbing her arm, their fingers digging into Sarah's skin. They made a looking gesture with their fingers and pointed at the peephole.

Sarah nodded, her throat tight. She pressed her eye to the small, fish-eye lens. There, standing in the dimly lit porch, with his shoulders hunched and his hair plastered to his forehead by the rain, was Ben.

A wave of relief, so intense it almost buckled her knees, washed over Sarah. "It's him!" she squealed, fumbling with the locks, her fingers clumsy with haste. "See, we were just being paranoid."

She threw open the door. "Ben! Oh my god, we were so worried! Why didn't you answer your—"

The words died in her throat.

The figure standing in the hallway *looked* like Ben, but... off. Sickly, almost translucent white skin stretched so tight over his cheekbones that he looked gaunt, skeletal. His eyes, usually bright with sarcastic humor, now appeared dull, unfocused, ringed with dark, bruised-looking circles that sank into his skull. He swayed slightly, like seaweed in a current. And the smell—a faint, cloying scent of damp earth, like freshly turned grave soil, mixed with something metallic, like old blood, clung to him.

"Ben?" Sarah repeated, her voice barely a whisper, the initial surge of relief instantly extinguished, replaced by a chilling, visceral dread. She instinctively squeezed the locket hanging from her neck. "Are you... are you okay?"

"Hey, guys," he said, his slurred voice missing its usual whip-like speed. He grinned, but it was lopsided and didn't reach his vacant eyes. "Sorry I'm late. Wasn't sure if I should drop everything and crash here instead of with Chloe." He swayed again, leaning heavily against the doorframe for support, his gaze drifting past Sarah to the interior of the apartment.

"Dude, you look like shit," Chris said bluntly, stepping forward, his own exhaustion momentarily forgotten in the face of Ben's horrifying appearance.

"Ben, what happened to you?" Maya asked, their voice tight with concern, while their hand instinctively reached for the protective amulets around their neck, their eyes wide with dawning horror.

"Ben" blinked slowly, his gaze unfocused, as if struggling to process their questions. "Just... tired," he mumbled, his voice a gravelly rasp. "Really tired. Can I... can I come in?"

He took a shuffling, unsteady step forward, towards the threshold of the doorway, towards the peachwood and line of salt Maya had sprinkled. Sarah, despite the wrongness, the screaming alarm bells in her head, felt a surge of pity. He looked awful. He needed help. He was her friend.

"Of course," she said, stepping back automatically to let him enter. "Come in, Ben. You're soaked. Let's get you warmed up."

As he lifted his foot to cross the salted threshold, the air suddenly crackled. He jerked back, his eyes wide in surprise. It was a violent, convulsive movement, as if he'd touched a live wire, an invisible barrier. A low hiss, like air escaping a punctured lung, or the sound a cornered animal might make, emanated from his throat.

He staggered back into the rain, his eyes—no longer dull and vacant—flashed with an unnatural, malevolent red light, like embers fanned in a blast of wind. The lopsided, sickly grin twisted into a horrifying snarl, revealing teeth that looked too long, too sharp, inhuman.

Then, with a speed that was terrifyingly unnatural, he turned and fled, his footsteps echoing eerily on the driveway as he disappeared into the darkness. A final, guttural growl faded away as it was swallowed by the storm.

Sarah, Maya, and Chris stared after him, frozen in a state of shocked, horrified disbelief.

"What... what the *fuck* was that?" Chris finally stammered, his face ashen.

"Guys, I... I don't think that was Ben," Sarah said.

She looked up to the peachwood hung over the door then back to her friends. Chris and Maya each nodded in silent understanding.

With a final glance into the storm, Sarah closed the door and locked it.

The silence in the house became a living thing, pressing in on Sarah, making it hard to breathe. The image of "Ben"—or whatever had been wearing his face—was seared into her mind—the sickly skin, the vacant eyes, that horrifying, unnatural snarl.

The peachwood above the door, or the salt, which had felt like such a flimsy defense moments ago, now seemed like the only thing that had stood between them and... *it*. The hand not holding the locket instinctively went to Auntie Lin's scarf, the scent of sandalwood and jasmine a flimsy anchor in the swirling chaos of her fear.

"If that was actually the Shepherd," Maya finally breathed, their voice trembling. They were clutching their tourmaline crystal so tightly their knuckles were white. "Then the wards... they stopped him. Or it. Whatever that was."

Chris was still staring at the closed door, his face a mask of disbelief and terror. The *tick-tick-tick* in his head, which Sarah could almost hear herself now, filled the void left by "Ben's" monstrous departure.

"It looked like him," Sarah said, her own voice barely audible. She replayed the way he'd recoiled from the threshold, the flash of red in his eyes over and over in her mind. Was that Ben's body being controlled like some freaky puppet show, or was it something pretending to be him? The thought made her stomach churn.

What had happened to her sarcastic, loyal friend? The flippant text message earlier now felt like a cruel taunt from the entity itself.

"We have to do something," Maya said, their gaze darting around the room as if expecting the Shepherd to materialize from the shadows. Their usual composure was frayed, their energy almost frantic. "We can't just sit here."

They wrung their hands, then their eyes lit up with a desperate idea.

"The hospital! We should call the hospital. Check on Chloe. And ask if Ben's there. Maybe he's still there—the *real* him—and he doesn't know what happened here."

Sarah looked at Maya. It was a long shot, a grasping at straws, but it was *something*. The alternative was to sit and wait, to let the fear consume them.

"You're right," Sarah agreed, though a cold knot of doubt sat in her stomach. If Ben was truly *taken* like Chloe, would he even be at the hospital? Or would he be like the thing that had just stood on their doorstep? Still, the slim chance that he's somehow still there, that he was safe, was a sliver of hope she couldn't ignore.

Maya pulled out their phone, their shaking fingers fumbling slightly as they dialed. Sarah watched, her breath held, as Maya asked to be put through to Chloe's ward, then inquired about her condition, their voice strained. A pause. "And... have you seen a young man, Ben? He might still be there... waiting with her."

Sarah studied Maya's face, trying to decipher the one-sided conversation. Maya's expression slowly crumpled.

"No... no, I understand. Okay. Thank you." They hung up, their hand dropping to their side as if the phone had suddenly become too heavy.

"Well?" Chris prompted, his voice raw.

Maya shook their head, eyes glistening. "The nurse said she hasn't seen Ben for hours. Then her voice got clipped before she hung up. All she said was, 'I have to go—we have a situation up here.'"

The fragile hope that had flickered within her died, extinguished by Maya's words. Sarah prayed that the situation at the hospital didn't involve Chloe. The darkness outside pressed closer, the storm a reflection of the turmoil raging within them. The *tick-tick-tick* grew louder, a mocking reminder of their dwindling time.

With a growing sense of helplessness, they realized there was nothing more they could do for Ben, not tonight. He was out there, somewhere in the storm-lashed city. Alone and vulnerable.

Exhaustion, heavy and profound, finally began to claim them. The adrenaline had worn off, leaving behind a bone-deep weariness and a gnawing, soul-crushing fear.

"We should try to get some sleep," Maya said finally, their voice trembling, though they tried to keep it steady. Their face was a mask of anxiety, the ticking in their head no doubt reaching a fever pitch. "Mr. Chen is working. We need to be rested... for whatever comes next."

No one argued. The thought of sleep though, caused panic to scratch at the door to Sarah's sanity. The prospect of facing Fén Yáng in her dream, in the vulnerable space between waking and oblivion made her sweat. But the thought of staying awake, listening to the storm and the insidious ticking, waiting for the demon to make its next move, perhaps to try the door again, seemed even worse.

They retreated to their beds, Sarah in her room, Maya and Chris opting to stay in the living room, closer to the warded door, closer to each other. The small, flimsy circle of firelight they'd created in the cave felt like a distant, impossible dream.

Sarah lay awake, thinking. Were Ben and Chloe, okay? And her father, who was uncharacteristically late—was he okay? Chloe was running out of time, and they needed Mr. Chen to hurry.

But a colder thought gripped her. The Shepherd was marking them, one by one. And she, for some terrifying, unknown reason, was being saved for last.

Chapter 24

The sickly green sky of the nightmare realm swirled and pulsed, a nauseating rhythm that made Sarah dizzy. One moment she was in her bed; the next, she was standing. The shift was seamless and disorienting, a lurch in reality that left her swaying.

Looking down, a wave of revulsion passed through her. Instead of the soft grass from her last visit, a foul carpet of blood-soaked fleece and slick, pink skin now formed the ground. The repulsive soil stretched out to the horizon. Gagging, she lifted a foot up and a string of viscous, flesh-colored fluid stretched from her sole before snapping. She covered her nose with a sleeve; the sickening smell of death was worse than the sight beneath her.

It was the same familiar place as before but changed in both subtle and not-so-subtle ways. Aside from the disgusting field of wool, there were a few new buildings placed at odd angles scattered around, more fences and a lot more mindlessly grazing sheep.

Her eyes snapped back to some buildings in the distance that were lying around like they were dropped haphazardly from the sky. She was startled when she realized they were recognizable, even though they were warped and perverted, there was no mistaking the ruined outlines. It was definitely Gu Mei. The position of each structure was off, but it was unmistakable, her ancestral village was here—or at least, some perverted replica of it.

Her eyes darted around the landscape, searching for any immediate sign of the Shepherd, but she was relieved not to find the demon. From past experience she knew not to let her guard down though; it was definitely out there. Somewhere.

The misplaced buildings loomed like grotesque monuments in the distance. Waiting. She decided that just standing around out in the open wasn't the smartest idea, so she took off towards the only place that felt "safe" in this nightmare—the imitation of Gu Mei. She tried hard to ignore the matted wool sucking at her bare feet with each step.

She studied her mother's house, which was canted at an impossible angle. She wondered if the ghost of her mother ever wandered there, exploring a well-known memory. Maybe her mother was there now.

Her eyes shifted over to the temple, which was unburied here in the nightmare, unlike the real one back in Gu Mei. She could just make out that the stone lions standing guard were weeping a thick black ichor. Despite the repulsive liquid oozing from the stone, she inexplicably felt a sense of peace emanating from it. She wondered if, maybe, instead of the home, Mei Lin's spirit was drawn to a place of tranquility that Auntie Lin provided growing up.

Each was a potential destination, or possibly a trap.

As she navigated a particularly dense thicket of gnarled, thorn-covered fences that shifted and writhed like living things, a noise caught her ears. It was faint at first, almost lost in the wind, but undeniably familiar. The calming chime of bells—the same ethereal bells back in the real Gu Mei.

A surge of hope flickered within her. Back in China, she had chosen to follow the rhythmic ticking that led her to her mother and the Relic, but here, now, was the opportunity to explore the alternative. Determined, she pushed through a gap in the thorny brambles, ignoring the barbs that tore at her clothes and skin, and stumbled into a small, unnaturally quiet hollow.

There, an old man stood amidst a field of grazing sheep. His semi-translucent form resembled smoke given human shape, the sickly green sky visible through his stooped shoulders. His clothes were the simple, worn garb of a traveling peddler from centuries past. Wisps of a long, grey beard clung to his chin, and his eyes, though ancient and filled with a profound sorrow, held a spark of weary recognition.

Standing patiently next to him was a dust-colored donkey, whose ribs protruded faintly beneath its thin hide. A brightly colored, though now faded, cart stood beside them both.

Recognition flashed in her eyes as he offered her a sad, knowing smile. It was *him*. The one she and her friends had seen on the rocky outcrop overlooking the road to Gu Mei. The one they thought was trying to warn them.

The donkey let out a soft, mournful bray, a strangely normal and comforting sound in this twisted landscape.

"You!" Sarah exclaimed in surprise as she bounded over to them. "I saw you, in Gu Mei," she said, looking over at the cart, where varying sized bells were tied along the top. "Were those your bells I heard at the ruins?"

Old Jian nodded slowly, his ghostly form wavering slightly, like heat haze above a summer road. He gave one of the bells a flick with his ghostly finger, releasing a musical note.

"Indeed, they were," he said, his voice a dry rustle, like autumn leaves skittering across stone. "I tried to guide and direct you, but the veil between worlds is strong, and sadly, the demon beat me to you. It pains me to say that I failed you then, child."

"Who are you?" she asked, stepping closer. For a stranger, his presence was strangely comforting and calming.

"I am just an old fool," he replied, still holding his sad smile. "The name is Jian. And this useless animal," he patted the donkey's neck, "is Chong." The donkey returned his look and let out an annoyed bray. Sarah couldn't help but smile too. But the moment of levity didn't last.

A sudden tremor ran through the fleshy ground, breaking their introductions short. The sky darkened for a moment as if a shadow passed overhead.

"It senses you," Jian hissed, his ethereal form flickering with alarm. "A lucid mind in its pasture... it is like a splinter in its flesh—felt but not yet seen. It will not tolerate it. Follow me! Stay low!" Jian urged, moving with a surprising swiftness for a spirit. Chong trotted silently beside him, the cart gliding over the foul ground.

Sarah scrambled after them, crossing the hollow, before ducking behind a thicket of writhing, thorny barriers that recoiled from Jian's ghostly presence. She ignored the few thorns that caught her clothing and peered through a gap in the vines, when she saw the Shepherd suddenly crest a distant hill—a towering, skeletal silhouette against the churning sky.

Fén Yáng paused at the top, searching the pasture for any sign of the intruder. Her heart stopped momentarily as its gaze swept over them, but it somehow didn't see them and continued looking. The Shepherd then lifted its arms into the air and bellowed an inhuman bleating sound that echoed across the pasture.

All around them, the grazing sheep froze, lifting their heads in unison. Their vacant eyes began to glow with a faint, malevolent red light. Sarah let out a small gasp when the sheep turned back towards the pasture. Gone was the empty look from before, replaced now with a freakish awareness.

"What the hell is this place?" Sarah whispered, pulling away from the fence, her heart hammering against her ribs.

"This is the Pasture," Jian replied, his voice a low rustle. "Its feeding ground, woven from the stolen memories and fears of its flock." He gestured with a trembling hand towards the sheep now moving with unnatural purpose, acting as the demon's eyes and ears. "They are the flock. Their spirits are being slowly consumed to sustain the demon."

She swept her gaze over the sheep and a strangled gasp caught in her throat. A hauntingly similar, glittery pink clip was fastened in the matted wool of one. On another, a similar pair of Ben's glasses were perched crookedly on its face.

"Are they...?" Sarah's voice trailed off.

"Your friends? Yes," Old Jian confirmed sadly. "Or specifically, their spirits. The Relic, when activated by the rhyme, opens a way for Fen Yáng to reach out, to *feed*."

"And my mother?" Sarah asked, tearing her eyes from the sheep and leaning closer to Jian, her voice tight with a desperate hope. "Mei-Lin? Is she here? Mr. Chen said she fought it."

A flicker of something akin to admiration crossed Old Jian's spectral face.

"Ah, Mei-Lin. A fierce spirit. Like her ancestor, Yu, but with more knowledge, more will." He paused, his gaze turning towards the distorted silhouette of her mother's house. "Yes, she is here. Trapped. Fén Yáng does not appreciate those who defy it. It takes a special pleasure in their torment."

Sarah's fists clenched.

"Where? How can I find—"

Her words were cut short as she gasped. A vine had extended from the fence and was slithering across her chest. She reached up in horror, grabbing at it, thorns cutting into her hand. She pulled, but it had already wrapped around her mother's locket on her neck and held fast. Beads of sweat began building on her forehead as panic began to set in.

"Easy, Xiao Láng," Jian said in a soft, soothing tone. "Steady yourself. I will be your *Shifu*—your teacher. I will show you the power you wield here."

More vines began snaking their way around her, their thorns cutting into her skin as they tightened. She struggled not to cry out, giving away their hiding spot as more and more grabbed her limbs.

"This place is made of memory and fear, Xiao Láng," he whispered, his voice urgent yet calm. "The demon is twisting them against you. You must twist them back. Command them."

A vine, larger than the rest, suddenly wrapped itself around her head and began to worm its way into her mouth. A frightened whimper escaped her as it squeezed inwards, the sharp thorns slicing at her lips. Blood began dripping from dozens of cuts over her body as she continued to struggle. She tried biting through the putrid vine in her mouth, but it was too hard.

"Close your eyes, Xiao Láng," Jian said in his calm manner. "The demon is imposing its will upon you. You can do the same. Visualize what *you* want."

Sarah's eyes were wide in terror as she choked on the vine pushing down her throat. But something about his calm voice, kept the panic away. Instead, she closed her eyes and focused on what he said. *Visualize what you want.*

She wanted the damn thing out of her throat.

She felt immediate relief. Her eyes flew open in disbelief. The vine remained wrapped around her, but it no longer wormed its way through her mouth. An exhilaration of power like she had never felt before filled her. She closed her eyes again and concentrated on the remaining vines.

The vines around her vanished.

She let out a low bark of a laugh in relief.

"Well done, Xiao Láng," Jian said, nodding, a huge grin on his face. "But we must hurry, the noise surely caught their attention."

Sarah peeked back through the opening in the fence, and sure enough, some sheep were trotting towards them.

Jian and Chong took off towards the temple in the distance, the cart pulled right behind them, their ethereal forms silent as they glided across the floor of flesh. Sarah didn't hesitate and quickly followed.

"How did I do that? What else can I do?" Sarah said in a low voice, as they continued to move from cover to cover. "With this power I mean. Can I just... will the demon to die?"

"Sadly, no," Jian chuckled. "It doesn't work that way. There *are* limits to your ability."

Sarah shuddered, but the resolve in her gaze didn't waver.

He stopped suddenly and crouched next to a warped and rotted ox cart that was covered in vines, waving for her to get low. Sarah's feet slipped on the slick wool beneath her. Luckily, Chong was solid enough to grab hold of, preventing her from falling into the muck. She gave him a quiet pat on the head in thanks, and he nudged her gently in response.

At first, she didn't see what caught his attention, but then two sheep emerged from behind another thicket of thorns. They moved with an eerie purpose, almost marching as they patrolled. Luckily, they didn't see or hear them and continued on, quickly moving out of sight.

"So," Sarah said as soon as the patrol was out of earshot. "Why am I different? Why am I aware?"

"That," Jian said slowly, holding up a finger, his gaze intense, "is because the demon, in its ancient cunning, made a... miscalculation. And where your mother's sacrifice comes into play."

"My mother's sacrifice?" she echoed.

Jian stood without answering, motioning for Sarah to move again. Sarah sighed and followed.

The group soon found themselves at the edge of Gu Mei. In the real village, the homes were well maintained and cared for, but here, in the nightmare, they were dilapidated and neglected. Most of the buildings were already collapsed and the ones that still stood weren't far behind. To Sarah, the village itself looked sick—as if it were decomposing.

They passed quickly through the central square, where it was quiet, and not a sheep in sight. As Sarah crouched from cover to cover, she suddenly realized why the village felt wrong. Besides the general degradation, and the lack of life, there was no dust here. She hated that dust but would have traded anything in this hellscape for it instead.

They climbed over a collapsed building, Jian's cart gliding over the stones as if weightless, and found themselves in front of the temple. Sarah, dusting off her hands, crouched just outside its familiar walls. Jian peeked over the lip for any signs of the demon or its flock.

"It is empty," Jian said, lowering himself next to her. "We will be safe here."

"Good," Sarah said, leaning against the stone wall. "I need a rest."

He pointed a wavering finger towards the distant, skeletal ruins that sat on a craggy hill, their silhouette a jagged tear against the sickly green sky. "Those ruins are an echo of the place where Fén Yáng's power was most potent in your world, where the bones of its first victim in this cycle lay, and where the object was recently unearthed. It is a place of recent trauma and strong connection for the demon."

Then he gestured towards the lopsided silhouette of Mei-Lin's house.

"Or it may be that her spirit is trapped in a place of deep personal significance, a place Fén Yáng has twisted into a prison of memory and regret. Her home. Maybe even the well. Places where her love for you, her fear for you, were strongest."

Sarah looked from the distant ruins to the warped image of her childhood home. Two terrible choices. Two potential traps. Sarah's blood ran cold at the thought of being back in those tight tunnels. The well. The narrow, suffocating darkness of the cave passage. The feeling of the walls closing in. It was bad enough in the real world but here where the demon could manipulate the landscape.

Sarah's knees almost gave out, but her unwavering resolve kept her standing.

"You must search within yourself to know for sure, Xiao Láng."

"If I do find her, can I even save her?" she asked. "I heard my mother found a weakness in the demon."

Old Jian nodded slowly. "Oh, she did. Mei-Lin was resourceful. She delved deep into the old lore, deeper than I ever could. She understood that Fén Yáng, for all its power, is an earth-bound entity. Its strength is rooted in the physical world, in the places it claims, in the objects it taints—like the lamp, like the well from which it may have first been summoned or drawn sustenance."

He looked directly at Sarah, his ancient eyes piercing.

"She discovered that Fén Yáng, despite its power, is bound by certain laws of nature. A spirit born of the earth could be returned *to* the earth. But what it required, I am not certain, other than a conduit... a willing spirit to guide the entity back, to seal the passage. A sacrifice."

Sarah's heart clenched. A sacrifice.

"My mother... the sacrifice you mentioned earlier...?"

"She intended to protect you," Old Jian said softly. "At any cost. She knew the risks. She knew the price. She was trying to perform the cleansing, to prepare the relic, when Fén Yáng realized her intent. It turned its full fury upon her. She managed to complete a portion, a shielding, but not the banishment."

Her mother's sacrifice. Sarah stared at Old Jian, the spectral peddler, her mind struggling to reconcile the image of her vibrant, laughing mother as a tormented spirit who had fought a demon and sacrificed herself to protect a child who wouldn't even remember the battle.

The full weight of her mother's love, her sacrifice, settled upon Sarah. She felt a surge of grief so profound it almost brought her to her knees, but with it came a steely determination. Sarah sat down, resting the back of her head against the cool stone wall, ignoring the foul slime beneath her.

Her mother had fought. Now, it was her turn.

"Wait," she said, straightening. "What shielding?"

His gaze flickered towards Sarah, filled with a strange intensity. "She used her remaining strength not to free herself, but to shield you. To place a partial ward upon a soul the demon had already brushed against."

Sarah's blood ran cold. *A soul the demon had already brushed against.* Her mother hadn't just been trying to protect her from a future threat; she had been trying to undo a damage already done, a connection already forged.

"She protected me?" Sarah asked in a whisper.

"She bought you time, child," Old Jian said softly. "She weakened the demon's claim on you, made you less susceptible to its immediate consumption. But the mark remains. And the entity... it is patient. It remembers. And I imagine it is angry." He looked towards the grotesque landscape. "And now, with the curse active again, with new souls feeding its power, it grows stronger. Your mother's sacrifice... it may not hold for much longer."

"Did she know I was connected to it? Even back then?" Sarah's voice was a raw whisper.

Old Jian nodded, his sorrowful eyes fixed on her. "Fén Yáng's touch, however slight, leaves a stain, like a taint on your spirit. The 'falling sickness' that later manifested... it was the festering of that initial wound, the demon's mark upon your spirit, a crack through which it hoped to one day reclaim you fully."

Her epilepsy.

Sarah's hand instinctively went to her head. All these years, she'd thought of her epilepsy as a weakness, a betrayal by her own body, a limitation. Instead, it was a curse, a scar from a battle she and her mother fought all those years ago. To first hear it from Mr. Chen and now Jian...

"*That*, however," Jian said, holding up a finger, then flashing Sarah a cunning smile. "*W*as its mistake."

Sarah frowned. "A mistake? How can a demon that powerful make a mistake?"

"Hubris, child," he said with a small chuckle. "For all its careful planning, it didn't anticipate... you. All of the lamp's mechanisms are designed to lull, to hypnotize, to weaken the victim's will and draw their spirit into the fold." He paused, his gaze piercing. "But for you... for one marked by the 'falling sickness' that Fén Yáng itself inflicted... what are flickering lights? What are repetitive, rhythmic sounds and shadows?"

Recognition dawned on Sarah, cold and shocking. The plane. The nightmare where the cabin lights winked out one by one, the terrifying, rhythmic ticking that had preceded her seizure. Chloe's livestream—the way the spinning sheep shadows had seemed to intensify, to writhe, just before the nausea and the overwhelming headache had forced her to look away. The very triggers that could send her own brain into chaos.

"My seizures," she breathed. "The lamp triggers my seizures."

"Indeed." Old Jian confirmed, a note of grim satisfaction in his voice.

He waved for her to follow him as he began walking, his eyes constantly on the lookout for any danger. Chong faithfully behind, tugging the cart along with him, the bells eerily silent. She struggled to stand up on the slick floor, then sprinted to catch up to Old Jian, falling in step beside him. She glanced back at Chong's cart and marveled at how the wheels glided over the vile soft wool.

"Fén Yáng," Jian continued. "Chose the lamp, thus creating a paradox for its claim on *you*. The very ritual designed to ensnare souls, the flickering light and rhythmic motion of the carousel, the elements that hypnotize and draw others into its full thrall... in you, they induce the very condition the demon itself bestowed upon you. A seizure."

"When your friends performed the ritual, or at the very least were exposed to its echo by watching it, their minds were open, vulnerable. They were drawn completely into the pasture, their consciousness submerged, becoming part of Fén Yáng's mindless flock. But you, Xiao Láng... when the lamp's ritual begins, when the shadows dance and the ticking starts, the mark of the demon upon you—your epilepsy—reacts. The seizure—the electrical storm in your brain, it *shatters* the ritual's hold before it can fully take you. It acts as a shield of sorts."

Sarah stared at him, her mind reeling. Her epilepsy. The curse that had defined so much of her life, the source of so much fear and shame was actually a protective shield? Her greatest vulnerability, her greatest shame, was a unique, if painful, strength. It didn't stop Fén Yáng from pulling her into this nightmare realm, but it prevented her from becoming one of the lost sheep. It allowed her this terrifying lucidity, this agonizing awareness.

"So, when Chloe... when she used the device..." Sarah struggled to articulate the thought. "And when I watched her livestream, the flickering, the clicking... that's why I felt so sick? Why I looked away just before...?"

"It was your body's defense, child. Imprinted by your mother's sacrifice and the demon's own mark. Your mother's love, in a way, turned the demon's own curse against itself, forging your affliction into an unexpected, albeit perilous, armor."

Sarah stopped short in front of the weeping statues, her feet slipping in the damn muck again. She used Chong's head for support; a fact the donkey didn't seem to mind.

Perilous armor. The phrase echoed in Sarah's mind. She was walking this nightmare landscape with her eyes open, while her friends were lost, unthinking. But she was still *here*. Still *aware*. And the Shepherd was still hunting.

"You are still at risk though, Xiao Láng," Jian said. "Even though this is a place between places, what happens here is real. You have some control, some power, but make no mistake, Fén Yáng is furious you have resisted, and it is stronger than you."

"I can't hide," she said. "My mother needs me, I—"

A rustling from behind them made her stop and spin around. There, emerging from some thorny bushes, was a sheep. It stepped out and froze when it saw them. It didn't make a noise or move, it just stood there, its glowing eyes staring unblinking. The lack of response was more terrifying than any alarm it could have made.

"It knows we are here!" Jian said in a loud panicked voice. He glanced around, trying to find a place to run, or hide. "Get inside the temple! Hurry, Xiao Láng!"

He turned towards the weeping statues without waiting to see if she followed his command and started to mumble something under his breath. She didn't hesitate though and sprinted for the temple doors. Chong and his cart following behind.

When she turned around at the entrance, she watched as Jian began waving his hands through the black ichor dripping from the stone lions, still whispering under his breath. Across the courtyard, another red eyed sheep stepped through the bushes, then another. Then even more appeared from down the road.

"Whatever you are doing, you better hurry, Jian!" she yelled.

He didn't respond. He kept mumbling and waving.

She caught sudden movement in the distance that was too fast, too large to be a sheep. A dark blur heading straight for them at a terrifying speed.

"It's coming, Jian!"

As if right on cue, the black ichor began to spread out from the statues. At first, it was a thin tendril, but the tendrils started to flatten and stretch in midair. As it expanded more and more, it began to cover the temple around them, forming a glistening dome. It made a wet slopping noise as it rolled over the stones, stretching like oil, distorting the green sky outside into a sickly ripple.

Sarah gasped in wonder.

The temple plunged into darkness as the ichor spread over them, blocking out most of the sickly green light from above. The thin fluid continued up and over the temple until they were completely enclosed.

Jian stepped back to examine his work and nodded before turning and racing towards Sarah.

"This won't hold for long," he said, running. "Inside, quickly."

Sarah was ushered inside just as something large smashed against the wet curtain behind them, causing the ground to shake. The strange liquid shield didn't budge though; luckily it was more solid than it appeared. Jian closed the doors quickly as another collision rang out, dust falling around them from above. Darkness swallowed them as the only light source from outside was cut off.

A loud, frustrated bellow rang out across the pasture.

They were safe. But now they were trapped.

CHAPTER 25

Debris rained over Sarah as The Temple shook again. She coughed as she breathed in the dirty air. Unable to see in the dark, she stumbled away from the door, tripping over something hard on the floor.

"Jian!" she called into the darkness, her voice shaking. Even though she had just met the man, the sudden thought of being alone without him and Chong terrified her.

"I am here, Xiao Láng," Jian answered gently nearby, instantly putting her at ease. "Remember our first lesson on control."

She closed her eyes and focused, trying to steady her heavy breathing.

"In this realm," he continued, "you can create just as you can destroy. Focus your will like before. Do you wish to see? Then visualize what you desire."

What she desired. She clung to those words. She hated the dark—it reminded her of the day the Still Alive Five was formed. She concentrated on that thought, on that hate, and started to will it away. She didn't care how; she just wanted the darkness gone. A low hum reverberated around her, then the floor trembled, sending a tickling sensation up her legs. She *pushed* against the gloom with her mind.

"No!" Jian cried out in panic, cutting through her concentration. "Child, stop! Do not *unmake*! Create light, don't destroy the dark! Candles, Xiao Láng, think of candles!"

Candles?

She flinched as a loud splintering crack rang out. Her eyes shot open and found that The Temple was now bathed in the soft lighting from dozens of newly lit candles along the walls. The dancing flames cast disorienting shadows that could be seen through Jian's ethereal form. He was standing across from her, looking down with terror in his eyes.

Following his gaze, she gasped at the sight. A dark fissure, jagged as a lightning strike, split the floor between them, tearing a darkness deeper than The Temple's gloom. A wave of grave-cold air washed over them, mysteriously carrying the faint scent of ozone with it.

Confused, Sarah stepped away from the fissure, bumping into a trembling Chong. Jian's frightened eyes softened slightly when he realized she had calmed her thoughts then he let out a ghostly breath in relief.

"What...what happened?" she asked, with wide eyes.

Jian took a deep breath. "Are you familiar with Yin and Yang?"

Sarah nodded.

"This... place, it both exists and does not at the same time."

"A place between places..." she breathed, remembering what he told her earlier.

"Exactly," he said, stroking his thin beard. "Just like Yin and Yang, opposites yet balanced. To force your willpower in a positive way, or to create, is balanced. To push a negative thought or destroy is unbalanced."

Sarah shook her head confused. "I don't understand."

Jian stroked his long wispy beard with one hand. For the first time since meeting him, he seemed flustered.

"These lights you created," he said, gesturing to the lit candles along the walls. "Are additions from your spirit. The darkness is a product of the nightmare realm itself. Just like you cannot simply erase the demon out of existence here, you cannot remove darkness either. To do so would destroy the very realm, including you and everyone's soul trapped here."

"But what about the vines from earlier? I willed those away."

"Ah, good question, Xiao Láng. The vines were a manifestation of Fén Yáng, not the nightmare realm itself."

"I think I understand," she lied, studying the rift she had created.

"The demon is not powerful enough to create such a place as this, it has merely found a way to... repurpose it, I suppose. Though, the laws of the Universe are beyond my simple understanding."

Sarah brushed some dust from her face, then studied The Temple around her. As her eyes adjusted to the low light of the candles, she realized the stone walls weren't empty, they were covered in vast, faded murals. She carefully stepped around the deep fissure in the ground and walked over to study the paintings.

Her breath hitched. The artwork was incredibly detailed and beautiful. They depicted what looked to be a millennia-long war. In one panel, a serpentine, dragon-like creature rose from a river, its claws snatching villagers from a sinking barge. In another, a monstrous wolf with matted, fleece-like fur and burning red eyes tore through a line of spearmen. A third showed a large sea creature with long tentacles and a chitinous beak sinking an old ship.

"It really can change its shape," Sarah whispered, tracing the outline of the dragon with a trembling finger.

"Yes," Jian murmured, his spectral gaze sweeping over the violent tableaus. "It is a creature of the earth, a *Yaoguai*. A shapeshifter. It preys on belief and fear. A village that fears the river dragon will see a dragon. One that fears the forest wolf will see a wolf."

Sarah's eyes scanned the murals, searching for any hint of victory. In most, the humans were losing, their bodies broken. But in a small, damaged corner of the dragon mural, a monk stood on a cliffside, striking a massive temple bell. From the bell, golden, concentric rings of energy pushed the monster back into the water.

"They fought back," Sarah breathed.

"They always fought back," Jian said proudly. "With blessed iron, with peachwood, with faith... and sometimes, with sound. They were all fighters, like you Xiao Láng."

Sarah turned from the mural, her brow furrowed. "Why do you call me that? *Xiao Láng*? Little wolf."

"What else would I call you?" Jian asked, his eyes filled with a deep seriousness.

"Mr. Chen... he calls me *Xiao Yáng*. Little Sheep."

"I've no doubt this Mr. Chen is a good man," Jian said with a smile. "He sees a gentle soul caught in a storm, a lamb that needs a shepherd for protection."

Jian took a step closer to her.

"But I am a spirit. I see differently. I saw you command the thorns to release you. A sheep does not do that. A sheep is prey. A wolf... a wolf bites back."

"But I'm not," Sarah replied with a shake of her head. "I was terrified. I *am* terrified. I feel like a sheep."

"Fear is the water the wolf drinks before the hunt." He gestured to the murals again. "Fén Yáng has spent millennia conditioning its prey to think of themselves as nothing but a mindless flock. It is how it feeds, how it wins."

Jian's eyes suddenly hardened as they bore into hers.

"You are a wolf walking among the sheep. It is time you see it too."

Sarah frowned. She wasn't entirely convinced.

Outside The Temple, the sheep began to bleat an annoying chorus that grated on her nerves. It was then she noticed the shaking had stopped. Had Fén Yáng given up, or was it looking for another way in?

"It is plotting," Old Jian answered, understanding the look in her eyes. "Drawing its power while it waits for us to make a mistake."

She almost believed him, but she caught his quick glance at the hole she created. He quickly looked back at her; his ghostly face etched with a guilt that transcended time.

"Do not blame yourself. It is my fault, Xiao Láng. In this place, I am the only guide you have—a poor master for a student with such power."

"What do you mean?"

"I was the one who started this cycle," he confessed, his voice a dry rasp of regret. "I gave the lamp to your ancestor, Yu. Because I am a coward. It... felt wrong. Dark and cold. It whispered in my sleep. I wanted to be rid of it, so I gave it to a desperate woman in exchange for a sip of water. I knew it was dangerous, and I did nothing. My spirit, and that of my faithful Chong, became tethered to its fate, bound to witness the sorrow that I..."

His voice trailed off as a guttural laugh bellowed from the rift in the center of The Temple. Sarah spun towards the noise, where a reddish glow appeared in the hole. The light grew brighter and brighter as the horrible mocking laughter became louder.

A long, pointed claw, black as obsidian, hooked over the edge of the pit. Then another. Slowly, horribly, the Shepherd began to emerge. Its elongated sheep skull, slick with the same black ichor as The Temple guardians, rose from the darkness. The two points of malevolent red light in its sockets burned through the gloom, ignoring the spectral form of Jian and locking onto the one living, breathing soul in the room. Onto Sarah. Its jaw unhinged in a silent, grotesque grin.

Sarah was paralyzed; her breath caught in her throat. This was it. The Shepherd had found her, and she had accidentally created the opening it needed.

"No," Old Jian whispered. He looked from the emerging demon to Sarah's pale face. The centuries of regret in his eyes hardened into a diamond-sharp resolve. "Not again. I will not stand by and watch."

He turned to her, his vaporous form suddenly blazing with a pale, determined light. "Find your mother. I will buy you an escape!"

He quickly spun towards his cart and with a practiced flick of his wrist he rang one of his bells. The sound was a high-pitched chime that echoed in the stone hall before feeding back on itself, growing in intensity.

The Shepherd cried out in pain.

He flicked another bell, this one slightly lower pitched, adding to the resonating hum of the first bell. The two rings overlapping each other into a crescendo that hurt Sarah's ears. The Temple groaned and shook.

"Take Chong and run!" Jian shouted, as he rang another bell.

The Temple began to fracture, sending pieces of stone raining down around them. The Shepherd, still standing at the edge of the rift, screamed in pain while covering its ears with its claws. One of the doors to the temple suddenly shattered from the pressure of stones collapsing on it, sending splinters of wood flying.

Jian shoved her hard towards the new opening, the force of his ghostly push surprisingly solid. As she stumbled back, he slapped Chong on the rear, sending the donkey running after her. He grabbed the back of the cart and pushed, charging *towards* the demon. With a shout, Jian leaped onto the rolling cart, grabbing the largest, most ornate bell.

Jian gave Sarah one last smile before swinging at the last bell with all his might. Sarah turned and ran as fast as she could towards the gap in stone, when the sound from Jian's final bell hit her.

It did not ring. It *exploded* with pure, resonant sound. A shock-wave of silver light and deafening noise erupted from the bell, slamming into the Shepherd. The demon shrieked—a high, piercing sound of static and grinding stone—and recoiled, its form flickering as the pure tone disrupted its hold on the pasture.

The sonic blast tore through The Temple like a tsunami. The ceiling split, the walls groaned. The Shepherd, stunned and disoriented, stumbled back into the gaping hole.

Sarah and Chong were thrown into the air by the shockwave. Stones rained down around them as they flew through the air, Chong braying helplessly. She flailed her arms just as she and Chong were thrown out of The Temple, the massive lintel above the doorway crashing down where they had just been. An explosion of stone and dust erupted from behind them as the temple collapsed. Sarah hit the foul woolen earth hard and rolled from the momentum, as pieces of stone crashed around her. Large pieces just narrowly missing her.

Chong landed hard next to her, bounced and came to rest on top of her before slowly sliding off. Dazed, the two of them lay there, unmoving in the muck, trying to catch their breath as small pebbles showered them.

Finally, her ears ringing, Sarah pushed herself up and gulped at the sight. The Temple was nothing but a pile of groaning, settling rubble. She shook her head, unable to comprehend how close she had been to being buried—like Jian and the Shepherd were. She looked up towards the swirling green clouds and silently thanked the brave Jian. The demon was gone—for now.

A shuffling sound reminded her that she wasn't out of the woods yet. She looked over at the sheep. The red light in their eyes had faded to a dull glow. They stood frozen for a moment, confused, the Shepherd's controlling consciousness momentarily shattered. But it didn't last long.

The sheep shook their heads, as if clearing cobwebs from their mind, before turning their focused gaze back on her. They stepped closer as they surrounded her, hunger filling their eyes.

She scrambled backwards, her hands slipping in the wet fleshy soil. A dust-colored blur suddenly shot past her with the sound of a desperate, defiant bray.

It was Chong.

He charged straight into the flock with a fury, his teeth tearing flesh and wool, his back legs kicking with such force they shattered skulls. The sheep turned their attention from Sarah towards the crazed animal. The ferocious assault momentarily distracted the flock, which fell back in confusion, creating an opening.

Sarah didn't hesitate.

She jumped up and ran, diving straight through the preoccupied flock. Sheep towards the back noticed her escaping and tried to cut her off, but she twisted out of the way without slowing down. She almost lost her footing when one particular sheep with a pink hair-clip lunged for her, its teeth snapping at her thigh, but she narrowly dodged it and continued on.

With a cry of triumph, she broke through the last of the sheep and into open pasture.

Her smile died on her face as a cry of utter pain and anguish erupted from behind her. She looked back just in time to witness the sea of red-stained wool part for a second. For a single, heartbreaking instant, she saw Chong's bloody face. His eyes, no longer frightened, were locked on her, calm and resolute. Then the flock closed in, and he was gone.

"No!" Sarah cried out.

She hesitated. Torn between helping and fleeing, a wild cry of rage caught in her throat. Jian and Chong's sacrifice had bought her a chance—a chance she couldn't squander. As much as it pained her not to fight, Sarah knew there was no time for heroics.

With a final, choked sob, she turned from the slaughter and fixed her gaze on the prize her new friends had died for: the lopsided, nightmarish silhouette of her mother's house.

CHAPTER 26

The final sounds of Old Jian and Chong haunted Sarah as she plodded along towards her mother's home. Soon the destroyed temple faded in the distance behind her along with the last of the trailing sheep. A cold resolve was beginning to displace the initial shock. She was no longer a sheep meandering aimlessly in a field of secrets, she was a wolf on the hunt.

The ground beneath her bare feet, the grotesque carpet of blood-flecked fleece, squelched and shifted on its own, as if the very earth was a dying animal. She shifted her attention from the vile carpet and focused on the distorted silhouette of her mother's house which was perched precariously on a lopsided hillock. The structure was a broken mockery of the real home back in Gu Mei.

She knew that this place, once a symbol of love and connection, was now likely being used as a prison for her mother's spirit. The well in its courtyard—no doubt a mirror of the one from which the Relic was born—felt less like a feature and more like bait.

She took a deep breath to steady herself and immediately regretted it, the foul air—a mix of wet wool, decay, and that faint, unsettling metallic tang—made her gag anew.

Sarah took another careful step towards the house, and the pasture suddenly awoke. The gnarled, thorny fences shifted, their branches scraping together, then reaching out like skeletal arms, barring her path. The ground beneath the wool rippled, making each step a treacherous hazard. Illusions flickered at the periphery of her vision: Chloe's face, pale and vacant, her eyes staring blankly from the matted wool of a nearby sheep; Ben's glasses, cracked and bloodied, lying half-buried in the filth; Maya's protective amulets, tarnished and broken, scattered amongst the thorns.

The Shepherd had her scent.

"No," Sarah gritted through clenched teeth, pushing the horrifying images away. "You won't break me."

The path—if it could even be called that—leading up to the house began to narrow. The air grew thick, heavy, pressing in on her from all sides. It was a familiar sensation, one that always preceded the crushing grip of her claustrophobia. The sickly green sky pressed lower, the swirling clouds taking on indistinct, leering faces that sneered down at her. The thorny fences closed in, scraping at her skin, tearing at her clothes, forming a suffocating tunnel.

Her breath hitched. Her heart started hammering against her ribs. The walls of the thorny passage began to pulse, to breathe, to *constrict*. She could feel the familiar tightness in her chest, the rising panic that threatened to steal her air, to paralyze her.

She forced herself to take a ragged breath, then another. She focused on the image of her mother's face, the strong, smiling woman from her memories, the woman who had sacrificed everything to protect her. That image became a buoy keeping her afloat.

Taking inspiration from Old Jian's teachings earlier, she closed her eyes, shutting out the maddening whispers on the wind and pictured the peachwood branch Mr. Chen had given her. She focused on its smooth, cool surface, its faint, clean scent. A ward. A shield.

She imagined its protective energy surrounding her, pushing back the encroaching darkness, widening the suffocating passage.

She opened her eyes and took a sharp, involuntary intake of foul air through her teeth. Her hand, empty a moment before, now gripped a solid, very real peachwood branch. The branch pulsed with a defiant warmth that pushed back the darkness around her.

The thorny walls began to recede, just enough that she could squeeze through. The crushing pressure in her chest let up. There was no time to marvel at her newfound power; she just pushed forward, one painful step at a time, ignoring the thorns that ripped at her skin and the whispers that slithered at the edge of her hearing.

She ducked under an overhang of vines and gasped, sliding to a halt. Hundreds of sheep, standing double file and facing each other, lined the path to her mother's house. They stood there, unmoving, watching her with an unnerving, collective intelligence. They didn't seem interested in stopping her, just on waiting.

She swallowed. The only way was through the gauntlet. She took a careful step forward, her muscles tense as she remembered what happened to Chong; but the sheep didn't move. She picked up her pace, eager to get past the flock. Sweat dripped from her forehead as she inched by sheep after sheep. If they decided to attack...

"Your mother's not here, little lamb..." a slow guttural voice bleated from the flock. *"She's lost... forgotten... part of the flock now..."*

Her head spun around, searching for the Shepherd, but he was nowhere to be seen.

"So much pain... Just let me sleep Sarah... why can't you mind your own business...?" another voice, a twisted mockery of Chloe's, giggled.

Chloe?

"I'd make a joke, but... you already are one." The contorted imitation of Ben mocked from somewhere in the flock.

She glanced at a nearby sheep and its jaw moved, releasing a twisted mimicry of Maya. *"You are so irritating. Always acting like the victim."*

Sarah let out a terrified cry, recoiling from the horror. The sheep all began to chuckle an obscene imitation of a human's laugh. Gritting her teeth, she tried to ignore them, focusing on her destination instead. As terrifying as they were, she knew they were just tricks of the demon. She knew there was a sliver of truth to the words—a fact that stung—but she refused to let the poison take root.

Then a new voice slithered in from the flock.

"Sarah... my sweet xiao tiānshǐ *."*

It was her mother's, gentle and warm, the sound she had chased in her dreams for years. Tears instantly welled in her eyes, blurring the malformed landscape. For a single, fragile moment, she believed.

"I died for you. Please, turn around." The words continued, still filled with warmth, but covered in a sweetness that felt... slimy. The gentle cadence began to stretch, the vowels elongating unnaturally, like a recording played too slow. *"Why can't you just be a good girl and listen?"*

"No!" Sarah cried. "You aren't real!"

"Of course I am real. You must leave Sarah!"

"I... I can't, Mom," Sarah stammered. "I need your help."

"My help?" The warmth in the tone began to curdle, flattening into a cold, mocking tone. *"How dare you! I gave everything for you,"* it hissed, the syllables sharpening into venomous points. The voice was deepening, losing its feminine quality, becoming a resonant, gravelly thing that vibrated in the air around her.

Then, the memory shattered completely. The bellow exploded from the flock, no longer a whisper but a deafening, monstrous bellow that was both a sheep's bleat and a rockslide. The sound ripped through the pasture, filled with ancient, bottomless rage.

"YOU SELFISH BRAT!"

Sarah flinched, tears rolling down her cheek. It had almost fooled her. Clenching her fists, she wiped the salty liquid away angrily and focused on placing one foot in front of the other. If the demon thought it was breaking her, it was sorely mistaken. Its taunts only caused anger to swell inside her, a deep-seated bubble of resolve rising to the surface like lava in a volcano. For so long she had been hiding from herself, afraid of the past, ashamed of what she was. She was determined to end this cycle.

Finally, scratched and bleeding, she burst out of the thorny passage and into the warped courtyard. The air here was even heavier, colder, making her already labored breathing even more difficult. The house loomed before her, its windows like vacant, staring eyes, its doorway a gaping, shadowed maw. The scent of jasmine, cloying and sweet, battled with the overwhelming stench of decay.

The well—not quite where it was in the real Gu Mei—sat in the center of the courtyard, a dark and silent beacon. The heavy wooden lid was slightly askew, a sliver of impenetrable blackness visible beneath. It was so dark it felt more like a void, a place where light itself died. Just like that strange vision she had at the real well. The faint ticking sound, the one caused by that cursed Relic, emanated from its depths, a rhythmic, hypnotic pulse.

Sarah approached it cautiously, her every instinct screaming at her to turn back, to flee. This was a place of power for Fén Yáng, a place of evil. But it was also where her mother's spirit might be trapped.

As she neared the edge, the ground beneath the matted wool became slick, almost greasy. The clicking from the well intensified, vibrating through the soles of her bare feet, up her legs, into her very bones. She felt a strange, irresistible pull, a hypnotic beckoning, urging her closer, closer...

She leaned over the stone lip, her heart pounding and pushed the wooden lid off. It slid easily, making surprisingly little sound, before thudding to the ground. She peered down into the inky blackness.

It was deeper than any well should be, an impossible abyss that stretched down into the very bowels of this nightmare realm. A cold, damp air, thick with the smell of grave soil and something ancient and foul, rose to meet her, making her nostrils burn.

Then she heard a faint, choked whisper, from the depths.

"*Sarah...?*"

Again, it sounded like her mother—trembling and filled with fatigue, but with a hint of hope and surprise. This didn't seem like the mocking imitation from earlier; this felt truly *hers*.

"Mom?" Sarah cried, her voice cracking. "Mom, I'm here! I'm here to help you!"

A scraping sound echoed from deep within the well. Then, slowly, a hand emerged from the darkness, clawing its way over the stone lip. Skeletal fingers, nails broken and caked with dirt, gripped the edge with a desperate strength. The skin was a pale, translucent gray, stretched tight over bone, mapped with a network of dark, spidery veins.

Sarah stumbled back, bile rising in her throat at the hideous sight. The bright, cheerful woman from her memories was gone. In her place was this tortured obscenity.

Another hand followed, then a withered arm, then a hunched shoulder. Slowly, painfully, a decaying figure began to pull itself from the darkness. It was her mother, but ravaged, rotten, her body emaciated, her clothes tattered and filthy, the remnants of the vibrant silk dress Sarah had seen in the photographs were a disgusting brown. Her once beautiful black hair was thin, matted, streaked with a lifeless gray.

But her eyes, though sunken and shadowed, weren't vacant. In their dark, tormented depths, something flickered. Her soft gaze swept over Sarah, a flicker of a mother's worry still shining in their depths.

"Māmā?" Sarah whispered, more tears streaming down her face, the sight a fresh, excruciating wound upon her already grieving heart.

Mei-Lin's decayed hand, skeletal and trembling, reached towards Sarah, her dark, hollow eyes filled with an agony that transcended death. "Run, Xiao Láng... run... it's a trap..." The slow, raspy words came out in a desperate, urgent plea. Each breath a painful test of will.

But Sarah couldn't run. Not now. Not when her mother was right there, inches away, a ravaged shell of the woman she had longed for her entire life. The initial wave of horror, the revulsion at the decayed form, was quickly overwhelmed by a desperate, aching love.

"Mom!" Sarah choked out, tears streaming down her face, the salt causing the scratches on her cheeks to sting. "Mom, no. I found you. I found you." She sobbed in defiance, and took a hesitant step closer, ignoring the stench of the grave that clung to her mother's spirit. "I'm here. I'm going to help you."

A faint roar rumbled its way up from the bottom of the well. The demon knew she had found her mother and was coming. It sounded distant for now, but they both knew it was getting closer. They didn't have much time.

A flicker of fierce, protective love, sparked in Mei-Lin's shadowed eyes. Her lipless mouth worked, and this time a sliver of strength was behind it. "Sarah... my brave little wolf..." The voice was fragmented, but it was *hers*. "You should not... be here. I saved you... protected you. Please."

"I had to come, Mom," Sarah said. "I know about Fén Yáng. About the Relic. Old Jian told me. You... you found a way to fight it, didn't you? A ritual?"

Mei-Lin nodded, a simple, slow movement that made sickening popping sounds as tendons snapped. "Yes... a way... to bind it. To seal it." Her rotting form unraveled before Sarah's eyes, skin falling off in wet patches, pus oozing, and one of her eyes, detaching from whatever held it, began a slow, grotesque slide down her cheek. "But it must be done... in both realms. Both here," she gestured weakly at the nightmarish pasture, "and in the... waking world. Together. A mirror ritual. It must be trapped... *underground*... in both."

Trapped underground. In both realms. Sarah's mind raced. The cave. The well. But how?

"I tried," Mei-Lin moaned, a fresh wave of anguish contorting her decayed features. "But... I couldn't reach it... *here*. Not like this. Not like you. You, Sarah... are special... the mark it left on you... it allows you to walk this pasture with open eyes. You... you can *act* here—and it hates you for it."

Sarah's heart pounded. Her epilepsy. Her curse. It was the key. The reason her mother had failed, and the reason she might succeed.

"But how, Mom?" Sarah pressed, sensing a shift in the oppressive atmosphere, a subtle darkening of the already sickly green sky. "How do I do it? What's the ritual?"

"The ritual must... be performed somewhere that... resonates with you, somewhere... personal," Mei-Lin said between gasps, pointing at Sarah's heart with her bony hand. "And I believe... the Shepherd hates itself, hates... seeing itself. Even though... it wasn't in any of... the texts, I always... had a suspicion. Demons... are products of their own... weaknesses, and the Shepherd is a shape-shift—"

Mei-Lin's remaining eye suddenly widened in stark terror. She spun around, towards the gaping maw of the well. "No time..." she rasped. "It's here..." Her voice dissolved into a choked gasp. She turned back to Sarah. "I love you—"

Before Sarah could react, before she could ask another question, a torrent of massive, bony, black arms, slick with black ichor and tipped with razor-sharp obsidian claws, erupted from the depths of the well. They were impossibly large, impossibly strong, moving with a terrifying, predatory speed.

They wrapped around Mei-Lin's fragile, rotting form, crushing her in their wretched embrace. Bones snapped. With a wet pop, her other eye detached, then swung uselessly from its exposed nerves. Mei-Lin let out a gurgling, agonizing scream, before she was violently ripped back down into the blackness of the well.

"MOM!" Sarah shrieked, lunging forward, her hands outstretched.

But it was too late. Her mother was gone, again. Swallowed by the abyss. She clenched her jaw. A burning rage began to boil inside her, causing her cheeks to turn a fiery red. It was a wave of pure hatred that frightened even her.

And then, the arms came for her.

They shot out from the well like striking serpents, coiling around her ankles, her wrists, her waist, their touch icy cold, their grip like bands of steel. Sarah screamed, a raw, primal sound of terror, and defiance, struggling against their relentless pull.

One of the claws, sharp as a shard of volcanic glass, raked across her forearm, tearing through her sleeve, ripping a searing line of pain. Hot blood, shockingly real even in this nightmare realm, spilled from the wound, staining the matted wool beneath her.

A monstrous, inhuman sound ripped through the air, a nasty parody of a sheep's bleating, amplified a thousand times, vibrating through Sarah's bones, rattling her skull. The sound, the very essence of the demon, echoed through the pasture, a chorus of pure, unadulterated malice.

She was being dragged, inexorably, towards the dark opening of the well. She kicked and thrashed, clawing at the arms, but their grip was too strong and the ground too slick. The stone lip of the well scraped against her back, the cold, damp air from its depths washing over her, thick with the stench of decay and ancient, unimaginable evil.

The world narrowed to the black, suffocating opening of the well. She was pulled over the edge, into the abyss with a final cry.

She fell.

And fell.

And fell.

The darkness was absolute, a crushing void that pressed in on her from all sides. The well was impossibly deep, a bottomless pit leading to the very heart of the nightmare. There was no air, no light, no sound but the frantic hammering of her own heart and the faint, fading echo of Fén Yáng's monstrous bleating.

The walls began to close in.

The stone, or whatever nightmare substance formed the shaft of the well, pulsed, began to breathe, to constrict around her. Her claustrophobia, a lifelong torment, a fear her mother had shared, a vulnerability Fén Yáng clearly knew and delighted in exploiting, surged with a vengeance.

The passage narrowed, the walls scraping against her shoulders, hips, and chest. She ricocheted from one side to the other, the cold, damp stone a series of brutal impacts against her skin. The pressure squeezed the air from her lungs, stealing her breath. Panic, raw and primal, clawed at her throat. She was slowly being trapped. Squeezed from each side. Buried alive.

Her lungs burned. Black spots danced before her eyes. The last vestiges of her consciousness, her very sanity, began to shatter under the unbearable weight. The walls were inches from her face, but unseen in the absolute darkness, the pressure unendurable.

Just as the last spark of her awareness threatened to wink out, as the crushing darkness prepared to swallow her whole, a searing white light exploded down below her in the well.

"The wood, Sarah!" Her mother screamed, a final sound of defiance in Fén Yáng's hold. Then, with the fading light, she was gone—a final sacrifice to save her child.

The peachwood branch! In the back of her fading mind, she realized she was still holding the branch. With the last of her remaining power, and emboldened by her mother's sacrifice, she stabbed the branch into the wall of the well and let out a primal scream.

A deep roar of frustration erupted all around her.

Sarah bolted upright in her bed with a strangled scream tearing from her throat, her body drenched in a cold sweat, her arm burning with a searing pain. She gasped for air, her lungs aching, her heart hammering against her ribs as if trying to escape her chest.

She was awake. She was back. But the terror, the claustrophobic horror of the well, the image of her mother being dragged into the abyss, the chilling certainty of her own failure clung to her like a suffocating shroud. The experience had been more real, more terrifying, than any dream she had ever known. She had faced the Shepherd, and she had now seen its power firsthand. But her mother, with her last breath, had given her a map.

The Shepherd had wounded the wolf, but for the first time, the wolf knew exactly where to find its throat.

Chapter 27

Sarah winced in pain, clutching at her arm where The Shepherd's claw had torn her flesh in the dream. She half-expected to find blood and torn skin but found only her half-healed scar. The cut she'd received in the ruins of Gu Mei had been fading away to a faint red line and no longer tender to the touch, but the nightmare had made it burn anew.

Outside, the storm was raging with undiminished fury, wind and rain lashing against her windowpane, a chaotic symphony that matched the tempest inside her. Below the burning anger in the pit of her stomach sat the cold acceptance of defeat. Again, she'd found her mother, only to watch her ripped away. Maybe for good this time. Her mother's final act had shoved her out, saved her from that dream-death, but to what end?

She'd failed. Failed her mother. Failed everyone.

She let out a scream of pure frustration, burning her throat from the effort.

An urgent knock came from the bedroom door before it flung open. Maya's head appeared, their face pale and etched with concern in the dim pre-dawn light. Chris was a protective figure right behind them, his eyes dark with exhaustion.

"Sarah? You good?" Maya whispered, stepping into the humid, stale air of the bedroom. "Is *it* here?"

Sarah couldn't speak, only shake her head, tears of frustration and grief stinging her eyes. The anger extinguished itself, replaced by a cold ash in her belly. The sense of being a wolf, a hunter, had vanished; in its place stood only a girl in a sweat-soaked t-shirt, the phantom ache in her arm a searing reminder of her failure.

She hadn't been a hunter; she'd been bait. The Shepherd hadn't just defeated her; it had made a mockery of her hope, dangling her mother's spirit before her only to snatch it away. What good was her rage against a power like that? It felt like a child's tantrum against a hurricane.

Chris followed Maya in, the both of them looking relieved, though his movements still heavy with the unnatural lethargy that plagued him. "Almost thought we'd find you like Chl—" he cleared his throat. "Well, we're just glad you're okay," he said, his voice raspy. The constant *tick-tick-tick* that they heard was getting louder for them now, a goddamn drum solo in their skulls. "You were really letting it out."

"It... it was my mom," Sarah choked out, burying her face in her hands. "I found her. At the well in Gu Mei. But it was a trap. The Shepherd killed her in front of me. It... it almost crushed me." She shuddered. The memory of the walls closing in, the suffocating pressure, sent a fresh wave of nausea through her.

Maya sat on the edge of the bed, placing a comforting hand on Sarah's trembling shoulder. "Hey, it was a dream, Sarah. A horrible one, but it wasn't real. You're here. You're safe."

Only it *was* real. Old Jian had confirmed it. That pasture, a hellish reflection of the Shepherd's domain and its feeding ground. What good would it do to tell them the truth, she thought. Her friends had been through enough as it is, no need to burden them with more. Not now, anyway.

"We need to check on Chloe," Sarah said sitting up, pushing aside the damp blanket. "Has anyone heard from Ben?"

Both Maya and Chris shook their heads. Last night's encounter with Ben flashed in her mind. At least there was no sign of him in her nightmare, not as a trapped soul like her mother, or a mindless sheep like Chloe. She hoped that meant he was okay.

"Maybe this is another one of Glitch's pranks," Chris said hopefully, while helping Sarah up off the bed.

Sarah smiled, but it didn't reach her eyes. "Maybe..."

Maya checked their phone and let out a small groan, then held it out for Sarah to see.

The viral "40 Winks Challenge" had continued its insidious spread overnight. More teenagers had fallen into unexplained comas. The demon's curse was accelerating, empowering it more and more with each passing minute. Another video was trending, DONT WATCH ALONE: #CityOfSleep GUY THROWS HIMSELF OUT OF WINDOW, but it was missed by the group, buried amongst the mass of other viral videos.

They dressed in silence, the only sounds the howling wind and the relentless rain. "When's this damn storm gonna pass?" Chris muttered. No one answered. Sarah found a note from her father on the kitchen counter that read: *We WILL talk more tonight.* But what more was there to say if he still refused to believe? And where had he been all night?

The hospital, which had been a portrait of controlled chaos yesterday, had since shredded the canvas. The air itself was a chaotic hum of crying, frantic announcements, and the squeal of gurney wheels on linoleum. Every chair in the waiting area was taken, forcing families to huddle on the floor, their faces illuminated by the cold, merciless blue of their phone screens as they searched for news. With no more space in the already overflowing hospital, patients were lined up in the hallways now. This has spread much faster than they could've imagined; it was becoming an epidemic.

"Oh my god," Sarah breathed, her hand flying to her mouth.

"They just keep coming," Chris muttered, his face ashen. The lethargy seemed to weigh him down, his shoulders slumped, his movements slow, as if he were wading through water. The ticking in his head, Sarah imagined, must be deafening here, amidst so much despair.

Ben was nowhere to be seen. Sarah's heart sank further. She tried his phone again. Straight to voicemail.

They made their way to Chloe's room, a small space dominated by the rhythmic beeping of monitors. They weren't surprised to find new patients lining the room now since space was at a premium, but they were surprised to see the window was broken. It was covered in a sheet of plastic that was held in place by tape around the edge in a hasty attempt to block out the raging storm outside. Wind pushed against the sheet, pulling it away from the wall, breaking the seal and letting rain splash inside.

Chloe still lay in bed, a pale, fragile doll amidst the stark white sheets. But she looked worse. Visibly more diminished than yesterday. Her skin, once vibrant and glowing, was now a dull, almost translucent gray, stretched tight over her cheekbones. Her usually bright pink hair appeared faded, lifeless. She looked shriveled. Like a flower left to wither in a crypt.

Sarah felt a wave of nausea. The Shepherd was feeding on her friend. This was what it did. It slowly drained the life force, consumed the spirit. This was what had happened to her mother, what was now happening to Chloe, and what would happen to all of them if they couldn't stop it. Anger bubbled inside her again.

Chris ran up to Chloe's bed and sat on the edge, leaning over her, taking her frail hand in his. "Hey, babe, I'm here." He gently brushed a strand of her hair off her face with his free hand. "I love you, babe; you know that, right? Even though you drive me crazy." He gave a small chuckle and kissed her forehead. "I'm going to kill whatever did this to you, babe. I swear it."

A nurse bustled in, a young woman with kind but tired eyes peeking out from above a face mask. She started, surprised to see them gathered around Chloe's bed. "Oh," she said. "I didn't realize anyone was here." The nurse glanced at Chloe, then back at them, her expression softening with pity.

"What the hell happened here?" Chris asked, glancing at the broken window while rubbing the tears from his face with the back of his hand.

The nurse looked surprised. "Oh, you... haven't heard?" Her eyes widened slightly. "Oh, god. I am so, so sorry. I just assumed... with you all being here for... for Chloe..."

Sarah tensed, the nurse's words a dissonant chord in the already cacophonous symphony of her fear and grief. "Heard what?" she repeated, a cold dread coiling in her stomach, tightening its grip around her heart.

"Your friend Ben—" The nurse cut herself off, wringing her hands nervously.

Ben. His name hung in the sterile air of Chloe's hospital room, heavy and ominous. Sarah felt the blood drain from her face. The unanswered texts. The calls going straight to voicemail. The unsettling, out-of-character message "he" had sent before they went to Mr. Chen's. The figure at the door of her apartment.

"What about Ben?" Chris demanded, his voice rough, his lethargy momentarily forgotten. He stood up, fists clenched.

The nurse flinched at Chris's voice and dropped her gaze to the floor. "There's someone here you should talk to," she stammered, her professional composure crumbling. "Follow me."

Sarah shared a confused look with her friends before following the nurse out into the bustling hallway. The nurse motioned for them to wait while she walked up to a large, sweaty and weary-looking police officer, who was talking with other staff at the nurse station. She couldn't make out what was said, but the officer looked up at her, his brow furrowing, before walking over to them. The nurse hurried away, disappearing into the throng of people shuffling about.

The large officer stopped in front of them, the sweat dripping from the thin hair that was combed tightly to the side of his balding head.

"I'm Detective Graves. Are you the friends of Benjamin Lee?" he asked in a thick New York accent, flipping open a notepad and removing a pen. Sarah nodded. "I'm afraid I have some bad news. Your friend had an accident last night. He... fell through the window there." He pointed over his shoulder towards Chloe's room. "And unfortunately, he didn't make it."

The words struck Sarah in her gut, causing the room to spin. Ben fell? He was dead? No. Not Glitch, with his stupid jokes and his fierce loyalty. Not Ben, who was just with them last night, arguing, scared, but *alive*.

Maya gasped, their hand flying to their mouth, their eyes wide with disbelief. Chris stared at the detective, his face losing all its color. He blinked once, slowly, as if the words were in a foreign language he was struggling to translate. His mouth opened slightly, then closed without a sound. He looked from the detective to Sarah, then back again, his brow furrowed not in sadness, but in pure, blank confusion, as if waiting for someone to deliver the real punchline.

"An accident?" Sarah finally managed to choke out, the words tasting like ash in her mouth. "What kind of accident? He fell? How did he fall through the window?" The image of "Ben" at her door, his sickly pallor, the red glint in his eyes, the way he'd recoiled from the threshold... was it even really him? Or was it *the Shepherd* playing with them?

Detective Graves shrugged, though his eyes were filled with pity. "I'm sorry, I have to ask. Can you think of any reason he would have jumped? On purpose? Was he showing any signs of depression? Maybe he was recently dumped by a girlfriend?"

"What? No. No, nothing like that. Why?" Sarah asked.

"Well, I checked the security feed from last night. He was the only person in the room, other than the poor girl in the coma of course." He frowned. "But he was in some kind of hurry, ran in the room like he was being chased by a ghost, right before... well, you know." He wiped the sweat dripping from his brow with the back of his sleeve.

"He wouldn't do that, sir," Chris said, finally speaking up. "He was the happiest out of all of us... I think."

Detective Graves looked over at Chris and scowled. Something Sarah noticed he was good at.

"You think? Well, maybe he tripped while playing on his phone then."

Playing on his phone and tripped? The explanation was so mundane, so absurdly normal, that it felt like a deliberate, cruel poke at them. Ben, for all his quirks, wasn't clumsy like that.

"That's not what happened," she whispered, the words catching in her throat. Sarah's legs gave out. She sank onto the floor, the hallway spinning around her. Maya was beside her instantly, their arm around Sarah's shoulders, though Maya was trembling themself, their face a mask of shock. Chris stood there, frozen, his eyes fixed on the detective, his expression unreadable.

"We need to see him," Maya said, their voice choked with unshed tears.

Detective Graves hesitated. "I'm sorry, not yet. He's with the medical examiner now. He's still being examined."

Procedures. Formalities. While their friend lay dead, a victim of an ancient evil that no one else could see, no one else would believe. The injustice of it, the sheer, horrifying absurdity, threatened to consume Sarah.

"Can we see his phone?" Sarah asked in a shaking voice.

The detective didn't hesitate before responding. "I can't give you that just yet." He wiped his brow again, then looked over his shoulder at the crowd of people. "It's part of my investigation." He put away his notepad. "Listen. This city has gone to shit. All these cases coming in is overwhelming us. I don't know if its drugs or what, but something is going on and I can't be everywhere at once." Detective Graves pulled out a few business cards and handed one to each of them. "If you think of anything that might help, give me a call."

With that, he spun around and walked away, leaving Sarah and her friends with no answers.

Hot tears flowing down her face, Sarah pulled out her phone. There was only one person left who might understand, who might be able to help them make sense of this escalating nightmare. Mr. Chen. She wanted to share with him what she learned as well.

Her fingers, trembling with adrenaline, fumbled to find his contact. She hit dial, pressing the phone to her ear, praying he would answer, praying he would have some answers, some sliver of hope to offer. The phone rang. Once. Twice. Three times. Then, it clicked over to his familiar, slightly formal voicemail greeting.

"Greetings. You have reached Thorne's Curios. Please leave a message after the tone, and I will return your call at my earliest convenience." Beep.

Sarah hung up, a fresh wave of worry washing over her. Mr. Chen always answered his phone, especially if he knew they were expecting him. He had promised to call them the moment he found anything more about Fén Yáng.

"He's not answering," she said, her voice hollow.

"Try again," Chris urged, his voice raspy.

She did with the same result. Voicemail.

"Maybe he's just busy," Maya offered, though their voice lacked conviction. "Or his phone died. The storm..."

But Sarah knew. Deep in her gut, she knew. Something was wrong. Terribly wrong. The Shepherd, Fén Yáng, it wouldn't stop with Chloe and Ben. It was hunting them. All of them. And Mr. Chen, with his ancient books and his dangerous knowledge, would be a prime target. He assured them he was protected there, but with the Relic in his possession, so close...

"We need to go to his shop," Sarah said, pushing herself up from the floor, a new, desperate urgency fueling her movements. "Now."

They didn't argue. The thought of what might have happened to Mr. Chen, their last potential ally, their only source of real information, was too terrifying to contemplate. Sarah couldn't let what happened to poor Ben happen to Mr. Chen too, not if there was a chance she could save him. Chris took a last look at Chloe, a burning anger in his eyes, before leaving.

The drive to Chinatown was a blur of rain and silent tears. Maya drove on autopilot, their eyes red-rimmed, their usual careful precision replaced by a reckless urgency. Chris sat beside them, staring blankly out the window, his face a mask of stony sorrow and a new look of determination. Sarah sat in the back, quietly replaying the details of what her mother had said in the nightmare.

When they finally reached Thorne's Curios, Sarah's heart sank. The usually vibrant, bustling street had fallen eerily quiet, the storm having driven most people indoors. But it wasn't just the weather. An unnatural stillness hung around Mr. Chen's shop, a sense of emptiness.

The narrow storefront was dark. No warm, inviting glow spilled from the windows. No scent of jasmine tea and incense wafted into the street. The faded gold calligraphy of the sign seemed to mock them, a relic of a time when the world had still made sense, before the Shepherd had come calling.

Sarah pushed open the heavy wooden door, the brass bell above it emitting a single, mournful, dissonant jingle that echoed in the sudden, oppressive silence of the shop.

The interior was a disaster.

The carefully curated chaos, the whimsical clutter that had once defined the shop's unique charm, had become a scene of violent upheaval. Books lay splayed open on the floor, their fragile pages torn and trampled. Glass display cases were shattered, their contents—delicate porcelain figurines, ancient coins, tarnished silver lockets—scattered like broken teeth. Tapestries were ripped from the walls, scrolls unfurled, and torn, African masks stared up from the floor with vacant eyes amidst the debris, some cracked or splintered. The air, usually thick with the comforting scents of jasmine tea, old paper, and incense, was now acrid, metallic, with an undercurrent of something sickeningly sweet, like rotting fruit.

Sarah's breath caught in her throat. Maya let out a small, choked gasp, their hand clamping over their mouth to stifle a scream. Chris, his lethargy pushed aside by a surge of adrenaline, shouldered past them, searching for a threat.

"Mr. Chen?" he called out, his voice rough, echoing unnaturally in the ravaged space. "Mr. Chen, are you here?"

Only the drip, drip, drip of water from a cracked pipe somewhere in the back answered him, a metronomic counterpoint to the frantic pounding of Sarah's heart. The faint, insidious *tick-tick-tick* that had plagued her friends pulsed in the very walls of the shop, louder now, more insistent, as if the Shepherd itself were counting down the seconds to their demise. Sarah still couldn't hear it, but she could see the way it affected her friends—Maya's eyes kept darting around and the way Chris flinched at every creak of the floorboards.

"Stay behind me," Chris demanded quietly.

They moved cautiously deeper into the shop, their footsteps crunching on broken glass and scattered debris. The destruction was systematic, malicious. Vases shattered, maps torn, statues destroyed. It wasn't a robbery, nothing of value seemed to be stolen—it was a violation, an act of malevolence.

"What happened here?" Maya whispered, their voice trembling. They picked up a small, jade Fu Dog statue, its head cleanly severed from its body. "Who would do this?"

Sarah didn't answer. She didn't have to. They knew.

They reached the small alcove in the back, the place where Mr. Chen kept his most precious texts, where he had shown them the terrifying illustration of the Grave Goat. The low table was overturned, its contents—ancient books, scrolls, teacups – scattered across the floor. The large, leather-bound treatise on *Yaoguai* lay open, its pages ripped and stained with something dark and viscous.

In the very back of the shop was the small, windowless room he used for storage and private consultations—his office. The door, usually closed, was ajar, a sliver of deeper darkness beckoning them forward. Chris pushed it open slowly, the light from his phone trembling.

The smell hit them first—a coppery, metallic stench mixed with sickeningly sweet rot that made bile suddenly rise in Sarah's throat.

Then, they saw him. Or what was left of him.

He was pinned against the far wall, not by nails or ropes, but by what looked like long, black, obsidian-like spikes that protruded from the wall itself, piercing his frail body, holding him aloft in a grotesque parody of crucifixion. His eyes, magnified behind his cracked glasses, were wide open, frozen in an expression of unimaginable terror and agony.

But it was what had been done to him that shattered Sarah's remaining composure. His skin had been flayed from his body, peeled back in long, ragged strips, stretched taut and pinned to the walls on either side of him, forming a pair of gruesome, leathery wings. They were dark, almost black, glistening wetly in the flashlight beam, like the wings of some monstrous, demonic insect.

And the top half of his skull was gone. Crushed, or maybe bitten off, it was impossible to tell through the gore. All that remained was a horrifying, ragged mess of bone, brain and blood. The image of the crushed skulls of the mother and child in the ruins flashed in Sarah's mind, the same brutal signature.

Sarah let out a choked, guttural sound and doubled over, retching violently onto the floor. Chris stared, his face a mask of white, frozen horror, his phone clattering from his nerveless fingers to the floor, plunging them into near darkness before Maya's shaky beam found them again.

Sarah felt the world tilt, the sounds of her own ragged breathing, Maya's choked sobs, the relentless drip of water, fading into a dull roar. She couldn't scream. She couldn't move. She could only stare at the horrifying tableau, at the desecrated remains of the kind, gentle man who had been a mentor of hers for years, who had tried to help them, who had been their last hope.

Fén Yáng. The Shepherd. This was its macabre work. It wasn't just a murder; it was a warning to them. And at the base of the gruesome display, placed with deliberate, profane care, lay the brass Relic.

Maya, their face pale but eyes blazing with a cold, hard fury Sarah had never seen in them before, stepped forward. They reached into their bag, their hand closing around something—a small, intricately carved wooden athame, its blade dark and polished.

"We... we need to... to cover him," Maya whispered, their voice trembling but firm. "We can't... we can't leave him like this."

But before they could do anything, before they could even process the full extent of the horror before them, a sound from the front of the shop made them jump.

The soft, rhythmic *jingle* from the bell above the front door.

They each froze—afraid to make any noise. They were trapped. Trapped in this charnel house, with the mutilated body of their friend, and the entity that had done this... perhaps still lurking in the shadows, waiting.

Now, someone—or something—was joining them.

CHAPTER 28

A short hiss escaped from Maya's throat as they grabbed Sarah's shoulder. Sarah flinched, her hand flying to her mouth to hold in the scream that fought to climb out. They exchanged terrified glances. Trapped. With poor Mr. Chen in the back room, and now someone or *something*, entering the shop.

Chris put a finger to his lips and mouthed, *"Stay behind me."*

Heavy footsteps creaked on the old wooden floorboards in the front of the store, moving with a slow, deliberate confidence.

"Sarah? Are you in here?"

It was her father. Sarah's heart skipped a beat at the sound of his voice. Chris and Maya noticeably relaxed as well. Sarah was first to move as relief broke her paralysis, pushing past Chris's protective stance.

Dr. Láng stood in the doorway of the alcove, his trench coat damp from the persistent storm, the worry lines around his eyes deep. "Sarah, thank goodness. I was so worried when you didn't answer your phone after... I heard about Ben." He paused, his gaze sweeping over the ransacked room. "I had a feeling you might come here. Mr. Chen always had a soft spot for you, for your mother."

"Dad? What are you doing here?" she managed, her voice barely a whisper. She ran over and gave him a firm hug, surprised but glad to see him.

"Looking for you, of course," he said, returning her embrace. "Are you alright, sweetheart? You and your friends? You all look shaken." He took a step further into the alcove, his gaze scanning the destruction around the shop. "Good heavens... what happened here? Mr. Chen... is he...?"

"He's dead," Chris choked out, his voice raw. "Something tore him apart." He pointed to the back where Mr. Chen's body was displayed like some sort of macabre experiment.

Dr. Láng stepped hesitantly towards the room where he lay, peered in for a moment, then recoiled, his face a mask of disgust. "Monstrous," he whispered, shaking his head. "Absolutely evil. We need to call the police immediately." He pulled out his phone and began fumbling with the screen, his movements shaky.

"It was the demon," Sarah stated, carefully watching her dad for any acknowledgement of the proof before his eyes.

"No, a break-in, clearly," he said dismissively, still looking at the phone as if figuring out how to use it. "Vandals. Drug addicts, perhaps. Chinatown has its share of troubles. Poor Chen. Such a senseless tragedy."

He rubbed his chin. "We need to get you all out of here. This is no place for you." He finally looked up, his gaze sweeping over them. "Are you hurt? Did they attack you too?"

"We're okay," Maya stammered, still pale but regaining a sliver of their composure. "We just found him like this."

Dr. Láng nodded, his gaze lingering on Maya, then Chris, then settling on Sarah. "Good. Good. That's a relief."

He began nonchalantly rummaging through the mess, phone forgotten, picking up objects, studying them for a few moments before setting them back down. "When I heard about Ben, I knew

I needed to find you. I should have listened. To you, to Mei-Lin." He slammed his fist down on Mr. Chen's front desk, causing dust to fly up in a cloud.

"Dad, it's okay." Sarah laid a hand on his arm to calm him. "Who could believe all of this? Really believe?" She gestured around the room. "I'm sorry for how I treated you. You were only trying to help."

He smiled at her with an approving look. Sarah pointed at the phone in his hand. "We can talk about it later," she let out a harsh laugh at the irony of her own words. "Right now, we should call the police."

"Ah, yes. Yes." He started fumbling with the phone again, then paused. He was looking at her with emotionless eyes. "We should call the police, but you guys must be starving after all this. We should get some food."

Sarah stiffened. Food? At a time like this?

"That... sounds good, Dad." She looked over at Chris and Maya in disbelief, but they were still in such shock over Mr. Chen, that they didn't even notice her. "Can you cook my favorite?"

"Your favorite? Of course. We just need to stop at the grocery store and get the ingredients. Come on, I'll take you all."

"Thank you, Dad." Sarah smiled, glancing to the side. "I could really go for some spicy ramen right now."

Dr. Láng returned her smile. "Me too, it's perfect food for this dreadful weather."

Before anyone could react, before Maya or Chris could sense the shift in her demeanor, Sarah moved. She lunged forward, grabbing a sharpened peachwood branch from the table next to her. With a guttural, animalistic cry, she slammed the pointed end of the branch directly into the chest of her father.

His eyes widened in shock, then he let out a sound that was not human. Not a gasp of pain, not a cry of surprise, but a deafening, horrifying *BLEAT*. The sound of a thousand sheep screaming in agony, amplified, distorted, a sound that clawed at their sanity.

His body convulsed violently. The familiar features of Dr. David Láng began to waver, to distort, like a reflection in troubled water. The kind eyes burned suddenly with that malevolent fire Sarah knew so well. His skin darkened, began to smoke, the form flickering between man and monstrous shadow.

Then, the deafening bleat shifted into a booming laugh. A perverted mockery of a sound that rattled the remaining glass in the shop. The twisted figure of her father started to dissolve. Not into blood and gore, but into a swirling vortex of black, acrid dust and shadow, which then blew away, sucked back into the unseen cracks of the violated shop, leaving only the lingering scent of ozone and ancient decay.

Sarah stood panting, the peachwood branch still clutched in her trembling hand, staring at the empty space where the imitation of her father had stood. Maya and Chris stared at her, their faces masks of shock and disbelief.

The silence that followed was absolute, broken only by Sarah's ragged breathing and the relentless drumming of the rain against the shattered storefront.

"Sarah?" Maya finally whispered, their voice barely audible. "What in the actual *fuck* was that?" Sarah looked at Maya and tilted her head. Maya didn't have to be told. They all knew it was the Shepherd.

The lingering smell of ozone hung heavy in the ravaged antique shop, mingling with the horrifyingly sweet, metallic scent of death from the back room. Sarah's chest heaved, the peachwood branch sticky with blood in her trembling grip. The image of the thing that had worn his face dissolving into dust replayed in her mind, a sickening loop. Chris stood frozen, his face a sickly grey, his eyes wide and staring at the empty space where Dr. Láng had been.

Slowly, the initial shock began to recede, replaced by a cold, nauseating terror and a fresh wave of anger. It wasn't just Mr. Chen. It wasn't just Ben. The Shepherd, Fén Yáng, had worn her father's skin, had spoken with his voice, had tried to manipulate her. The violation of it, the intimate horror, was a fresh reminder.

"How? How did you know?" Chris finally asked.

"It was too obvious. Almost like it wanted me to know," Sarah whispered. "That fucking thing was playing with me. Teasing me. When it got my favorite food wrong, I knew," Her gaze darted towards the back of the shop. "My dad knows it's always pizza. Not to mention, he hates spicy food, calls it 'culinary arson.'"

Maya sank onto an overturned crate, their legs seemingly unable to support them. "Your favorite food? That's how you knew?"

Sarah nodded, the movement making her head spin. "Sort of. In the nightmare, with Old Jian... he told me the Shepherd would use everything I hold dear against me. My mother... she tried to warn me in the well that it was a trap. This..." she gestured vaguely at the chaotic space, "this was another one."

She then summarized to her friends what Old Jian and her mother's spirit had revealed in the nightmare realm—Fén Yáng's nature, its connection to the Relic and the well, her mother's attempted ritual, the truth about her own epilepsy created by the demon's initial touch and, in a strange twist of fate, a shield by the demon's own hubris. She explained how the lamp's flickering lights and rhythmic sounds, meant to ensnare others, triggered her seizures and prevented her from being consumed.

Chris, who hadn't moved since the Shepherd took her peachwood to the chest, finally slumped against a debris-strewn shelf, the fight draining out of him. The persistent, insidious *tick-tick-tick* that had become the soundtrack to his fear pulsed with every heartbeat. "So, what now?" he asked, his voice hollow. "Your mom knew how to stop it? This ritual?"

Maya, despite their pallor, looked at Sarah, a spark of desperate hope in their eyes. "Sarah, my Wiccan abilities... I think it's time. Mr. Chen was dismissive against this magic. But your mother said the ritual had to be performed in *both* realms. What you can do in that nightmare place I can do here. We need every edge we can get, and I have an idea."

Sarah looked at her hands, then at the peachwood branch. Maya was right. Her connection to that other place, her painful lucidity there, was their only unique weapon. "I think you're right. But am I strong enough? He already beat me once."

Chris pushed himself upright, a flicker of his old determination returning, though his face remained grey with exhaustion and dread. "We don't have other options, Láng. Your mom fought. Chen fought. Chloe and Ben..." His voice cracked. "We have to fight too. I'm tired of running."

Sarah wasn't convinced but was surprised at how inspired she was by his optimism. Plus, the anger that was already burning deep inside her started to boil over. She looked Chris straight in the eyes and nodded.

Chris turned to Maya. "Great! What do we need?"

Maya gave them a short list of items, and they began a frantic search of the devastated shop. Most of Mr. Chen's ancient texts were destroyed, ripped and stained. They found a few more intact branches of peachwood, and a small, unopened pouch of coarse sea salt. Most importantly, Maya found a handful of various mirrors that they felt were the key to defeating the Shepherd after hearing what Sarah's mother told her in the nightmare. The lamp, still in the back room, near Mr. Chen's desecrated body, seemed to mock them.

"We need to perform the ritual," Sarah said, her voice gaining a shaky confidence. "Mom said it needed to be somewhere personal to me, somewhere underground, in both realms. And she suspected mirrors... that the Shepherd hates seeing itself."

"Underground?" Maya frowned. "Like the cave in China?"

Sarah shuddered. "No. Not the cave. Some other place. Some-place that means something to me... to us."

Chris looked at her, a dawning understanding, and horror, in his eyes. "You don't mean..."

Sarah met his gaze. "Yes. The sewers. Under Northwood High."

Chris and Maya gave each other a look that was thick with a shared trauma. Northwood High. The place where their child-hoods had shattered, where their unlikely friendship had been forged in the crucible of unimaginable violence.

"No," Chris said, his voice flat. "Absolutely not, Sarah. Any-where but there."

"It has to be there, Chris," Sarah insisted, her own fear battling with a desperate certainty. "It's personal to me. To us. It's under-ground. It's... it's where I first became afraid—truly afraid."

Chris looked to Maya for support, but they looked away.

Sarah pressed on. "I can't think of a better place that's personal to us underground." Chris didn't blink. "Look, you know I don't like it either, but if we are right, then this is our chance to fight back. Everyone's sacrifice was for this, right here, right now. They died to give us *this* chance, and I'll be damned if I'm going to let them die for nothing. I'm going, with or without you. So, choose."

He stared down at her, unmoving, anger and fear in his eyes, but she didn't back down. She stared back up at him defiantly, waiting for him to make the first move. Without a word, he abruptly turned and stomped to the room where poor Mr. Chen's body still hung. He emerged moments later, carrying the cursed lamp, its brass sheep seeming to gleam with malevolent amuse-ment in the dim light. He didn't speak, just handed it to Maya, who quickly wrapped it in another layer of cloth from their bag and shoved it deep inside.

Sarah didn't show it outwardly, but she was close to tears. She was so relieved that Chris decided to go with her that her knees almost gave out. She looked to Maya.

"What about you Maya? Are you up for this?"

Maya had a look in their eyes that Sarah had never seen before. "Let's fuck this demon up."

Maya's response was so out of character that Sarah let out an incredulous bark of a laugh. Chris, just as surprised as Sarah, joined in. Even Maya cracked a smile, a deep blush rising on their cheeks. It felt good to laugh and release all of the pressure that had been building inside them.

The laughter quickly died as Sarah's gaze fell back upon the room where Mr. Chen's body lay displayed. "What about Mr. Chen?"

"I hate to say this, Sarah," Maya responded with a pained look. "But I don't think we should call the police yet. We don't have time to waste answering their questions. We need to hurry."

Chris let out a sudden sharp laugh that startled both Sarah and Maya, causing them to jump. They looked at him incredulously.

"Sorry," Chris said, blushing. "I know this is terrible, but I could almost hear Ben making a joke about how Mr. Chen isn't going anywhere..."

Sarah was about to lay into him for the inappropriate comment, but she bit her tongue. The thought of Ben, being there with them, breaking the tension with his bad jokes was somehow comforting. She didn't laugh—she just laid a reassuring hand on Chris's shoulder, letting him know she missed Ben too.

With the hard decision to leave Mr. Chen's mutilated corpse made, they gathered their things from the wreckage of the shop and headed for the front door. Sarah paused at the threshold and turned, forcing herself to look back one last time.

She scrunched her ears. From somewhere in the back, she thought she heard the sound of pages fluttering in a breeze.

Chapter 29

The journey over to Northwood High was a somber affair. The storm had finally lessened slightly, but the sky remained a bruised purple, the rain a steady, miserable drizzle. The city felt muted, as if holding its breath, waiting. As they drove, the unspoken memories of their past hung heavy in the SUV.

"I still hear them sometimes," Chris said quietly, breaking the long silence as they pulled up to the imposing, gothic-style building of their old high school, now dark and deserted on a Saturday. "The screams..."

"I remember the smell," Sarah whispered, her hand instinctively going to her nose. "Old water, sewage, sweat, dirt, our fear. It felt like the walls were closing in on me."

Maya nodded, their own eyes shadowed. "Me too. Huddled in that pipe... I remember thinking every sound was him coming for us." Maya shuddered as they parked the car in front of the memorial that now stood guard at the entrance. The three of them sat in silence for a few moments, each of them building the courage to confront the one place they had all swore never to visit again.

"Let's do this." Chris suddenly blurted out loud, hopping out of the car into the pouring rain. Sarah and Maya quickly followed, spurred into action by his lead. They ran past the memorial erected for the victims, refusing to look. But Sarah could feel its gaze upon them—a towering slab of silent judgment.

"The access grate is behind the gym," Sarah yelled, her voice barely carrying through the storm. They rounded a corner and found it down the rain-slicked alley, but the access grate looked worse than they remembered. Nature had tried to reclaim the spot. Thick, thorny vines, that were eerily similar to the ones that writhed in Sarah's nightmares, choked the entrance, their tendrils woven through the bars of the grate like skeletal fingers. Orange-brown rust covered the metal itself, the hinges seized by years of neglect.

"Shit," Chris muttered, yanking uselessly at the grate. It didn't budge, the metal groaning in protest. "It's rusted shut."

Sarah stared at the sealed tunnel through the bars, into the darkness that seemed to loom larger, calling to her. Claustrophobia began to claw at her with its familiar grip.

"Guys, we need to hurry," Maya said, their voice tight with urgency as they began tearing at the thorny vines with their bare hands. The thorns bit into them, drawing blood, but they didn't seem to notice, their movements frantic. "Help me."

Chris and Sarah joined in, ripping at the tough, woody stems. The thorns tore at their clothes and scratched their skin as well. Thin lines of blood, mingled with the cold rain, dripped from their hands as they worked. The vines were stubborn, seemingly fighting them with each pull, but after a few agonizing minutes, they had cleared enough of the vines to get a firm grip on the bars underneath.

"Together," Chris grunted. "On three. One... two... THREE!"

They heaved, their feet slipping on the wet pavement, their muscles straining against the unyielding metal. For a long, straining moment, nothing happened. Then, with a prolonged, tortured screech of rusting metal, one of the hinges gave way.

"Again!" Chris yelled.

They heaved again, and the grate finally tore open, slamming against the brick wall with a deafening clang that echoed in the deserted alley. They paused, panting in the cold rain, their chests heaving. Chris moved first, preparing his flashlight and readying his peachwood spear. Sarah, however, remained frozen, staring into the black maw.

"Hey."

Maya's voice was soft, cutting through the sound of the rain. They had stepped in front of Sarah, blocking her view of the dark tunnel. Maya gently took Sarah's hand—the one she'd scraped raw on the thorny vines. Their thumb brushed over Sarah's bleeding knuckles, a touch so tender it felt like it could extinguish the world's pain.

"You aren't alone," Maya said, their dark eyes searching Sarah's, their usual calm now a fierce, protective focus. "I'm here with you. You can do this, okay?"

In their gaze, Sarah didn't just see a friend. She saw the quiet strength that had anchored her for years, the unwavering loyalty that had followed her across the world and into this literal hell. The world narrowed to the space between them, the chaos of the storm and the dread of the sewer momentarily fading into a muffled roar. For a heart-stopping second, Sarah felt the insane urge to lean forward, to close the small distance between their faces.

Instead, she just squeezed their hand back, a silent promise passing between them. "Okay," she whispered, nodding her head. The moment broke as Chris called from the edge of the opening.

"You guys coming, or are you gonna let me face the goat-demon alone?"

Maya let go of Sarah's hand, the loss of contact leaving Sarah's skin feeling cold. They shared one last look, before turning to descend into the oppressive darkness. Chris led with his large flashlight, its beam cutting a swathe through the gloom, reflecting off the slick, curving walls of the tunnel. Maya followed, their phone casting its own light which danced nervously around.

The thick, cold air wrapped around them, a familiar, suffocating blanket of damp concrete and decay. Every drop of water echoed like a gunshot in the narrow tunnel. Sarah pressed her arms out against the walls, as if she were preventing them from closing in around her. A physical means of pushing back the rising tide of her claustrophobia. This was a place of ghosts, and not all of them were supernatural.

They moved in silence, their footsteps splashing in the shallow, grimy water, the beams of their flashlights cutting nervous paths ahead. It was Maya who stopped first, their light fixed on a small recess in the tunnel wall.

"Guys... look."

A small, pathetic pile of withered flowers lay propped against the weeping concrete wall, their petals turned to brown mulch, their plastic wrapping clouded with grime. A single, deflated football lay beside them, its skin brittle and cracked. A makeshift memorial.

The memory hit them all at once, a collective, silent gasp of shared trauma. They didn't need to ask. They all knew where they were.

"This is it," Chris whispered, his voice rough, his usual bravado gone. "This is the spot. Only twenty more feet and..." He swallowed hard.

Sarah's breath hitched. Twenty feet. That's all it had been. Twenty feet of concrete had separated their terrified, huddled forms from the place he died. She remembered the sounds—the frantic, pounding footsteps, a single, pleading cry cut short, and then the final, deafening bang, followed by a silence more terrifying than any noise.

"I'll never forget the sight," Maya said, their voice hollow, their gaze fixed on the dead flowers. "After... when the police led us out. Poor Jayden... and him."

Chris nodded, his jaw tight. "He had a rifle. I remember the mess." He didn't need to elaborate. The image was seared into all their minds: the last victim, a promising star football player and senior named Jayden, and the gunman, another senior named Mark, his face a ruin, lying in a pool of blood right here. The end of a massacre.

Sarah felt a fresh wave of nausea. The Shepherd fed on death, on despair. It was no wonder this place felt so charged, so potent. They had survived one monster here, only to return to fight another.

Sarah tightened her mouth. "C'mon." She turned and splashed her way down the tunnel. "Almost there."

They reached a wider junction, a raised circular chamber where several tunnels converged. "This is it," Maya said, their voice echoing strangely as they immediately began to unpack their Witch Bag with ritualistic familiarity, everyone made an obvious effort to avoid looking down the tunnel where they had hidden all those years ago. The dark void held repressed memories; it called to them, threatened to remind them of the horror they faced that day, long ago.

Maya began to draw a large circle on the damp floor with the coarse sea salt, then smaller, protective circles within it for each of them. They carefully placed thirteen candles around the outer salt ring and lit them one-by-one, all while chanting something under their breath. Sarah couldn't help but notice that the flickering candle lights did not help the creepy atmosphere of the dark sewer. Last, they arranged the mirrors around the inner-most circle, angled inwards towards where they would place the Relic once they were ready.

"The mirrors should amplify and reflect any energy," Maya explained, their voice tight. "If your mother was right, if it hates its own reflection, this might contain it."

"*If* we can even get it in there," Chris responded skeptically.

Maya continued, ignoring his comment. "The salt, the peachwood, they're traditional wards. They should offer some protection." They looked at Sarah, their eyes dark with worry. "Once we place the Relic and it starts, once you're... there... it'll be up to you. You have to find a way to trap it in the nightmare realm, to seal it underground there, while we try to do the same here."

Maya took Sarah's hands. Their welcome grip was surprisingly strong. "Sarah, listen. Remember, when you're in the nightmare the Shepherd will use your fears, your memories. But you said the old man from your dream said you could act there, that your lucid state is a weapon. Wiccans believe we can influence the world around us, not by force, but by being in tune with it, by coaxing it. Dream-walking... it's similar. You've done it before, remember? You summoned the peachwood in your nightmare. You can shape that place, Sarah. Bend it to your will. Find its weaknesses. Use its own nature against it."

Sarah nodded, remembering the unexpected appearance of the peachwood branch in the nightmare. It *had* felt like she'd willed it into existence. Maybe Maya was right. If she could control and manifest objects like the branch in the nightmare, what else could she do?

With a deep breath, Maya let go of Sarah's hand and placed the Relic in the center of the salt circle. Chris stood beside them, his face grim, his hand gripping a long, sharpened piece of peachwood like a spear.

Sarah took her place within her own smaller circle. Her heart hammered against her ribs. The air in the sewer tunnel was cold, damp, pressing in on her. The *tick-tick-tick* that Chris and Maya heard was growing louder, more insistent, a maddening rhythm that echoed the frantic beating of her own heart.

Maya looked up at both Chris and Sarah. "Ready?"

Chris nodded, but Sarah noticed something out of the corner of her eye. "Maya." She pointed down at the ring of salt.

Maya followed Sarah's gaze and cursed at what they found. "Oh, I am so sorry, guys," They reached over and fixed the outer ring of salt that had a small gap in it. "I can't believe I missed that..."

"Jesus, Maya," Chris blurted. "What would have happened if Sarah didn't catch it?"

Maya looked horrified at the thought—their face went white.

That was all the answer Chris needed. "Just concentrate please." He turned his back to the two girls in a protective stance, holding the stick in one hand and the flashlight in the other, all while scanning the dark room.

Maya lit the candles in the Relic with a shaking hand. The small flames flickered, casting dancing, distorted shadows on the curved sewer walls. The tiny brass sheep began their slow, relentless journey, and a sound filled the chamber, soft at first, then growing in insistence.

Tick. Tick. Tick.

Sarah closed her eyes, her voice trembling as she began the rhyme, joined by Maya and a reluctant Chris.

"Little Bo-Peep has lost her sheep, and doesn't know where to find them..."

The carousel spun a little faster causing the shadows to writhe.

A wave of dizziness washed over Sarah. The expected pressure building behind her eyes. But this time, she didn't fight it. She leaned into it. Each word, each flicker of light was an attack on her senses, but she let the waves wash over her.

As they chanted, the temperature in the sewer plummeted. The shadows on the walls coalesced, taking on horrifying, recognizable shapes. A muffled gunshot echoed from the depths of the tunnels, causing the three of them to jump. Then another. Screams, young and terrified, clawed their way out of the very brickwork.

Chris cried out, clutching his head, his face contorted in fear. "No... stop it!"

"Concentrate, Chris!" Sarah barked.

A faint, ethereal figure shimmered at the edge of the candlelight—Ben, his eyes wide with terror, his hand outstretched. "Sarah... Maya... don't! You don't understand! It's a trap! He's using you!" Just as fast as he materialized Ben was gone, disappearing back into the darkness.

They had prepared for this and mostly ignored the distractions. Slowly, as they continued chanting, their fear built, causing the incantation to become more and more out of sync, but they remained steadfast.

More figures emerged out of the darkness, both familiar and unfamiliar. Each apparition begging. Pleading. Victims from the school shooting, students they had known and lost, appeared at the edge of the light. With wide, terrified eyes, the ghosts of their former classmates reached for help from the group protected in the inner circle.

"Please, no!"

"Help!"

"Don't shoot!"

They were forced to watch as one ghostly student after another was executed, their spectral forms dissolving only to be replaced by a new face contorted in terror. The words of the rhyme caught in Sarah's throat, her voice hitching. The line of salt, the faces of her friends, the very stone beneath her feet began to blur at the edges, the world dissolving into a smear of sound and terror. The unending assault of tragedy and horror pushing her to the brink of insanity.

From the damp wall directly opposite Maya and Chris, a deeper shadow detached itself, flowing like viscous oil. It solidified, taking on the grotesque, towering form of the Shepherd, its sheep-skull head tilted, its burning red eyes fixed on Maya. It took a jerky step towards them.

"...for they were still—"

Right before they finished the rhyme, the world exploded for Sarah. The pressure in her head became unbearable. The flickering light, the rhythmic clicking, the chanting, the terrifying apparitions all overwhelmed her senses. Her body convulsed. The last thing she saw before oblivion claimed her was the ring of candle lights blowing out just as the Shepherd reached for Maya.

Chapter 30

Maya saw Sarah collapse out of the corner of their eye, her body jerking violently within the salt circle, and a choked gasp escaping her lips. Even though there was no wind, the ring of candle lights blew out all at once.

Panic seized Maya—they wanted to rush to Sarah, but the towering horror of the Shepherd demanded their attention. Its clawed hand stretched towards them, its fetid breath washing over them in a foul wave of decay. The outer protective circle of salt flared with an almost invisible blue light as the Demon's shadow touched it. The Shepherd recoiled with a guttural hiss, its red eyes blazing with frustrated fury.

It couldn't cross.

Enraged at being thwarted by Maya's mysterious Western magic, its form wavered, then melted back into the deepest shadows of the sewer tunnel, vanishing as if it were never there. However, the spinning shadows from the Relic continued to writhe around the room, mocking them with each pass. The presence of the Demon lessened, the chilling echoes of the school shooting faded out, the spectral voices blew away like whispers on the wind.

Then, a figure appeared out of the darkness of a tunnel—Chloe, her pink hair dull, her eyes vacant and confused.

"Chris? Is that you? Babe... help me... I can feel it feeding on me...it hurts...."

Chris, who had been paralyzed when the Shepherd appeared, now snapped back to action by Chloe. Tears streamed down his face.

"Chloe... babe... I'm here..." He took a step towards her, his foot scuffing the edge of Maya's larger salt circle.

"Chris, no!" Maya shrieked, their voice hoarse. "Don't break the circle! It's not her! It's a trick!"

Chris paused, his foot right at the edge of the salt barrier. Chloe, or what looked like Chloe, shuffled across the floor on bare feet towards him and stopped just outside the barrier. She stood just inches from him, her eyes moist with tears, a look of pleading in them that tore at his heart.

"Babe, it *is* me, really me." Chloe lifted her hand and placed it gently against the invisible barrier that prevented her from reaching him. A faint bluish glow radiated outward from her hand, illuminating the protective shield, but she didn't recoil from it like the Shepherd did. "I don't know how I got here. Please, babe, let me in. I don't want to die."

Chris glanced over at Maya with a look of desperate pleading, as if asking for their permission to let Chloe in. Maya gave him a sad shake of their head and mouthed '*no*'—their heart breaking at the sad sight of him. Seeing their two friends in the clutches of the Shepherd was hard enough for them; they couldn't imagine the pain Chris was going through.

He turned back to Chloe who was still pressing on the barrier. "I'm so sorry, babe." He held up his hand next to hers as close as he dared without actually touching. "Why can't you cross, Chloe?"

Chloe looked at the faintly glowing shield around her hand. "I don't know—"

Something abruptly shifted in the darkness behind her. "Chloe, behind you!" Chris shouted.

Chloe turned just as a figure materialized out of the shadows. It wasn't the Shepherd. It was something out of their worst nightmares. A tall, lanky teenager in a black trench coat, his face pale and emotionless, his eyes holding a terrifying, vacant emptiness. Mark. The gunman.

Chris froze, the color draining from his face. His breath caught in a strangled gasp. "No..."

The illusion of Mark moved with an unnatural smoothness, raising a semi-automatic rifle. It pointed it directly at Chloe. The sound of the charging handle racking a round into the chamber was deafening in the silence of the sewer. It was a sound that echoed from the depths of their worst memories causing all of them to wince.

"Chris, don't look!" Maya screamed, recognizing the Demon's trick. "It's not real! It's feeding on your fear!"

But Chris couldn't look away, his eyes locked on the specter from his past. He was torn between the instinct to protect and shield and the terrified teenager he had been that day, hiding just twenty feet away.

Time slowed to a crawl as Chris tensed, his thoughts flashing to the past. He relived the countless nights spent crying in the shower after the massacre. Feelings of guilt and what-ifs breaking him apart. What if he had tried to help Jayden? The others? Instead of hiding like a coward. Would he have stopped the shooter?

Mark's finger twitched on the trigger.

Chris's fists tightened—his decision made. He wouldn't lose Chloe or anyone else to that piece of shit. Chris lunged. His foot kicked open the salt barrier, breaking the seal.

Next, everything happened so fast.

"No!" Maya cried, as the illusion of Mark disappeared.

Chris slid to a confused halt as the object of his rage vanished. Giant insect-like claws suddenly grabbed Chloe out of the darkness from the opposite direction of Mark's illusion, yanking her backwards.

Chloe let out a surprised yelp.

The long form of the Shepherd rose up from behind her. With a slow and deliberate movement, the Demon opened its foul mouth while staring Chris down with its malevolent red eyes.

"Chris," Chloe whimpered with pleading eyes, her arms held out towards him.

Before Chris could react, the Shepherd bit down. A wet, percussive *CRUNCH* echoed in the sewer chamber, a sound of impossible force. A spray of warm red and gray matter exploded with such force that it splattered against Maya's cheek across the chamber. The Shepherd tossed Chloe's limp body at the stunned Chris, who fell over backwards as he caught her. He landed awkwardly on his ass, his foot twisting at a sickening angle beneath him as he bounced.

The Shepherd slid back into the shadows. Chloe's very real body lay crumpled on the floor in front of Chris as an unnerving silence descended upon the sewer chamber, broken only by the methodic ticking of the lamp and Sarah's choked, unconscious breaths from within her own circle. The sudden quiet was almost deafening, more terrifying in its implications than the chaos that had preceded it.

Maya was a statue, afraid to move or make a sound. Their eyes darted around the room, watching every shadow that seemed to coil, ready to spring at them.

Chris, unable to look away from Chloe's remains, unconsciously wiped a hand across his face to clean it, which only smeared the blood that had splattered there. Pieces of Chloe's flesh dropped from his hand as he pulled it away, making a soft squishing sound as they hit the damp stone.

Her death was so quick that Chloe's heart hadn't yet given up. Blood spurted out from what remained of her head in rhythmic pulses, then pooled around her body. Steam rose from the hot blood as it wormed its way along grooves in the cold hard floor towards Chris. There was no telling how much time went by before Maya mustered the courage to break the stillness.

"Chris," Maya hissed, trying to get his attention. When he glanced over at them, they nodded their head at the salt line. "Fix it. Quickly!"

Chris, eyes wide in shock, and unable to stand, slowly shuffled over to reconnect the line. The salt was quickly turning to a thick mud-like substance as it absorbed Chloe's bodily fluids. But before he could rearrange the protective ring properly, Maya let out a soft wheezing sound behind him. He stiffened when he saw what made Maya gasp.

Against the wall across from him a new shadow began to bleed outwards. A large, narrow body pulled itself free from the brickwork, its shadowy form solidifying, its red eyes burning with an ancient hunger.

A snake, larger than any they had ever seen, coiled around itself and stared at Maya with a burning hunger. Instead of scales, it was covered in a patchwork of wool and decaying flesh, pus oozing out from open sores, making a stomach-turning squirting sound with each movement. An unnatural bleating sound began to erupt from the monster which started as a low rumble and built to a crescendo of noise.

The nightmare made flesh slowly slithered towards them.

Chris panicked, and with hands shaking uncontrollably, pushed too much salt to the side, opening the ward even further. The demonic snake sprang at them with impossible speed. It reached out for Maya when Chris, with a defiant roar, launched himself forward with a protective fury.

His twisted foot made a loud cracking sound, breaking into pieces as he leapt towards the Shepherd—but it didn't stop him. He threw himself in front of Maya, the sharpened peachwood branch held high.

The creature, incredibly fast, ducked under his wild swing. Chris's triumphant yell died in his throat as the snake's tail whipped around his legs, pulling him off balance. Chris tried jabbing his peachwood at the large body twisting around him but couldn't get enough leverage to puncture the oozing flesh.

With another twist the snake wrapped around his torso, pinning his arms to his side and fully engulfing him. He struggled to free himself as the snake began to constrict, squeezing tighter and tighter.

Maya watched, unable to move. A command shouted in their mind—HELP HIM. DO SOMETHING—but their body refused to listen.

A horrifying gurgle began to escape from Chris as he struggled to breathe. "Run..." He gasped before his body gave out. With a final, nauseating crunch, Chris's body broke in the snake's grip. His eyes popped from their sockets by the impossible pressure and flew across the room like discarded marbles.

The snake uncoiled, and Chris's corpse crumpled to the ground like a puppet with its strings cut, landing beside Chloe with a dull, final thud. As the peachwood spear clattered uselessly away, his crushed body settled, its eyeless sockets staring straight at Maya; or at least, it would have, had he any eyes left. Blood gushed from a mouth that was hanging open in a crooked manner.

Maya screamed and stumbled backward into their inner circle, their body knocking over one of the mirrors and breaking the seal. The snake turned its gaze on them, its movement now slow and calculated. With a loud monstrous bleat, it slithered towards them.

Maya had nowhere to go, they were trapped.

As the Demon, in snake form, wormed through the broken salt line and towered over them, the frantic drumming in Maya's chest simply... stopped. The stench of rot, the cold of the sewer, the burning red eyes of the beast—it all became distant, like a scene observed from very far away.

So, this is it.

A brief wave of sadness washed over them for having failed their friends, but a swell of pride pushed it aside. They had overcome so much tragedy together, traveled China and faced a literal Demon—the thought of dying alongside these friends gave them peace.

Maya closed their eyes and reclined back as insect-like chitinous arms tore out from the snake's skin and reached for them. As they braced for the inevitable, they felt their hand brush up against something. Their eyes flew open, and they looked down, ignoring the claw inches from their face.

They had found Chris's peachwood.

Chapter 31

The sewer, with its stench of damp concrete and mildew, was ripped away, replaced by a roiling green sky of the Shepherd's Pasture. It snapped into existence above Sarah, an unsettling canvas of churning clouds like waves on an angry ocean. She reeled, the phantom sensations of the world she'd just left—the oppressive darkness, the rhythmic ticking, the hard concrete floor—still clinging to her like a residue.

She gagged as the foul air hit the back of her throat like a wet film, causing bile to rise. She bent over, trying to hold her stomach contents in, when she noticed she was standing on a churning slurry of decay. A gruesome quicksand of shifting fleeces, splintered bone, and something soft and yielding that felt horrifyingly like flesh. The earth squirmed, a living mire that sucked hungrily at her ankles with every hesitant step.

A violent heave emptied her stomach, a sensation that felt uncomfortably real in this dreamscape. As she wiped the spittle from her lips with a shaking hand, she noticed she wasn't wearing her jacket. Instead, it was a thick, gray, and coarse wool coat. She rubbed the fur between two fingers, wondering if she had subconsciously manifested the clothing, or if this was another trick of the Shepherd.

Láng!

Sarah flinched as her name boomed through the very fabric of the hellscape, a sound that resonated from every direction at once. The mocking imitation of her family and friends along with the guttural bleating of the Shepherd itself—all echoed in a chorus of voices that vibrated in her teeth before fading away.

She clenched her fists at her sides. The resolve she'd found talking to Old Jian, the burning ember of her mother's sacrifice, the anger from her friends suffering and Ben's death, had all been tempered in the crucible of her previous defeat. She didn't hear a mocking threat of her name. She heard a war cry instead.

With a focus of thought, a sharp peachwood branch appeared, clutched firmly in her right hand. It felt solid, real, its surface a stark contrast to the soft foulness under her. It hummed slightly against her warm skin with a faint, cool energy, a small reminder of the power she wielded here.

Looking around to get her bearings, she wasn't surprised to see everything was still bathed in a depressing mix of grays and greens; a sickly luminescence that seemed to ooze from the clouds themselves rather than shine through them. The distorted, nightmarish effigies of Gu Mei's buildings still littered the landscape, though more numerous now.

Her mother's house leaned at an angle that made the world tilt, its roof tiles like broken teeth. The temple squatted in the distance, stone lions weeping a slow, black ooze that wasn't water. And the ruins on the hill appeared to breathe, the stones subtly shifting, rearranging themselves with a faint, dry scraping sound, like bone grinding against bone.

Nothing was still. Everything writhed under a heatless shimmer, the very air buzzing like a fly caught in a web. Even the fences of gnarled, thorny branches twisted and squirmed. They contracted and expanded rhythmically, like the ribcage of some unseen beast, their razor-sharp thorns glistening with a dark, viscous fluid. Passages that had been open moments before would seal themselves with a dry, scraping sound, while new, equally uninviting paths would tear themselves open in the shifting slurry of death underfoot.

And then there were the sheep. She saw one first, then another, then her brain finally assembled the horrifying whole. They weren't grazing; they were waiting. Hundreds, no, *thousands* of them stood unnervingly still, a silent, white sea of wool under the sickly green sky. And they were all looking at her.

As she took a single, hesitant step, a thousand shadowed heads swiveled in perfect, silent unison, a ripple of motion that was as precise as it was unnatural. Their eyes weren't vacant this time; they were black pits filled with a collective, desperate plea for help—a plea a thousand times more terrifying than any empty stare.

The air began to vibrate with the sound of their bleating, a low, guttural hum that wasn't a chorus but a single, multi-throated groan of agony. Each one was an accuser, a memorial to a soul she'd failed. And though the Shepherd was nowhere to be seen, she knew it was out there, watching.

She had a purpose now, a desperate, burning clarity. Her mother had said the ritual to bind the Shepherd, to seal it, had to be performed in both realms, somewhere personal, somewhere *underground*. The sewers beneath Northwood High were the waking world's battleground. Her battle was somewhere here. Now.

A pang of worry for how her friends were handling the fight in the real world shot through her, but she forced it away. She needed to focus. Here, in this psychic sewer of the Shepherd's making, she needed to find the anchor of the demon's spirit, the knowledge Mei-Lin had died to pass on. Old Jian had believed her best bet was at the ruins, an echo of the cave where the lamp was found, or the well at her mother's home. Both choices made logical sense to her and seemed the obvious choices.

The well in the distorted courtyard of her mother's nightmare-house had been a direct conduit for the Shepherd's power before, a place where it had manifested its physical, monstrous arms and dragged Mei-Lin back into the abyss. The memory of the closing walls suffocating her was still as fresh as a newborn lamb. The thought of willingly approaching that dark maw again, especially knowing it was a direct line to the Shepherd, gave her chills. But a sudden thought occurred to her.

Back at the well, it had taken the demon several minutes to reach them once it had realized she had reconnected with her mother. It hadn't been waiting there for them. No, the well was too obvious of a hiding spot, same as the ruins. She was beginning to understand the way the Shepherd thought—and how the fucking thing thought it was so clever.

She scanned the hellish pasture looking for any signs of where the Shepherd would hide, anything out of the "ordinary"—at least as ordinary as anything could get in this hellscape. Her sharp eyes caught something in the distance past her mother's house.

The mudslide. The place where her Auntie Lin, and countless other villagers, had perished. A place of death, despair, and disturbed earth—prime territory for an entity like the Shepherd.

Against the large slope of wet mud was a festering brown scar, an oozing dark, viscous substance that steamed faintly in the green light. It wasn't there on her last visit with Old Jian. The pasture was *changing*, reacting, growing more complex with each new soul Fén Yáng claimed from the viral challenge.

She immediately knew that was the place.

"Got you," she whispered.

The maddening wail from the sheep abruptly stopped.

In its place, an ethereal chorus of "Little Bo-Peep" began like whispers carried on a fall breeze. The words then twisted into obscenities, promises of pain, whispers of her deepest failures. The surface nearby suddenly squelched, and one of the thorny fences directly between her and the mudslide-scar began to intertwine, its branches twisting together, forming a dense, impenetrable wall.

Sarah gripped the peachwood branch. "Not this time," she breathed, her voice a low growl that surprised even herself. She recalled her mother's words from the well—"You can *act* here."

She closed her eyes, not against the horror, but to channel her will. She pictured the thorny barrier parting, the branches recoiling as if burned. She poured all her anger, all her grief for Ben, for Mr. Chen, for her aunt, for the countless others, into that single mental image.

When she opened her eyes, she flinched in surprise at the sight. The thorns directly in front of her were ablaze. She had expected something subtle, but this surprised even her. Her shoulders pulled back slightly, confidence swelling in her. This world, Fén Yáng's world, could be bent, and she had that power.

The fire sputtered, dying much quicker than she anticipated as the nightmare fought back for control. As soon as the flames were low enough, and before the vines could recover, she plunged into the gap without hesitation. Even still, the thorns reached for her, tearing at her, but she pushed through, bursting out the other side. Her heart pounded not just with fear, but with a wild, fierce exhilaration. For the first time, she didn't feel like a hunted sheep. She was becoming a hunter.

Emboldened by her minor success, she marched onward towards the mudslide looming in the distance. The trek towards the scar was a relentless struggle as the whispers grew louder, more personal, twisting her memories, using the voices of her loved ones to taunt and demoralize. She made her way past many of the sheep who still stared, letting out an occasional bray. Watching. Waiting.

Shivers ran up her spine each time she brushed past one with the thought that she could be one of them soon. Would she be conscious? Would she feel pain? She shook her head to clear those thoughts. That's exactly what the Shepherd wanted, fear and doubts.

With each step, Sarah's resolve hardened. This was its game. And she would not play by its rules. She lowered her head and concentrated on placing one foot in front of the other. She ignored the phantom calls of Old Jian and her mother, one pleading for her to go to the well, the other echoing from the distant ruins. She recognized that the voices were tricks meant to lure her from the true path. A crooked smile stretched across her face as she trudged onwards towards the scar.

The nightmare began increasing its efforts to slow or stop her. The further she walked, the more resistance she came across. The sickly green sky above wept a viscous, oily rain that stung her skin and made the "ground" more slippery. More vines tried to sneak in and block her path, wind pushed her, lightning crashed around her, fierce rain whipped at her face, but she willed them all away. The journey was just as mentally draining as it was physical.

After dismissing another assault of thorny vines, she looked up in exhaustion, trying to gauge her remaining distance. A cry of frustration erupted from her when she realized she seemingly hadn't actually made any progress. The scar waited just as far out of reach as when she started, mocking her, another trick of the Shepherd and its nightmare. Next to her, sheep watched with sympathetic eyes.

Her knees gave out, and she collapsed into the mire with a wet, sloppy squelch. Frustration boiled over into a choked sob as she slammed her fist into the decaying fleece—more furious at herself than the demon. She had thought herself cleverer than the Shepherd, had become overconfident, and had fallen for the Shepherd's ruse.

Defeated, she laid her head against the muck, her nose filled with the stench of rot. The soggy, cold slurry of decay pressed against her cheek. But she ignored the repugnant feeling while her mind raced with ideas.

Despair, colder than the festering pasture beneath her, threatened to overwhelm her. But deep inside she felt a flicker of warmth; a small spark of anger that she clung to like a beggar with their last coin. Sarah realized she couldn't walk to the scar, but she'd be damned if she was going to give up. Her mother didn't give up, and neither would she.

She attempted to stand, but her bare foot slipped in the slick mire, and she again fell to one knee with a moist squelch. Her hand sank into the soft earth and her fingers brushed against something hard and round. At first, she thought it was a smooth stone, until she felt it move.

Sarah snatched her hand back with a choked cry. She stared at the spot her hand had just been. The slurry of decay swirled away for a brief second, revealing a pair of terrified human eyes staring up at her from the very earth itself. A mouth, caked in dead flesh, opened in a silent, pleading scream before the mire flowed back over it, swallowing the face once more.

A wave of horrified understanding washed over her. She looked out at the vast, undulating landscape. The ground was *breathing*. That soft, yielding texture under her feet was *alive*. The entire pasture, the very earth she stood upon, was a mass grave of thousands of still-conscious, tormented souls, their bodies fused into the earth, their faces just beneath the surface.

Sarah froze in terror. She could feel each wave of flesh roiling beneath her, each one another life stolen by the Shepherd. She couldn't move—dared not move. The thought of her walking over those poor people this whole time was unbearable. Every step she had taken, every gurgle of the foul sludge under her bare feet, hadn't been on lifeless flesh and bone. It had been on top of still-conscious, silent screams of a thousand trapped souls.

To take another step would be to press her heel into another forgotten victim's eye, to grind their agony deeper into this living hell. This, she realized, was the Shepherd's game. To make her the willing instrument of their torture. To walk through this world would mean trampling on countless victims, making her an accomplice to their suffering. To stand still meant surrender.

It was a clever trap.

No. She would not play its game or its rules.

"No more," she breathed, her voice raw.

If she couldn't walk *across* them, she would have to find another way. She stood back up, careful not to slip again as a desperate idea began to form. She couldn't go *to* the scar. But what if...

Closing her eyes, she ignored the feel of the yielding flesh beneath her, ignored the silent screams she could now almost hear. She focused her mind's eye on the two points of power in this realm: herself, and the demon's hiding place. She visualized the Shepherd, not as an all-powerful monster, but as a frightened, cowering sheep, hiding in its dark chasm.

The sheep was prey, and she was the wolf.

She then visualized a string, a shimmering cord of pure will, connecting her to that animal. She wouldn't walk the string. She would *pull* it.

With a mental heave born of pure, desperate determination, she reeled the string in. The sensation was bizarre: a non-physical lurch, like the world was rushing past her while she stood still. The Shepherd—her prey—thrashed against her imaginary line, but Sarah held on tight, her grip forged by the desperate need to lift her feet off the suffering soil.

She gave the image of the sheep a final, sharp mental tug and opened her eyes.

She was standing at the mudslide.

She blinked in a mix of elation and shock, half-surprised her plan had actually worked. As the disorientation of the shift faded, she lifted a foot off the ground in a panic, worried she might be stepping on a poor victim, but thankfully found only wet mud. Gone was the sea of souls.

With a sigh of relief, she turned her attention back to her true goal and was surprised to see the scar was actually a large tear in the side of the earth that opened down into utter darkness. From its depths, she could feel a cold, ancient presence radiating outwards, a palpable sense of malice that made the peachwood in her hand grow noticeably warmer, like some magical demon dowsing rod.

This was it. The entrance to the Shepherd's lair.

CHAPTER 32

The hole at the heart of the mudslide physically pulsed with a dark energy. Each subtle beat radiating the frigid cold of death. The peachwood in Sarah's hand throbbed in sync with each wave, though it held a contrasting warmth, a small, defiant armor against the overwhelming malice that radiated from the darkness.

This was definitely the place. The festering heart of the Shepherd's domain in this twisted pasture, a gaping wound from which the nightmare bled. If the Shepherd wanted to hide here, then she would just have to trap it where it felt safest.

She took a step towards the opening, then another, the muddy earth of the scar trying to suck her down, to claim her before she even reached the precipice. The green, roiling sky above pressed closer, indistinct faces formed in the clouds, contorting into leering, hungry masks, their silent observation a pressure on her spirit. Her breath hitched, the familiar tendrils of claustrophobia tightening around her chest, the air growing thick, but she was ready for this and forced them back, her resolve a cold, hard diamond forming in her belly.

This ends now. One way or another.

As she yanked her foot out of the sucking mud and onto the hard lip of the opening, a voice slithered into her mind, a mental intrusion, an oily insinuation of thought that belonged to the Shepherd.

Little lamb, so determined to be devoured. What is your plan? Do you truly think you can destroy me here? In my pasture? Where I feed? The mental assault was layered, a chorus of all the pain it had inflicted, each syllable laced with an ancient, chilling amusement that scraped like a rusty blade across her sanity.

Your mother screamed so deliciously before I devoured her. Your friends... they barely whimpered as their pathetic lives were extinguished. You can hear them, can't you? Wailing like all the other bleating fools in my flock.

Indeed, the chorus of disembodied bleating from the pasture beyond the mudslide intensified, each cry a needle of grief twisting in Sarah's gut. She ignored the cries, and the sickening images it tried to force into her mind. She focused on the fear it was trying to instill, the cloying dread it exuded, and she let that very fear become the blueprint for her plan.

She closed her eyes, not in surrender, but in a desperate act of creation. She remembered the oppressive darkness of the well, the crushing pressure of the earth, the childhood terror of small, enclosed spaces where monsters were undeniably real. Her biggest weakness. She let that fear bloom, gave it form, painted it onto the canvas of this nightmare realm with the brushstrokes of her will.

When she opened her eyes, the gaping maw of the mudslide scar was gone. In its place stood a small, cramped space, the walls close, unyielding, made of a dark, sweating stone that appeared to drink the bilious green light, the texture like cold, damp flesh. The air was thick, stale, each breath tasting of mildew and old blood. It was her childish vision of the school sewer.

With a deep breath, Sarah ducked and crawled into the narrow tunnel. She didn't remember willing the peachwood to glow so brightly, but she was thankful it was. The darkness was absolute here, but the soft glow from the wood she held lit the passage just enough for her to press onwards.

Scared, little lamb? The Shepherd's words oozed into her mind, the sound filthier than before. Each syllable felt like slimy tendrils worming around her brain, each a violation of her body that gave her goosebumps. It was a perverse invasion of her body. *How... predictable. Cowering in the dark, just as your kind always has. Do you feel the walls closing in? Do you feel the panic, that delightful little flutter of a trapped animal, rising in your breast?*

Just outside the glow of her peachwood a monstrous shadow, blacker than the sweating stone, began to coalesce, pulling itself from the very fabric of the oppressive gloom. It was tall and had to bend over in the narrow tunnel. Its limbs were like twisted branches, its sheep-skull head tilted with a predatory curiosity, the bone stained with the dried blood of countless victims. The two points of malevolent red light that served as its eyes burned through the dimness, fixing on her with an intensity that felt like a physical touch.

The Shepherd braced its long, branch-like arms against the walls and pushed. With a loud crack, the stone slid away, expanding the tunnel. Then it pushed up, the narrow tunnel began stretching and cracking higher as the Shepherd straightened. The sound of all the stones shifting was like bones breaking. Small rocks rained down on top of them, kicking up a cloud of dust that threatened to blind her.

The Shepherd took a slow, deliberate step through the cloud, the sound of its clawed feet scraping on the stone floor echoing in the stifling confines. It raised one of its impossibly long, insectoid arms, the gesture almost casual, dismissive. Illusions of her mother's face, contorted in agony, and Ben, broken and bleeding, and of Chloe, a mindless, bleating sheep, assaulted her mind.

The demon's mouth didn't move when it spoke next, its thoughts still slithering inside her mind. *They suffer because of you, little lamb.*

Their pain is your masterpiece. Oh, how you have satiated me more than I could ever have imagined. I have waited so long for this.

Sarah pressed herself against the back wall, making herself small. The Shepherd could sense her will weakening and slowly pressed closer but still remained cautious. Not yet, she thought.

"Please," she whispered, letting her voice tremble, letting the fear she held for her friends, for her mother, for the tattered remnants of her own sanity, coat the word. "Let them all go. I... I will come with you."

You? The Shepherd was closer now, looming over her, its fetid breath washing over her in a choking wave, the stench of the grave mixed with the acrid odor of burnt wool and rotting fruit. *Oh, little lamb, you have already fulfilled your purpose. I have no need of you anymore. I will savor your despair and feast on your fading hope until nothing remains but a hollow, bleating shell. You, who dared to walk my domain with open eyes, you who carry the failed defiance of your mother in your very blood, you will be a special, exquisite addition to my flock.* It raised a clawed hand, the obsidian talons glinting, poised to strike, to rend, to claim.

"No," Sarah breathed, and then her eyes snapped open, the feigned terror within them igniting into a blaze of pure, unadulterated fury that burned away the cloying fear. "You will be *mine.*"

She lunged at the demon with a speed and ferocity that surprised her just as much as it did the Shepherd. The creature, caught completely off guard, flinched away as she swung with the peachwood, its red eyes wide in surprise. One of her wild swings connected as the Shepherd raised an arm to block, the peachwood slicing through its grotesque skin with a searing flash of light. The demon made a satisfying cry of pain as a dark mist the color of coal sprayed from its wound.

The demon quickly retreated just out of the reach of her light. Without waiting for the damn thing to collect itself and go on the offensive, she willed a path into existence, the hard stone beneath her feet immediately dissolving, creating a deep escape. She jumped into the opening of her creation and slid along a damp narrow path of stone that led downwards.

The tunnel she descended reminded her of those old, haunted carnival slides that her dad would take her to as a child, but this one was much more terrifying. It began twisting and turning but always continued down. Above her in the distance she could hear the Shepherd roar in anger as it began to follow her.

The demon fought to overpower her influence over the nightmare with its own, trying to exert its control on the nightmare around her. Tree roots began to reach out from the walls, grasping at her, trying to slow her down. She swatted at them with her wooden weapon, causing the roots to let go and shrivel away. The walls constricted, threatening to swallow her, but she forced them apart with a mental push born of both intense fear and anger.

The clever thing even tried drowning her, as water burst through the walls quickly filling the narrow tunnel. Again, she twisted the attempt back with a surge of will, forcing the rushing water to part before her, creating a pocket of dry air in the deluge.

The sound of the demon's roar at being thwarted, that terrible mix of bleating and thunder, was music to her ears. She closed her eyes, smiled and focused her mind on where she wanted to go.

The tunnel ended abruptly, spitting her out into a dark recess. Sarah let out a cry of pain as she landed awkwardly, her legs buckling, then tumbled with the momentum. Luckily, she kept her grip on the peachwood, her only source of light in the vast darkness around her. There was no telling just how big the room was past the soft glow from her glowing peachwood. She hoped this was the place she wanted.

Sarah stood, her legs protesting with a sharp pain, but she forced herself steady. The rumbling sound of the Shepherd crashing through the slide above her was fast approaching and she had nowhere to run.

Then, the sound of the demon's pursuit went silent. The sudden quiet left only the ringing of tinnitus in her ears. She shook her head trying to clear the noise, so she could listen. Standing poised, her heavy breathing rasping in her throat, she waited. Her eyes tried scanning the oppressive dark beyond the small circle of her light. Nothing. No sound. No movement.

She quickly scratched at an itch on her cheek with the back of her free hand, while turning in circles, trying to keep an eye on every direction at once. She desperately needed light—and she knew she could make it—but it wasn't time. Not yet.

The unnatural silence stretched on. This was nothing like the silence of the caves in Gu Mei, at least in that darkness, there were *some* sounds. Water dripping. Bugs scurrying. Hell, even the sound of bats was preferable to this nothingness.

She scratched her cheek again.

"What are you waiting for?" she yelled into the void, more to fill the unbearable silence than getting answers. There was no answer.

The irritating itch bloomed on her cheek again, but she ignored it, her attention on the opening above her. Her hand tightened around the peachwood. Her muscles coiled. Sweat dripped from her brow. Silence.

Then, the itch suddenly flared into a sharp pain. She gasped in shock, hands flying to her face. Her fingers found something under her skin, squirming. She screamed as the skin on her cheek tore open. A faint, wet tearing sound, like old parchment being ripped, echoed in the silence. She looked down at her hand. It was slick with blood. Her blood. The itch was now a splitting pain as her skin began to peel open, not from an external cut, but pulled apart from within by thin, fibrous threads.

Out of desperation, she pressed down on her cheek harder, trying to hold her ripping skin together, but the thing inside her pushed out. A scream caught in her throat, turning into a choked, gagging sound. Through the bloody, spreading tear in her own flesh, a tiny, monstrous head began to emerge. She felt it wiggle and writhe under her hand as it emerged, she also felt... wool.

It was a sheep, no bigger than her hand, its wool stained with her blood, its miniature black eyes glittering with an ancient, familiar malice. It pulled its impossibly small body through the wound, its tiny hooves scraping against her cheekbone. It was a grotesque and obscene birth, a violation so profound it shattered her sense of self.

Without thinking, she switched from holding the monster in, to pulling the damn thing out. With a cry of revulsion, she grabbed the miniature horror and ripped it from her face, a flap of her own skin tearing away with it. The tiny sheep landed on the floor in front of her with a wet smack.

The repulsive creature started trembling, as it began to grow.

The sound it made grew into a symphony of horror—the wet pop of dislocating joints, the loud crack of rapidly elongating bones, the sickening tearing of wool and decaying flesh. It unfolded like a piece of gruesome origami, a grotesque marionette pulled by unseen strings. The tiny form cracked and popped, its limbs stretching into insectoid appendages, its skull elongating into the familiar, blood-stained bone, its body swelling into the towering, nightmarish form of the Shepherd.

It rose before her, its red eyes flaring with a burning hatred, the tatters of her own bloodied skin still clinging to its foul hide. It stared Sarah down and snarled, exposing its razor-sharp teeth. She watched in horror, as the Shepherd's mouth began to open. It opened much too far, its jaw bones making a sickening snapping sound.

It unexpectedly reached inside its own mouth, down into its bowels and began to pull something out. At first, it didn't register to Sarah what the Shepherd had in its claws, but when she finally recognized what it was, she retched. The demon tossed the remains of her mother's crushed head at her feet.

Sarah's legs gave out and she fell backwards onto her ass, right next to her mother's remains. Her eyes fixated on what was once such a beautiful, loving face.

Tick. Tick. Tick.

This is your legacy. The foul voice mocked, worming its way into her mind again. *So much struggle, and for what?*

Sarah crawled backwards away from the demon. The Shepherd inched towards her, keeping pace with her slow retreat. It took its time, knowing it had her cornered with nowhere to go. Stalking its trapped prey with the confidence of a predator. The sharp pain in her torn face and aching legs became an unbearable firestorm that burned through her remaining adrenaline. She was so tired, both physically and mentally.

Tick. Tick. Tick.

All the effort your mother made to hide you from me. The Shepherd shuffled closer and closer to her. *Her sacrifice... and you came to me. You are responsible for all of this little lamb. If you had never come to my cave, your father and your friends would still be alive. And now, after all this time, you will join my flock. I have you.*

Sarah suddenly stopped crawling and looked up at the Shepherd with a sudden intense gaze that lacked any sign of exhaustion. The demon paused in confusion.

"You're wrong," Sarah growled, lifting her glowing peachwood in front of her, its blue light flaring brighter. "I have *you!*" With a shout, she twisted around and stabbed at something behind her. A soft yellow light burst into life, illuminating the room around them, melting the oppressive darkness away.

The sudden light revealed they no longer stood in a claustropho-bic hole, but at the bottom of a vast, circular chamber, a well of impossible depth and breathtaking design. The walls, curving upwards into the light, were lined, not with stone, but with hundreds upon hundreds of pristine mirrors, each one framed in polished, now-glowing peachwood, each angled slightly inwards. In the very center of the chamber, resting on a pedestal of what looked like white, veined marble, sat the Relic, its tiny sheep gleaming from the freshly lit candle.

Primal fear gripped the demon once it realized what was happening. It sprang forward at her with terrifying speed, but Sarah was faster. She waved her hand, focusing her mental will above her. A hole opened in the ceiling, the stone melting away like sugar in warm water. An abrupt searing white light poured down from the opening far, far above. The light, a pure, concentrated sunbeam from the well's distant mouth, struck the lamp, igniting its metallic surfaces, and then refracted, exploding outwards in a blinding cascade, caught and amplified a thousandfold by the ring of peach-wood mirrors.

The sheep on the lamp began to spin.

Tick. Tick. Tick.

The Shepherd shrieked. The sound wasn't an insidious whisper in her mind this time; it was a physical, ear-splitting scream of pure agony that tore through the chamber. The demon recoiled, its shadowy form flickering violently, erratically, as the concentrated light, imbued with the purifying energy of the peachwood and the multiplied torment of its own reflected image, struck it from every conceivable angle. It tried to shield its burning red eyes, but there was nowhere to hide, no shadow to offer respite. Its own hideousness, its own darkness, its own ancient evil, was reflected back at it a thousand times, becoming a torment of self-realization it could not escape, a truth it could not deny.

"TRICKERY!" it howled, its voice losing its layered, confident quality, now thin, reedy, shot through with genuine pain and disbelief. Its towering form spasmed, trying to shrink away from the light,

from its own myriad reflections. *"YOU WILL PAY FOR THIS! I WILL TEAR YOUR SPIRIT TO SHREDS! I WILL TORTURE YOUR FRIENDS FOR ETERNITY!"*

But its threats were hollow, undermined by the raw terror that now laced its tone. Its form began to shift uncontrollably, a desperate, chaotic dance of horror. One moment it was the towering, skeletal sheep-demon, its bones cracking and reforming—the next a churning vortex of shadow and matted wool, lashing out blindly—then what looked like a dragon, each transformation more horrifying, more unstable, more agonizing than the last. The mirrors showed every excruciating permutation, every shred of its monstrous nature, forcing it to confront the totality of its evil.

The peachwood frames around the mirrors began to sing, a low, resonant hum that vibrated in Sarah's bones, a chorus of defiance that pushed back the demon's dark energy, that reinforced the integrity of the light-filled prison. The lamp in the center pulsed, its light no longer dim and insidious, but now a brilliant, steady beacon, seemingly empowered by the sunlight from above, its tiny sheep no longer harbingers of doom, but silent, gleaming sentinels. Those bronze sheep now cast clear and distinct shadows across the chamber, each shadow amplified by the mirrors. Round and round they spun, with each pass the shadows turned on the Shepherd, reaching for it, pulling, scratching.

The Shepherd thrashed, its multi-jointed limbs flailing, its screams echoing and re-echoing in the mirrored chamber, each reflection a fresh torment, each angle a new perspective on its own damnation. It lunged, not at Sarah, who stood small but resolute at the center of the light-filled arena, but at its own reflections, clawing at the mirrored surfaces with its obsidian talons, trying to extinguish the unbearable images of its own abomination. But the mirrors held, the peachwood still glowing with an inner light, protecting the mirrors from the Shepherd's assault.

Tick. Tick. Tick.

Sarah watched with pleasure as the demon that had haunted her since childhood cried and writhed in pain. For the first time, the lamps methodic ticking sounded like music to her ears. A music that was no longer meant for her or her friends, it was meant for the Shepherd. She took joy in the knowledge that she had beat the demon at its own game, had used its own malice and hubris against it.

Black, viscous ichor, the very substance of its malevolence, began to seep from its shifting form, sizzling and smoking as it touched the light-drenched marble floor, leaving scorch marks where it spattered. Its screams became gurgles, its movements more spastic, less controlled. The red light in its eyes flickered, dimmed, pulsed erratically, then sputtered like dying coals in a forge.

Sarah held up her hand in front of the demon, and focused her willpower on the final piece to her trap. Old Jian's largest bell materialized in her grip. Sarah held up the peachwood to it. Everything went quiet as the demon saw what she held, its eyes widening in terror.

"I'm the Shepherd now!" she screamed, as she swung the peachwood at the bell with all her might.

Time slowed for a heartbeat as the branch connected. Then, light and sound erupted in a single, deafening explosion. The shockwave rippled outward from the bell and crashed into the demon. With a final, ear-splitting shriek that tore at the very fabric of the nightmare, the Shepherd, Fén Yáng, the Grave Goat, *burst* into dust. Its monstrous form unraveled into a swirling cloud of black, acrid mist that was then sucked upwards, drawn inexorably towards the distant opening of the well, vanishing into the pure white light like a phantom at dawn.

The ticking stopped.

The mirrored walls shattered around her, sending shards tearing into her skin. The peachwood frames splintered, their glow snuffed out. The brilliant sunlight from above wavered, softened, then blinked out. The very ground beneath Sarah's feet trembled, and the illusion of the well chamber began to unravel, the fabric of the nightmare tearing apart like a worn, ancient tapestry being pulled by a single, decisive thread.

As the reality unraveled around her, she felt a shift internally. Closing her eyes she could feel the same sensation she had when she traveled to the chasm, like a movement through space. She opened her eyes.

She was standing back outside on the surface. A wave of dizziness washing over her as she adjusted to her new location. Out of all the horrible experiences in the nightmare, she would miss that feeling the least.

The sickly green sky of the pasture was again overhead, but it too was cracking, great rents of pure white light spreading across its nauseating surface, as if the false sky itself were shattering. She watched as the clouds of faces each silently burst like dandelions blowing away in a strong wind. The hard stone below was now the fleshy ground, but it too began dissolving into nothingness. The distorted buildings of Gu Mei in the distance crumbled into silent dust, while the thorny fences withered and vanished like burnt paper.

Where the pasture had been, where the endless flock of tormented sheep had grazed on their own misery, there was now a gentle, undulating landscape of soft light. And the sheep, their woolen forms shimmered, then solidified. One by one, they changed; their vacant, pleading eyes cleared, and dawning recognition replaced the mindless terror. They became human again.

Sarah found herself standing on a precipice of cool, clean darkness, the last vestiges of the Shepherd's realm dissolving around her like smoke. And then, they were there, coalescing from the fading light, their forms whole, their spirits finally, blessedly, free.

Her mother, Mei-Lin, no longer decayed and ravaged, but radiant, her dark eyes filled with an immeasurable love and a profound pride that made Sarah's heart ache. Auntie Lin stood beside her, her kind smile finally unburdened by sorrow, the vibrant plum blossom scarf around her neck glowing softly. Her father stood on the other side of Mei-Lin, his arm draped around her shoulders, his face beaming with pride.

Then, there was Chloe, her pink hair as bright as Sarah remembered, her usual mischievous grin lighting up her face, and already striking a pose. Chris, tall and strong, wrapped his arm instinctively around Chloe's shoulders, a look of bewildered relief on his face. Poor Chris, if his spirit was here then that meant... she let out a little sob at the implication.

Ben, his glasses slightly askew, a sheepish but undeniably genuine smile spreading across his features as he met Sarah's gaze. And in the back stood Mr. Chen next to Old Jian, who gave Sarah a nod of approval while patting a happy Chong.

"Māmā," Sarah whispered, the word a release of emotion pent up for years. Tears streamed down her face, tears of grief, of exhaustion, of a love that had bridged worlds and faced down demons. Mei-Lin reached out, her hand warm, real, tangible against Sarah's cheek.

"My brave little wolf," she said, her voice the melody Sarah had yearned to hear for so long, clear and strong. "You did it. You freed us all."

Chloe bounced forward, her energy irrepressible even in this ethereal space. "Seriously, Sarah, that was insane! Way better than any escape room! Though, not gonna lie, the ambiance was a bit much." Chris smiled, showing off one last flex of his biceps.

Ben gave a thumbs-up. "Not bad, Láng. Not bad at all. You can be my player two anytime."

Sarah laughed, a sound of pure, unadulterated joy, a sound that felt alien and yet wonderfully familiar, even as the light around them began to glow brighter, pulling at them, a gentle but insistent summons. They had so little time.

She turned and hugged her mother, a fierce, desperate embrace, trying to absorb a lifetime of missed moments, of unspoken love, into a single, perfect, heartbreaking instant. "I love you, Mom. I'm so sorry."

"There is nothing to forgive, Xiao Láng," Mei-Lin whispered, kissing her forehead. "I am so proud of you. Be happy. Live. For all of us."

"You know what that means, right?" her father asked, his eyes sparkling. "It means, go cook all the pizza delivery you want. You've earned it."

Then, one by one, they began to fade into a bright light, their forms becoming translucent, their smiles serene, their essence returning to the gentle peace that lay beyond the nightmare. Mr. Chen with a proud smile. Old Jian with a flourish. Chong with a heartfelt bray. Auntie Lin, with a toss of her colorful scarf. Chloe, blowing a kiss. Chris, a final, grateful nod. Ben, with a sly wink. They all slowly vanished—their souls released, finally free, ascending into the light.

Her mother was the last to go, her image lingering for a precious moment more, her love a tangible warmth that enveloped Sarah, a shield stronger than any peachwood. Then she too was gone, leaving Sarah standing alone, in a quiet, peaceful emptiness, the echoes of their love the only sound.

The Shepherd was gone. The curse broken. And Sarah Láng, the girl who had once been a fragile sheep, was finally, truly, a wolf. And the hunt was over.

CHAPTER 33

T he first thing Sarah noticed was the silence. No ticking. No whispers threading through her skull like barbed wire. The absolute silence felt like cotton balls pressed against her eardrums.

She rolled over from her back onto her hands and knees, groaning in pain with the movement. Her skin pressed down onto the cold, damp concrete of the sewer, sending a chill that traveled through her body.

Then she noticed the darkness. For a brief, heart-skipping moment she thought she had gone blind, but as her eyes gradually adjusted to the void around her, she realized she could just make out a faint light. To her right, a dying flashlight cast a weak, barely visible beam across the floor, painting long skeletal shadows on a slimy stone wall.

The reality of where she was came flooding back. Sarah shuffled over to the flashlight, her hands sliding over the damp and slimy concrete. Picking it up, she slapped it against her palm, causing the light to surge in brightness.

The soft glow gently pushed through the gloom, painting a scene of grim disarray. The salt circles were scuffed and smeared into the grime. Overturned mirrors reflected distorted slices of the chaos. And in the center of it all, still resting on its makeshift pedestal, was the brass candle holder. It was inert. Silent. The malevolent energy that had pulsed from it was gone, leaving only a piece of cold, tarnished metal. No whispers. No pull. And no accursed ticking.

Then she saw Chris and Chloe.

A hollow, animal sound tore from her own throat. They lay crumpled near the edge of the outer circle like discarded dolls. Chris's body was a broken ruin, twisted at an angle that defied the limits of human anatomy. His face, what was left of it, was a mask of blood and terror, the sockets where his eyes had been, stared blankly into the darkness. Chloe, once vibrant and full of life, was now just a ruin of bone and gore, unrecognizable save for the garish, happy colors of the clothes she wore.

Tears carved clean paths through the filth on her cheeks as she crawled towards them. "No," she sobbed, her hand hovering over his leather jacket, unable to bear the finality of touching him. She looked over at what remained of Chloe. "I'm so sorry. I'm so fucking sorry."

"Sarah?"

The voice, shaky but blessedly real, cut through her sorrow. Sarah's head snapped up to see Maya emerging from the shadows of an adjacent tunnel. Blood matted their hair, and their clothes hung in tatters, but they were standing. Maya was alive.

"Maya!" Sarah scrambled to her feet, nearly falling in her haste. They crashed into each other's arms, clinging with desperate intensity. The fierce, painful hug confirmed they were both still solid, still breathing, still tethered to the world of the living.

"I thought you were dead," Sarah choked out, pulling back to study her friend. "Did you kill it?"

"It almost had me," Maya breathed, their eyes wide with remembered terror. "After you went down the Shepherd came right for me. But Chris... he... he froze." Their voice broke as they got a distant look in their eye. "Just as it lunged for me, something happened... something distracted the thing. It stopped and looked over at you, Sarah. Chris saw his chance and tried to run away, but it was so fast, Sarah." They pointed a trembling finger at Chris's body. "It just crushed him. He didn't even have time to scream."

Maya took Sarah's hands in hers, squeezing them tight as they continued. "After it killed him, it was still staring at you. Like it had forgotten I was even there. That's when I saw the peachwood. I grabbed it, and... well." They looked down at their hands, which were smearing something black and viscous over Sarah's. "It just came apart. Like smoke. We did it, Sarah. We actually fucking won."

Sarah was stunned. They had pulled it off. Battling in two separate worlds—two fronts of the same war, they had won.

"I can't believe it," Sarah whispered, her eyes glancing over at the now-inert Relic. "We actually did it."

Maya nodded, following Sarah's gaze. "Once *it* was gone, I went outside for help. My phone had no signal down here." Maya looked back at Sarah and let out a soft gasp. "Your face," Maya whispered, their thumb gently tracing the edge of her torn skin. "Are you okay? What happened in there?"

"I'm fine. It doesn't hurt," Sarah lied without elaborating.

Maya's concerned gaze dropped from her shredded face to the ruptured scar on her arm. In the quiet ruin of their world, surrounded by the bodies of their friends, something shifted. The space between them, once filled with the easy camaraderie of friendship, was now charged with something fragile, desperate, and new.

Maya brushed a stray hair from Sarah's face with a gentle touch, then leaned in slowly, giving Sarah every opportunity to pull away. But Sarah didn't move. She couldn't. She watched as Maya's eyes fluttered closed, and then their lips, chapped and cold, met hers.

The kiss wasn't gentle or romantic. It was a raw, desperate reaffirmation of life. It tasted of salt, and grief, mixed with the coppery tang of blood. Yet, the unpleasant taste didn't stop them from holding it. A surge of warmth flooded through Sarah causing her skin to prickle.

After what seemed like both an eternity and a heartbeat at the same time, they broke apart, resting their foreheads together, their breathing mingling in the cold air. Sarah blushed as the reality of what they had just done in front of their dead friends hit her.

What was that? Oh God, I shouldn't have done that. Not here.

Maya saw the distressed look in her eyes and pulled her close into a tight, reassuring hug. In that safe space, held in their arms, Sarah couldn't stop the floodgate of tears from opening up. They both started crying openly now—for their lost friends, for the nightmare that was finally over, and for the impossible victory that had cost them everything. The tears eventually dried up and they stood there holding each other, both afraid to be the first to let go.

Sarah was first to break the silence. "Poor Chloe. How did she even get here?"

Maya looked over at Chloe's mangled corpse, their eyes focused on the body, studying her. "I don't really know," they said after a slight pause. "Chris and I thought she was just another vision. A trick by that fucking demon, but..." Maya's voice trailed off, unable to finish.

In the following silence, the reality of what came next crashed down on the two of them. Maya pulled away from Sarah and dried their eyes with a dirty sleeve. "We should go take care of poor Mr. Chen after we talk to the police."

Sarah simply nodded, her hand lingering slightly on Maya's arm before walking over to the Relic sitting unassumingly in the center of the room. She stood over it for a moment, contemplating whether to leave it or not. It looked so ordinary now—just a piece of tarnished metal sitting on the makeshift altar. But she couldn't take the chance. Couldn't risk someone else stumbling across it, starting the cycle all over again. She snatched it up with an aggravated motion and handed it to Maya, who shoved it deep into their Witch Bag without a word.

Together, they limped toward the surface, leaving the dead behind them in the darkness.

The gray world above felt alien after the suffocating darkness below. Rain fell in sheets, washing some of the filth from their skin but not the memory of what they'd seen. Police sirens wailed in the distance, growing closer. Sarah leaned against the wall to the gymnasium in an attempt to stay dry, and for support while she tried calling her father. She needed to be sure.

The phone rang once, then went to voicemail. A cold knot formed in her stomach as she dialed the university instead. A kind, hesitant voice on the other end gave her the news. He'd been found in his office. An aneurysm, they said. So sudden. So peaceful.

She'd heard that explanation once before. She knew the truth.

Without any emotion, she thanked them for the information, like they were simply discussing the weather, then hung up. The fire of her anger, her grief, her fear—it was all extinguished, leaving only a pile of cold ash where her heart had been. They had won, but at what cost? The weight of it all was almost too much. First her mother, now her father. Chloe. Chris. Ben. Mr. Chen. Auntie Lin. The names scrolled through her mind like a death toll. Gone. Everyone, gone.

Everyone except for Maya.

Two patrol cars and an ambulance screeched to a halt at the mouth of the alley, their flashing red and blue lights reflecting off the rain-streaked bricks. Sarah was surprised when the strobing lights didn't aggravate her epilepsy. She heard doors slam, and two figures in uniform came running around the corner in practiced urgency.

The first officer to meet them was a heavy-set man in a detective's trench coat. As he stepped closer a flicker of grim recognition crossed his face. It was Officer Graves.

"Goddammit," he muttered under his breath, a sound of pure professional exhaustion. He looked from Sarah to Maya, his gaze lingering on their bloodied, filth-caked forms. "You two again." It wasn't a question.

Sarah didn't say anything. She just stared back, the sight of him a brutal reminder of what she had lost. Graves's professional mask settled back into place, but his eyes were filled with a deep weariness. He gestured towards the open sewer grate. "Don't tell me you found more of your friends down there." His voice was flat, devoid of sarcasm, as if he was already steeling himself for the worst possible answer.

The world around Sarah suddenly went gray. The sounds of Officer Graves, Maya, the rain, all of it, faded into background noise. Sarah became mentally lost in a fog, and everything became a blur. She was vaguely aware of being guided, of more flashing lights, of questions she couldn't answer.

In her fugue state, she didn't hear Maya, who was lying for both of them. It was a necessary fiction about finding their friends, a story that felt flimsy even to their own ears. But in a world that refused to see monsters, they knew it was the only story that would be heard.

Sarah briefly came out of her stupor when a paramedic, who was dressing her wounds, flashed a light in her eyes. She looked up at them in confusion, unable to make out what they were saying. They gently helped lift her up—she hadn't even realized she was sitting—and led her to a waiting ambulance where she and Maya were loaded into the back.

The inside of the ambulance presented a jarring world of sterile white, a sharp contrast to the filth of the sewer. Each bump and sway of the vehicle was a dull, distant sensation. Sarah stared at the ceiling, watching the reflection of passing streetlights glide across its surface. The paramedic's voice was a muddled hum, a meaningless drone from far away. She thought she heard him say she was in shock.

Yeah, no shit.

Maya's hand found hers, a small point of warmth in the cold pressing at her heart. Sarah squeezed back, a reflex, the only proof she could offer that she was still there, still tethered to the living.

Once at the hospital they were quickly wheeled over to a small, curtained-off cubicle in the emergency room. They passed by dozens of comatose patients who were still stacked in the hallways due to a lack of space. All still unmoving, with open eyes, staring but not seeing. What was the point, she thought. All that sacrifice, and it made no difference for these poor people.

A doctor, her face a mask of professional empathy, asked questions Sarah couldn't process. A nurse took her blood pressure, her touch gentle, but impersonal. Time became a thick, syrupy thing, stretching and compressing without logic.

Sarah didn't know how long they sat there, two tormented souls who were more mentally beaten than physically. She watched the clock on the wall, but the hands didn't seem to move. The ticking was gone from her head, but this mechanical version, slow and steady, was its own kind of torture. Each second that passed was another second that her family and friends were dead.

Then, through the fog, a sound broke through. It was a shout from down the hall. At first, they thought it was a cry of pain or fear, but the next words heard were joyous ones.

"She's moving! She's awake!"

Sarah's head lifted slowly. Another cry echoed from a different room, this one a sob of pure, unadulterated relief. A nurse rushed past their cubicle, her expression one of stunned disbelief. Then another. The rhythmic beeping of the monitors in the hallway began to change, their steady, monotonous tones becoming quicker.

The air in the ER, once thick with despair, now charged itself with a new, frantic energy. A palpable current of disbelief and burgeoning hope. Through a gap in the curtain, Sarah saw a woman drop her phone, her hands flying to her mouth as she stared at a stirring figure on a gurney.

"What's going on?" Maya whispered, their voice raw.

A doctor rushed by, calling to a colleague. "It's the coma patients! They're waking up! All of them!"

Sarah and Maya exchanged a look, a silent, wild question passing between them. The noise grew, a cascade of happy, weeping families flooding the hallways, nurses and doctors rushing to keep up with the sudden, inexplicable wave of recovery.

A young woman, not much older than Chloe, was wheeled past their cubicle, sitting upright, her eyes bleary but open, her parents clinging to her, their faces streaked with tears. A teenage boy stumbled out of a room, supported by a nurse, his face pale but alive, so alive, as his father enveloped him in a crushing hug.

Sarah felt her own breath catch in her throat. She pushed herself off the cot, Maya following close behind, and they stepped out into the hallway. They were surrounded by miracles. Everywhere they looked, families were being reunited. The vacant, staring eyes that had haunted the hallways were now clearing, focusing, blinking back at a world they had been snatched from. The symphony of anguish had been replaced by a chaotic, beautiful chorus of joy.

She glanced over at Maya, who was frowning. "Maya?"

Maya returned her gaze before responding. "These people will never know who saved them. The price we paid. It's... not fair."

Sarah didn't respond. They were right. A bitter mix of jealousy and pride swirled inside her as she watched more and more loved ones reunited. These people would go home. Her friends would not.

"Well, the world might not know, but I do," Maya said, wrapping an arm around Sarah's shoulder. "*You* saved them, Sarah. You broke the curse."

"*We* did it, Maya," Sarah corrected, watching a mother kiss her son's forehead, watching a father laugh through his tears. Each reclaimed life stood as a testament to the lives that had been sacrificed—to Chris's bravery, to Ben's loyalty, to Chloe's spirit, and to her mother's eternal love.

A single, hot tear traced a path down her cheek. A tear from a well she had thought dried out earlier that day. It wasn't a tear of grief, it was a trickle of relief, and of an aching pride for the friends she'd lost.

The hunt was finally over. Fén Yáng, the Wool Eater, the Shepherd—was destroyed. And she, Sarah Láng, the girl who had once been a fragile sheep herself, lost in a pasture of fear, was left as the shepherd over her flock of survivors.

Epilogue

The phone's violent buzzing against the countertop below startled Sarah, and her hand slipped on the ladder rung. She steadied herself, then stretched to place the final book on the highest shelf of Thorne's Curios. The call would have to wait. A small, unbidden smile touched her lips. She knew who it was.

She leaned back to admire her work. For the first time since inheriting the shop, the cluttered maze of Mr. Chen's peculiar filing system had been tamed into something resembling order. The transformation had taken months, but seeing the clear pathways between shelves and the logical arrangement of inventory filled her with quiet sense of accomplishment.

Flutter. Flutter.

Sarah paused, listening. Pages rustled somewhere in the back—probably another draft from a gap she'd need to find and seal. The building's bones were old, full of gaps that let the outside world seep in through cracks and forgotten spaces.

The amount of work to be done as a business owner was staggering. It deepened the respect she had for Mr. Chen, even though it had taken her ages to tame the organizational monster he had created.

Mr. Chen definitely had a peculiar way of arranging things, to the point where she was impressed that he could find anything at all.

When she learned Mr. Chen had left her the shop upon his death, she'd nearly sold it just to avoid the overwhelming task of re-arranging the inventory. Now, standing in the clean, well-lit space that had been her childhood sanctuary, she was grateful for the impulse that made her stay. The shop had given her a sense of renewed purpose in the hollow weeks after burying what remained of her old life.

She picked up the phone after climbing back down and smiled to herself at the name on the screen. Maya, of course.

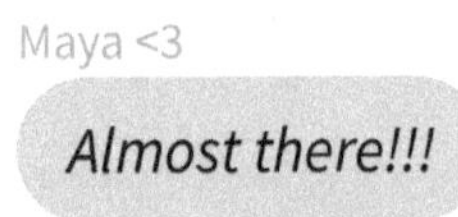

Perfect timing, with the shop finally ready to reopen.

They hadn't seen each other since the night at the hospital. Maya had needed space—"to reconnect with nature and process everything," they'd explained—leaving Sarah to rebuild alone. Until the other day when they finally reached out to let Sarah know they would be returning.

Feeling invigorated at the thought of seeing her friend again, Sarah made her way to the back storage room, no longer needing to navigate the narrow pathways that had once snaked between towering book stacks.

She opened a box of incense, selecting sticks at random until the scent of jasmine made her stiffen. A wave of sorrow rolled over her when the scent hit her nose—nostalgia instantly taking her back to the village of Gu Mei, her Auntie Lin, and of course, her mother. She lit the stick, deciding the timing was appropriate with Maya arriving soon, letting the sweet smoke carry her memories to every corner of the shop.

She grabbed a slice of cold pizza from the box she had been working on for the last few hours and took a bite while surveying her handiwork. She smiled, a genuine, unburdened smile. The shop was ready.

Well, almost.

Dusting the pizza crumbs from her hands, she walked toward the back of the shop, not far from where she had found Mr. Chen's body all those months ago. There, tucked away in a dark corner sat the once cursed Relic. It was a dull, unexceptional trinket now. Looking at the damn thing, no one would ever guess at the horror it had imposed on the world. Sarah, unafraid, picked it up with bare hands, testing as she did every day for any whisper of malevolent energy. Nothing. Just cold metal against her palm.

Satisfied that the Relic remained dormant, she placed it on the small wooden altar she'd made to remember and honor Mr. Chen's sacrifice. She'd debated whether displaying the instrument of Mr. Chen's death was respectful or grotesque. But the old man had faced this thing knowing what it was, knowing what it could cost him. He'd stared into its malevolent heart to protect her and her friends. In Sarah's mind, the lamp had become a symbol of his courage—proof that ordinary people could stand against impossible darkness.

Flutter. Flutter.

With a groan, Sarah grabbed a lit incense stick and began pacing the back room, watching the thin smoke trail for signs of moving air. When she turned toward the far wall, the smoke wavered as if pushed by invisible fingers.

Flutter. Flutter.

"Got you," she muttered, getting on hands and knees to follow the draft.

It led her to a small wooden shelf against the far wall. It was an unused section of the store she had only rummaged through briefly, mostly filled with old, worthless trinkets and baubles she wasn't quite sure how to organize yet. She set the incense stick on an empty shelf and started moving items around, searching for the source of the noise.

Flutter. Flutter. Flutter.

Her phone vibrated from an incoming message. It was Maya again.

Maya <3

Did you find my gift?

Gift? No. What gift?

There. In front of you.

Worms of ice crawled down her spine. She grabbed hold of the shelf from the side and with some effort pulled it away from the wall, the legs screeching as they rubbed across the hard floor. The damn thing was so heavy she only managed to pull it out just far enough to squeeze her small frame behind it.

As she squirmed between the wall and the old shelf, she couldn't help but pat herself on the back for overcoming her claustrophobia. A few months ago, the tight space would have sent her into a spiraling panic. Now she felt only determination. The trauma had changed her in some ways, strengthened her in others.

Thunder rumbled outside the shop from an approaching storm. The interior of the shop darkened slightly as clouds moved in and blocked the sun. Sarah didn't notice, her attention was fully on the task at hand.

There on the floor, lodged behind the shelving and the wall, was a book. With a grunt, she squeezed into the gap and reached down into the darkness, her fingertips brushing against something solid. Thoughts of bugs or any other dangers lurking in the crevices never even crossed her mind. Something compelled her to end this annoying sound as quickly as possible.

Her fingers wrapped around the object. She pulled it free, and with another grunt of effort, managed to stand back up. Panting, she held the book in the dim light of the shop. A flash of lightning illuminated the cover, and she gasped.

Flutter. Flutter. Flutter.

It was hard to see but she thought it was—no, it couldn't be.

Another flash proved her wrong.

It was Maya's journal.

The blood-red title on the cover read '**The Shepherd.**' Sarah's hands trembled as she traced the letters with her fingertip. She opened it and started to read. Struggling in the dim light.

It began: *The sound of ringing bells sliced through the thick dusty silence that clung to the village of Gu Mei.*

Goosebumps erupted on her arms. She flipped a page. Then another. Her heart began to hammer against her ribs as she read. It was all there. The trip to Gu Mei. The cave. The ruins. The whispers from the demon. Ben's death. Mr. Chen's death. Chris's final, heroic moments in the sewer. Everything. Word for word.

Her story. Their story. Maya had written everything—and more—in a journal that shouldn't be this complete. How had they managed it? The image of Maya, always scribbling furiously in that journal, flashed into her mind.

She flipped faster, the pages a blur, noticing each section started with a verse from the "Little Bo-Peep" nursery rhyme. She had to see how it ended. She found the last entry, her eyes scanning the text frantically.

...She flipped faster, the pages a blur, noticing each section started with a verse from the Little Bo-Peep nursery rhyme. She had to see how

it ended. She found the last entry, her eyes scanning the text frantically. Suddenly the bell to Thorne's Curios rang out from the front of the store...

Suddenly the bell to Thorne's Curios rang out from the front of the store.

Sarah's head snapped up, her blood turning icy cold in her veins. The words on the page matched reality with terrifying precision, as if Maya's diary was writing itself in real time. The journal wasn't predicting reality; it was narrating it.

"Maya?" she called out, her voice cracking. "Is that you?"

Silence.

She scooted out from behind the shelving and turned on her phone's light, shining it on the journal. She should stop reading. Should throw the diary away, run from the shop, never look back. But the compulsion was too strong. She had to know how it ended. Had to see what came next.

She flipped to the end:

She heaved a sigh, and wiped her eye,

And over the hillocks went rambling,

And tried what she could, as a Shepherdess should,

to tack each again to its Lambkin.

The final verse. The completion of the ritual.

A howl of pure malevolence erupted from somewhere in the shop. A mix of a sheep's bleating and something not-quite human. The sound came from the walls themselves, from the very air around her.

"No, no, no," Sarah whispered, understanding flooding through her with sick certainty. "How?" She had read the complete nursery rhyme. The demon had found a way to get her to finish the curse. But it was dead. She had killed it. *They* had killed it.

Lightning flashed again. Maya stood right behind her.

They smiled.

But it was not Maya's smile.

It was the Shepherd's.

The grin came as a slow, deliberate stretching of the lips, a grotesque pulling of skin that revealed too many teeth. Teeth that were too long, too sharp, inhuman. Its mouth kept stretching impossibly wide, skin splitting at the corners as black ichor began dripping from its chin. The smile became a smirk. The eyes that looked like Maya's burned with triumphant red fire.

Sarah knew immediately she had been deceived.

She had been so overconfident in her cleverness, she hadn't recognized the truth back in the sewers. Maya had never actually defeated Fén Yáng.

The demon had won.

The journal tumbled from Sarah's nerveless fingers, pages fluttering as it fell.

You were such a good shepherd, Sarah, the demon said, its voice a sound like breaking glass and screaming sheep inside her head. Its mouth did not move. *You led so many sheep to the slaughter for me. Every last lamb.*

As it spoke, the shop began to change around them. Books flew from their carefully organized shelves, pages ripping free to swirl in an impossible wind. The lamp on Mr. Chen's altar pulsed with renewed malevolent light, its brass surface growing hot enough to char the wooden altar beneath it.

The demon stretched and grew before her eyes. Maya's skin began tearing open as the demon grew larger, unable to contain the hard thorny form inside. The evil grin expanded so far, Maya's head split open in two with a sickening crack.

The cycle begins again. The creature continued, its smirk so wide Sarah could see down its throat into an abyss that had no bottom. *I have a new shepherd now.*

A frightened whimper escaped her lips. She had been wrong. Her mother was wrong. All of them—so incredibly wrong. The whole time she misunderstood the warnings that were right in front of her. Fén Yáng was never the Shepherd; she was.

For Sarah Láng, there was nowhere left to run. No more tricks, no one left to help her. The trap was sprung, and the wolf was caught. The demon leaned in closer, so close that Sarah could smell the rotten decay on its breath. The last thing she heard before her world went dark was the sound of pages turning in an endless book, writing itself forward into darkness, one victim at a time. It was the maddening sound of a curse beginning anew. A curse that had found its new Shepherd.

FÉN YÁNG LOOKS AT YOU.

ABOUT THE AUTHOR

A.J. BUSA is a Florida-born author who now crafts his tales of terror from the long shadows of Pikes Peak in Colorado. Inspired by a childhood defined by his parents' passion for the dark and the written word, he has authored a prolific catalog of screenplays and short stories that blur the thin line between reality and the obscure. He writes full-time, always searching for the horror that waits just out of sight.

For more information visit:
www.phylumbooks.com

www.ingramcontent.com/pod-product-compliance
Lightning Source LLC
Chambersburg PA
CBHW050506110726
47899CB00005B/1351